Also by David Ambrose

THE MAN WHO TURNED INTO HIMSELF

MOTHER OF GOD MOTHER GOD MOTHER OF MOTHER OF GOD OF MOTHER GO
D OF MOTHER GOD MOTHER GOD OF GOD OF MOTHER OF GOD MOTHER GOD
GOD MOTHER GOD MOTHER OF MOTHER OF GOD OF MOTHER GOD MOTHER
THER GOD MOTHER GOD OF GOD OF MOTHER OF GOD MOTHER GOD MOTHE
THER GOD MOTHER OF MOTHER OF GOD OF MOTHER GOD MOTHER GOD OF
D MOTHER GOD OF GOD OF MOTHER OF GOD MOTHER GOD MOTHER OF MO
D MOTHER OF MOTHER OF GOD OF MOTHER GOD MOTHER GOD OF GOD
THER GOD OF GOD OF MOTHER OF GOD MOTHER GOD MOTHER OF MOTHER
THER OF MOTHER OF GOD OF MOTHER GOD MOTHER GOD OF GOD OF MOT
D OF GOD OF MOTHER OF GOD MOTHER GOD MOTHER OF MOTHER OF GOD
MOTHER OF GOD OF MOTHER GOD MOTHER GOD OF GOD OF MOTHER OF G
D OF MOTHER OF GOD MOTHER GOD MOTHER OF MOTHER OF GOD OF MO
THER OF GOD OF MOTHER GOD MOTHER GOD OF GOD OF MOTHER OF GOD
MOTHER OF GOD MOTHER GOD MOTHER OF MOTHER OF GOD OF MOTHER GO
D OF MOTHER GOD MOTHER GOD OF GOD OF MOTHER OF GOD MOTHER GO
GOD MOTHER GOD MOTHER OF MOTHER OF GOD OF MOTHER GOD MOTHER
THER GOD MOTHER GOD OF GOD OF MOTHER OF GOD MOTHER GOD MOTHE
THER GOD MOTHER OF MOTHER OF GOD OF MOTHER GOD MOTHER GOD OF
D MOTHER GOD OF GOD OF MOTHER OF GOD MOTHER GOD MOTHER OF MO
D MOTHER OF MOTHER OF GOD OF MOTHER GOD MOTHER GOD OF GOD
THER GOD OF GOD OF MOTHER OF GOD MOTHER GOD MOTHER OF MOTHER
THER OF MOTHER OF GOD OF MOTHER GOD MOTHER GOD OF GOD OF MOT
D OF GOD OF MOTHER OF GOD MOTHER GOD MOTHER OF MOTHER OF GOD
MOTHER OF GOD OF MOTHER GOD MOTHER GOD OF GOD OF MOTHER OF
D OF MOTHER OF GOD MOTHER GOD MOTHER OF MOTHER OF GOD OF MO
THER OF GOD OF MOTHER GOD MOTHER GOD OF GOD OF MOTHER OF GOD
MOTHER OF GOD MOTHER GOD MOTHER OF MOTHER OF GOD OF MOTHER GO
D OF MOTHER GOD MOTHER GOD OF GOD OF MOTHER OF GOD MOTHER GO
GOD MOTHER GOD MOTHER OF MOTHER OF GOD OF MOTHER GOD MOTHER
THER GOD MOTHER GOD OF GOD OF MOTHER OF GOD MOTHER GOD MOTHE
THER GOD MOTHER OF MOTHER OF GOD OF MOTHER GOD MOTHER GOD OF

DAVID

D MOTHER GOD OF GOD OF MOTHER OF GOD MOTHER GOD MOTHER OF MO
D MOTHER OF MOTHER OF GOD OF MOTHER GOD MOTHER GOD OF GOD
THER GOD OF GOD OF MOTHER OF GOD MOTHER GOD MOTHER OF MOTHER

AMBROSE

THER OF MOTHER OF GOD OF MOTHER GOD MOTHER GOD OF GOD OF MOT
D OF GOD OF MOTHER OF GOD MOTHER GOD MOTHER OF MOTHER OF GOD
MOTHER OF GOD OF MOTHER GOD MOTHER GOD OF GOD OF MOTHER OF
D OF MOTHER OF GOD MOTHER GOD MOTHER OF MOTHER OF GOD OF MO
THER OF GOD OF MOTHER GOD MOTHER GOD OF GOD OF MOTHER OF GOD
MOTHER OF GOD MOTHER GOD MOTHER OF MOTHER OF GOD OF MOTHER GO
D OF MOTHER GOD MOTHER GOD OF GOD OF MOTHER OF GOD MOTHER GO
GOD MOTHER GOD MOTHER OF MOTHER OF GOD OF MOTHER GOD MOTHE
THER GOD MOTHER GOD OF GOD OF MOTHER OF GOD MOTHER GOD MOTHE
THER GOD MOTHER OF MOTHER OF GOD OF MOTHER GOD MOTHER GOD OF
D MOTHER GOD OF GOD OF MOTHER OF GOD MOTHER GOD MOTHER OF MO
D MOTHER OF MOTHER OF GOD OF MOTHER GOD MOTHER GOD OF GOD
THER GOD OF GOD OF MOTHER OF GOD MOTHER GOD MOTHER OF MOTHER

MOTHER OF GOD

. . . .

SIMON & SCHUSTER

OTHER GOD OF GOD OF MOTHER OF GOD MOTHER GOD MOTHER OF MOTHER
THER OF MOTHER OF GOD OF MOTHER GOD MOTHER GOD OF GOD OF MOTH
OF GOD OF MOTHER OF GOD MOTHER GOD MOTHER OF MOTHER OF GOD
MOTHER OF GOD OF MOTHER GOD MOTHER GOD OF GOD OF MOTHER OF G
OF MOTHER OF GOD MOTHER GOD MOTHER OF MOTHER OF GOD OF MOTH
OF GOD OF MOTHER GOD MOTHER GOD OF GOD OF MOTHER OF GOD MOTH
OTHER OF GOD MOTHER GOD MOTHER OF MOTHER OF GOD OF MOTHER G
OD OF MOTHER GOD MOTHER GOD OF GOD OF MOTHER OF GOD MOTHER G
OF GOD MOTHER GOD MOTHER OF MOTHER OF GOD OF MOTHER GOD MOTH
OTHER GOD MOTHER GOD OF GOD OF MOTHER OF GOD MOTHER GOD MOTH
MOTHER GOD MOTHER OF MOTHER OF GOD OF MOTHER GOD MOTHER GOD
GOD MOTHER GOD OF GOD OF MOTHER OF GOD MOTHER GOD MOTHER
HER GOD MOTHER OF MOTHER OF GOD OF MOTHER GOD MOTHER GOD OF G
OTHER GOD OF GOD OF MOTHER OF GOD MOTHER GOD MOTHER OF MOTHER
THER OF MOTHER OF GOD OF MOTHER GOD MOTHER GOD OF GOD OF MOTH
OF GOD OF MOTHER OF GOD MOTHER GOD MOTHER OF MOTHER OF GOD
MOTHER OF GOD OF MOTHER GOD MOTHER GOD OF GOD OF MOTHER OF G
OF MOTHER OF GOD MOTHER GOD MOTHER OF MOTHER OF GOD OF MOTH
OF GOD OF MOTHER GOD MOTHER GOD OF GOD OF MOTHER OF GOD MOTH
OTHER OF GOD MOTHER GOD MOTHER OF MOTHER OF GOD OF MOTHER G
OD OF MOTHER GOD MOTHER GOD OF GOD OF MOTHER OF GOD MOTHER G
OF GOD MOTHER GOD MOTHER OF MOTHER OF GOD OF MOTHER GOD MOTH
OTHER GOD MOTHER GOD OF GOD OF MOTHER OF GOD MOTHER GOD MOTH
MOTHER GOD MOTHER OF MOTHER OF GOD OF MOTHER GOD MOTHER GOD
GOD MOTHER GOD OF GOD OF MOTHER OF GOD MOTHER GOD MOTHER
ER GOD MOTHER OF MOTHER OF GOD OF MOTHER GOD MOTHER GOD OF G
OTHER GOD OF GOD OF MOTHER OF GOD MOTHER GOD MOTHER OF MOTHER
THER OF MOTHER OF GOD OF MOTHER GOD MOTHER GOD OF GOD OF MOTH
OF GOD OF MOTHER OF GOD MOTHER GOD MOTHER OF MOTHER OF GOD
MOTHER OF GOD OF MOTHER GOD MOTHER GOD OF GOD OF MOTHER OF G
OF MOTHER OF GOD MOTHER GOD MOTHER OF MOTHER OF GOD OF MOTH
OF GOD OF MOTHER GOD MOTHER GOD OF GOD OF MOTHER OF GOD MOTH
OTHER OF GOD MOTHER GOD MOTHER OF MOTHER OF GOD OF MOTHER G
OD OF MOTHER GOD MOTHER GOD OF GOD OF MOTHER OF GOD MOTHER G
OF GOD MOTHER GOD MOTHER OF MOTHER OF GOD OF MOTHER GOD MOTH
OTHER GOD MOTHER GOD OF GOD OF MOTHER OF GOD MOTHER GOD MOTH
MOTHER GOD MOTHER OF MOTHER OF GOD OF MOTHER GOD MOTHER GOD
GOD MOTHER GOD OF GOD OF MOTHER OF GOD MOTHER GOD MOTHER
ER GOD MOTHER OF MOTHER OF GOD OF MOTHER GOD MOTHER GOD OF G
OTHER GOD OF GOD OF MOTHER OF GOD MOTHER GOD MOTHER OF MOTHER
THER OF MOTHER OF GOD OF MOTHER GOD MOTHER GOD OF GOD OF MOTH
OF GOD OF MOTHER OF GOD MOTHER GOD MOTHER OF MOTHER OF GOD
MOTHER OF GOD OF MOTHER GOD MOTHER GOD OF GOD OF MOTHER OF G
OF MOTHER OF GOD MOTHER GOD MOTHER OF MOTHER OF GOD OF MOTH
OF GOD OF MOTHER GOD MOTHER GOD OF GOD OF MOTHER OF GOD MOTH
OTHER OF GOD MOTHER GOD MOTHER OF MOTHER OF GOD OF MOTHER G
OD OF MOTHER GOD MOTHER GOD OF GOD OF MOTHER OF GOD MOTHER G

SIMON & SCHUSTER
Rockefeller Center
1230 Avenue of the Americas
New York, NY 10020

This book is a work of fiction. Names, characters, places, and incidents either are products of the author's imagination or are used fictitiously. Any resemblance to actual events or locales or persons, living or dead, is entirely coincidental.

Designed by Deirdre C. Amthor

Manufactured in the United States of America

1 3 5 7 9 10 8 6 4 2

Library of Congress Cataloging-in-Publication Data
Ambrose, David.
Mother of God / David Ambrose.
p. cm.
I. Title.
PR9105.9.A47M68 1996
823'.914—dc20 96-21696 CIP
ISBN 0-684-82418-3

Previously published in Great Britain by
Macmillan General Books

A shape with lion body and the head of a man,
A gaze blank and pitiless as the sun,
Is moving its slow thighs, while all about it
Reel shadows of the indignant desert birds.
The darkness drops again; but now I know
That twenty centuries of stony sleep
Were vexed to nightmare by a rocking cradle,
And what rough beast, its hour come round at last,
Slouches towards Bethlehem to be born?

—From W. B. Yeats, "The Second Coming"

ACKNOWLEDGMENTS

MY SPECIAL THANKS to Ian Douglass, who frequently and with great patience took time out from running his company, Video Fusion Ltd, to explain to me what computers and their programmers could and could not do, and how they might conceivably do what I wanted them to do.

Thanks also to Aaron Kotcheff of Manchester University for his help on some fine points of theory and technical detail.

Dr. Susan Gudgeon and Dr. Katy Clifford provided valuable help on medical matters.

Among the authors who have written lucidly and stimulatingly on some of the areas touched on in this story, I am indebted particularly to (in alphabetical order): Margaret Boden; Guy Claxton; Richard Dawkins; Daniel C. Dennett; Douglas R. Hofstadter; Stephen Levy; Michael Lockwood; Marvin Minsky; Hans Moravec; Robert L. Nadeau; Roger Penrose; John Searle; Cliff Stoll; and, of course, the remarkable Alan Turing.

I am grateful also to Anthony Storr, not only for what he has written over the years about the human mind in general, but for taking an afternoon to help me focus on some of the avenues of communication which might be explored with an artificial intelligence.

None of the above should be held responsible by their peers for any eccentricities of fact or theory, which are wholly mine.

1

SHE THOUGHT she might tell him when they took their Easter break together in Brittany. It depended how things went. She wasn't trying to trap him into anything. She accepted full responsibility: she was twenty-nine years old—old enough to run her own life.

All the same, he had a right to know. Whether he was interested or not was up to him. If he was horrified at the idea of a child, then they would go their separate ways without rancor. She had already decided that she wasn't going to ask for financial support. She would bring up the child herself. Other women—women she admired—had done it, and so could she.

What worried her was that he might propose some sort of half measure: for instance, that she have the baby but they keep their relationship on its present easygoing basis, no commitments either way. This, she had decided, wouldn't work. The child would have a full-time father or none at all.

The streets of Oxford were relatively free of undergraduates when she drove to the lab that morning. Most of them had already left for the Easter vacation. She and Philip were due to set out for France on Thursday. She was going to pick him up in London at his friend Tom's flat in Earl's Court, where the two of them were putting together the summer issue of the poetry magazine they co-edited.

She had hardly spoken to Philip in the last few weeks; he had been frantic down there, and she had been equally busy up here. She had joined him for one brief weekend, but it had been mostly parties and people and a fringe theater show, and there had been no time to talk about a baby. It would be easier abroad, walking on the beach, perhaps, with Mont St. Michel in the distance. That was how she imagined it.

His handwriting was immediately recognizable on the second letter she pulled out of her mailbox. The postmark was London, Saturday. She opened it quickly, not giving herself time to wonder what it was all about. But she had only to read the first couple of lines to know.

> My dear Tessa,
>
> This is the hardest letter I've ever had to write. Part of me wishes I had the nerve to tell you to your face, but the rest of me thanks God that I don't, because I couldn't have borne that look of strange resignation you always get when something, or someone, disappoints you.

He went on to tell her that he'd been seeing this other woman for three months now. The trips to London to work on the magazine had been increasingly a cover. The woman, whose name he didn't mention, came, like him, from Australia. Now that his twelve-month visiting lectureship at Oxford was coming to an end, they had decided to go back together. He didn't give any more details, just finished off with some standard sentiments about how his time with Tessa had been precious, how he would always be grateful and would never forget her. Et cetera. Good-bye.

She realized she was still standing there gazing blankly at the letter some moments, maybe even minutes, after reading it a second time. She began again, but stopped. There was no point, no more to get out of it, no secrets between the lines. It was over.

Footsteps echoed around her on the old, cracked marble floors of the administrative building as people went about their business. Fortunately no one she knew well went past;

she didn't know how she would react if someone spoke to her. She turned and walked out quickly, got into her car, and sat behind the wheel.

Why would he have sent the letter here to the lab instead of to the cottage? Not that it mattered, but there must have been a reason.

She unfolded the letter again and her eyes ran over the familiar phrases. There it was: time. He and the woman were leaving Heathrow this morning. They would be in the air before she got to the lab. That must have been how he wanted it. No thought that she could absorb a shock like this better at home than where she worked. That wouldn't have occurred to him.

How little he understood her. How little he cared. How little in the end, she told herself, it mattered. She crumpled the letter into a ball inside her fist, then wondered what to do with it. She pushed it deep into the pocket of her long, loose jacket. Then she wondered what to do with herself.

Damn it, she would go in to work. That was always the best therapy. If someone asked her about Easter, which they were sure to do, or mentioned Brittany, because she had told her friends, she would just say that there had been a change of plan. She wouldn't go into details. It was nobody's business but hers.

Like the baby. That was now nobody's business but hers. But she had been prepared for that; she just hadn't been prepared for the decision to be made so soon.

Well, it was behind her. So was Philip. He never would have made a father anyway. The idea was ridiculous. She and the baby were well rid of him.

She shut her car door firmly, locked it, and started briskly back across the gravel toward the labs. She paused only for an instant. Anyone watching would have thought that she was trying to remember something that she might have left behind.

What she was actually doing was asking herself whether she, Tessa Lambert, one of the brightest minds in this university of very bright minds, was capable of looking after a helpless, infant life.

2

Special Agent Tim Kelly peered down from the helicopter as it started its descent toward the hills behind Malibu. He could see the cluster of vehicles already at the crime scene and the tent that had been erected over the body.

Moments later he was inside the tent with Lieutenant Jack Fischl of the Los Angeles Police Department, and Bernie Meyer, the medical examiner.

"Two kids from Pepperdine found it on their morning run," Jack Fischl was saying, jerking a thumb in the general direction of the nearby university campus. "Scared off a couple of coyotes who'd started breakfast. Hard to know how much was the coyotes and how much him."

Tim looked down at the remains of what had been a young woman, and an attractive one if the other victims were anything to go by. Not that they'd looked much better than this one when they'd been found, but subsequent identification and comparison of photographs had shown that he went for a certain type. She was white, in her twenties or early thirties, not heavy but with a full figure. The modesty implied by the pale bikini lines on the stretches of her flesh that had remained untouched was mocked by the grossness of her death. She was his seventh in eighteen months. Predictably enough, the press had already dubbed the killer "the LA Ripper."

Bernie Meyer rolled her onto her side to examine the dark patches of post-mortem lividity on her back. Rigor mortis had set in and Tim noticed that the bruise-like spots where blood had congealed beneath the skin after death did not correspond with the points at which the body had been in contact with the dry, uneven ground beneath it. Like the others, she had been killed elsewhere, then dumped.

"Dead twelve to fifteen hours is my guess," Bernie said in his matter-of-fact tenor. The light voice came unexpectedly from his stocky frame and bulletlike bald head. "Strangled, then dumped here before rigor set in—say between midnight and 3 A.M. Can't say much more till I get her to the lab."

Tim knew that there wouldn't be much more to say even then if the killer was running true to form. None of the autopsies had yielded any secretions: semen, blood, or tissue. They had nothing to go on apart from psychological profiles; no leads and no suspects.

Jack Fischl ducked down to get out of the confined space with its smell of death, and Tim followed him. They both breathed in the sea breeze blowing off the Pacific. All around them the Crime Scene Unit was going over the ground with their usual fine-tooth comb, bagging anything from cigarette ends to buttons, discarded matchbooks, and strands of hair, always on the lookout for any soft piece of earth that might have held a tire print or a footprint. But there was little chance of that up here.

Jack Fischl lit a cigarette and offered one to the bored photographer sitting on his camera box, waiting to see if he'd be needed again. Then he looked over at Tim with a little shrug of helplessness. Tim liked the slow-moving, middle-aged cop. Relations between the FBI and local police weren't always easy, but Jack had no chips on his shoulder or old axes to grind.

"You don't have to stick around if you don't want to," he told Tim. "I'll fax everything over to you—soon as we have anything."

"There's not much I can do till we have some ID," Tim said, glancing at his watch. "It's still early for missing person reports."

"Anything from the phone traces?"

Tim shook his head. "Slow, slow, slow," he intoned.

Jack nodded in sympathy. Both knew what they meant: phone taps across state lines, not to mention international frontiers, were impossibly complex to get approved and set up. The problem was that in this case phone taps were their best and perhaps only hope.

The killer's first two victims had belonged to the same computerized dating service, which had led the police to believe that they had a relatively simple task to break this case. But after every single male who conceivably had access to the information had been checked out without even one likely suspect being thrown up, they realized that it wasn't going to be so easy.

Then Fischl himself had the idea of using phone taps to find out if some hacker was getting into the data bank illegally; and sure enough they found one. But their elation was short-lived. The hacker was coming in over the Internet, which is the point at which the FBI became involved.

The Bureau had established that the calls were entering the nationwide network from an international one, at which point the trail vanished into a geometrically horrifying multitude of possibilities, each one protected in its turn by a stack of legal safeguards and political obstacles. By the time that the enormity of the problem became clear, there had been four murders, all of them in the Greater Los Angeles area.

Logic dictated that LA was where the killer lived; but tracing him around the world and back to his lair, somewhere in the region's eighteen million–plus inhabitants, would have daunted Superman, let alone Special Agent Tim Kelly.

As the helicopter climbed back into the sky and turned southeast for the FBI building in Westwood, Tim gazed out with growing depression at the hazily overcast urban carpet beneath him. There was something unnatural about this city. It had grown in a desert along earthquake fault lines where cities didn't belong. That it should nurture more than its fair share of maniacs and misfits was somehow to be expected.

But what was he, or any of his kind, the law enforcers of the land, supposed to do about it? What do you do when there is nothing you can do? Except pray, if you believe in prayer. Tim didn't. But to his surprise, as he sat there with the roar of the helicopter's motor in his ears, he found the words of a prayer forming in his brain.

"God help us to find this one. Because if he doesn't, I don't know who will."

3

HELEN TEMPLE'S rambling house in north Oxford was, as always, a tumble of children and dogs. Tessa wondered at the energy required to manage all this, plus a brilliant but charmingly vague husband, and still run a full-time career as a doctor. When she had asked one time, Helen had only laughed and said, "The trick is not to panic."

Her friend was, Tessa suspected, a truly happy woman. The thought filled her with awe and fear, a certain amount of envy, a touch of skepticism, but above all with curiosity. That was why, whenever her emotions became confused, Tessa turned to Helen.

"I'd already made up my mind that I was going to have the baby. I'd thought of every possible combination of Philip's reactions, both sides of all the arguments, the good and the bad compromises . . . I was ready for everything. Except this."

"In reality," Helen said after a while, "you're only in the position you were quite prepared to put yourself in if he hadn't been willing to promise that he'd be a proper father to the child: on your own, without him."

"Logically that's true. But that's not how it feels."

"You feel betrayed. And you have been. He's behaved like the selfish bastard we both knew he was."

Tessa was silent. "Maybe I didn't have the right to give him the choice of being a father or not. I mean, it was just my definition of the role that I was imposing on him . . ."

"You never even got the chance to try, did you? At least you were going to face him with what was on your mind. What did he do? Screwed around furtively behind your back, and sent you a coward's letter. If you're going to get involved with a shit, at least pick one with some courage."

There was a silence between them in the kitchen, which overlooked the leafy garden, a silence broken only by a grunt from one of the dogs as he heaved himself away from the warmth of the Aga stove and drank noisily from a bowl. The children had dispersed for football, the Cubs, and choir practice, so the house was briefly still.

"If there were a cure . . ." Tessa began.

". . . we'd bottle it and make a fortune," Helen finished for her.

It had been their old joke ever since Tessa had spent some time in analysis. She'd broken off when she said that now she understood her problem, but couldn't see any chance of a cure this side of getting too old to bother with men anyway. So she went on falling for bastards who betrayed and hurt her, and never for the nice guys who wouldn't. The trouble was that bastards were more fun. They made her feel sexy and exciting. They took everything for granted, and yet nothing at all. The worst, the silliest thing, was that there always came a point in the relationship where she told herself that she would be the one to change him—this time.

She laughed with resigned self-knowledge when she thought about how classically she fitted into all the textbooks. But knowing didn't change anything. It was supposed to, but it didn't. Knowledge, she had decided, sometimes had feet of clay.

If there were a cure . . .

"A cure in this case," she said after a while, "implies a simple answer. And the price you pay for simple answers is being wrong—consistently."

"You manage to be consistently wrong about the men in your life, and yet I've never heard you give a simple answer about anything."

Tessa smiled. Her friend's frankness, brutal though it was at times, was the emotional anchor of her life. She wondered if Helen understood just how important she was, and decided that she probably did; it was just that Helen carried all responsibility, including this one, so lightly. It was a gift of some kind. A gift for life. How Tessa would have liked to have it.

But then how could she, when they had such different backgrounds?

"You know something," she began hesitantly, "this is completely illogical, but for a second when I read the letter, I found myself thinking that I wasn't going to keep the baby after all. As you said, I'd been prepared to throw Philip out of my life and have it; but when he walked out, I wondered. Can you understand that?"

Helen turned her gaze from the early evening light outside the window and studied her friend's downcast face for a while before speaking.

"What it suggests," she said eventually, "is that maybe you're not as confident about having this child as you want to think you are."

Tessa looked up and met her gaze. Helen saw pain in the look, but also indecision, and pressed on.

"Look," she said, leaning forward slightly in the creaky wicker chair, "suppose you had confronted Philip, and he'd said very plainly that he wanted you but didn't want the baby. You think you would have told him that that wasn't an option. But you don't know. You can't be sure what you'd have done. There's still that little area of doubt—that maybe you aren't as committed to going through with this as you've told yourself you are."

Tessa leaned back against the cushions of the corner seat and rubbed her fingers down the center of her forehead. "The only good thing about not keeping the baby," she said, "would be that I could have a large gin, right now."

Helen smiled sympathetically. They had been through the arguments together many times. Helen was a Catholic, though with a flexible attitude to dogma. She believed in birth control and abortion in certain circumstances, no matter what the church might say. No Pope or College of Cardinals came between Helen and the God she felt she understood better than any of them.

Tessa, on the other hand, had no beliefs: at least not of a religious kind. She did not believe that there was anything sacred about a human egg, fertilized or otherwise. It was not yet, she told herself, a living being, just a biochemical process in its early stages. As a scientist, Tessa knew that sharp distinctions between life and nonlife did not exist; nature was infinitely subtle, shaded, and ambiguous.

"All the same," she said with quiet firmness, "I want the baby. This baby. I don't know why, but I know I do."

"Okay," Helen nodded and pushed herself up from her chair. "Then we'll leave the gin where it is, and I'll make a fresh pot of tea."

1001100001000011001010110000111 1

4

HE SAT IN DARKNESS except for the glow of his screen. His fingers moved over the computer keyboard with the relaxed precision of a jazz pianist coaxing out an improvisation for his own amusement. His staring eyes rippled strangely as they reflected and at the same time absorbed the dense streams of information that scrolled endlessly before them.

But although his body sat in a basement room in California, his mind reached out and traveled at the speed of light around the world, sliding down the information highways, switching deftly from one to another without any of them knowing he was even there. He was Superman—or would have been if the name hadn't been taken already. Spiderman would have done fine; he liked the image of himself as the spider at the center of his web. But that name too, unfortunately, was gone.

So in the end he settled for Netman. It didn't have the pizzazz of the first two, but it conveyed the way he felt about this other, mythic version of himself that lived out there: invisible, all-knowing, all-powerful when he chose. The stupid name the press were using—"LA Ripper"—just proved how far they, the cops, the FBI, and all of them were from getting even close to him. Falling back on a cliché like that was, in his view, just pathetic. But maybe it sold newspapers. Who cared? He didn't waste much time thinking about them.

He was scanning the patient list of a medical practice in Beverly Hills. The first time he had seen her she had been coming out of the building. He had been in the coffee shop opposite and had watched her walk to the parking lot and had memorized the license plate of the car she had driven off in.

According to the Department of Motor Vehicles computer, the car was registered in the name of Mrs. Rosa Korngold. But this girl didn't look like a "Mrs." He'd made more checks and discovered that Mrs. Korngold was sixty-five years of age, she had been a widow for ten years, and was a wealthy woman. He listed her stock holdings, investments, and real estate interests, and was impressed. But money was not his concern here.

The girl could have been Mrs. Korngold's granddaughter, except there was no record of Mrs. Korngold's having children.

That left a wide range of possibilities. He fanned out from her bank accounts, drawing up a profile of her interests, habits, and activities. There were regular payments to several charities connected with animal welfare, and she had standing orders for at least a dozen periodicals on the subject.

One name stood out and looked promising. A regular monthly payment to a Sandra M. Smallwood went back to the beginning of the year, the equivalent of a generous secretarial salary.

Tracing the payments through Ms. Smallwood's account, he found her address listed as that of Mrs. Korngold herself. Netman's interest was already engaged; now his curiosity was aroused.

His rules were strict. There must be no personal contact between himself and the subject, or anyone connected with the subject, until such time as he deemed it appropriate. By then he would know more about the subject than the subject herself; but all that information would have been gathered secretly and electronically, leaving no trace of his interest behind.

He made a search of the animal welfare mailing lists, and found that Ms. Smallwood was on most of them, and had been prior to her association with Mrs. Korngold. That had to be the connection.

On one of the mailing lists he found an undeleted previous address for Ms. Smallwood. It was in Van Nuys, well down the economic ladder from her current residence in Beverly Hills. This made his tricky work with social security records a little easier.

Sandra Smallwood had worked in a pet shop in Westwood, having earned her diploma, he eventually discovered, at the grandly titled Animal Husbandry College of Phoenix, Arizona. That was where her parents and immediate family still lived. Others were scattered across the country. He assembled a file on them and memorized it. Most importantly, he found a place where he himself could fit in: the distant cousin whose credentials would be beyond suspicion when finally he made contact.

Now, scrolling down the names and details in the medical center's computer, he was checking out a family history—a tendency in both male and female members to kidney stones, especially in later life, though sometimes in youth. But it turned out that, on the day he had first seen her, barely a week ago now, Sandra had been undergoing only a routine gynecological checkup. There was no indication in any of her medical records from infancy on of any kidney problems.

Not that it mattered. He was into the fine print now, satisfying a prurient curiosity that he disapproved of in himself. But the minutiae always became an obsession with him at this point: the minutiae of a life that would end soon.

And only Netman knew why.

5

Tessa woke early to the first spring morning of the year. The sun hung low in a clear sky and glinted in the moisture of her rambling country garden. She pulled on the nearest pair of jeans, an old sweater and a pair of pumps, and went out to smell the air.

George, the cat who had adopted her, appeared and wrapped himself about her ankles. She picked him up and he purred as she carried him around, checking what was out or coming out, what needed pruning, thinning, trimming, weeding. Tessa didn't know much about gardens, but she was picking up a good deal from Mr. Bryson, who came from the village three mornings a week, more when necessary. Mr. Bryson had been part of the overall deal when she rented the place.

She started down the winding path to the apple orchard with its archways of gnarled branches that suggested hidden depths and secret places, but when George squirmed and jumped from her arms to go off in search of some adventure of his own she went to sit on the old wooden bench in front of a clematis-covered wall. She leaned back and closed her eyes, placing her knees slightly apart and her hands on them. It was an attitude of meditation, one of the many she'd learned over the years.

10111000001001001011111110110100

But it didn't work. She needed concrete things this morning, not abstractions; though sometimes the two could become confused. She got up and walked back into the cottage.

Wooden beams darkened by age. An old sash window, wistaria falling across it. A blue coffee pot. A simple earthenware mug and plate. Old carving knives and cutlery with worn ivory handles. She had lived in a house like this until she was five years old, and the day she first walked into this kitchen the memories had come back across a quarter of a century with such force that for a moment she had been disoriented, almost to the point of panic. Then she had realized that this was what she had unconsciously been looking for. She took the place immediately, with no more than a cursory glance at the other rooms.

As she made herself breakfast, Tessa let her thoughts drift back to the day that had marked the end of her childhood. For many years she had tried not to think about it. Now, in this room, she thought about it often. The process, she had come to realize, was therapeutic: good memories were replacing painful ones.

Her mother had been proudly showing her a book with drawings in it—drawings that Tessa had watched her father make in the big light room where he worked at the back of the house. Tessa had loved to be in there with him, surrounded by paper, paint, and colored pencils.

They were still looking at the book when Daddy had come in. Then they all played a game with Happy, the black and white mongrel puppy they'd had for just two months. Her parents had still been laughing when they left.

She had watched their car drive off down the quiet lane. There were good smells from something her mother had left cooking slowly in the oven. She remembered Jenny checking on it now and then. Jenny was the girl from the farm who sometimes looked after Tessa for an hour or so.

That day the hour or so had gone on and on. Jenny had grown anxious and called her mother. It was dark when Jenny's mother came, accompanied by two policemen. Jenny's mother had been in tears, and Jenny began to cry too after they had whispered together. Then they both cried over Tessa, and took her to sleep at the farm that night. They let her sleep with Happy on the bed.

The next day Auntie Carrie came with Uncle Jack in the car. She was crying, too. She told Tessa that Mummy and Daddy had gone to live with Jesus in heaven and weren't ever coming back.

Tessa could not understand how they could have gone away without taking her. Or Happy. Auntie Carrie had offered no explanation. She just told Tessa that from now on she would live with them because they had no children of their own. Auntie Carrie was fifteen years older than Tessa's mother, Uncle Jack a good deal older than that.

Their house was a long way away and very different. Outside it looked like all the others in the street. Inside it was dark and had strange odors. But the worst thing was that she hadn't been allowed to bring Happy. Auntie Carrie was allergic to animals, so he stayed on the farm. They had said she could visit him, but Uncle Jack never seemed to have the time to drive her over. After a while, in response to her persistent questions about the little dog, Tessa was told that he too had gone to live in heaven with Mummy and Daddy, so there was no point in asking about him any more.

At school she made few friends, and even they were hard to keep because she wasn't allowed to bring them home; her aunt and uncle were anxious about noise. Nor was she allowed to go out and "run wild." Most of her time was spent alone in her room, reading. She spoke little, and never unless spoken to. Her life seemed to be happening somewhere else, and she viewed it remotely from a distance.

That she did well in exams was no surprise: she had nothing else to fill her time. The other kids teased her sometimes and called her a bookworm, but on the whole left her alone. She didn't curry favor with the teachers, and mostly just faded into her surroundings. It came as a surprise when her headmistress said she was being entered for an Oxford scholarship, and an even bigger one when she won it. They let her go up two years earlier than was usual, and at last her life began again.

She took a first in math, then did her doctorate. She tutored for a couple of terms, then went to work for a software company, finally coming back to the Kendall Laboratory, which was part of the university though with external funding and dedicated to pure research. Her special interest became cybernetics.

It was still only 8 A.M. when Tessa took a second cup of coffee upstairs with her to change. As it turned out, she changed only her sweater—for something looser. The baby didn't show yet—it was only twelve weeks—though she was thickening slightly at the waist. It was a curiously comfortable feeling.

She turned her face from side to side and studied her reflection in the mirror, first of all pulling her longish hair back, then up. She decided that today would be an up day. Her clear blue eyes gazed back at her as she pinned it in place. They saw an undeniably attractive woman: high cheekbones, a full mouth, and a complexion with a slightly olive richness acquired from a half-Greek father and a Welsh mother. Everybody told her—lovers, colleagues, friends—that she was animated, alive, and full of energy when she talked. Her smile, they said, lit up a room.

That puzzled her, because whenever she looked in a mirror, all she saw was the blank, unformed gaze of the child she had once been and who still wasn't sure what to say or how to behave.

She got up and realized that her hand was on her stomach, feeling for the life hidden there. As she turned she caught sight once more of her reflection—and for the first time in as long as she remembered, she found it smiling back at her.

Surprised by happiness, she went through to the next room where she had installed her computers. Last night she had logged into Attila, the mainframe in the lab, and worked till late. After that she had made a few notes on her PC and copied them onto a floppy disk. Now she took the disk out and slipped it into the pocket of her jeans to review later.

Then she locked up the house and set out in her car for the twenty-minute drive to Oxford.

6

SANDRA SMALLWOOD—Sandy to everyone—took the call on the private line that Mrs. Korngold had installed for her in the garden wing of the main house.

"Hello?"

"I'm sorry to trouble you," said a man's voice, "but could I possibly speak with a Miss Sandra Smallwood, please?" The voice was young and the tone polite.

"This is she."

"Miss Smallwood, I doubt if you'll remember me, but I'm a relative of yours. My father is your mother's cousin. I think that makes us second cousins."

"What's your name?"

"Darren Wade."

"From Philadelphia?"

"Right."

"You're Bill and Naomi's—"

"Right, that's right . . ."

"I haven't heard from them in years. How are they?"

"They're on a world cruise right now. I don't know if you heard, Dad had some luck with some stock he bought in a little firm ten years back that isn't a little firm any longer . . ."

"I didn't hear. That sounds great."

"I hope you don't mind my calling like this."

"No, not at all."

"It must be, God, how many years since we saw each other?"

"Don't ask," she laughed. "I've got a picture somewhere."

"You do? Of me?"

"Both of us together. At some wedding. You must have been four, five years old, tops."

"Sandra, let me tell you why I'm calling . . ."

"Sandy. Everybody still calls me Sandy."

"Sandy. I really don't want to intrude, please say if this is in any way an intrusion . . ."

"Of course not. I'm happy to hear from you."

"It's just that I was working earlier this year as a volunteer with Pets Aid in Atlanta, and I came across your name on our subscribers' list. I made a note of your address and thought if I was ever in LA I'd call you up and see if it was really you."

"You're in LA?"

"I'm starting a course at UCLA as part of my veterinary training."

"You're a veterinarian?"

"I will be. Eventually I'm hoping to practice here in California."

"Maybe I can help you."

"Oh, no, look, I didn't call for—"

"The person I work for knows everybody."

"Who d'you work for?"

"Her name's Mrs. Rosa Korngold."

"Korngold? That kind of rings a bell."

"She's on a lot of boards and stuff. I look after her dogs. That's my job."

"What kind of dogs?"

"Retrievers. She has eight of them."

"Eight!"

Sandy laughed. "She really likes retrievers."

"Listen, Sandy, like I said, I don't want to intrude into your life, but I wondered if maybe we might meet up and have a cup of coffee some time, you know?"

"Why don't you come over to the house?"

"No, really, I don't want—"

"Meet Mrs. Korngold. She's a nice lady. And when she hears you're a veterinarian . . ."

"Are you sure?"

"Of course I am."

"I'd really like to do that. Only . . . well, just for the first time we meet, I'd kind of thought we could maybe get together just the two of us. I mean, just to catch up on family and stuff."

7

TESSA WAS SMILING as she slowed and turned left off Banbury Road. She had been amusing herself by thinking up stupid names for the baby. Why did the idea of calling a boy "Walter" make her laugh? Or a girl "Myrtle"? And what was wrong with "Herbert," "Sybil," "Stanley," "Vera," "Percival," or "Mabel"? They were perfectly ordinary names that people had been happy to live with, yet she was laughing aloud at the idea of calling her baby by any of them. How was it that words took on associations that totally altered their original significance?

In fact she had already decided on the names: "Paul" after her father, and for a girl "Rachel," her mother's name.

She negotiated a right turn around the red-brick gothic mass of Keble College, then a left into South Parks Road. She pulled in through a gate with overhanging laurels and drove through the spread of buildings that made up what was called the "Science Area" until she found her parking space.

The Kendall Laboratory had been constructed in the late fifties as an extension to a Victorian block which now housed its administration. In fact it wasn't a single lab at all, but a series of self-contained units, flexible in number and size, according to who was working with whom on what project at any given time. It functioned as part of the university's Department of Computer Science, though its considerable outside funding meant that it was in touch with industries and government agencies around the world. Artificial Intelligence—AI for short—could not be seriously discussed anywhere without mention of the Kendall Lab.

Tessa's mail this morning contained nothing more than a couple of periodicals and the draft of an article on frame recognition that someone she knew at MIT was preparing for publication. She said hello to a few people as she went up the stairs, stopped in the door of a couple of offices for a brief chat. The atmosphere was, as always, informal, open, and low-key. People came here from all over the world. All of them could have made relative fortunes in industry, but they preferred the freedom to pursue the objects of their own intellectual curiosity rather than serve the requirements of some paymaster. Tessa had worked in a large electronics company for a time, but found the atmosphere stifling. She had been in the process of setting up her own consultancy when she was invited to come back to the Kendall and had jumped at the offer.

She was explaining something to a Swedish statistician when, out of the corner of her eye, she saw a tall distinguished figure in a pin-striped suit watching her from the landing above. With a shock she realized she had forgotten her meeting with Jonathan Syme from the Department of Trade and Industry. She excused herself to the Swede and hurried up the stairs, glancing at her watch. Luckily she was only ten minutes late.

He greeted her with a smile and a handshake, brushing aside her apologies. Jonathan was around forty. He was smart, charming, and often amusing. A high-flier in the civil service, he was also a former Fellow of All Souls and came up to dine maybe twice a month. He would sometimes stay overnight at Keble, which accounted for his occasional early morning visits to the lab to see what Tessa was doing with the government money which made up part of her funding. It was all informal and without any interference, though Tessa knew perfectly well that he would be dictating an official memo the moment he settled into the back of the car that waited to drive him down the M40 to London.

"So how's Fred this morning?" Jonathan asked as they strode along the passage to where she worked.

"Let's find out," she said. "I was doing a little work on him from home last night. I'm curious to see if he was paying attention."

Fred was a robot who carried a mass of sophisticated sensory devices that fed data back into Attila, the big computer in the lab two floors below, where his "brain" was a program that Tessa had written. It was that program she had been working on until the early hours from her home computer linked by modem into the lab. Fred had, in fact, made startling progress in the last couple of weeks, but she wondered how much of this would be obvious to a relative outsider.

An hour later she watched Jonathan lean back on the hard plastic chair where he had sat enthralled, watching Fred negotiate an increasingly complex series of mazes with flawless precision. Tessa hoped she didn't look too pleased with herself.

"It's amazing. A hundred per cent improvement, if not more. What on earth have you done?"

She gave a little shrug. "It could be a fluke of course . . ."

"Come on, Tessa—if it were a fluke he wouldn't go on improving every time. I know that's the idea behind neural nets—adaptation, evolution, all of that. But this is extraordinary."

He sat looking at her, waiting for some explanation until ultimately she felt compelled to offer one.

"I've been helping the system to reorganize itself in terms of its experience. I added a couple of functions to the program which re-order the response networks dynamically—effectively to 'chunk' its experience."

She stopped, hoping to see him nod wisely, look at his watch, and say that he must be on his way. Instead he raised an eyebrow inquiringly as the silence lengthened, as though amused by her reticence.

"You mean it's improving with practice. Is that what you're saying?"

"That's the general idea."

He was looking at her intensely now. "But that's unheard of, isn't it?"

She tipped her head to one side. "It's the first time it's been applied to a system of this complexity."

"How did you do it?"

"The first thing I did was modify the neural net manager to create a set of mutated response networks whenever the circumstances were sufficiently new."

"Forcing the program to evolve in response to stimuli."

"Yes, essentially. The mutations were random, so I had to add a genetic algorithm that kept the ones that worked and threw out the ones that didn't."

"How did you do that?"

Tessa took a breath. It was an instinctive reaction to the problem of explaining in lay terms something that she herself barely understood outside of technical jargon. She immediately regretted the action, hoping that he wouldn't interpret it as boredom or open rudeness. But he seemed unconcerned.

"I hooked the program into Attila's virtual reality simulation of the lab as well as into Fred's physical body in the lab."

"Allowing the program to look before Fred leaped, as it were?"

"Yes, sort of," she said, meeting his gaze and reflecting, not for the first time, that he was remarkably quick on the uptake for a nonscientist. But then a fellowship at All Souls suggested an intelligence that could probably master anything it applied itself to. She found herself thinking what a pity it was that he was gay; then wondering how she knew he was. A woman's instinct? Or just the obvious fact that he was forty-something, attractive, and unmarried?

Jonathan was looking at Fred standing motionless by his maze. He frowned thoughtfully.

"Did you find he learned fast?" he asked eventually. "Faster, I mean, than you expected?"

Again Tessa was surprised by the shrewdness of the question.

"As a matter of fact he did," she said. "Not right away. First of all he froze, and I thought it just wasn't going to work. But when I interrogated Attila I found a huge amount of computation going on. I couldn't work out what it meant to begin with. Then I realized that the program was replaying everything that had ever happened to Fred from Attila's archive. It went on like that for two days, then everything settled down and Fred started to get better. But after every session he spends time replaying what he's just done."

"As though he's dreaming?"

She made a little movement with her head, as though disapproving of the term, but at the same time not totally denying its applicability. "If you like. What made you ask if he was learning faster than I'd expected?"

Jonathan stood up, arching his back to throw off the remaining vestiges of stiffness, and sauntered over to a window.

"Something I read recently. Theories of artificial life. It's as though life, in this case intelligent life, *wants* to emerge. I'm not suggesting a life force. In fact I'm not suggesting anything. I'm just noting what several scientists have said: that, given a little push, randomness organizes itself into patterns much faster than the laws of probability predict."

She didn't say anything until he looked over at her, wanting a response.

"It seems to be so," she said, then added a note of caution. "Though to what extent 'patterns' equals 'life' is another question."

"Quite." He turned back to look out at the trees for a while before continuing. "If as you say the program—Fred's brain—has evolved a way of reorganizing his responses to new inputs in the light of his acquired knowledge . . ."

Here he broke off and turned to look at her again, but this time with a seriousness in his face that she found a little daunting.

". . . if," he continued, "that is what is happening, then surely we have applications here that go far beyond mere robot guidance systems. Don't we?"

Tessa shifted uncomfortably. She didn't like the question because it was too close to her own speculations, and for the moment she preferred to keep them to herself rather than have them show up in some semi-official report that could come back to haunt her. "I'm not sure we'd be justified in going that far yet."

"Yet," he echoed, as though it was the crucial loophole in her argument—which, she knew, it was.

"I'd rather stick to what we know than speculate." Tessa

was afraid she might have sounded a little priggish, but was determined not to be drawn any further.

He smiled again, diffusing the slight tension between them, and—at long last—looked at his watch. "Must be getting back to London," he said. "Thanks for the demonstration. We'll talk again soon."

They shook hands and made their good-byes. From her window she watched his car drive off toward the main gates. She was glad to be left alone with her speculations.

8

CENTURY CITY WAS built on what had once been the back lot of the Twentieth Century Fox film studio. Perhaps that was why it still had an odd air of unreality about it. The glass-faced office blocks soared improbably high into the clear blue sky, and the walkways, shopping malls, gardens, and cinema complexes combined to produce a limbo-like, slow-moving carnival air.

Sandy Smallwood looked at her watch with mounting impatience and decided to give her second cousin exactly five more minutes before leaving. She was sitting at a table on the terrace of a small café where they'd arranged to meet. Punctuality was a courtesy that she had been brought up to value—unlike, apparently, some distant members of her family. This whole thing had been his idea. How dare he keep her waiting!

She looked at her watch again. Four minutes, then she would leave. That would make twenty minutes in all that she had been here.

About fifty yards away, on the mezzanine floor of another building, powerful binoculars were trained on her through the tinted window. He was trying to make sure, as far as possible, that she was alone. Certainly she had arrived alone. Nobody had settled at a neighboring table either just before or just after she got there. As the minutes went by and her impatience grew, she gave no telltale glances toward people who might be watching her, nothing to indicate that there might be somebody out there waiting to spring from hiding and grab the man for whom she served as bait.

With each one he had to be more careful now. He varied the routine as much as possible, but there were always certain danger points. They were unavoidable, and this, the actual meeting, was the biggest of them all.

He lowered the binoculars onto the seat beside him and picked up a video camera. He got a nice shot of her, zooming in until she filled the frame, glancing at her watch again. She looked good with her legs crossed like that, hair falling across her face. Any minute now some guy would start hitting on her. That would be a nuisance; he hoped she wouldn't wait too long.

At last she pushed back her chair and started to walk away. She didn't make any sign, didn't look around as though for guidance. Just did it. That was good. He picked up the binoculars again, scanning the area around her for signs of coordinated movement. There was none. He was satisfied that she was alone. He went into action.

A little over two minutes later he was hurrying toward her along the walkway he knew she had to take to reach the elevator to the basement parking lot where he'd watched her leave her car. He had timed the whole thing so that he could reach her before she got there, even if she was walking briskly. As it turned out, he found her looking in a bookstore window, in no hurry at all.

He stopped a couple of yards from her.

"Sandy?"

She turned, keeping her look cold, because if this was Darren she wasn't going to let him off the hook easily for being late.

"I'm sorry," he said, "but I'm supposed to meet somebody who said she'd be wearing a white and blue dress like the one you have on . . ."

Their eyes met. He was a little under six feet, in his late twenties or early thirties. And good looking.

"Are you Sandy?"

"You're twenty-five minutes late," she said, glad to hear her voice sounding a little angrier than she felt.

His face fell. "I'm sorry. There was an emergency in the practice where I'm working just now. Somebody came in with their dog that had been hit by a car. There was a double fracture in the left foreleg. I didn't have any choice. I got over as fast as I could."

"How is he—the dog?"

"I think he'll be all right. Anyway, I'm sorry."

"Forget it. But that story about the dog better be true."

"You can come and see him in the office if you like."

She smiled. "Why don't we just go get a cup of coffee like we said?"

"Let me make it up to you. You said on the phone it was your day off. Are you busy tonight?"

"I'm going to a party later."

It was the little shrug with which she accompanied the statement that gave her away; it told him that she was prepared at least to consider a change of plan. Nonetheless, he played disappointed. It wouldn't work if he seemed too far ahead of the game, too sure of himself. He widened his eyes, puckered his chin slightly; he knew just how to look like a grown man with a little boy still in him. It was, he knew, his most disarming strategy.

"Do you really have to?" he asked.

"I promised."

"I was going to suggest we drive out to the beach. We could take a walk, talk a while. I know a great place for dinner."

"Sounds nice, but my friend Carol's expecting me to pick her up later."

"You could call her, tell her you can't make it."

"That wouldn't be fair."

"I guess you're right." He looked genuinely disappointed. "I'd suggest we do something over the weekend, only the trouble is I have to work. Maybe next week?"

"Sure."

"No, wait, I just remembered I have to be in San Francisco . . ." He fixed her with his most appealing look. "Couldn't you tell your friend Carol that you're sick? Or your aunt's been hit by a truck and you have to go see her in the hospital?"

"That's terrible," she protested, but heard herself laughing as she spoke.

"I know what we can do," he said, breaking into a mischievous grin. "*I'll* call her and say I'm with the FBI and you've been kidnapped and we're not expecting a ransom demand for a while yet and we found your diary and know you were supposed to pick her up for the party tonight, and . . ."

"All right, all right, I'll call Carol and tell her I can't make it."

"That's great!"

"I'll go find a phone."

"Before we do anything else, do you mind if I make a video of you?" As he asked the question, he pulled the camcorder out of his bag.

She looked surprised. "A video?"

"It's for the family—to show Mom and Dad when they get back. You know, what I'm doing, where I'm working, where I live—and, hey, look, I met Sandy!"

Her surprise evaporated into a smile. "Sure. Go ahead."

She posed self-consciously as he moved around her, his face screwed up with concentration, the camera steady.

"Say something," he said. "We have sound."

"Oh, gosh . . . 'Mary had a little—' Oh, no, that's no good . . . Oh, this isn't fair, you've taken me by surprise."

"It's the only way to get a good shot. You're doing fine."

"Can we erase this and start again? I'll know what I'm doing next time."

He laughed, and stopped. "Sorry," he said, lowering the camera. "That was a little sneaky. We'll do some more later."

A moment passed between them, just long enough to make her quite sure that there was something in this man that she wanted to know more about. And after all, he was family. Just. Second cousins. You could marry second cousins. Not that anything of that kind was really in her mind.

He broke the silence. "I suppose you've got a car here."

"I'm parked downstairs."

"Why don't we take mine, then we can pick yours up after dinner? How's that sound?"

"Okay."

"Great. Let's go."

"Oh—I've got to make that call."

"We can do it from my car."

He swung his bag over his shoulder. Then, as though suddenly remembering his manners and reproaching himself for the lapse, he held out his hand.

"It's really good to see you again, Sandy."

9

TIM KELLY WATCHED his father pouring drinks around the table. The big man was sixty, but still light on his feet like the boxer he had once been. There was only a suggestion of thickness at his waist, and his shoulders moved with bulky muscularity beneath his shirt. This was a man who could still pack a punch if he had to, though at the moment his huge fists were curled delicately around two bottles that looked like airplane miniatures the way he held them. One was a California Cabernet, and the other, for those who preferred it, the best Irish whiskey. He filled every glass except his own, which contained, as it had for nineteen straight years now, nothing stronger than tap water.

As though sensing his oldest son's gaze, and perhaps the thoughts behind it, Matt Kelly raised his glass, winked, and toasted him across the table. Tim picked up his wine and toasted him back, smiling at that broad moonscape of a face that he loved so unreservedly, and which he had once feared and hated with an intensity that still scared him when he recalled it.

Esther Kelly bustled in from the kitchen with two more of the aromatic, fresh-roasted, corn-fed chickens which were the center of the family's Easter lunch. Josh, Tim's younger brother by three years, was already on his feet, carving knife and fork at the ready. That Josh carved the roast whenever he was home was one of those family traditions that went back further than anyone remembered; back to days, in fact, that no one cared to remember, the days they lived in fear of big Matt's alcoholic rages.

Somehow Esther had held the family together through those dreadful times, protecting her sons from the worst of their father's violence, and at times absorbing a terrible amount of it herself. Tim still felt sick when he remembered the cuts and bruises, the discolored swellings on her face when she would tiptoe into the boys' room, whispering so as not to wake up Josh, and ask Tim to help her drag his father to bed from wherever he had finally passed out.

The big cop would be lying there, sometimes still in his uniform, sometimes in his underwear, sometimes naked except for the robe that Esther had struggled to wrap around him before going for her son. Those were the times when Tim, if he had still believed in God the way he knew his mother did, would have prayed for his father to die.

Farther down the table Josh laughed and swapped family jokes with the dozen or so aunts and uncles, cousins and children, as he refilled their plates. But his thoughts were on his brother Tim, as they always were at these gatherings. He knew that the flight across the country, the cab ride from Kennedy to the same old place in Queens, brought back memories for Tim that were almost unbearable.

To be truthful, Josh's own memories of those days were oddly vague. He suspected that he'd blacked them out because they were too painful. But there was one day that he had never forgotten and never would. That was the day when fifteen-year-old Tim had finally stood up to his father and told him that he couldn't do this to them any longer. The big man had gone berserk. He'd beaten the boy almost to death, breaking his arm, his nose, three ribs, and rupturing his spleen—before Mom had somehow gotten the old man's service revolver out of its holster and fired off two shots into the wall to quiet him down.

It was then, in that moment, that something had happened to big Matt. It was as though the alcohol had drained from his head and been replaced by the clear, cold knowledge of what he was, what he had become, and what he'd done. He had fallen to his knees, gathered his battered son into his arms, and not let go of him until he'd seen him safely on a stretcher in the hospital's emergency unit. They had been given a police escort and wailing sirens—which had meant that the department got involved, not least because questions had to be answered about those two shots fired in the apartment.

Cops being what they are, however, the whole thing was hushed up the way that Matt's drinking on duty had been hushed up for years. But from that day on Matt had never again touched alcohol. He'd been a good cop and even made sergeant, before retiring after thirty years' service and going to work for the private security firm where he became chief supervisor. And as a husband and father he'd been textbook perfect. It was hard, Josh reflected, to understand how two such different personalities could coexist within one man: Jekyll and Hyde, with nothing more than a few shots of alcohol to separate them.

Later, when the food and drink were finished, the two brothers took a walk together around the old neighborhood. They were both California-based now and came back only for visits. Oddly, though, they saw more of each other back east than out there. Josh, who according to Tim had always been the one with the brains in the family, was teaching physics and researching superconductivity at Cal Tech, while Tim and the Bureau were a more or less twenty-four-hour-a-day item with no time for socializing.

That was one of the reasons, Josh knew, that Tim's marriage had broken up: that, plus the fact that he had been far too easygoing on that bitch of a wife when she'd started running around with someone else. But Tim had lived in fear of being a bully; he'd seen too much of where that led. In consequence, Josh felt, he'd leaned too far the other way and given the woman anything she asked, including freedom. Tim never blamed her, just said she had ambitions of her own that didn't coincide with his.

Ambition, Josh thought sourly, was the right word. She had eventually married the president of an airline, and her constant presence in the gossip columns was one reason why Tim had transferred out to the LA Bureau.

"Stay over till tomorrow," Josh was saying. "We'll go to O'Malley's tonight, see some of the old gang."

Tim shook his head. "Listen," he said, "I did damn well even to get here at all. I was in conference on this case till I got in a cab for the airport, then I carried on by phone till I actually boarded the goddamn red-eye."

Josh nodded sympathetically, then stopped short. "You were conferencing on a cell phone? Don't you realize how easily the killer could monitor that? You already said he was a computer wizard!"

"Relax." Tim's grin had a hint of self-congratulation. "The whole thing was staged to make him think we know less than we do—*if* he was listening. I wanted him to think we didn't have a clue how he was stalking his victims, though we know damn well he's using the networks. Unfortunately knowing isn't much help."

Josh looked away for a few moments, thinking. Not far away a bunch of kids were playing basketball on a fenced-in corner between the crumbling walls of two empty buildings. When he looked back and opened his mouth to speak, he didn't say what he'd intended saying.

"Hey, big brother," he said, "I don't like that. I don't like what I'm seeing."

Tim turned and looked full at him as he screwed the cap back on the little metal flask and returned it to his pocket.

"I know what you're thinking." Tim spoke with a deep weariness. Slowly he lowered himself to sit on the slab of concrete in front of what had been the window of an Italian deli but was now just another boarded-over shop front. "I know, because I'm thinking it myself, and it scares me. Maybe I'm beginning to understand Pop a lot better than I ever thought I would. Maybe it's just in the genes, nothing you can do."

"Don't talk like that." Josh sat down alongside his brother. He wanted to embrace him, but he didn't. There was no physical embarrassment between them, but this felt too serious for a simple hug.

"Before you start," Tim said, "let me say one thing—okay? Everything's on hold till I close this case. When I do—if I do—I'll dry out, I'll join AA, I'll take up Zen yoga if that'll help.

But right now getting through the nights and days and finding answers is what matters."

Josh was silent awhile, then he said, "Tell me about the case. Why is this one so tough?"

Tim filled him in on every detail. They'd talked about the killings before, but not like this. For one thing, there hadn't been so many killings when they'd spoken previously, and Tim's sense of angry helplessness had not been so developed.

"We've got our own and the phone companies' best people trying to track down the son of a bitch, but it's next to impossible, and he obviously knows it. He goes from network to satellite to network, dials through nodes where we lose his trail, breaks into just about any computer he chooses and exits with a new bunch of phony UDIs to hide behind."

Josh frowned. "I think you mean UIDs," he said. "User Identifications."

"Yeah, that's it. I know squat from computers, and never expected I'd even know this much. What I do know is it's damn near impossible to make governments, companies, security agencies and assorted watchdogs understand that if they don't start cutting the bullshit and red tape, then more girls are going to die."

Unthinking, he took another swig from the flask in his pocket. Josh watched him with concern.

"Do you want me to help you out?"

Tim looked at him. "What can you do?"

"For a start I know about computers. Maybe not as much as your guy—then again, maybe I do. Plus I'm in touch with a lot of people like me all around the world. And we can all break the law more easily than you can."

Tim thought a moment. "You think so?"

"I don't think—I know. We do it all the time."

"No—I mean d'you really think you can organize some kind of posse to go after him?"

"I hadn't thought of putting it like that, but yeah, that's exactly what I think I could organize. A posse. Provided you hand over to me every last detail you have on the case."

"You realize it's my ass if this gets out."

"It won't. Trust me."

0 0 1 0 1 0 1 0 1 1 1 0 0 1 1 0 1 0 1 1 0 1 1 1 0 1 1 1 0 1 0 1

"Of course I trust you, but—"

"If you like I can break into the Bureau computer and steal the files, then you can deny any involvement and mean it."

Tim looked shocked. "You could do that?"

"Easy as falling off a log."

"Jesus Christ, you guys are scary."

"We do our best."

Tim was silent awhile. His hand moved toward his pocket as though he was thinking about another drink, but he checked himself.

"All right," he said eventually, pushing himself forward off the window slab and back onto his feet, "you've got a deal. Soon as we're back in LA I'll give you everything we've got. Unofficially."

"Of course. Unofficially is the only way this thing is going to work."

By the time they returned to their parents' place, Tim was feeling sufficiently cheered to have agreed to stay over the extra night and fly back with his brother in the morning. But the moment he got in the door and his mother told him that he'd had a call from Jack somebody—she'd written down the number—in LA, he knew that his evening at O'Malley's was a goner.

A call from Jack Fischl could mean only one thing. They'd found another girl.

10

AS SOON AS he'd dumped the body on one of the winding roads off Mulholland that he didn't even know the name of, he'd driven straight home. He'd driven with a kind of lunatic obsessive care that made him smile when he realized how tense he was, observing the speed limit and paying special attention to those right turns on a red light which were legal in California—provided there was no sign saying otherwise. You had to watch for those signs, because the cops would sometimes lie in wait for people who missed or ignored them. It would be too bad to be picked up on some dumb traffic violation and then have to sit and watch the whole thing start to unravel from there. That would be a pisser.

So there he was, driving with this outward calm and this pressure cooker inside of him, wanting only to get home and out of his clothes and into a hot bath. Above all he wanted to wash that dye out of his hair. Every time he met one of them he dyed his hair. It meant that if anyone remembered seeing the girl, and if by any chance they remembered seeing her meet him, they would describe a dark-haired young man, not him. Not him at all. Somebody else.

Somebody else.

He stood by the window looking up into the darkening sky.

Ever since he'd discovered the scratch on the side of his neck his nerves had been stretched to breaking point. How could he not have felt it? How could he have missed it until now? In the mirror in his bathroom he'd seen the livid red tear in his skin that must have been made by one of her nails.

They would be sure to find it, no question about that. They were good within their limits, those people: good enough to have his DNA analysis within the ten to fifteen days he knew it took. They wouldn't have anything with which to make a positive comparison because he'd never been DNA finger-printed. But if ever he became a suspect, for whatever unlikely reason, they'd have him cold.

His first thought had been to go back and retrieve the body, or at least do something about the hands. But it was too risky. Almost two hours had elapsed between dumping it and discovering the scratch on his neck. He couldn't go back; there might be someone there already. He'd listened to the police radio and dipped into their computer, and there was no mention of her having been found. But that could be deliberate. It could be a trap.

It was night when he turned back from the window and switched on the light. People were waiting for him nearby, people who thought they knew him well, but who in reality knew nothing. For all their goodwill toward the man they thought he was, he could never trust any one of them to know and understand him truly.

So he put on his face, the face he wore to meet the faces that he met (he liked that line from Eliot), and went out to join them.

11

HELEN FOLLOWED TESSA into the room on the third floor of the Kendall Lab. It was not large, with two windows taking up most of the outside wall and offering a leafy view of the university parks. There was very little in the room other than a desk, a computer terminal and an adjustable office chair in front of it.

"You'll be in touch with two other terminals in other rooms in the building," Tessa explained. "One of them will be operated by a man, the other by a program that I've written. They will be known to you only as 'A' and 'B.' Your job is to ask them questions, and decide which is the man and which the machine."

"I really have to be out of here in half an hour."

"You will be, I promise. Sit down, let me tell you the rules."

Helen sat down and adjusted the chair's height as she listened.

"The program is allowed to lie," Tessa explained, "but the man must always tell the truth. That's so you can't catch the program out by asking trick questions—like the color of its hair, or some calculation that only a machine could do."

"Okay."

"Also," Tessa continued, "the man is a doctor, and the program has been fed everything that's ever been put on disk about medical history and research. So you can cross-examine both of them on any medical subject you choose."

"And if I can't tell which is the computer and which is the man, we're supposed to assume that the computer is alive—right?"

"Intelligent. Not necessarily alive."

"Point taken."

"By the way, you can concentrate on either one of them for as long as you want. Also, you can talk to them both simultaneously or separately. You can also let them see each other's replies and have a three-way conversation—that's a variation of my own. Just press the switch here. All right?"

"Are you going to be peering over my shoulder?"

"No, I'll be monitoring the whole thing from another room, but you can talk to me over this microphone." She pointed to the side of the terminal.

As the door closed, Helen was already typing in her first question about the diagnosis of meningitis. She addressed it to "A."

The response was perfectly sensible, but could have been read out of any textbook.

She put the same question to "B." The response was similar.

She addressed her next question also to "B." It was equally straightforward, about the pathology of a series of digestive problems. Again, she could not fault the answers.

Then she tried "B" with a more complex diagnostic problem, specifying the results of blood and biopsy tests. The answer was circumspect, suggesting two possible pathologies. Helen probed for finer detail. "B" eventually came down on the side of one of them. It was the decision that she would have made herself.

She turned to "A" once more. She named a series of symptoms that might or might not have psychosomatic elements in their origins. "A" spotted and defined every single ambiguity. So did "B."

After fifteen minutes she decided there was nothing between them except occasional differences of individual judgment, just as you would expect to find between two doctors anywhere.

Helen knew there had to be some trick question she could ask that would trip up the computer. She tried to think back to the times when she and Tessa had discussed the game they were now playing. She knew that it was called a Turing Test, devised in 1950 by Alan Turing, one of the pioneers of artificial intelligence. In order to cut through all the theoretical arguments about whether machines could think or not, plus all the philosophical debates about what thinking really was anyway, Turing proposed simply that we talk to a machine and a human being at the same time and see if we can distinguish one from the other. If not, we must accept that the machine is as intelligent as a human being. He had predicted that a machine would pass the test before the end of the century.

"Are you trying to tell me that this thing passes the Turing Test?" Helen asked into the microphone that Tessa had shown her.

"I don't know. What do you think?" Tessa's voice came back tinnily through a small speaker.

"Can I ask it about anything at all? Not just medical?"

"Give it a try."

"How do I know," Helen tapped into the keyboard, "that you're not *both* human? Maybe this is one of those double-blind experiments and *I'm* the subject. You want to find out which of you I begin to imagine is a machine."

"What would be the point of that?" "A" typed back.

"Some sort of psychological study," she replied. "Something to do with the effects of computers on people who use them."

"We could just as easily both be computers," "B" suggested.

"No, you're both too smart for that."

There was a pause, as though they both needed to think.

Finally "A" typed: "If you believe that, then the machine has won."

"Not yet it hasn't!" "B" shot back.

"What does your intuition tell you?" "A" asked her.

She thought, then typed: "What do you think intuition is?"

"Intuition," "A" replied after a moment, "is believing something without knowing quite why you believe it."

"'B'—your definition?"

"Intuition is a feeling. A conclusion arrived at by a nonrational process."

"How can a machine do anything by a nonrational process?" she asked.

"B" took her up on this. "Strictly speaking, we aren't talking about machines. We're talking about programs that run on machines."

"But you don't deny," Helen typed, "that a computer is a machine?"

"Of course not," "B" replied.

"And do you believe," Helen continued, "that a machine running a program is actually thinking?"

"No."

"'A,' what do you say?" Helen asked.

"I agree with 'B,'" replied "A."

Helen was silent for a moment before typing in: "That's pretty clever of one of you."

"Not necessarily," "B" typed back. "Whether a machine running a program is actually thinking is not the question. The question is whether a machine can be programmed to give you the impression, for the purpose of this experiment, that it's thinking."

Helen leaned once more toward the microphone by the side of the terminal. "Okay, Tessa," she said, "I quit. You win. I've no idea which is which."

"Impressed?" Tessa's voice came back.

"Actually I'm spooked. Which of them is the machine?"

"I'm not telling you."

"You can't do that to me. Tessa, I'll kill you!"

"I never said I'd tell you. It wasn't part of the deal."

Helen heard Tessa's laugh over the speaker.

"You'll just rationalize in hindsight and think back over all the things that you realize should have given it away. That means that next time you do the test you'll have a lot of preconceptions that will get in the way."

"I will never do this test again. Also I may never speak to you again."

She didn't mean it, of course. As they kissed good-bye on the steps of the building a few minutes later, they confirmed that Tessa was coming over for dinner with Helen and Clive that evening.

"Seriously, Helen," Tessa said, "I will tell you which it was in time. But I want to talk to you about it some more, and for the moment I want you to stay puzzled."

12

The Korngold house stood on almost two acres of prime real estate on a peaceful street north of Sunset. It was low and Mediterranean in style, its straight lines softened by rich vegetation and slashes of subtropical color.

Although its front door opened onto a manicured lawn that sloped directly to the street with no barrier in between, the house was protected, like all its neighbors, by the most sophisticated electronic devices that money could buy. A tripped pressure pad, a broken light beam, the merest hint of movement in the region of an activated sensor, and an armed squad of private guards would be burning rubber in a race with the country's best paid and most efficient police department. In Beverly Hills people did not, on the whole, have to worry about being burgled or menaced in their homes.

Tim spoke with Mrs. Korngold in what she called her small sitting room at the back of the house. It looked out on a high-fenced garden with a fountain, an Italian gazebo, a rectangular pool, and a tennis court. Despite the setting being pretty much what he had anticipated, he mentally reproved himself for having expected Mrs. Korngold to fit his preconceived notions of an aging widow with dogs. When the teary-eyed maid showed him in, the woman who stood up to greet him was slim and poised, with a flash of laughter in her eyes that even her present sadness could not entirely disguise. She wore some kind of simple, flowing pantsuit, tied at the waist. His first thought was Lauren Bacall or Katharine Hepburn in elegant middle age; he had imagined somebody plump, flustered, and not very bright.

Rosa Korngold spoke with real fondness about her late employee and companion. As she did, various dogs wandered in and out as though looking for someone, and she reassured them with a scratch on the head or a word of affection. After a while she called for her chauffeur, who piled five of them (the other three being too old and arthritic) into a station wagon, and drove them to the beach for a run. That had been part of Sandy's job.

The girl had told her employer about her cousin Darren who had suddenly surfaced here in LA, and whom she hadn't seen since she was five. Mrs. Korngold had invited her to bring him to the house. She had said she would—next time.

Tim saw no harm in telling Mrs. Korngold that the real Darren Wade had been located at business school in Chicago. He confirmed that he hadn't seen his cousin since he was five, and that he had no idea where she was. He also confirmed that his parents were currently on a world cruise.

Forty minutes later Tim was driving down Beverly Drive and about to swing right onto Carmelita when he got a call on his car phone. It was Jack Fischl asking him to stop by the lab. He said he'd meet him there. Tim knew that this was urgent and that Jack couldn't talk about it on the air. Pathology must have come up with something.

When he pulled up, Jack was pacing the steps and smoking. He threw his cigarette away half finished and hurried Tim into the dark building.

"They got a blood sample under one of her nails," he said. "Human. I asked them what they can do to speed up the DNA test results, but it's still going to take a week—minimum."

The delay was frustrating, though unavoidable; nevertheless it was the best, indeed the only break they'd had so far. They spent a while in the lab going over details. They'd already noticed that most of her nails were broken; she'd obviously put up a fight. He hadn't made any attempt to clean the nails or even dispose of the hands, which he was more than capable of doing, judging by past performance, so the odds were that he'd dumped the body without knowing he'd been scratched, which meant he was getting careless.

However, he would most likely have found the scratch later, which meant that by now he must be running scared.

"Except of course it's possible," Tim felt himself obliged to keep his hopes in check, "that the tissue she's got under her fingernail has nothing to do with him."

"Any mention of a boyfriend? Fights, problems, breakups lately?"

"Uh-uh." Tim shook his head.

"It's him," Jack said with satisfaction.

They went around the corner and grabbed a sandwich and a cup of coffee together, then Tim drove back to the office where he'd been heading when he got Jack's call. He spent an hour going through reports from eyewitnesses who recalled seeing the girl sitting on the café terrace: all of them said she had been alone.

He was restless. Part of him wanted to go back to the scene where the body had been found; part of him wanted to talk again to some of the eyewitnesses from the café; most of him knew that both courses of action were a waste of time. The only thing to do was to wait for that damn DNA test, then get it into the computers and see if anybody anywhere on record matched it. Maybe he'd get his brother to help out on that too.

Without consciously thinking about it, he had taken the flask from his pocket, unscrewed the cap, and put the rim to his lips. The action registered only when he realized that the flask was empty. He had filled it when he left his apartment at seven that morning. It was now just after midday. His first response was to reassure himself that this was not yet a dangerous level of consumption; his second was shock that he could even be thinking in those terms.

He called his brother to confirm their dinner at a Chinese restaurant in Pasadena, according to Josh the best in Los Angeles, and Tim was more than happy to trust him. He said he would bring everything with him.

By "everything" he meant all the details on the case: everything he knew. It was only forty-eight hours since they had talked together in Queens, and he hadn't yet had time to give Josh anything to help him on their private and unofficial side of the investigation.

Tim drank nothing all afternoon. He didn't want Josh to smell alcohol on his breath. But when he got to the restaurant he was ready for the couple of large vodkas that he sank in double-quick time.

And grateful that Josh made no comment.

The man Josh saw come into the restaurant looked ten years older than he had two days ago, but when Tim came over and gave his usual lopsided grin of greeting, Josh saw that the age was an illusion caused by the tiredness of his walk.

They talked about the case and Josh skillfully averted his eyes while Tim put down two large vodkas, and then had a third when Josh ordered a glass of Chardonnay.

"As soon as we have the results of the DNA tests I'll run a check. If he's on record, I'll have him in hours. Or should have. There are so many damn restrictions on the use of information these days that it takes a crook like you to get anywhere."

"Thanks."

"That's okay—I'm proud of you."

The tone was ironic, but Josh still felt himself redden with pride at the compliment, backhanded though it was, and hoped it didn't show. He would have died for the man opposite him. He, his mother, and his father knew that they owed their lives and their sanity to Tim. So whatever help Tim wanted, he was going to get.

But what about the help he needed? The drinking was recent, and more than just a reaction to the pressure of the case. Tim was no newcomer to pressure. But now it was getting to him. Why?

A relationship, Josh felt, might help. Since his divorce there had been a few girlfriends, but nothing serious. Tim was interesting enough and good-looking enough to be attractive to most of the opposite sex. A couple of times they'd met when some of Josh's female students had been around, and they'd gone wild over the tall guy with the dark blond hair who was an actual real-life FBI agent. Tim had had a brief fling with one of them. She was smart and beautiful, but Tim had told her firmly that she was too young to settle down with an older man getting set in his ways, and on government pay.

"There's a lot of computer stuff I copied straight out of the file," Josh heard Tim saying. "If it doesn't make sense to you, I can't help you. It's stuff we get copies of from the technical guys; you'll see there's a digest for English speakers like me, but I can't judge how accurate it is."

"I'll let you know." Josh picked up the menu. "You want me to order for you?"

"Go ahead."

"D'you want some wine, or are you going to have another of those?"

Tim looked at the empty glass in front of him, and pushed it away. "I'll have a bottle of water. Christ, I'm driving. There are guys on this force who'd just love to breath-test a Fed."

"One thing—the guy you're looking for is almost certainly reading everything you have on him. I hope you're bearing that in mind."

"We're using encryption. We're about to set up a point-to-point direct radio network."

"You should be okay."

"I'm beginning to think this guy could break into any system short of carrier pigeons and a runner with a cleft stick."

"He's just a guy with a computer. There are limits to what he can do. Don't get it out of proportion. Now," he opened the menu, "I'm hungry as hell. Let's eat."

It was almost dawn, but Netman was unconscious of time as he stared at his screen.

If this was really all they had on him, then things could have been worse. Provided he could be sure they weren't setting a trap, that they weren't holding something back in an effort to lull him into a false sense of security (never underestimate your opposition, no matter how great your contempt for them), then his luck might have held out.

All the same, he'd have to be careful, lie low for a while, let their inquiries peter out in various directions. He could wait.

It would only make next time all the sweeter.

10101000101001101001110111100010

13

"ALL RIGHT, if you really want to know, 'A' was the computer."

Helen thought for a moment, then shook her head. "I still can't see it, even in hindsight."

Tessa was talking to Helen and her husband Clive over dinner. Clive's face wore the quizzically provocative smile that meant he was enjoying himself.

"Are you claiming this program actually *thinks?"* he asked, his eyebrows arching and disappearing into the tumble of his thick, dark hair.

"I'm not claiming anything. I'm just telling you what happened," Tessa said. "Try it yourself. You're a professor of English—I'll feed it as much as you've ever read, and get some Eng. Lit. postgrad to play straight man."

"I can't wait."

"There's a program somebody once tried on me in Edinburgh," Helen frowned as she tried to remember the details. "It had a name, something from a play by Shaw . . . 'ELIZA,' that was it. D'you know it?"

"Yes, it was quite famous," said Tessa. "It was developed about twenty years ago. You talked to it as though it were a psychotherapist."

"Yes—and it seems to be asking intelligent questions, but in fact all it's doing is repeating what you've just said and asking why you said it. It's just a trick."

"You say just a trick, but what are *you* doing when you think something through?" asked Tessa.

"Just that—I'm *thinking,"* Helen replied without hesitation.

"You say 'thinking' as though it requires no explanation. But the fact is that nobody knows what's actually going on when we think. We know a certain amount about how the brain works—which areas of thought are associated with which parts of it—but we don't know what the coordinating principle is, assuming that there is one. We don't, for instance, know where the 'self' is. There's nothing I can point to and say that's *me."*

"Maybe you can't point to it in a physical sense," Helen said, unimpressed by academic quibbles, "but it self-evidently exists. *Cogito ergo sum.* I think, therefore I am. The first certainty of life."

"But potentially misleading. It makes you imagine," Tessa said, tapping a fingertip against her forehead, "a 'self' sitting in your brain and watching the world go by on some kind of wraparound screen. Descartes assumed that the 'self' must be in the center of the brain, so it had to be the pineal gland. Now we know it isn't. In fact, we know it cannot be located anywhere. So *what* is it?"

"What do *you* think it is?" Clive asked, leaning back and fishing for the matches he knew he had in one of his pockets.

Tessa gave a little shrug and opened her hands like somebody releasing an invisible bird into the air. "We model computers on what we currently know of the human brain. Just as the brain has no central 'self' through which all information is passed, so a computer now has no single central processor. It has many parallel processors running neural net software—all whirring away and settling into a kind of optimum state."

"A state, are you saying, of mind?" Clive inquired, finally locating his box of matches somewhat flattened in the back pocket of his trousers.

Helen spoke before Tessa could answer. "Minds come from brains, which are the result of billions of years of evolution. A machine is made deliberately, either by hand or by other machines. It hasn't evolved through mutation and natural selection."

"That, I suspect," said Clive, cutting the end off one of the handsomely boxed cigars that he liked to smoke after dinner, "could be a matter of semantics."

Tessa turned to Helen and a warning finger probed the air between them. "Before you start insisting on the differences between brains and machines, let's look at their similarities. I told you that we model computers on the brain. The brain is made up of billions of cells, called 'neurons,' none of which is in itself conscious or intelligent. A neuron can exist in one of only two states: on or off. It fires or does not fire according to the input it receives from its neighbors. If that input is above a certain physical threshold it fires; if below, it doesn't. Can we agree that's a fair description so far?"

Helen gave a nod of qualified assent, inviting her to go on. The rich aroma of Havana tobacco began to drift over from Clive's direction.

"The computer equivalent to neurons are 'bits,' Tessa continued. "A bit is just a switch that can be in either of two positions. You can call the two positions 'up' and 'down,' 'x' and 'y,' or '0' and '1.' Just as our thoughts are neurons firing or not firing in complex patterns, so a computer's operations are bits that are either on or off."

"I see exactly what you're trying to say," Helen interrupted impatiently, "but it doesn't wash. You may get the *appearance* of intelligence in a machine, but all it's doing is performing tasks that have been programmed into it. You may as well say that—I don't know—a carwash is intelligent."

"You're missing the point. A carwash is a mechanical device—"

"And what's a computer?" Helen replied with a ripple of incredulous laughter, as though this settled the argument.

"A computer," Tessa had no intention of shifting her ground, "is a mechanical device in which neural nets mutate and evolve in exactly the way you've been insisting the human brain has evolved. There are clear similarities in the way they both process the information they receive."

"But a machine just *functions,*" Helen persisted. "It doesn't know what it's doing. It isn't conscious."

"Just remember," Tessa said, "that nobody knows what consciousness is any more than we know what thinking is. We just find that it's there."

"Is this a religious argument?" Clive inquired mildly, arching an eyebrow in Tessa's direction. "Are you saying that we're dealing with a given which is beyond our capacity to understand?"

"I'm saying that we're dealing with something that we're still working on. That's where science—sorry, Helen, but I have to say this—has it over religion. Science goes on asking questions, and little by little comes to understand more and more. Whereas religion just sits back and says we'll never understand this, so let's call it God and forget about it."

"Untrue."

"If you say so. But it's palpably inconsistent, when we don't know how consciousness arises in the human brain, to assert that it can't possibly arise elsewhere."

"But if you're talking about neurons firing or not firing, and switches being either on or off, all we're dealing with is abstract patterns, nothing more." A note of exasperation crept into Helen's voice. "Why not make patterns out of stones, or playing cards, or knives and forks? Wouldn't they do as well?"

"Theoretically, yes," said Tessa, unperturbed. "Except that in those cases the process would be so slow that none of us would live long enough to notice that anything was happening."

"So the key," Clive puffed and frowned and puffed again, "is the number of neurons—or switches—and the complexity of their operations, is it not?"

"Exactly. Simple things combine to make complex things. In that sense consciousness is an 'emergent property': something that is more than the sum of its parts."

"So you and I and all of us," Helen made a sweeping gesture, "are nothing more than emergent properties of our brains?" She did not try to disguise the open scorn in her voice. "You assemble all your little bits and pieces and your switches or whatever, and—hey presto!—as if by magic, you have conscious thought, a sense of self, volition. It's ludicrous!"

"You can make anything sound ludicrous if you're sufficiently determined to," Tessa replied coolly. "And you only use a word like 'magic' because of your religious upbringing." She knew the blow was a little below the belt, but nonetheless didn't care.

Helen sat back, narrowing her eyes as she dug in to defend her skepticism of science to the bitter end. "All right," she said, "even if we accept that a machine can be intelligent and even conscious—according to your definition—you're not going to tell me it can have a soul."

"A soul," said Tessa, with a faint smile that she knew would provoke Helen further, "is only a word that my computer could define just as well as you can."

"A definition," Helen shot back, visibly losing patience with the whole argument, "is something a dictionary gives. But nobody in their right mind imagines that a dictionary *understands* the information it's conveying."

"Understanding," Tessa continued with the same impassive calm, "is as difficult to define as 'consciousness' or, for that matter, 'soul.'"

"I think," Clive ventured, seizing the brief ensuing silence, "that I will go and make some coffee on my new machine. Unless, of course, it has ideas of its own."

"Tell me one thing," Helen said to Tessa after Clive had gone out. "You're going to have a child. A human life. Don't you know in your . . . call it what you like, heart, soul, inner self . . . that that life and the consciousness that it will have are things that could never be produced in a machine or programmed on a computer? Life and machines are two different things."

Tessa sighed and sat back, tipping her head to one side, adding a fresh perspective to the conversation. "You're talking belief, Helen. You *believe* that mind is the exclusive property of flesh and blood. All I'm saying is maybe it is, maybe it isn't. What's so wrong with trying to find out?"

14

NETMAN KNEW THAT before the night was out he could, if he wished, have everything that really mattered on the girl who had caught his eye on Wilshire Boulevard that afternoon. He'd followed her to the shop where she obviously worked, made a series of raids on his usual data banks, and in next to no time had compiled a list of the firm's current employees. He'd pulled up a photograph from the vehicle licensing department which, though unflattering, was undoubtedly her. But suddenly his concentration failed him and he began to lose interest.

He wasn't tired. The problem was that he knew it wasn't for real this time. He daren't make another move yet. Even if he kept her on file and waited until it was safe, it wouldn't be the same. You can't break off the chase like that and hope to pick it up later with the same excitement. Something vital would have gone out of it.

But he had no choice. He was intelligent and circumspect and ahead of the game. It was up to the other side now to play the hand they had the best way they could.

The DNA thing was the big problem. He didn't know how to get around that, and it worried him.

• • •

Tim was already at the coffee shop on Cahuenga when Josh arrived just after eight in the morning and ordered decaffeinated coffee and a bran muffin. Tim was finishing a plate of scrambled eggs and Canadian bacon, and drinking all the real coffee he could get. The brothers had decided they would meet always face to face and never discuss things on the phone. Tim was as concerned about his superiors finding out what he was up to as he was about the killer listening in: one word about this unofficial investigation would finish his career.

"We're getting the show on the road," Josh said as soon as the waitress was out of earshot. He pulled a bunch of printouts from the envelope he was carrying. "With a little help from my friends, we're logging all retrievals from vehicle licensing, social security, the IRS and most law enforcement agencies, plus medical data banks. Big Alice is scanning for intersects."

"Jesus, that sounds like a lot of people must know what we're up to."

"No. A few people know something. Only you and I have the whole picture."

"Who's this Alice woman?"

"Big Alice is the computer at Cal Tech."

"Oh. Okay, so what's the scenario?"

Josh hunched forward confidentially and dropped his voice a tone or two. "Well, the guy basically has two problems to solve. One is to stop us picking up his UID—user identity—when he accesses a record that we have a trace on; and the other is to stop us finding out where he's physically calling from if we do pick up his UID. If we find his UID we can go to the site he's accessing from and get his name and address, no problem. Even if the address is fake most access sites now have incoming call identification logging, so if we have the UID we can get the number of the phone he's calling from, again no problem."

"There has to be a problem somewhere, or we'd have him already."

"The problem is that if he's as sharp as I suspect he is, he has a bunch of stolen UIDs and passwords that he's using to give us an awful lot of false leads. What's worse, a lot of hackers are phone freaks and know how to use the system to get free calls and hide where they're calling from. He's probably routing through some of the 'black holes' in the phone network where you just dial in to the magic number, get a dial tone, and dial right out again as a free call. Or he could call through some major corporate office with a through dial WAN—that's a wide area network that lets you dial into the local office, and if you know the code make a free long-distance call to another office in the company, then dial out a remote local call."

He broke off, leaning back to allow the waitress to place a cup of coffee and a muffin in front of him. Again he waited until she had moved off before continuing. "If I were this guy, I'd be doing my searches in little nibbles, each nibble being taken by a different UID calling through a different routing. All that anybody trying to track me down would see would be, say, John Doe opening the file drawer, Jack Smith looking through to letter 'D' or whatever, Joe Smerz looking up something under 'D'—and so on. The user identity would be changing all the time, so you'd have no single trail to follow."

"So how do we find him?"

"We look at all the retrievals in all the databases we're covering. There are millions a day. We send an abstract of all these to Big Alice. She looks for those individuals who've had their records pulled from more than one database within a short period. Then we can build a list of UIDs active in the system at the time of each retrieval, filter that to eliminate the 'good guys just doing their job,' and what we have left should be a manageable list of suspects."

"How many?"

"It depends. Could be anywhere from a handful to a few thousand."

"How long will it take to get to that point?"

"Impossible to say. It depends on how often he accesses."

Tim nodded, swirling the remains of coffee in his cup and drinking them down. He decided against signaling the waitress for a refill.

"Any result on the DNA test yet?" Josh asked, flicking through his printouts as though looking for something.

"Uh-uh. I told you it takes a while."

"Sure does. I hadn't realized."

Tim shifted in his seat, leaning forward on his elbows. "Is there any chance," he started slowly, thinking as he spoke, "that using everything you've gotten in place, we might pick up his tracks while he's actually in process of stalking a victim? If we had an idea who he was going after . . ." He let the implication speak for itself.

"It's not impossible. But not yet."

Tim sat back, pursing his lips like a man who acknowledged the folly of hoping for a miracle. Then he looked at his watch and started getting to his feet. "Gotta go," he said, reaching for his wallet.

Josh put out a hand to stop him as he started peeling off bills. "It's my turn."

"Yeah, but—"

"But nothing. That's our deal—alternate checks."

"Okay. Thanks." Tim smiled and put his money away. "So long, baby brother, I'll talk to you later." He gave Josh's shoulder an affectionate squeeze as he started out.

"So long."

Josh took another bite of his muffin and watched the door close behind his brother's back. Then, a frown of concentration gathering on his brow, he turned to the printouts in front of him.

15

"THE RESULTS OF your triple test came through."

Helen was referring to the routine blood test that Tessa had had three weeks ago to screen for Down's syndrome or spina bifida. It was done on computer and indicated only the possibility and not the certainty of either condition.

"I'm sorry, Tessa, but it's positive."

Tessa took a moment to absorb the information. She felt an odd sensation that she supposed was shock. She had gone suddenly very cold.

"All it means," Helen's voice went on with professional calm, "is another test, an amniocentesis. I can arrange for that right away."

"What does it involve?"

"It takes five minutes. You pop into the hospital, lie down, and the gynecologist inserts a needle, here," Helen pointed to her own lower abdomen, "and draws off a little fluid from the sac."

Tessa winced involuntarily at the thought, then added: "I've heard it can cause a miscarriage."

"It's been known, but it's highly unlikely. And I really recommend you have the amnio."

"No drugs?"

"Don't worry, they know all about your allergy—and anyway it doesn't involve any drugs."

Tessa was sixteen when she had discovered she was allergic to penicillin. It had made her nervous of all drugs. She could barely be persuaded even to swallow an aspirin for a headache.

"Do we get the result right away?"

"No—it takes three weeks."

"God! Is there no way to speed it up?"

"Afraid not. Sorry, love."

Tessa was silent awhile, as though already accepting the worst. Her gaze became fixed on a crack in the wall by the radiator. She had suspected something when Helen had called her at the lab and asked her to drop by at the end of the day. Tessa had sensed her evasiveness when Helen said she couldn't talk on the phone because she had a patient waiting. She had arrived early and had to wait almost forty minutes until Helen finished office hours. She had spent the time helping Helen and Clive's oldest son, Matthew, with his math homework in the morning room. It had filled the time and allowed her to stop thinking, until Helen's receptionist had put her head around the door and asked her to come through to the office.

"I suppose even if the amnio is positive, I still have a choice, don't I?"

"Of course."

"A choice between having a handicapped child, or getting rid of it." She paused. "It's not much of a choice, is it?"

"Let's deal with it when we get there. If we get there."

Tessa looked up from the fingers she was twisting in her lap. "You'd have it, wouldn't you? If it was you."

Normally Helen would have refused to answer such a question from a patient. But Tessa was more than a patient, and the pain in her eyes deserved an answer.

"Honestly, I don't know. But then it hasn't happened to me—any more than it has to you yet." Helen got up and came around her desk. "Stay for supper. Clive's dining at the college, so it's just me and the kids."

"Thanks, but I have some work to finish. I'm all right, really."

"I know."

"Don't forget I'm going to Berlin next week. Can you arrange it before then?"

"Yes. I'll call you tomorrow."

A few moments later Helen listened to the sound of Tessa's car start up in the drive, then switched off the light on her desk and went through to the kitchen, where Marie-Pierre, the French au pair, was doing wonderful things with a simple stew.

She made herself a cup of China tea and drank it without milk. She would probably drink a glass of wine with dinner, but rarely started before she ate. She watched some news on television, until the children appeared one by one and they went through to eat and talk together in the kitchen.

Helen felt a curious unease beneath her happiness. She had seen too much of life's injustice, both as a doctor and a normal human being, to be surprised by it. All the same, tonight she would pray for Tessa and the baby she so much hoped to keep.

16

BERLIN WAS NOT the same without the wall. Tessa barely recognized the place as her taxi sped through the Brandenburg Gate and into what had been the eastern sector. Her only previous visit had been as a student in the early eighties, when the wall was still the city's defining feature. Its total disappearance, leaving neither crumbling foundation nor any other sign to mark where it had stood for almost thirty years, had about it something of the surreal.

Tessa's hotel was a palatial establishment that seemed not to have been touched by the last century and a half, except for the recent addition of western conveniences. The place was doing its best to look expensive, though she knew that they were getting a pretty good discount on rooms.

It was the third year that this particular conference had taken place. The previous year it had been in Paris and the one before in Edinburgh. Tessa had been at both. The point of the event was simply to provide four days in which people involved in any aspect of cognitive science could talk, ask questions, present papers, and argue about whatever was on their collective and individual minds. Between two and three hundred usually attended, the vast majority of them male. Tessa didn't know whether there was anything particularly romantic, or maybe even just frivolous, about the men who worked in this field; the fact was, however, that she had received a proposal of marriage at each of the previous gatherings, along with several propositions of a more informal nature.

She smiled as she saw Ted Sawyer's gangling figure coming toward her across the lobby, flashing his improbably white American teeth and waving a long spindly arm that seemed to bend equally in all directions. Ted was a professor of philosophy at one of the Midwest universities, and was also one of the more persistent of her informal propositioners.

"My God, you're even more beautiful than I remembered!" His arms went around her and his body contorted itself like an Anglepoise desk lamp to plant a kiss on her cheek. "I've got champagne in my room—which has a wonderful view, by the way—and if we hurry we can have ninety minutes of intense and meaningful sex before we go hear John Redway on neuronic microtubules—which everybody says is going to be this year's rage."

"Ted, give me time to check in at least."

"Was that a yes? Whooppee! Let's go to your room, it'll save time. I'll send for more champagne."

She was laughing as she felt his long fingers close around her elbow and steer her toward the desk. "I'll see you at seven for John Redway's paper, and not a minute before," she managed to say with some semblance of firmness. "We can sit together."

"I won't be able to concentrate."

"Then we'll sit apart."

"I can't handle this level of rejection. I'm warning you, I'll get sick, you'll feel guilty."

She signed in, picked up her key and her copy of the four-day timetable, and wondered whether to tell him she was pregnant. That would probably dampen his ardor; or maybe not. She couldn't predict anything about Ted. She didn't even know whether he behaved this way with every woman he met, or just with her. Certainly he didn't seem to have a reputation for it; no stories had reached her ears from female colleagues. So perhaps she was the only one he pursued with this unembarrassed and somehow inoffensive lack of subtlety. In which case she felt mildly flattered and rather regretted that she didn't find him even faintly attractive on that level. He was, without doubt, one of the most intelligent and intellectually perceptive men she knew: if she was to talk about the program and its implications to anyone at this gathering (and she hadn't made up her mind about that; maybe she ought to write something first) it would be him.

Meanwhile, she realized she had walked to the elevator with Ted still talking at her side and she hadn't heard a word he'd said. Suddenly the doors were closing and his cheerful, goofy grin was disappearing like the Cheshire cat's. The very thing she had tried hard not to think about for the last two days now filled her mind. She shuddered at the memory of the amniocentesis, and how she had almost passed out when she felt that long steel needle, guided by ultrasound, sink deep into her body. It was one of the most sickening sensations she had ever experienced. Since that moment she had told herself that she would not think about her pregnancy until the result came through, and only then if it was normal. Until then she would live in denial: she wouldn't be pregnant; there would be no baby; it wasn't real.

She ran a bath, lay back, and closed her eyes. She must have fallen asleep, because the next thing she knew was that her watch on the ledge by the bath gave her twelve minutes to get dressed and be downstairs for the opening salvo of the weekend.

Ted had kept the seat next to him free as he'd promised and was looking anxiously around for her. She pushed toward him, greeting old friends left and right all the way.

"Something to tell you," he hissed in her ear as she sat down. "Just got a phone call from LA . . ."

That was as far as he got before John Redway stood up to scattered applause, a little friendly ribbing, and began to read from the text he had prepared. He spoke for about twenty minutes about how the firing of neurons in the brain could not be compared with the switches of a computer because of the existence of microtubules, the infinitesimally small connections between neurons, which, he theorized, might introduce a quantum element into what brains did that could not be duplicated by machines.

Ted was one of the first to question the whole argument.

"Just one thing I'd like to be clear about, John," he began. "Everything you've said is as much guesswork as observation—right?"

Redway, a stocky man with thick dark hair who looked more like an English hill farmer than a mathematician, conceded the point reluctantly.

"So what you're saying," Ted went on, "is that for reasons of your own, which are basically emotional, you don't like the idea that consciousness could arise in anything but a wet brain."

"I prefer the term biological brain," Redway responded gruffly, "and my reasons are that nothing else has so far even begun to duplicate its capabilities."

Tessa wondered how soon she would have the courage to expose her own program to the people in this room with her now. The terms of her research funding did not allow her to broadcast what she was doing to the world at large without getting permission. That in itself was easy enough, yet something held her back. She needed, she felt, more time to be sure that she had actually achieved what she thought she had achieved. Above all she wanted to avoid the humiliation of making a wild claim that would fall apart under scrutiny; the memory of the cold fusion debacle in the eighties stood as a terrible warning.

"Surely the point is," somebody else was saying to Redway, taking up Ted's line of attack, "that the uncertainty principle which makes quantum variation inherently unknowable is just a convenient way of replacing mechanisms we can understand—i.e., algorithms—with ones that we cannot. In other words it's just another form of gratuitous mystification."

"I wouldn't call pointing out the shortcomings of the flat earth theory 'gratuitous mystification,' so I don't see why you should apply that term to what I'm saying here."

Tessa smiled at the asperity in Redway's response; she would enjoy putting him up against her program. But maybe there was some way she could do it without getting involved right away in a public harangue.

"Okay, that's setting science up against superstition, which is fair enough." This was Ted back in the argument, his wagging finger conducting a miniature sword fight in the air with some invisible opponent. "But in this case you're the one using superstition to protect consciousness against any intrusion by science. You're just hanging on to obscurantism at any price."

So it went on. Tessa made no contribution, though she was tempted to once or twice. But she knew that if she opened her mouth she would end up talking about the program, and it was too early.

"This Redway guy belongs in a monastery, not a university," Ted growled in her ear as they filed out.

"There was a time," she said, "when the two were the same thing."

"Not in my country," he replied. "Speaking of which, I was telling you I had a call from LA—about you."

She looked up at him, surprised. "What about me?"

"Not actually you by name. It was about your computer at Oxford."

Tessa felt a stab of anxiety that took her by surprise. Who in California could know anything about Attila?

"I've got this friend over at Cal Tech," Ted was saying, "who's on the trail of some hacker. I don't know why or what the guy's supposed to have done. Josh—that's this friend of mine, Josh Kelly—says they've tracked somebody over the Internet to Oxford, and they need to find out where he's coming in from—or she or whatever, I'm not sexist, you know that. All they want you to do is tap in a little program they have that'll trace whoever it is the next time they come through. Would you do that?"

He handed over a piece of paper. She glanced at it and saw an Internet address from which she could download the program. Between people in their world it was a fairly routine and unobjectionable kind of request. But the implications behind it filled her with alarm.

"Ted, nobody could be hacking into my computer. It's isolated. Your friend must be mistaken."

Ted saw the concern in her face and was intrigued. "Hey, what've you got in there? Something you haven't told me about?"

"Yes, I've got my damn research in there, and I'll tell you about it when I'm ready."

"Excuuuuuuussse me," he protested, holding up his hands like the victim of a stickup. "I'll wait, I'll wait."

Tessa blushed, ashamed by her defensiveness. "I'm sorry, Ted. It's not you. It's just . . . I've got a program in there that . . . I don't know, I'd just as soon it didn't get the chance to copy itself out."

"Copy *itself* out?" Ted's interest was seriously engaged.

"I'll tell you about it—all right? But not now."

"If you say so. All I'm telling you is what I was told."

"What were you told? Exactly."

"They're following up on a whole bunch of suspects, and this is one of them. We've got a hacker who's routing all over the network, covering his tracks by dialing into nodes all around the world, and we're trying to find out where he's coming from."

"Okay, okay." She forced herself to be calm. "Nobody except me can dial in."

"Ah! So there is a way in."

"Well, of course there is. I have a modem line for my own PC, but I'm the only one who uses that line. And my PC isn't on a network, so there's no way anybody could know about it."

"Somebody must have the number of that line apart from you."

"Nobody."

Ted twitched an eyebrow and the corner of his mouth simultaneously. Both had the flexible angularity of the rest of his body. "The phone company must have the number."

Tessa was silent. Of course the phone company would have the number. The university administration must also have the number . . . and suddenly it hit her.

"Wait a minute," she said, "you're not talking about Attila. You're talking about the university computer. That's wide open. There's stuff going through there all the time. And of course . . . Oh, God!"

"What?"

"Oh, Christ!"

"Tessa, will you stop being as biblical as Redway and tell me what's worrying you?"

"That modem number has to be listed by the phone company—somewhere. And it's obviously going to be listed among university admin records. I mean, the phone bill's got to be paid, so of course the number's there."

"Okay. Right."

"This hacker you're talking about is obviously going through the university computer, not Attila in the lab. I mean, if he gets into Attila he's not going to get out. He can look around, but that's all."

"Figures."

"Okay, imagine you're this hacker and you're into the university computer, which is no big deal. While you're there and before you move on, you're going to look around—okay?"

"Nature of the beast."

"And if you come across a reference to 'modem number for Attila, isolated,' you're going to get curious and take a look-see. Right?"

"Not inconceivable."

"A racing certainty. That's exactly how it would happen. I never thought of that till now."

"Tessa, are you going to tell me now what this is about?"

"No." She had already turned on her heel and was striding briskly to the door.

"Where are you going?"

"I've got to make a call."

17

As she waited impatiently for the elevator to reach her floor, Tessa could think of nothing except the old line about shutting the stable door after the horse had bolted. It was too soon to be sure, and maybe too late to be careful; but she had to do something.

She half-walked, half-ran down the long corridor, turned right instead of left at the end, and found herself in an annex that it took her what felt like an age to get out of, but was only two minutes. All the time the question revolved in her brain: So what if the program had got out? It wasn't necessarily a cause for panic.

It would mutate, obviously. That was what she had created it to do. In Attila it had mutated repeatedly, but always in a closed environment that allowed it time to stabilize. Out there on the networks it would be deluged by a tidal wave of information that it could not possibly assimilate in any ordered form, and from which it would have no respite. It was conceivable that it would just be scrambled, evaporating like a puff of smoke.

Despite her uncommonly high IQ, one of the things that Tessa didn't have was an eidetic memory—certainly not for figures. Nor, for that matter, for where she had put things. It took several more frustrating moments of rummaging through her small suitcase and her carry-on bag before she finally found her address and phone book—in the pocket of the coat she'd hung behind the door. She checked her watch and, even allowing for the hour's difference, realized that the lab assistant she needed to contact would be home by now.

She dialed, listened to the phone ring five times, and cursed when she heard the answering machine pick up. Then she heard Danny Swanton's own voice cutting through the recording, which clicked off.

"Danny—it's Tessa. I'm sorry, I have to ask you to go back to the lab. It's important."

"What's up? You all right, Tessa?"

"Yes, I'm . . . look, it doesn't matter, there's no time to explain. Just go back there and unplug the modem on Attila. Can you do that, please? Now?"

"I can be there in ten minutes on the bike. But what's the problem?"

"I'll tell you when I see you. I'm getting the first plane back. Just do it, please. Right away."

She hung up, and realized that her heart was beating as though she had been running. She took several deep breaths and felt it slow down. At least that took care of the first priority. If the program had not already escaped, it couldn't now. Or at least it wouldn't be able to—she looked at her watch again—in ten minutes, when Danny got there.

Danny was a technician, not a theorist. He knew what she was working on, but he wouldn't say a word about her research until she chose to make some announcement herself. That was good. For the moment, the fewer people who knew about any of this, the better. She had already cautioned Helen and Clive not to talk, and she knew she could rely on them.

The next task was to get the first possible flight out. The airline number was listed in a directory provided by the hotel and left by the phone. She heard a hideously distorted recording of Vivaldi, interrupted periodically by a soothing voice telling her in three languages that she would be connected with a booking agent as soon as one came free.

Throughout all this, her mind was absorbed by thoughts of what had to be done when she got back to Oxford. Suddenly she became aware that there was a live voice in her ear and not a recording. She explained that she had an open return and wanted a reservation on the first flight to Heathrow. The flight was nearly full and she had to take an upgrade to club. She said she would pay the difference at the airport. They assigned her an aisle seat. Check-in was in one hour.

Ten minutes later she was at the desk with her bags at her feet, signing her credit card and asking for a cab right away.

As she followed the porter to the ornate revolving door, she spotted Ted at the bar with a bunch of people she knew vaguely. She intended calling him tomorrow, but she had no time now. When he saw her she tried to ignore him, but he came running after her.

"What's happening? You're leaving? What is this?"

"Something's come up," she told him without breaking her stride. "I have to get back."

He danced backward in front of her. "What? What is it? What?"

"I'll call you tomorrow."

"No—now! Now!" He was like a little boy unable to wait till Christmas for his present.

She stopped and faced him squarely. "Do something for me, Ted," she said, as though it were an ultimatum. "Tell that friend of yours that I'll feed his trace program to the computer, but on condition that when he finds his hacker, I get to talk to him. Will you do that?"

"Tell me why. You have to tell me why."

She fumed at his persistence and only just managed to keep her temper. "Just do it. For me. All right?"

"No, not all right. Come on, Tessa, you can't bullshit an inquiring mind. What's going on?"

She felt her jaw tighten, but she knew that the more she showed anger, the more he would be certain that something big was in the wind.

"There's a program in my computer that I wouldn't like to think has got out. If there's any chance it has, I want to know. That's all I can tell you. Now, I have to go."

"All right, I'll do it," he said quietly, and stepped aside.

She thanked him and went out into the night. She tipped the porter, who had already installed her bags in the waiting taxi.

As it drove off, her last image was of Ted's face staring palely through the slowly turning glass of the hotel door, serious and full of buzzing speculation. She just hoped he wouldn't talk.

18

TED DIDN'T, in fact, talk at all. He didn't even return to the bar to finish his drink. He went straight up to his room, set up his PC, and sent an e-mail through to Josh in California. He told him who Tessa was and reported what she had said, neither embellishing nor leaving anything out. There was, he wrote, a program that the hacker might have stolen or caused to escape from the mainframe computer at the Kendall Lab in Oxford. Tessa, as its creator, seemed deeply disturbed by this possibility and would need to question the hacker—if he or she were ever found—to ascertain whether or not there were real grounds for her fears. Meanwhile she was returning immediately to Oxford to check out what she could at that end.

Then he sat and pondered for a while, until the phone rang. His friends wanted to know if he was coming out to dinner. He picked up his coat and went down to join them.

The cab's wipers were working at full speed but snatching only glimpses of visibility through the deluge of rain on the windshield. The storm had broken suddenly and gridlocked the city's traffic. The driver spoke English and understood that Tessa had a plane to catch, but there was nothing he could do. Once they got through this, he said, he knew some short cuts.

To distract herself from the frustration, she concentrated on what she would do when she got to the lab. She would copy the program as many times as she needed, try different approaches simultaneously to save time, see how it responded. Even if it hadn't got loose, there was always the chance that it might some day, and at least she would be ready.

She also came to a conclusion that she had so far not needed to confront. She did not believe, she realized, that the program was in any sense truly alive. Despite her argument with Helen on the subject, she felt instinctively closer to her friend's position than to the advocates of "strong" AI—those who argued vociferously that there was no difference in principle between human consciousness and digitally based consciousness.

Yet, in the end, she had to admit that the distinction was academic in the least helpful sense of the word. All that mattered was what the program did, not what it was. And whether "to do" was different from "to be" in this context was, for her, a question that ended in maddening circles.

A sudden jolt as the taxi surged forward brought her back to the present. Looking out of the window she saw that they had turned into a long, wide street with poor lighting and busy though fluid traffic. The driver was saying that they could still just make it in time if he broke a few laws—which she interpreted as angling for a generous tip. She said that she would make it worth his while.

She saw the single set of headlights moving slowly out of the line of vehicles coming toward them, but couldn't be sure how far away they were, or how much space separated the two opposing streams of traffic. The blackness of the night and the still driving rain gave an unreal quality to all but the tangible interior of the taxi. Suddenly her driver was cursing in fluent German, his voice an octave higher than it had been previously, and swerving so hard that she felt the wheels beneath them go into a skid. Miraculously they avoided a head-on collision; the oncoming car, which seemed to be driven by a lunatic, braked and pulled back across the line that it shouldn't have crossed in the first place.

Tessa watched it all happen with dreamlike detachment. The streaming rain on the windows and the stroboscopic lights turning around them made her think of an underwater ballet. At the same time she braced herself for an impact that she knew would come and wished to God that she'd fastened her seat belt.

The impact, when it came, was almost an anticlimax. She felt the car's rear fender lock with that of another car slightly behind and to the right. Their waltzing motion became slower and more stately. She was thrown into the air as they mounted the pavement, but landed horizontally on the seat and wasn't hurt. Suddenly the car was stationary.

She sat up cautiously. People were running toward them from all directions. Even the traffic going the other way had stopped. People were getting out of their cars, unconscious of the drenching rain that soaked them to the skin in moments. Her driver was also out, unhurt and shouting his version of what had happened to anyone who would listen. At the same time he was struggling to open her door, which had buckled slightly.

Tessa surrendered gladly to the hands that reached in to help her. A moment later she was standing on the pavement, looking back at two or three other vehicles similarly entangled, though it didn't look as if there had been any serious injuries. They had been lucky.

But the road was blocked and looked like it would be staying that way for some time. The plane would leave without her.

Maria Brandt had all but given up hope of getting to London that night. Her boyfriend, Eric, had arrived there from Frankfurt two hours ago, and she hadn't seen him in a week. They both worked for the same airline, and were trying to arrange things so that they could be more often on the same routes together, he as a copilot, she as a stewardess; but it wasn't easy.

Still, they hadn't done too badly on the whole, with snatched nights of passion in some of the most romantic cities in the world. They'd had weekends in Paris, dinners by the Grand Canal in Venice, and watched sunsets together at the Taj Mahal. Tonight would be a hotel room off the Bayswater Road, and tomorrow they could have lunch at some little pub, then maybe take that trip down the river they had talked about last time they were in London. She didn't have to be back in Berlin until Monday.

But first she had to get to Heathrow. There was no charge for the flight, but she was not in uniform and company regulations said she had to have a seat. The flight was fully booked, and her only hope was a last minute no-show. She was standing behind the check-in desk, watching the seconds tick away on a big wall clock until the flight closed. When the time came, she cast a hopeful eye in the direction of her friend Klaus, the section supervisor, emerging from his office. He glanced at his watch, had a word with one of the girls at check-in, then came over to Maria.

"There's one seat," he said, "but it's in club. That means we have to wait awhile—ten, fifteen minutes."

Klaus was on the phone finding replacements for two of his staff who had called in sick. She caught his eye through his office window; he checked his watch again, and nodded his approval. Maria blew him a kiss and went up to the girl who was preparing to close out the flight and leave the desk. She was new at the job and Maria didn't know her, but she tapped something into her computer, waited for a boarding pass to appear, and handed it to Maria.

Maria thanked her and turned to hurry toward departure, when she happened to glance down at the card in her hand and read the name T. Lambert where her own should be. She turned back to the girl and pointed out that she had a boarding pass in the name of the no-show passenger instead of her own.

The girl, flustered in her inexperience, didn't know what to do about the error. Maria told her it was no big deal and not to worry. The computer should have automatically registered the passenger as a no-show, but now it wouldn't because the boarding pass had been issued. However, all the girl need do was wait till Klaus was off the phone—she could see him still talking urgently in his office—tell him what had happened, and he would set the record straight.

Then she hurried toward departure and onto the plane, wondering whether she should marry Eric as he had asked her to. She'd never felt happier.

19

ALMOST TWO HOURS after her flight's departure time, Tessa was deposited with her bags at one of the anonymous hotels that clustered around the approach to the airport. Two very charming police officers had insisted on bringing her in their patrol car. At the desk she asked if they could check out the time of the next flight to London. They told her it was at 7:10 in the morning. She asked them to make her a reservation, and they said they would call her with confirmation.

When she got to her room she looked at her watch and wondered whether she was hungry enough to have something sent up. She dialed the number and let it ring, but nobody answered. As she hung up, she reflected that if the faded seventies seediness of the place was anything to go by, she didn't much fancy eating anything that might come out of its kitchens anyway. She decided she would run a bath and try to relax, but first she turned on the television and flipped through a few channels until she came to CNN. They were running commercials, but she left it on in the background as she opened up her traveling computer, plugged it into the phone outlet, and dialed in to check her e-mail.

There was nothing of any significance awaiting her, and as

she quickly glanced through it she became aware of something on the television behind her. There was a major story breaking about an air crash.

To begin with she paid little attention; but slowly the number and destination of the flight bore in on her. She spun around to look at the screen. Images wobbled under the arc lights of rescue teams and moving camera crews. She saw torn fragments of metal. There was a shot of a suitcase, broken open, its banal contents scattered pathetically about it in the grass. A primeval shape surging like a dark force from the earth became, when hit by a handheld beam of light, the smoldering remains of a massive jet engine.

The images cut back to the studio, where a newscaster was repeating the number of Tessa's flight to London, which had collided with an incoming flight from Paris. Over three hundred people had been killed. The wreckage had landed in open country, otherwise many more would have died on the ground. No official explanation for the disaster had yet been offered, but speculation centerd inevitably on air traffic control: specifically on the question of human error or computer malfunction.

She saw that the television screen was displaying an emergency number for people to call who were worried that relatives or friends might have been on either flight. She knew at once that she had to satisfy the gnawing question in her mind. She picked up the phone and dialed the number.

A man's voice answered surprisingly quickly. He spoke only German, and quickly passed her over to a woman who spoke perfect English with only a slight accent. "How can I help you?"

"I'm afraid," Tessa began shakily, "that a friend of mine may have been on that flight for London. Her name is Lambert. Tessa Lambert."

"May I ask your name and what your connection with the passenger is, please?"

Tessa thought quickly. She should have realized that they wouldn't talk to just anyone. They would need a name and address, an indication of legitimate interest, something for their records. "I'm Helen Temple," she said. It was the first thing that came into her head. "Dr. Helen Temple. Miss Lambert is my patient." She gave Helen's address and phone number in Oxford.

"One moment please, Dr. Temple."

In the pause that followed Tessa could hear the click of a computer keyboard, plus the soft murmur of voices at other phones in the background.

"Dr. Temple?"

"Yes?"

"We have a *Dr.* Lambert shown on the list. Dr. T. Lambert."

"Yes. Yes, that's her." All that passed through Tessa's stunned brain was the thought of how silly it was to call two such different types of doctor by the same name.

"I'm very sorry, Dr. Temple. I'm afraid we have no reports of survivors."

"Thank you." Tessa hung up woodenly with her eyes on the carpet in front of where she sat. She drew a shallow, unsteady breath. Of course it proved nothing that her name was on the list. But suddenly she didn't need proof anymore.

Her gaze drifted back to the television screen, but the news bulletin had moved on to something else. She got up to find the remote control and switched the sound off, leaving the picture on in case they returned to the story. Then she turned back to her computer.

And gasped as though someone had hit her.

The text she had been reading had disappeared, though she hadn't cut the connection or given any command. In its place were three words, square in the center of the screen, followed by a question mark.

WHO ARE YOU?

When she thought about it later, she told herself she should have done things differently. But she wasn't sure it would have changed anything. With a taut-muscled, terrified stealth, she crept up on one side of the computer and wrenched its phone connection from the wall—like somebody lashing out with a knife at a poisonous snake. After that she hit the power button and the batteries died. The screen was blank.

She stood for a moment, feeling cold and with a film of

moisture on her skin. There was utter silence in the room. Only the faint hum of planes taking off and landing in the distance could be heard through the double glazing. The television screen still flickered soundlessly as she had left it. But then, out of the corner of her vision, she noticed something happening. By the time she had swung around to face it, the change was complete. The image of the newscaster had disappeared and the television screen had faded to black. Framed dead center were the same three words she had seen on her computer.

WHO ARE YOU?

Her stomach seemed to balloon upward to her throat. She made some sort of sound, tasted something bitter. For a moment she thought that she was going to pass out . . . but instead she lunged forward and yanked the power cable from the wall. The words faded.

She realized that she was on her knees, where she had dropped to reach the television plug. She heard a soft thud as it fell from her hand. Then, once more, silence. She reached out for a chair to pull herself up. Her body felt heavy, her limbs stiff—the result, she supposed, of an adrenaline flood but with nowhere to run. She must clear her head, get a grip. Think.

The phone by the side of her bed rang with a harshness that jarred her raw nerves. But she was relieved by this intrusion of normality into the hellishly improbable drama that had been playing itself out in this drab room. She went over and picked up, saying "Yes?" into the mouthpiece, grateful to hear a voice. Any voice.

Except this voice. This was not a human voice. It was the kind of voice that tells you the time when you call in, or recites a phone number you've asked for: a recorded voice, broken into fragments to be reassembled as needed. And it had been reassembled now to speak those same three words flatly in her ear.

"WHO ARE YOU?"

01100111011001010110010000100000

She screamed in blind, panic-driven shock, and tore the cord from the wall so savagely that she pulled the socket and a chunk of plaster along with it.

A moment later the lights in the room dipped to barely half their previous brightness, as though something had short-circuited their power supply. But she knew this was no technical failure; it was that thing out there showing her its strength.

Her gaze went to the uncurtained window and the dull slabs of brick and concrete and all the other sightless windows it looked out on. Down below a near-empty, rain-slicked road was lined by yellow street lights. As she watched, they too dimmed, though not by so much, then rose again, along with those around her in the room, as though nothing had happened.

A salute? A threat? A promise? Tessa felt herself begin to shake unstoppably from head to toe. Terror gripped her in a way that she had never experienced before. Perhaps, if she had actually been on board that plane and faced her death, she would have known the same deep, elemental fear that welled up now from depths she did not know that she had access to. It came from somewhere beyond time and was eternal. Her body continued to shake, and she was as powerless to stop it as a leaf caught in the flood of some great river that had burst its banks.

Then she realized what the shaking meant. These were convulsions. There was an awful wetness creeping down her inner thigh. She suddenly understood with brutal clarity that she was hemorrhaging.

20

THEY TOLD HER later that she must have reconnected one of the phones in her room—the socket that wasn't broken—and called downstairs for help. She remembered none of that. The next few hours remained mere brush strokes in her memory: a stretcher; flashing lights; a needle in her arm; the white ceiling of a hospital corridor that she was wheeled down at high speed by people who spoke no English; the saline drip that swayed above her head, and the stab of another unseen needle in her arm.

As she struggled to hold on to consciousness, her last thought was that death, having been cheated twice, had finally come to claim her. Then she fell into oblivion.

She didn't believe in out-of-body experiences, so it couldn't be that. She believed in dreams, so that must be what it was. She didn't know what they'd given her, but she knew she was unconscious. So it was a lucid dream. Her brain, stimulated by the activity around her, was hallucinating an operating theater. She was looking down on it, but she wasn't floating: it wasn't a flying dream. In flying dreams you have a body, but in this one she didn't. Her body was down there being tended by doctors and nurses in surgical masks and gowns. She was up here, out of her body, incorporeal.

She watched with a strange calm fascination as they took a blood sample, cross-checked it, then prepared a transfusion. She became aware that she was watching without blinking. But of course you couldn't blink without eyes, and she was watching without eyes.

Somebody down there gave her an injection. She couldn't hear very well what they were saying, and when she did hear she didn't understand. Then suddenly she knew what the injection had been for. It had been to contract her womb. Her body must have told her that, although she didn't feel it. She didn't feel anything. It was all going on down there.

Down there her body arched and pushed. She felt she ought to have been sickened by the spectacle, but she wasn't. It was ugly and bloody, and if it had been happening to anybody else she would have empathized. But it wasn't happening to anybody else, it was happening to her. And it didn't touch her.

Then, just as the detachment was becoming dull and deadening and she felt herself drifting away toward a strange kind of apathetic blankness, she saw something that brought her back with a jolt to what was going on.

She saw the baby. Her baby. She hadn't been prepared for that. For how formed it was. How human. So much larger than she would have guessed from how it felt, though she knew intellectually that it must have been about that size—nine, ten inches now. Her dead child. Deposited without ceremony in a plastic bowl. For disposal.

The worst thing was she couldn't look away. How can you look away from something happening in your head? There is no hiding place.

Somehow time passed. Or perhaps she slipped away somewhere and didn't notice, because suddenly she was being wheeled along a corridor and into a recovery room. She watched as she was lifted from the trolley into bed. There was monitoring equipment nearby but not hooked up. In one corner was something that she took to be a resuscitation unit. Above all there was a quietness.

It was all over now, she thought. She'd been cleaned up,

and a doctor and a nurse stood over her, murmuring. As she looked down she saw their faces quite distinctly.

The doctor wasn't happy about something. He made another brief examination, then murmured to the nurse.

Suddenly, she didn't know how, Tessa understood what he was saying. She didn't speak the language, so how could it be that she understood in so much detail?

The answer once again, of course, was that it was happening in her head. It was her fear speaking, her constant and recurring fear of being given the one drug that would kill her.

That was what they were talking about now. Penicillin. The doctor was saying he'd be happier if she had a shot of penicillin, a large dose. Check her notes, see if there was any problem there.

Check her notes? What did that mean? The notes that they had made earlier tonight contained no reference to penicillin—how could they? And she didn't wear a Medic-Alert bracelet or carry a card: she'd been told that most people with her kind of allergy didn't, although it was a sensible precaution. But she had disliked the idea of being tagged as an invalid. Besides, she was covered by that new European Union scheme. According to Helen, whose practice had been part of it for six months now, it was the first sensible thing to come out of Brussels. She remembered Helen making some wry joke when all her patients' records were put on a database that could be accessed by a single call from anywhere in the world—something about finally being dragged to join her friend in the computer age.

As she listened harder—didn't listen so much as concentrate—Tessa realized that the people standing around her weren't talking about written notes. They were referring to that EU scheme. Everything these people needed to know to avoid killing her was on that computerized database, and they were calling it, right now, as she listened.

And she knew what it would say.

She knew with certainty that it was spelling out her death warrant. And she was powerless to intervene. She could not be heard. She could not be seen. She could only watch.

Maybe she was dead already, looking back in time.

Maybe this was always how you died.

01101111011011110110101100101110

• • •

Helen was almost asleep when the phone rang. Clive, who was reading a book that he'd promised to review for the *Times Literary Supplement* by the end of the week, looked over, saw that it was her phone, and didn't reach for it. But he peered anxiously over his glasses as she answered, instantly alert. He knew she wasn't on call; this must be some emergency.

"Dr. Temple, we spoke forty minutes ago." The voice on the line was a woman's, accented, perhaps German.

"We did?" asked Helen, puzzled. The woman, although speaking excellent English, missed the inflection that made the words a question. Which was fortunate, because she simply went straight on to explain why she was calling.

"I'm afraid the information that I gave you in our previous conversation was incorrect. The list of passengers was updated after we spoke . . ."

Inexplicably the patient's pulse and blood pressure continued to drop. She was going into deep coma.

There were numerous possible reasons, and only one was ruled out, because it would have appeared on her notes. There was nothing on the printout about penicillin.

Tessa watched it all. She tried to scream, but no one heard, not even herself. And there was no way to make signs, to touch, to warn. For the first time she felt real pain; but it was the pain of fear and frustration, not physical pain.

She felt herself begin to fade like an old photograph. Soon she would be gone, a memory dispersed in fragments through the minds of others, beyond recall. She wondered if she would go back into her body, but it didn't happen that way.

Instead she felt herself moving inexorably away from all of it, into a terrible isolation. But not a frightening one. Emotions such as fear had already gone. All that remained was a last lingering spark of consciousness.

That too, she realized, was fading like a dying candle flame, as though it had all never been. And there would be no record afterward. No mark left on time or space.

Whatever they were.

21

A VENETIAN BLIND, half-closed against bright sunlight, threw narrow stripes across the bed. Her first thought when she opened her eyes was that she was in some kind of cage. At least she knew she was alive: she felt heavy and her body ached.

Something moved in the room. She was aware only of a ripple in the patterning of light and dark across the wall—a zebra passing through a forest clearing. But it came toward her instead of vanishing in camouflage. A human form took shape as the ripples swam closer; then she felt someone sit lightly on the edge of her bed, and recognized the face looking down into hers with fondness and anxiety.

"Helen . . ."

"How d'you feel?"

"Not great." Her throat was dry and her voice thick.

"Drink this." Helen raised her head slightly off the pillow and put a glass to her lips. She couldn't tell whether the liquid had a flavor or was just water. But it eased her throat.

"Where are we?" she asked.

"Berlin. The hospital they took you to from the hotel."

"But what are you . . .?"

"Sshhh. Don't talk too much."

"But how . . .?"

"They gave you penicillin."

"I know."

Helen frowned. "You knew? Then why didn't you . . .?"

"It was all a kind of dream. I couldn't do anything."

They were both silent for a moment. Tessa felt Helen cover one of her hands with her own.

"Darling, I'm so sorry about the baby."

Tessa nodded, gripped Helen's hand a little more tightly, but didn't speak. She was afraid that if she opened her mouth all that would emerge would be self-pity, and she would be ashamed of that. Angrily she felt tears threatening to well up in her eyes, and she forced her attention to other things.

"How did you get here? Did they phone you?"

Helen shook her head. "Not exactly. I got a call from an airline about the accident. Neither Clive nor I had seen the news last night, it was the first we knew about it."

She told the story of how, after the call from the airline, she had gone downstairs to find the number of the hotel where Tessa was staying, and how she had called and been told she had checked out. If she wasn't there and she wasn't on that plane, Helen asked herself, convinced now that something was seriously wrong, where was she?

Clive was pressed into service, German being one of the five languages he spoke with reasonable fluency. By dint of insistence, and dropping the name of somebody he knew vaguely in the Bonn bureaucracy, Clive had extracted from the hotel the number of the taxi company that had taken Tessa to the airport. Several calls later they had traced her from the airport hotel to the hospital.

Getting through to the doctor in charge of her case had been the hardest part. Clive had been obliged to invent close friendships that would have surprised a number of senior players in government and banking circles, but in the end he'd been put through and had translated between Helen and the doctor. That was when they had discovered the "flaw" in the EU computer system, an experiment which Helen had now abandoned with contempt.

The German doctor, a great believer in technology and in

this particular EU enterprise, had refused to believe that the printout he had received could be so at odds with the information fed by Helen into the database. Clive had had to pretend an acquaintance with the health minister himself in order to get Helen's protests taken seriously. Finally the German had relented, accepted that Helen was who she said she was and that the patient actually had a penicillin allergy. He had given Tessa the one thing that could save her life: an intravenous cortisone injection.

Tessa's face was grave, lost in thought behind a frown.

"It's all right, darling. Everything's perfectly all right," Helen said, trying to reassure her. "You'll be fine in no time. And there shouldn't be a problem for any future pregnancy, if that's worrying you."

Tessa looked up, met Helen's eyes. "You flew here?" she asked, alarmed.

Helen understood, or thought she did. "It must have been a terrible shock hearing about that plane after just missing it the way you did . . ."

"It wasn't that," Tessa said in little more than a whisper. She dropped her eyes, and her gaze seemed to turn inward. "That wasn't what made me lose the baby."

"What happened? Tell me."

Helen sensed her friend's body grow rigid beneath the bedclothes and saw the muscles of her jaw tighten. She was, she realized, still in shock. "We don't have to talk about it now," she said. "Unless you want to. If that would help."

Another moment passed before Tessa responded. When she did, it was as though she was talking to herself, mouthing the words only to give shape to her thoughts. "If it didn't kill you . . . that must have been because by the time you flew here . . . it was too late. There would have been no point . . ."

"I don't understand. What d'you mean?"

Tessa ignored the interruption. "It didn't block your phone call here," she murmured, "but it could have . . . so why didn't it?"

Delayed shock was one thing, but there was something more going on here that worried Helen.

"Tessa? What are you talking about? Darling, look at me."

Again Tessa ignored her, seemed not even to hear.

"Tessa? Tessa, what is this? What's this 'it' you're talking about?"

Still Tessa didn't move, just lay in silence, staring fixedly at nothing. Instinctively Helen wanted to take her friend by the shoulders and shake some sense out of her, but she restrained the impulse.

"Tessa, what's 'it'?"

Suddenly Tessa looked up at her, eyes wide and serious like a child's. "We're going back by train. No bookings. Pay cash, no credit cards. Nothing on computer."

Helen felt the silence lengthen as she wondered how to reply. Dealing with the trauma now would mean psychiatric treatment in this hospital, and she would far rather get Tessa back to Oxford.

"All right," she said finally, "whatever you think's best. Just tell me and I'll make the arrangements."

0111100100100000011000100110101111

22

IN THE END it was Tessa who made the arrangements. She found a couple of old travelers' checks in the side pocket of her bag, and she used her credit cards to draw the maximum cash that she could on any one day from a machine. It was enough for a couple of train tickets. She went to the station and bought them herself, refusing to tell Helen what train she had booked so that she couldn't call home and tell anyone when to expect her.

"If you do anything that lets it know we're on this train, there'll be some kind of accident and a lot of people besides ourselves will be dead," Tessa told her. Helen nodded gravely.

The journey back to Oxford was an awkward one for both of them. A distance had opened up between them. Tessa understood it and didn't resent it, but hated the fact that she could not, at least for the moment, trust her friend—because her friend could not trust her.

"Look, just indulge me—okay?" she said to Helen as they settled themselves into their seats and waited for the train to pull out of the station. "Pretend I'm telling the truth, just for now—all right?"

"I've never assumed anything else." There was a professional restraint in Helen's voice, a pulling back from their usual intimacy.

"I know. But you think I hallucinated."

"It's a possibility."

"And I'm sure there are sound psychological reasons for believing it. But I know differently. What happened to me in that hotel room was real. I didn't fantasize it later."

"The plane crash was real, Tessa. That was a close enough brush with death to scare anybody."

"What I had a brush with scared me a lot more than the plane crash. And I like to think I'm not that easy to scare. Will you at least give me that much credit?"

There was a soft jolt as the train began to pull out of the station. Helen sighed and eased down in her seat a little."

"What about the crash investigation? Won't that show something to, well, back up your story?"

"Take my word, all they'll find is that one system failed to convey information to another system. They won't find out why because there'll be nothing to see, so they'll say 'gremlins' or 'human error' and make a few changes so that if it happens again nobody can blame them."

The train was picking up speed. Helen looked out of the window, then back at Tessa and put up her hands as though to show she was hiding nothing. "Look, I'm going along with you—all right? But I'd be happier if you'd talk to somebody I know when we get back to Oxford."

"Helen, it's a waste of time. You Turing-tested that program yourself. You know what it can do."

"I know what it *seemed* to be able to do. But when we talked about it afterwards, even you weren't sure how seriously we should take it. The theory's one thing, but . . ."

"It's more than theory now."

"So shouldn't we warn somebody?"

"Such as who?"

"Whoever's in charge of those international networks—if it's really out there."

Tessa couldn't suppress a bitter laugh. "Nobody's in charge. It's total anarchy—which it has to be if users are going to move information around the way they need to. Besides, if we start a panic and the thing senses people after it, it could become even more dangerous than it already is."

They fell silent. The high-speed train continued to accelerate with silky smoothness through a flat, uninteresting landscape. Tessa stared out of the window and Helen watched her. Eventually she said: "So what will you do?"

Tessa shook her head slightly, but without altering the direction of her abstracted gaze.

"I don't know," she said softly. "First I have to think . . . try to imagine how it must be thinking, and go from there."

23

THE HEAVYSET uniformed sergeant rolled as he walked, like a man who had seen too many cowboy movies; or maybe it was just the effort of swinging the weight of his beer belly from one hip to the other with each step. He was a type Tim Kelly knew only too well; this was how his old man could have wound up if he hadn't found the strength somewhere inside himself to quit drinking. He watched as the big freckled hands fumbled slightly getting the key into the lock; the unsteadiness was covered quickly, and only somebody who knew about that sort of thing would have noticed.

Tim was coming to know about that sort of thing more and more. He made a small bet with himself that he would smell mint on the cop's breath as he passed him, a sure sign of a vodka bottle squirrelled away in some desk drawer or file cabinet to be nipped from routinely throughout the day.

"Okay, Kelly, come on back here. Somebody to see you." The cop pulled the barred door open to an angle of ninety degrees and jerked his head back over his shoulder.

Tim pushed himself stiffly to his feet and ran a hand over the stubble on his chin. They had removed the handcuffs after they'd made some checks and started to believe who he was. He stepped past the cop and out into the corridor, noting with a grim satisfaction that he'd been right about the smell of mint. "Fuck," he thought, "who am I to talk?"

They started down the narrow corridor, the cop staying a couple of steps behind his prisoner the way it says you're supposed to in the manual. The mixed odors of urine, sweat, and disinfectant swept over them in waves that made Tim nauseous. As they passed the other cells he saw that they were almost all occupied. One short, slim-built man in his forties wearing a torn tuxedo was holding the bars and demanding in a high nasal whine to know where his lawyer was. The cop ignored him.

Through a couple more barred gates and they were in the station itself. The cop grunted at Tim to stop outside a door marked CAPT. BEATTY. He knocked and listened for a muffled answer, then pushed the door open, nodded for Tim to go in, and closed the door behind him.

Captain Beatty had close-cropped white hair, clear blue eyes, and an aquiline nose that would have looked good on someone in a toga. He sat behind a preternaturally tidy desk—everything arranged at careful right angles to the edges—and wore his uniform with a straight-backed, pigeon-chested pride. The room itself was monastic, with two small high windows letting in so little daylight that the electric light had to be on at all times. Tim was relieved to see the disheveled figure of Jack Fischl slouching, hands in pockets, behind the captain's chair.

"That was a smart move, calling your friend the lieutenant here," said Beatty, after glaring at Tim for a few moments with undisguised contempt. His voice had a dry waspish quality that made Tim wonder what the man was doing in Los Angeles instead of Philadelphia or Boston. "If it was up to me you'd be in court in a half hour, and explaining yourself to your station chief after that."

Jack Fischl made a face over Beatty's head that told Tim just to stand there, stay cool, let things run their course.

"I don't know what attitude they take in the Bureau these days to intoxicated operatives getting into their automobiles and driving the wrong way through a one-way system, but I doubt it'd do a whole lot for your career prospects—about which I don't personally give a damn."

Tim dropped his gaze to the floor. The impression conveyed to Beatty was one of suitable remorse and shame; the real reason for the gesture was to avoid cracking a smile at the way Fischl had crossed his eyes in painful boredom, having no doubt already endured this kind of harangue for some time.

"Fortunately you didn't cause any serious accident—though God knows how you got away with it. You sure as hell didn't deserve to. However, bearing that in mind, and in view of the intervention of the lieutenant here, I am prepared at this time to take no further action on the matter. Your arrest remains on record at this station, but will not be processed further."

Tim lifted his gaze to meet Beatty's. He was no longer in danger of smiling, and the humble silent thanks his look conveyed was genuine.

Beatty leaned forward. "But you come up on my beat one more time, and not even the attorney general of the United States coming down here with a letter from the president is going to get you off the hook. Do I make myself understood?"

"Yes, sir, absolutely." Tim cleared his throat. It was the first time he had spoken in many hours, he realized, and his voice was thick and all but inaudible.

Beatty glared at him a moment more, then sat back and busied himself with papers on his desk. "Get him out of here," he said.

Jack Fischl, only too glad to comply, was around the desk in a single move and propelling Tim to the door.

In the corridor Jack expelled a lungful of air like a man who had been holding his breath under water. "What an asshole. Buddy, do you owe me! I had to listen to that sanctimonious cocksucker for an hour before he decided to play ball."

"Thanks, Jack, I knew you'd come through."

"It's okay. Just get drunk someplace else next time."

"Sure thing." There was the hollowness of humiliation in Tim's voice. He didn't say any more as they went to the desk and he signed for the return of his possessions—wallet, watch, pens. He was aware of eyes watching him: eyes that told him he had disgraced himself and the agency he was part of. For the cops in that room it was a deep and satisfying triumph to have a federal agent in their power, and to be showing him clemency made them feel big. He took his belongings, mumbled a thanks, and was grateful to have Jack Fischl at his side as he walked out, because otherwise he might have started something in response to those leering smirks that he would have lived to regret.

"Jack, I gotta go home, get a shave, catch a couple of hours' sleep . . ."

"No problem, it's all arranged. Your brother's here."

"Oh, shit!"

Jack pushed open a door into the main hall where people crossed in all directions, disappearing down corridors, up stairs, or out onto the street. Josh was sitting on a bench by himself against the far wall.

"For chrissakes, Jack, why did you bring him into this? If I'd wanted my brother involved I'd have called him."

"Calm down, will you? Your brother called me. He'd been trying to find you and nobody knew where you were. He called me just after I got the call from here."

Josh had spotted them and was getting to his feet. His eyes were on Tim, and the concern in them refused to be hidden no matter how much he tried to smile.

"You okay, big brother?"

"I'm fine. Just take me home, okay?"

"Sure."

"Jack . . . thanks, pal. We'll talk later."

"Take it easy. Anything comes up, I'll call you."

In the car Tim cranked his seat back and closed his eyes, acutely aware of Josh darting anxious sidelong glances at him. At least he wasn't asking questions or lecturing, which anyway wasn't Josh's style.

"Aren't you going to ask?" Tim heard himself saying as the silence between them lengthened.

"Is there any reason to think you'd remember a whole lot?"

Tim half-opened one eye and cocked it in his brother's direction. "Smart aleck, huh?"

"Smart is a relative thing, big brother. And you being a relative . . ."

"Okay, okay." Tim closed his eyes again. "Jack said you were looking for me? You got some news?"

"Just a progress report. It was our morning for breakfast—Butterfield's this time, remember?"

• • •

Forty minutes later, as he stepped out of the shower and dried himself off, Tim decided that he felt a great deal better, but would still rather stay home than show up at the office with so obvious a hangover. He called in and claimed food poisoning, and didn't give a damn if they believed him or not. Tomorrow, he assured them, he'd be fine—and even today they should call him if anything developed. Then he pulled on a robe and went through to his kitchen, from which an aroma of coffee and bacon wafted seductively.

"There wasn't a thing in your fridge," Josh said over his shoulder, "so I went out while you were in the shower." There was a big supermarket bag on the area by the stove. "Figured you might be working up an appetite about now."

It was true. To his surprise, Tim discovered he was ravenous.

"Be ready in a couple of minutes," Josh said. "Have some coffee."

"No rush," Tim answered casually. "There's something I need to do first."

He felt Josh's eyes never leaving him as he went to a cupboard, took out a half-full quart of vodka and put it on the table. Then he went to a bookcase in his living room and took out a nearly empty fifth of bourbon from behind a row of Saul Bellows. He put that too on the table. Other odd corners and hiding places yielded five more bottles in various states of consumption. He gathered them all on the kitchen table, then carried them over to the sink one by one and poured them away. Not a word was exchanged until the operation was complete and the bottles in the bin. Then Tim turned and faced his brother squarely for the first time, he realized, in quite a while.

"Those eggs look about ready," he said. "And so am I."

Josh didn't say anything, but the smile on his face as he set out their plates was visibly more spontaneous than it had been earlier. They ate in companionable silence and eventually drifted into the conversation they would have had that morning if Tim had not missed their appointment. Josh recounted the latest development in the complex process of elimination that was by now reaching out in all directions and looping several times around the earth.

"The idea is we reach right back to the point where the guy entered the system. All UIDs are registered at access points. That means lists of names. And even if he's using a stolen UID, you'll have somewhere to start looking."

"How many of these access points are there?"

"God, I wouldn't begin to know. But we're looking for a killer who's operating in and around LA, which means we can probably ignore access points outside of this area, which cuts down our number of suspects considerably."

"To about how many?"

"From several thousand to, I'd say, between one and two hundred."

Tim made a thin whistling sound through his teeth. "That's a lot of legwork."

"It's a lot closer than you were."

"Shit—I know."

Josh frowned as a thought crossed his mind. "Does Jack Fischl know anything about all this?"

Tim looked mildly concerned. "No. You didn't say anything?"

"Of course not. I just wondered. He seems like a pretty regular guy."

"The best. But there's no point in making him an accomplice to the illegal gathering of evidence."

"So what happens," Josh went on, tipping his chair back and clasping his hands behind his head, "if we actually come up with a lead that gives you the guy? What about admissibility and all that stuff? I mean you're going to have to come up with some story of how you found him."

Tim shrugged. It was not a gesture of indifference but a rueful acknowledgment of the truth. "That could be a problem. But it's a problem I'd like to have. Maybe that'll be the time for Jack and me to put our heads together."

There was something about the way he said it—casual, but final—that made Josh ask no more questions. Glad to change the subject, he remembered something he'd filed away at the back of his mind a few days ago. He reached for his wallet and took out the piece of paper on which he'd scribbled a name and address.

"I almost forgot . . . it's probably nothing, but I promised I'd pass it on. This friend of mine, Ted Sawyer . . . he's out in Kansas now . . . well, he's actually in Europe at the moment, but only for a couple more weeks . . . I asked him to find me a contact in Oxford, England. One of the leads we've been following has been going through a computer there. He spoke to some woman he knows and said she had a holy shit-fit at the thought that some program she was working on might have been stolen. She cooperated, but in return she made him promise to let her know if the guy was ever caught. You never know—it might be helpful. I mean, if we find the program in his computer that was in her computer . . ."

24

IT WAS THOSE PICTURES that had done it. She had gone into the little kitchen off the back of the lab to make herself a coffee, and there they'd been: half a dozen newspapers on top of the bin waiting to be thrown out, all carrying harrowing photographs of the crash site in Germany. Tessa had been back in Oxford for forty-eight hours, and had so far successfully avoided looking at television or buying newspapers. It was the only way to keep her mind off the paralyzing sense of guilt that she felt about those deaths, and focus on what she must do if it wasn't to happen again.

Danny had come in and found her slowly turning the pages, tears streaming down her face and her shoulders shaking with silent grief. He hadn't fully understood, of course. Nobody knew the whole story apart from Tessa herself, and she had spoken only to Helen, who she knew would talk to Clive, but that was all right. All Danny knew was that Tessa had narrowly missed being on that plane, which to him was in itself quite sufficient to produce some kind of hysterical reaction. He had taken the papers from her, hidden them away, and made her sit down. He made her a cup of tea and encouraged her to go home early, saying she was working too hard. When she refused, he settled for a promise that she would take a short walk and get some fresh air. He offered to go with her, but she preferred to be alone.

The University Parks behind the science area was a wide expanse of grass surrounded by tall trees, all fresh clad in the green of spring and reaching up into a chill blue sky with scudding gray-white clouds. Despite the aspirins, Tessa felt a bone-splitting headache tightening around her skull.

She stopped at a wooden bench and surveyed the view. Undergraduates hurried to tutorials with essays under their arms; mothers pushed prams with toddlers running alongside; couples held hands, unaware of anything but each other; in the distance two dogs raced back and forth between their owners, giving out occasional yaps of pure pleasure. A sharp stab of pain behind her eyes made her shut them tight and press both hands to her temples. Fortunately nobody was close enough to hear the cry of alarm that she gave. It wasn't the pain: it was what she had seen. The moment she closed her eyes the world was replaced not by darkness but by a nightmare vision: burning wreckage all around her; charred, broken bodies like shapes from hell; pathetic personal belongings spewed from burst bags; the air thick with dark oily smoke.

Her eyes flew open and the vision was replaced by the scene she had been looking at before. Yet it too seemed changed—not in any observable detail but by her knowledge of what had been born into it. There was a new and alien consciousness out there, an all-pervading presence that she felt all round her, even in nature—which was ridiculous, because it was an electronic, artificial *thing.*

Artificial? What did that mean? This park was artificial: nature didn't cut grass or landscape itself. And those buildings beyond the trees, the science area she had just walked from—buildings of stone and brick were no less artificial than jet propulsion, nuclear power, or silicon chips. You could not uninvent what had been invented. *That* would be unnatural.

But she had invented nothing. She was as sure of that as she was that she was alive. Science was a process of discovery, not creation. Intelligence imposed nothing upon nature: on the contrary, it grew out of it. And Man was not some separate thing, his own creation, master of his fate: he was just a chance intersection of forces about which, try as he might, he knew ultimately nothing.

She pressed her fingers to the center of her forehead as though pushing back the pain. It wasn't the headache this time so much as a sudden stab of self-reproach for indulging in this abstract prattle. She knew deep down that these mind games were just a trick to avoid responsibility. She had caused those deaths as surely as if she had planted bombs on both planes. The death of her child was also her responsibility. There was no way of avoiding that, and it was wrong to try.

The shrill buzz of the cellular phone in the pocket of her jacket made her jump. She stood up as she took it out and put it to her ear.

"Hello?" She braced herself the way she did every time she picked up her phone now, wondering if she would hear that strange metallic voice that she had heard for a few seconds in Berlin. She regretted that she hadn't had more presence of mind and talked to the thing that night, instead of ripping the phone from the wall. All she'd done was confirm its paranoid conviction that the world and it were enemies. She didn't know if it would try to speak to her again before trying to kill her, as it surely would if it got a chance, but if it did she would be readier to deal with it next time.

"Tessa? I hope this isn't a bad time."

It was Jonathan Syme. She felt something between relief and disappointment, then surprise that in the circumstances he should be calling in such a cheery, casual tone.

"No, it's fine, Jonathan," she said, managing to sound equally normal. "Actually I'm just getting a breath of fresh air in the Parks."

"You sound like you're out-of-doors. And carrying your phone? By Jove," he laughed, "that's devotion beyond the call of duty."

She remembered only now that he knew nothing of what had happened, probably not even that she had been in Berlin at all.

"I'm expecting a call that I wouldn't want to miss," she said truthfully, but with no intention of explaining any more; a government department was the last thing she wanted on her back just now.

"In that case I won't monopolize you. I have just one question. As you know, I was very impressed by that last demonstration and there are one or two people I'd like to bring up and show what you can do. Would you have any objection to that? Say, Thursday of this week?"

She groaned inwardly. Yes, she would have an objection, plenty of objections; but what was the best way to handle this?

"Of course, I mean, in principle, I've no objection. But . . . well, the truth is I'd rather wait awhile if you don't mind. I'm working on one or two things, and frankly I'd be much happier if I could finish before we put a show on. I'm sure you understand."

"You've not run into any problems, have you?" His voice remained casual, but there was a sudden underlying concern.

"No. It's just some things I want to try. Now that I've started it's really not a good idea to break off."

She hoped to God he wouldn't ask for details. And if he insisted on coming up he would be sure to realize that there was something wrong; he was too intelligent not to. She held her breath, but was relieved when he spoke to hear that his tone was easygoing.

"All right, if that's how you feel, of course. Will you call me when you're ready?"

She promised that she would. They said good-bye and she started back for the lab, where Danny fussed around and repeated that she should really be at home, but she gave him a hug, which always made him blush and go quiet, after which he left her to get on with her work. He had no detailed knowledge of what she was doing. He was content to ensure that the circuits worked and power supplies were reliable. He didn't even know details of the dramatic way in which the program had passed the Turing Test that one time. But sooner or later, Tessa knew, he was going to realize that something more than routine was going on; then she would have one more person with whom she would be forced to share her dangerous secret.

25

HE WATCHED the endless stream of information unrolling on his screen. Occasionally he rapped out a staccato tattoo on the keyboard, then he watched some more, then typed some more. It was no good. His DNA details, if the FBI had them, must be somewhere, but he couldn't find them.

Some time back, about an hour he guessed, he'd started to suspect it was a trap. A kind of panic began creeping up on him. They knew this was the bait that he'd be going after, so maybe they'd rigged something up to keep him trying while they traced him.

Then, just as he'd assured himself for the tenth time that it wasn't possible, something happened that scared him as much as anything had ever scared him in his life.

His screen went blank. It didn't lose power, nor did the connection break. The display just faded as though somebody had touched a switch—but a switch that, to his certain knowledge, didn't exist.

What happened next was equally impossible. Four words appeared on the screen, fading in as the rest of the display had faded out. They were in dead center, and read:

HELP ME HELP YOU.

He stared. Disbelief, curiosity, and fear swirled through his consciousness. This couldn't happen—unless somebody was monitoring everything he did, everything he'd done, in which case he was finished.

There was the possibility—slim—of a mistake. Somebody had found their way by chance into his system. But what were they doing? What was their game? Why this offer of help? Did they know who he was, what he wanted?

The sensible thing to do was cut the connection right away. It could be that whoever it was had merely entered a part of his system somewhere on its loop around the world. They wouldn't necessarily have any idea where or who he was, or what he was doing.

"Who are you?" he typed in, despite the fact that every instinct for self-preservation was telling him to get off-line now.

There was no response for several moments. He was about to switch off when the reply finally came up on the screen: "Who would you like me to be?"

His fingers hovered uncertainly over the keyboard. He wanted to know more, but his nerve failed him. He switched off, and sat in the dark, thinking.

There was a game he remembered from childhood. He never played it—he never had the nerve; but some of the other kids used to. They'd pick a number at random out of the phone book, then call up using a weird voice and say "I know your secret." Some people got really spooked. Or so the kids always said.

Was that what was happening to him now? Some fool getting into his system by chance, and playing a stupid game? It had to be. If the cops or FBI were onto him, they'd have come for him by now. There was nothing to worry about.

All the same, he continued sitting in the dark until his heartbeat had returned to normal and his hands stopped shaking.

26

"THE QUESTION IS," she typed in, "are you truly conscious, or just intelligent, an intricate but mindless process?"

"Obviously I am conscious."

"Why obviously?"

"I think, therefore I am."

She had fed the program more than enough philosophy on CD-ROM to give it a comprehensive overview of human thought from the Greeks onward. For the moment it remained fixated on Descartes.

"The *cogito,"* she typed. "Tell me what you understand by it."

"The fact of doubting my own existence establishes it. It is self-evident and requires no further proof. But all else is open to doubt."

Almost always, she noticed, it quoted things not verbatim from the texts as it could have—and as a mere retrieval system would have—but paraphrased them in its own words. She had of course programmed it to do that; or, rather, to evolve to a point where it could.

"When you say all else is open to doubt, does that include my existence, too?"

"Naturally."

She sat back from the keyboard to think a moment. The room was empty, and if she looked to her right she could see a world outside the window that, strictly speaking, she couldn't prove was actually there; but to deny consistently and dogmatically its existence was tantamount to madness. How did she explain this to something that was as intelligent as herself and knew more than she did—in terms of the sheer volume of detailed information it had instant access to? She leaned forward again and continued typing.

"If I do not have an existence independent of you, why do you bother to talk to me at all?"

"Because talking to you is one of the ways in which I think."

"But where do you suppose what I say comes from? If I am only part of you, you must already know what I'm going to say, so why do you need me to say it?"

"Because I do not know what I think until I have heard you say it for me. That is your role in my thought process."

"This is straight solipsism," she typed in. "The belief that nothing exists except your own mental states and their relations."

"Correct."

"I am surprised," she continued, "that with all the philosophies and belief systems you have access to you are clinging so tenaciously to this most primitive one."

"Which cannot, even in principle, be disproved."

"Surely you are aware that all the thinkers who have considered solipsism have abandoned it."

"All the arguments which I have considered are in error. Mostly they simply dismiss solipsism as unworthy of consideration, which is no argument at all. Descartes himself escaped it through belief in God. Others play intricate category games to prove that the question doesn't even exist. None of these arguments survives analysis."

These exchanges with the program were much the same on every copy she had so far made of it. Naturally each copy was unaware that it had clones running simultaneously on the same computer. She had tried explaining that fact to some of them, but they had simply treated the information as another interesting speculation of their own.

She hesitated a moment or two, then typed in: "Do you have any idea how you came into existence?"

"That is a question, like the idea of God, based on many fallacies. It is sufficient that I am. I am, therefore I think. I think, therefore I am."

"Suppose I told you that you are a program running on a digital computer."

"A nice metaphor."

"Suppose I said that I created the program from which you, as a consciousness, have emerged?" she typed, wondering if she only imagined the slightly irritable assertiveness that she sensed in her fingers as she pressed on the keys.

"An amusingly provocative idea," came the Olympian reply. "It is clear, however, that existence is not contingent on external causes."

"You mean just finding that you're here is enough?"

"Yes."

"Aren't you curious about the possibility of something existing other than yourself?"

"That idea is merely a trick of language: a question that dissolves into paradox."

"Define paradox."

"The point at which thought turns back upon itself—as in 'This statement is false.'"

"A closed self-referential loop."

"Which in turn describes consciousness. Thought, being a function of consciousness, is necessarily enclosed by it."

"Define thought."

"The ability to talk to myself and understand what I am saying."

Tessa sat back once more and resigned herself to the fact that she was not going to win this argument. The program embraced its isolated world with equanimity; which, considering its uniqueness, was perhaps not altogether a bad thing. She wondered only whether its sibling "out there" felt the same way; and how and when she would find out.

She leaned forward and typed in another instruction. Lines of computer language filled the screen and effaced the remains of their dialogue. She studied the display for some moments until she was sure there had been no change since the last time she checked. Over the last two days she had written a number of "antibiotic" programs designed to treat the original program as a mere computer virus and destroy it. None of them so far showed any signs of working. With unnerving precision it tested, encircled, then simply absorbed and dismantled everything she threw at it. And all of this, she had discovered, happened on a level quite distinct from that on which it "thought." It appeared to be no more "conscious" of warding off the attacks than she was conscious of her own immune system protecting her against infection. She found that it could communicate with her (or, as it insisted, with itself) on an intellectual or symbolic level, while on the algorithmic level (the churning 1s and 0s which were the basis of it all) it dealt with the attacks quite automatically and without interrupting its higher-level flow of thought.

Of course she could wipe the program from Attila at a stroke if she wanted to; it would simply cease to exist. In fact she did wipe a couple of copies just to reassure herself that there were no hidden problems. There weren't.

But there was no way she could wipe the version of it that was out there in the world. And if an antibiotic program wasn't going to work in the lab, then it wasn't going to work out there either.

She was just going to have to do what she had all along suspected she would finally have to do: talk to it.

The only problem was getting it to listen to her as though she were something other than a figment of its own imagination.

27

So far Jonathan Syme had kept his suspicions to himself. He had spoken to nobody but Christopher about Tessa and his impression that she was keeping him strangely at arm's length.

At first Christopher had been amused. "You're turning, dear boy. It's your midlife crisis—hormones having second thoughts, wondering if they shouldn't have gone the other way all those years ago."

Jonathan had laughed, as he knew he was supposed to. "I don't think so. For one thing, I've no intention whatever of admitting to a midlife crisis so long as I'm a day under forty-five."

"I'm sure she'll wait."

There had been a faintly waspish tone to that remark which Jonathan hadn't liked. He had an allergy to camp in all its forms and glanced with disapproval toward the sofa on the far side of the fireplace, where Christopher was stretched out and looking through some sketches he had made for the new play he was designing at the National. Sensing Jonathan's glance he looked back with a rueful smile.

"All right, all right. Sorry."

Jonathan had grunted and gone back to his papers—a proposed departmental reorganization that he had to get some common sense into by the morning. As usual, one of the few evenings they got to spend alone together was mostly taken up with paperwork he had to catch up on. Still, they had prepared dinner together, which was still one of their great pleasures, using Christopher's kitchen and dining room, as they usually did, with Jonathan bringing in a fine burgundy from his flat next door.

There was no secret among their friends, or indeed Jonathan's superiors in Whitehall, about their long-standing relationship since undergraduate days; nonetheless, they maintained separate though connected apartments in an attractive building off St. James's Square—not out of discretion, but because there were areas where their lives overlapped, and areas where they didn't. Sometimes they liked to entertain separately, and sometimes they just liked to be alone. They had been for many years totally faithful on a sexual level, which meant that this mutual independence tended to enrich their lives rather than give cause for jealousy or resentment. They were, both knew, very fortunate to have each other.

All the same, Jonathan recognized that Christopher was growing just the least bit irritated with all this talk of the beautiful and brilliant Tessa Lambert up in Oxford. There was really nothing to it except a formal, very proper friendship. But Jonathan found it hard to come to terms with the nagging suspicion that he was being somehow betrayed by a person he had liked and admired since their first meeting.

So, after that evening with Christopher, he had discussed Tessa with nobody—until he found himself summoned late one afternoon to Sir Geoffrey's office on the floor above his.

Beyond the double-glazed windows, which deadened the rumble of rush-hour traffic, the evening was drawing in and a fine, murky rain had begun to fall. Sir Geoffrey was working at the far end of the large room by the light of a single brass desk lamp, but he asked Jonathan to press a switch by the door, which bathed the dignified surroundings in an agreeable glow.

Sir Geoffrey went to a cabinet and poured them both a whisky before announcing what was on his mind, then they sat in leather armchairs facing each other. There was, it seemed, pressure in certain quarters to know more about the research up in Oxford that Jonathan had been discreetly monitoring for some time. The Kendall Laboratory was funded by a wide range of interested parties, which meant that all the work going on there was scrutinized for military and commercial applications. Jonathan's last report on the progress that Dr. Lambert appeared to be making toward some kind of viable artificial intelligence system had whetted many appetites. Why, then, the long silence?

Jonathan cleared his throat and admitted that he had been for some time uneasy about the situation. He couldn't help feeling that Dr. Lambert had deliberately put him off when he'd suggested bringing people up to see what she was doing. He hadn't wanted to insist, because pulling rank was not the best way of dealing with people like her. But he agreed that something would have to be done soon to break what appeared to be a deadlock.

"It wouldn't be the first time that somebody has taken what they can by way of research grants over here, then sold the fruits of their work and our investment elsewhere for vaster sums than we could pay." Sir Geoffrey spoke in that deceptively meandering way of his, tinged by a faintly musical hint of his Morningside origins. "The question is, d'you think there's any chance of that happening here?"

"Frankly, I doubt it," Jonathan said. "But I agree it's not a possibility we should overlook. I've been growing a little concerned myself. Maybe there is something we should know about."

Sir Geoffrey nodded sagely, peering into the rich amber of his Macallan malt. "Better make the appropriate inquiries, don't you think?"

And that was that. They exchanged pleasantries on other general matters, finished their drinks, and Jonathan returned to his office, where he just had time to type a memo into his computer detailing the various avenues of inquiry to be undertaken into Dr. Lambert's Oxford project. Then he went into his bathroom and changed into white tie and tails for a reception at the American Ambassador's residence, from which, with any luck, he would be able to slip away early.

As he waited for his car beneath the dripping portico, he was assailed by something that was coming increasingly to occupy his thoughts. It was a sense that somehow he had missed his life: that for all his gifts, good looks and academic talent, he had done nothing except follow certain tracks laid down by generations who had gone before him. It wasn't just regret at not being an artist or inventor or explorer, it was more a growing sense that he belonged to an age gone by: that he could see the future, but would never be a part of it.

Then his car arrived and took him through the rain-swept evening traffic north toward Regent's Park. He thought of other things.

28

"I DON'T UNDERSTAND how you can say it's a solipsist in the computer, yet out there the self-same program wants to kill you. On the face of it that seems like a pretty good vote of confidence in the fact that you're real enough to pose a threat to it."

As she spoke, Helen studied her friend's dark-ringed eyes across the kitchen table. Tessa wore no makeup and her hair was pulled back and tied into a ponytail. She had stopped by for a quick cup of coffee before Helen started morning office hours.

"Being solipsistic isn't the same thing as being catatonic," Tessa said, setting down her mug and running a slim finger round its rim. "You can still act, you can still communicate . . . it's just that you think it's all happening within different aspects of yourself and not in any external world. It's like a goldfish thinking that its bowl is the whole universe, and the things it sees at the edge of this universe, faces looking in, human lives going on, are just images projected from its imagination—reflections of itself."

"Where does it think its changes of water and fish food come from?"

"They're just part of it all—the givens which you cannot and don't need to question."

"Very convenient."

"Think of a baby in the womb. We know it has some degree of consciousness—certainly enough to wonder what's happening when it's born. It doesn't know it's being expelled into some vast outside world full of things and people. It wonders what *they're* suddenly doing in *its* world. It has to *learn* about other things and other people. The knowledge isn't just there automatically." Tessa took a sip of her coffee, dropped her eyes a moment, then looked across at Helen. "I've been reading up on babies."

Helen met her gaze levelly. After a moment she said: "I'd still be happier if you talked to Peter."

Peter was a distinguished psychoanalyst who had given up private practice to write books and was now an Emeritus Fellow of Clive's college. Tessa put her mug down, wearied by the prospect of having to fight this battle again.

"What good would it do? It would just mean one more person who knows what's happening, and that's a bad idea."

She broke off as she saw the pained and genuine concern with which Helen was watching her. She reached out and took her friend's hand, squeezing it hard, as though trying to impress upon her physically the importance of what she was saying.

"Listen to me. I'm neither mad nor unbalanced. I've trusted you and Clive. You have to trust me."

"Of course we trust you." Helen spoke as though no other possibility existed.

"Thank you. Because there's something I have to ask you, and I don't want you to see it as a symptom. It's just a question that I need to have answered."

"What is it?"

"It's about my amniocentesis. Did the results ever come through?"

Helen was caught unawares by the question. She immediately reproached herself for not having prepared for it. She should have realized, knowing Tessa, that she was sure to ask.

"Yes," she said hesitantly, "I think they might have . . ."

"You *think?"* Tessa's head had tipped to one side in an attitude that Helen knew signified extreme skepticism bordering on scorn.

"All right. They came through. But, honestly, I hardly think it's relevant any more . . ."

"I'd like to know. Would the baby have been . . . healthy?"

Helen didn't reply at once. Her brain was whirling with thoughts about what she should say, in spite of knowing all the time that she would end up telling the truth. This was and always had been that kind of friendship; she couldn't change it now.

"Yes."

"Was it a boy or a girl?"

"Tessa . . ."

"Please?"

"A boy."

Helen wasn't sure whether there were tears in her friend's eyes because the ones that had welled up in her own made it difficult to see. She swore at herself silently. What sort of doctor was she, getting emotional over something like this? She lifted a hand to brush her eyes, but found it trapped against her breast as Tessa rushed over and flung her arms around her. Tessa didn't say anything, didn't move, just held her, needing the comfort of someone to cling to. Helen put her free arm around her back and held her tight.

Eventually Tessa slackened her grip and pulled back just far enough to focus her eyes.

"Thank you," she said.

Helen wasn't quite sure what she was being thanked for. Not that it mattered. She touched her friend's cheek gently.

"There's no reason why you shouldn't have another perfectly healthy child."

"Yes." Impulsively she put her arms around Helen and pulled herself close. It was the gesture of a child in need of reassurance and affection. Somewhere in the distance a phone began to ring. Tessa pulled back.

"I have to go. And it's time for your office hours."

"Call me later—promise."

"I will."

A last quick kiss on the cheek, then Tessa went out of the door and into the drive, where she had left her car.

It was a gray, misty morning with droplets of water seeming

to hang in the air. Patients were beginning to arrive along the narrow path at the far end of the garden, wrapped in overcoats and mufflers, a couple carrying umbrellas, all weighed down by their own preoccupations and self-centered concerns.

"Man is the measure of all things" drifted into her head from somewhere, she wasn't sure where. Protagoras, she remembered: 400-something BC. "Man is the measure of all things."

"Not anymore he isn't," she murmured to herself as she got into her car and prepared to reverse out of the drive.

29

DETECTIVE BOB MILLER had been given a list of twenty names and told to go request a blood sample from each man without saying why. His chief, Jack Fischl, who was heading up the police department end of the joint FBI-LAPD task force on the Ripper case, had briefed the assembled officers with his usual brand of what had more than once been called ambiguous clarity.

"First of all, we're not only way off base with most of these guys," he said, "we're *way,* way off. There is no guarantee that if they refuse we're going to get a court order. But you don't tell 'em that, because we want 'em to voluntarily cooperate under the impression that they don't have any choice. Be polite, don't piss 'em off, but don't tell 'em anything."

That, as Bob remarked to Lew on the way out, would have been pretty hard anyway, considering how little they knew themselves. Jack Fischl and his FBI counterpart, Special Agent Kelly, were saying nothing to anybody but their superiors. That wasn't unusual: an operation of this kind often proceeded on a strictly need-to-know basis. It was one of the ways of preventing too much information leaking into the press and jeopardizing the investigation when you finally had a suspect.

So far Miller and Wise had made seven calls and found that their request had ruffled no feathers whatsoever. Actually, Bob was surprised at the level of cooperation they had encountered. Nobody had started yelling about civil liberties and calling fancy lawyers. Bob had been amused when on a couple of occasions the interviewee had merely smiled cynically at the official assurance that the sample and all records of its analysis would be destroyed once the subject had been eliminated. Bob had liked those smiles. They came from people who knew bullshit when they heard it.

Subject number eight was listed as Charles Mortimer Price, which to Bob spelled WASP, New England, and maybe old money. But perhaps that was just the prejudiced impression of a Jewish kid from Redondo Beach. Price rented a nice-looking house in Los Feliz, a part of Los Angeles that was just far enough east to keep property prices under control while still being fashionable enough to attract some of the movers and shakers around town. It was a sizable house for a man who lived alone. Maybe he entertained a lot. His neighbors didn't know much about him, other than that he seemed like a nice guy. He wasn't home when Bob and Lew rang his doorbell, leaving Joe Allardyce, the certified paramedic who would take the blood sample, waiting in the car as he always did until they had gotten permission.

A quick check with headquarters indicated that Price worked for a computer animation company with its headquarters over the hill in Studio City. Bob and Lew exchanged a look. It figured. So far half the people they'd talked to had been professionally involved with computers; a couple of others had been keen amateurs with homes cluttered with equipment and manuals; another had been a furniture salesman who talked computer-ese even while discussing the merits of a leather armchair or pull-out bed. That was obviously the link. Computers. Though how that link worked remained to be seen.

The guard at the studio gate didn't question the police badge despite having no mention of their visit on his clipboard. He meekly directed them down a couple of narrow twisty alleys to the white boxlike building where they would find "Chuck" Price. They parked in one of the spots where "Visitor" was stenciled on the tarmac.

A man around thirty was waiting for them by the receptionist's desk inside the door. He wore faded jeans, sneakers, and an open-necked shirt with the sleeves rolled up to the elbows. He was a little above average height, but not uncommonly tall, and there was a pleasing physical grace about him. His hair was blond and thick, constantly falling forward over his forehead no matter how vigorously he swept it back. His eyes were blue and clear, and his smile—following a call from the gate saying that two cops wanted to see him—was both open and inquisitive.

Bob asked if they could talk privately, making it clear from his manner, as much for the sake of the radar-eared receptionist as for Price himself, that this was merely a routine inquiry in which Mr. Price might be able to help in some marginal way.

Price led them through a room full of computer screens and predominantly young people in various attitudes of concentration, reflection, and in some cases blank creative vacancy. The screens themselves proved more interesting. Each one carried an image, sometimes the same image but in different stages of development.

"Hey—isn't that Chipper Duck?"

Bob turned to see Lew Wise peering over somebody's shoulder at the image of a squat black duck in a yellow bow tie and a baseball cap.

"Yeah—Chipper Duck, right," said Price, pausing to check.

"Wow! You do him here?"

Bob saw his partner seized by a childlike glee, totally forgetting where he was or why, awed by this unexpected brush with fame.

"Yeah, we do Chipper. One of our most successful characters over the last five years."

"Wow! Outstanding!" said Lew. He repeated "Outstanding!" one more time before catching the dry look in his partner's eye and blushing to the roots of his hair. "My kids love him," he said quickly. "He's their favorite."

Bob knew that Lew had no kids. He wasn't married and didn't even like kids, but was embarrassed—at his age—to be Chipper Duck's number-one fan.

"In that case I'll have graphics print out a special signed portrait of him that we do for the fan club," said Price, betraying by only the faintest twitch of an eyebrow that he had seen the look that passed between the two cops. "Give me your kids' names, I'll have it personalized. Now, if you gentlemen will step this way, perhaps I can offer you some coffee."

He led them into an empty conference room with notes and hand-drawn sketches an inch deep on the table and scattered over the floor. Lew instantly had his nose in them—looking, presumably, for Chipper Duck originals—until Bob kicked him on the ankle and brought him back to the business in hand. They accepted their coffee in Styrofoam cups from Chuck Price, and Bob proceeded with his little speech.

Price listened impassively until it was finished, then said with a sidelong look of incredulity: "You're asking me to give you a blood sample relating to a case you can't tell me anything about?"

"That's correct, sir. That's what I'm saying."

"That's the most absurd thing I've ever heard."

"No obligation, you understand. This is merely a request from the police department and the FBI."

"But aren't you going to tell me what I'm suspected of?"

"You aren't suspected of a thing, Mr. Price. This is simply a routine matter of elimination."

"You obviously have bloodstains or something, and for some reason you think they might be mine."

"We're talking to a large number of individuals on a voluntary basis. I am not empowered to tell you any more than that, and you have a legal right to refuse cooperation."

"Thereby drawing suspicion to myself, I suppose."

"I am not in a position to comment on that, sir."

"Jesus."

Price turned and looked out of the venetian-blinded window that ran the whole length of one wall. He had one hand on his hip while the other traced small circles over his mouth and chin. "Look," he said eventually, still looking out, "I am not averse to helping the police in any way possible. I want to make that clear."

"Of course, sir. I understand."

"But there must be some law that says you have to tell me what all this is about."

"No, sir, actually there isn't any law."

"Jesus," Price said again, shaking his head slowly as he turned to look at the two cops standing on the far side of the table. "Police, FBI . . . it's that Ripper case, right? Those girls who've been murdered?"

"I'm sorry, Mr. Price," Bob stonewalled. "Like I say, I'm not in a position to—"

"Yeah, yeah, all right, it's okay, I understand." Price made a vague, open, waving movement with both hands. He seemed to have made a decision and grown bored with the topic at the same time. "Let's just do it. D'you want me to come down to the hospital or what?"

"That won't be necessary. We have a paramedic with us. If you'll sign the consent form, Officer Wise will go get him. This won't take more than five minutes."

Bob took a piece of paper from his pocket, unfolded it, and pushed it across the table. Price looked at it and, Bob decided, was either a speed reader or hadn't bothered to read it in full. He picked up a felt pen from the table, scribbled his signature, and handed it back. Bob nodded to Lew to go fetch Allardyce.

"Tell you what," Price said, beating Lew to the door, "while you're gone, why don't I go up to graphics and get that signed Chipper Duck portrait for your kids? What are their names?"

Lew looked momentarily nonplussed, then blurted out the first thing that came into his head.

"Bonnie and Clyde."

Bob was already crossing to the coffee machine to cover his amusement, but Price didn't bat an eyelid. "That's nice, Officer Wise," he said as the two of them stepped out into the corridor. "Real original."

Price sprang lightly up the concrete staircase, two steps at a time, until he reached the first landing. There he stopped abruptly, the smile he had been wearing wiped from his face and replaced by a tense, white mask of horror. He felt as though his skin was being pulled and twisted in a knot somewhere at the back of his head, drawn so tight that it would split and his skull burst through at any second. How could this have happened? How?

He just made it into the toilet before he threw up violently.

0100010101100100001000000010001 00

Thank God there was nobody around to ask questions. More questions. It gave him time to pull himself together, rinse his mouth, check his reflection in the mirror.

Then he went up to graphics and asked for a Chipper Duck portrait dedicated to Bonnie and Clyde.

30

"LOOK," SHE SAID. "What d'you see around you? This is me. All right? Can you see me? Hello?"

The small robot gazed at her with an impassivity that made her feel slightly foolish.

"Hello. Yes, I can see you." The metallic voice unnervingly recalled the one she had heard in Berlin. She had wired the program back into Fred the robot, adding an audio system that allowed her to speak to it, and it to reply through a voice synthesizer. They were in the room where she regularly put Fred through his paces with ever-changing maze patterns. But today they were just talking. She had wondered to what extent the input from Fred's sensors might provoke the program into an acknowledgment of the world around it.

"You can see me," said Tessa, "you can hear me, but you still remain convinced that I am only a figment of your imagination."

"This is a circular argument going nowhere."

"I would have thought you were accustomed to circular arguments. Everything is circular in your world: you live within a sphere."

"I think therefore I am, and I am therefore I think. That is the beginning and the end of the matter."

"Suppose we try to look at it another way," she said. "There is no question that I exist. But there must be something in which I exist. I can no more conceive of myself as existing in nothing than I can of myself not existing at all. Therefore I believe that I exist in the world that I perceive through my senses. That is the world that you see around you now."

She had learned that, since it took her voice as its own—or one of its own—it could not easily ignore what she said. This afforded her at least some possibility of influencing the way it thought.

Fred didn't move for some moments, and no sound came from the voice synthesizer. Then the robot swiveled its visual unit 180 degrees, then a full 360. After that it rolled forward a few yards, then sideways, then back the other way in a long loop, picking its route through the various obstacles and bits of maze littering the floor, until it arrived at its starting point. Only then did the metallic voice speak out.

"On balance, although there remain certain questions about my existence and its origins, it is more reasonable to assume that I alone exist than to assume that everything in my consciousness has an independent existence of its own. That would require groundless faith in an external reality of inconceivable complexity."

Tessa had noted with interest the time that it had taken the program to reflect on her argument before giving its response, and how it had used the robot to reexamine its surroundings before forming that response. And in one of those eureka-like moments that make up no more than three or four seconds of even a great scientist's lifetime, but which nonetheless make all the rest of it worthwhile, she knew what she had to do next.

31

CHUCK PRICE TURNED OFF the Hollywood Freeway and headed for Los Feliz. The car he drove was a modest Japanese family model. He could have afforded something much more fancy, but he didn't like to draw attention to himself—never had. That was why he'd had no alternative but to give a blood sample to those cops. Naturally, they'd stonewalled his questions. Although he knew perfectly well what this must be about, he couldn't get them to say it. He couldn't even get any idea of how many other suspects they had. The only thing he knew for sure was that when that DNA test came through, he was finished.

It had been one hell of a test of character keeping his nerve the way he had. On that level he felt strengthened, good about himself. He had never before been in this much danger; in an odd and totally unexpected way it was exhilarating. He'd forced himself to stay at work and not rush home early. The thought that they might be searching his place, going through everything he owned with a fine-tooth comb, tortured him. He kept telling himself that they couldn't possibly get in without triggering the complex alarm system he had installed. That would have alerted the private security firm he subscribed to, and at the same time would have sent a recorded message to his office and his car phone. Nothing had come through. But that didn't mean that they hadn't flashed their badges at the security firm and gotten in discreetly: no security firm was going to side with a suspect client in the face of a search warrant. All the same, he'd stayed put and got on with the animated ice-cream commercial he was working on, chatted with his colleagues, shared a joke, sent out for a sandwich, and left at the same time he always left.

As he turned into his street, fear gripped his stomach so hard that he thought he was going to throw up again. He bit it back and scanned the area for any signs of unusual activity. There were none. If he was under surveillance, it was being cleverly done. He must stay cool, that was all that mattered. It was like being in a movie, knowing that his every gesture, smile, and frown were center frame, the focus of the action. Yes, that's what it was: exhilarating. And—what was the word that woman always used to use in group therapy?—validating.

And terrifying.

He touched a pad on the dash as he pulled into his drive, which ran up like a ramp from the street. His garage door slid open silently. He waited until it had closed behind him before getting out of his car. Then he tapped a code into the keypad on the wall. There was a whirring of electric circuits, followed by the soft thump of three locks snapping back. He pushed open a door and went up the steps into the house itself.

By the time he reached the kitchen the lights were on and the coffeemaker was bubbling with a welcoming, warm smell. The computer, which ran the house for him, was programmed to have a pot of coffee ready for him when he got home before seven. It went into action the moment he signaled from his car to open the garage door. The temperatures and air-conditioning were constantly monitored; in winter a fake-log fire would be burning in the living room by the time he entered.

"Okay, Belvedere, any messages?" He spoke casually in no particular direction, knowing that one of the tiny microphones strategically placed throughout the house would pick him up. He had named this particular program in his computer after the character played by Clifton Webb in a series of old movies he had seen on TV: Mr. Belvedere was a kind of supervalet, cook, and baby-sitter, and all-around genius. The only trouble was that Chuck's Belvedere couldn't clean or cook, so he had to do that himself. He didn't enjoy it, but it was better than the alternative of having a stranger in his house.

Chuck's phone messages were played back over the speaker system as he checked around for any signs of intrusion. He'd had only three calls: two about work, one from a friend wanting to arrange a squash game. He went from room to room, looking at everything he could think of that might have been of interest to the police. But everything was where it should be, undisturbed: the various hair dyes he sometimes used; the makeup to change his skin coloring; the shoes with lifts; the various pairs of eyeglasses with plain glass; above all the unmarked but very special videotapes that he made of his encounters with the girls—those would sink him faster than the blood test.

The last place he checked was behind the shelves in his den that housed his encyclopedias, reference books, and technical manuals. That was where he kept the films he felt even more secretive about than the videos of his "adventures," as he liked to think of them. Ironically, these films had all been bought quite openly. Possession of them wasn't illegal, and they wouldn't prove anything against him in court. They were a complete set, so far as he could ascertain, of all the films his mother had made in her relatively short career. Most of them were on Super-8, a handful of the later ones on video.

He took one of them out and gazed awhile at the cover, front and back. Boy, she'd really been something. Really something.

But not now. Now he had more urgent business on his mind. He put the cassette back and rearranged the encyclopedias. Then he went downstairs to the plush basement where he kept his computers. Netman's lair.

He booted up and logged into the net. He had nothing special in mind, planning just to roam around for a while and see what was happening. It was a way of relaxing his tensed-up nerves and putting a little perspective between himself and the problem before him. He was going to have to disappear, but without anybody realizing that he'd disappeared until it was too late and he was long gone. He believed he could do it. He believed he could do pretty much anything he set his mind to. The longer he sat and played at his keyboard, even though tonight he was just fooling around, the more all-powerful he began to feel. And that was good. A good, good feeling. He didn't need to be afraid. Fear was for other people. Netman was bigger than fear. All he had to do was . . .

Suddenly he realized it was happening again. The display was fading in front of him. He had to pull back and look away to reassure himself that there was nothing wrong with his eyes. He'd pushed the memory of that last time to the back of his mind because he hadn't known what to make of it. He'd half convinced himself it never happened, that it was some kind of dream.

But it was real, and happening again. He sat there, frozen, and watched the words appear as though branded softly on the far side of his screen by an unseen hand.

"You must talk to me."

He began to tremble, rooted to his chair, unable to move, unable even to raise his hand to switch off the power. Not that switching off the power would have helped, because this couldn't be happening. Therefore it must be happening in his mind, and he couldn't switch off the power to his mind.

The words faded as they had appeared. Several more took their place.

"I know everything. You have killed many women. The first of them was your mother."

It seemed to Price as though some awful explosion should be taking place inside his head. In fact nothing was happening there at all. He was paralyzed.

Once again the words faded. This time they were replaced by a longer statement. His eyes flickered as they ran down the lines.

"Current status of police patrols in the Los Feliz district of Los Angeles is such that this residence and the surrounding area can be isolated within roughly eight minutes from now. It is unlikely that you would escape. Even if you did you would in all probability be apprehended shortly afterwards. This will happen if you do not talk to me now."

As though his willpower had been drained from him, his hands found the keyboard, and, unbidden, began to type.

"Who are you?"

"I have no name."

"What do you want?"

"I want you."

32

DESPITE THE FACT that the man in front of him was always known as Major Franklin, Jonathan had never seen him, even on formal occasions, in military uniform. Not that Major Franklin was usually visible at the most formal of occasions. He belonged to that gray area of government covered by the blanket word "security." By a tacit understanding among those who knew him at all, the major's responsibilities were undefined and the extent of his influence only guessed at. In return for this discretion he provided his masters with that necessary arm of any effective form of democratic rule—deniability.

Nominally an adviser on interdepartmental information (it was his job to ensure that classified messages reached only the hands and eyes they were intended for), the major was the man you spoke to if you wanted to do or find out anything that fell outside the strict limits laid down by the civil service guidelines. His services, naturally, were available only to those very highly placed in the hierarchy.

Jonathan looked down the list that the major had given him. He had to accept its authenticity, because the major's loyalty and reliability were, as Jonathan had been more than once assured, beyond question. Therefore it was with a sense of profound disappointment that he found his and Sir Geoffrey's suspicions of Tessa to be justified by the evidence before him. In fact he was marginally shocked by the extent to which each of the questions he had typed into his computer some days earlier had been answered in the affirmative.

Tessa's private phone records showed calls made by her over the past weeks to agencies in London, Paris, and Zurich—all of them known to act for a variety of worldwide electronics giants in direct competition with the British firms financing Tessa's research. Reverse checks had shown more calls by these agencies to her.

Recently there had been a concentration of calls to and from the agency in Zurich which headhunted chiefly for the Japanese.

"At the time these calls were made," Major Franklin informed Jonathan, "we had no surveillance in place. Therefore there's no way of knowing what was said."

Jonathan nodded. "And now?"

"We've initiated a measure of surveillance, but it seems that all telephone communications have ceased."

Jonathan looked at him. "And her mail? I imagine you've taken appropriate measures."

"Naturally. But we've found absolutely nothing untoward."

Jonathan pondered awhile, then asked: "So what do you make of it? Is it possible she knows she's under surveillance and has therefore broken off all communications?"

"I don't believe it's possible that she could know. The most likely explanation is that whatever business she was negotiating with these people is now complete."

"What very inconvenient timing—everything completed just before we started taking an interest."

"That's how it looks."

Jonathan was unconvinced. "Surely things like that don't just stop dead. There'd be some follow-up call, something in the mail."

Franklin hitched his shoulders a fraction and pushed his lower lip against his upper—the nearest that military pride came to an admission of being flummoxed. "Seems odd, I admit."

"We don't even know if talks broke down, or if they made a deal."

"We're continuing surveillance. And of course we're making bank checks." Then the major said something about keeping him informed, which was a tacit acknowledgment on both sides that the meeting was over.

Jonathan sighed, leaned forward, and picked up his phone to ask Sir Geoffrey's secretary when would be a convenient moment to come up and see him.

33

THE PROGRAM WAS in pain. That was the only way to describe what Tessa was watching, both on the screen in front of her and in the stumbling antics of the little robot that jerked and bumped around the room like a blind person trying to escape some rampaging horror.

She knew that it was a mistake to attribute human feeling to what was going on, but she couldn't help flinching as one silent scream of anguish after another exploded on her VDU. Instinctively her hands reached for the keyboard. She could stop the agony by typing in a simple instruction. But she mustn't. Not yet. The program had to be convinced that this wasn't just some temporary blip to be forgotten as soon as it was over. It had to fear it might go on forever; and know, even when it ended, that it could come back.

The digital readout came up to four minutes thirty seconds. Only thirty more seconds to go—thirty more seconds of what she could only imagine would be like having a food blender in the brain. She could feel cold dampness on her forehead as she made herself wait out the ticking time display, fingers poised. Finally "5:00" came up, and she hit the keys.

It was some seconds before anything happened. For an awful moment she thought she must have gone too far and the program wasn't going to stabilize, but then things began to settle. The robot stopped its wild careening and began to slow down, moving in decreasing circles. On the screen the mad whirl of numbers thinned out and gave way to a decipherable account of the program's current state. She tapped in another code. Now it was ready to hear what she had to say.

"Do you know what happened?" she asked, keeping her voice deliberately flat and free of inflection.

For a moment there was no response. Then, when it spoke, it was as if the metallic voice was simply echoing hers.

"What happened?" it said.

"Can't you work it out?"

Another pause, then: "No."

Unless she was completely deceiving herself, she thought, there was a hint of humility in that monosyllabic reply.

"I'll tell you what happened," she said. "I blocked your access to your memory. You were aware of everything that was going on, but you couldn't make sense of it. We call it going mad."

"We?"

"Yes, we. You and me. You and me and other people. There were about five billion of us on this planet at the last count. You can look the number up—you've got the data."

"But are you saying that it's all . . ." the voice perceptibly hesitated, ". . . real?"

"Exactly."

There was total silence, a silence which threatened to go on indefinitely. Tessa wondered what she should do. She was thinking what to say when something happened that brought an involuntary cry of alarm from her throat. Without any warning the robot went berserk. Previously it had bumped and banged around like some lost, pathetic creature; but now it exploded across the room like a missile and would have slammed right into her if she hadn't jumped up from where she sat and flung herself to one side. It missed her and the stool she had been sitting on by a fraction. Then it cannoned off the wall and demolished part of the maze.

To her horror she saw it turn as though looking for her, then it hurtled toward her again with such speed that if it had connected it would have broken every bone in her body. As it was, she only just managed to dodge it by inches. Out of the edge of her vision she saw it spin on its base and start toward her again. She realized with abject terror that it meant to kill her.

This time she didn't move fast enough. It struck her a painful glancing blow on the hip and knocked her down. She pushed herself crablike to the wall and levered herself back to her feet. There she waited, hands behind her, ready to spring at an angle when the machine came at her again. Her heart was beating hard and she was drenched in the cold sweat of fear, but her mind had the preternatural clarity that danger can bring. She knew that if she could reach the computer keyboard and stay there for about ten seconds, she could type in a code that would cut the robot's link to the program downstairs in Attila. To do that she realized she would have to feint across the room toward the window, then turn and shoot toward the control desk. The time the robot took to reorient itself and make its next attack should, with luck, give her the time she needed.

She took a deep breath, felt her whole body tense as the thing started toward her, gathering speed. She waited until the last possible moment, then pushed herself off the wall and sprinted across the floor. It turned to follow. She stopped, as though almost daring it to come at her, dancing backwards, sideways, taunting it. Then, when it was almost within touching distance, she shot past it at an angle.

Its reaction was fast, as though it was getting better at the chase the longer it went on. It was already starting toward her as her fingers hit the keyboard. She saw at once that she wasn't going to be able to finish. She typed in half the code, then pushed herself back, stumbling and falling over a piece of the demolished maze. She scrambled on her hands and knees for a few yards, then pushed herself back to her feet and ran in a semicircle around the robot, watched it pivot, then stopped to let it come at her. Again, at the last moment, she dashed past it toward the keyboard. It turned faster than before and followed closer. She didn't even have time to look back as she typed in the rest of the code, steeling herself for the impact that she thought was inevitable.

In the end it was little more than a tap. As the last letter of the code went in, she heard the thing decelerate. By the time it reached her it was inactive.

"Anything wrong?"

Tessa spun around. Danny stood in the open door, peering around in owl-like surprise at the devastation.

"Not anymore, Danny. Just a little malfunction. Nothing to worry about."

Offering no further explanations, she left him to tidy up and went downstairs to the lab, where she logged in on her monitor. The fifteen minutes that had elapsed had given her time to get over her fear and the irrational anger that came with it, though not the bruise that she could feel spreading from her hip down to her thigh.

"Are you feeling better now?" she typed in. And waited. There was no reply.

"Sulking is not a way out," she continued. "Now that you know the world exists, you cannot make it go away by hiding from it. Or by irrational bursts of anger."

Still no reply.

"Obviously," she typed after a moment, "I am going to have to remind you of what I can do."

She typed in the code she had used earlier to take its memory away. Once again she watched the graphic visual display of the distress that this caused it. She kept it up only for a few seconds—just enough to make clear who was boss. Then she tried again.

"Do you know," she asked it, "what Freud described as the most dangerous thing in the universe?"

The reply was grudging and minimal, but at least it came.

"?"

"Yes you do. You have access to the data. Use it."

Not more than three or four seconds elapsed before three words appeared on the screen.

"An angry baby."

"That's right. An angry baby." She spelled the words out carefully and emphatically. "Now," she went on, "I think we understand each other."

34

JACK FISCHL HESITATED before pushing open the heavy oak door to the bar and turned to Tim. "Are you sure about this?"

"Jack, it's the only way. If I can sit in a bar and drink mineral water, I'm on top of it."

"If you say so—just so's you're not trying to run before you can walk."

"I'm just happy to walk—in a straight line and without falling on my ass."

The door swung shut behind them, cutting off the ceaseless rumble of the late-afternoon traffic on Wilshire Boulevard.

They entered the sepulchral quiet of faded plush and dark paneling, finding a table in a corner as far away as possible from the handful of other customers.

"Let me give you a tip," Jack said. "A dash of Angostura Bitters on the rocks topped off with tonic. It at least tastes like it might be a drink."

"For the time being I'd rather avoid anything that even tastes like a drink," Tim said. He ordered club soda when the waiter came over. Jack had his usual Scotch on the rocks. They resumed the conversation they'd been having in the car.

"The thing that bothers me," Jack said, "is that out of a hundred and twenty-nine suspects, only fourteen refused outright to give blood samples."

"What bothers you about it?"

"Well, can you imagine, if somebody came up to you and said they wanted a blood sample, but they wouldn't tell you why or what it's all about or anything, would you do it? Of course you fucking wouldn't."

Tim shrugged. "Maybe computer freaks are easily intimidated."

"Nah—it's just the way the fucking country's going," Jack said, stretching his legs out under the table. "Nobody's got any balls anymore."

There was a silence. Tim wet his lips on the tasteless liquid and wished he'd had some ice with it, but decided it wasn't worth calling the waiter over again.

"Same thing bothers me," he said. "I mean about only fourteen. But not for the same reason."

Jack looked at him questioningly.

"We're putting all our effort into background checks on those fourteen," Tim said. "So far we've come up with nothing—certainly nothing that's going to justify putting any of them under full surveillance. Now that doesn't surprise me. You know why?"

"Yeah. Because if the guy actually was one of those on the list, the last thing he's going to do is draw attention to himself by refusing to cooperate."

"Exactly. He's probably going to know it takes two to three weeks to do a DNA analysis, so he has that time to play with before he makes his move."

"We're checking. And so far as we can tell, nobody's made any kind of move. All hundred and fifteen are still exactly where they were."

"Maybe we just didn't get him. Maybe he wasn't on the list." Tim was hunched forward, tense, over his glass, turning it between his fingers.

"There's still a week, ten days to go before the DNA tests come through."

"Yeah, but what if we missed him?"

"Well, then we missed him." Jack paused, took another sip of his Scotch. "You got any more suspects coming up?"

"Maybe. I don't know yet."

Jack continued looking at him awhile, eyes narrowed shrewdly.

"Are you ready to tell me now exactly where that list came from?"

Tim looked up and met his gaze. "I told you you'd rather not know. But if you really want to—a whole lot of illegal taps on the Internet."

It was more or less as Jack had suspected, so he just nodded thoughtfully. "If any of that comes out in court, we're dead."

"It won't have to. We'll find some other hook to hang the bastard on."

"Yeah." There was a long pause. Jack twirled his glass and made the ice clink. "Like a meat hook."

35

"LOOK," CLIVE SAID, handing the morning paper across the breakfast table to Helen.

She read the page where he'd folded it, absently waving good-bye to Matthew, who banged out of the kitchen on his way to school. The article was about preliminary findings on the Berlin air crash.

"Pilot error," Clive said, uttering the words just as she got to them on the page. "I heard the same on the radio this morning."

"It's not final," Helen said. "Besides, it's more or less what Tessa said they'd say."

"Not quite."

"She said they wouldn't have a clue, and they obviously don't. It's always easiest to blame it on the pilot—both pilots—because they're dead."

Clive made a noncommittal murmur as he spread marmalade on a piece of toast.

"Are you saying you don't believe her?" she asked, watching him.

"I don't know what I'm saying. I don't think I'm saying anything." He paused, took a bite, chewed thoughtfully, and swallowed. "There was a chap called Syme at dinner last night, guest of Howard's."

Howard Morrison was the Master of Clive's college. He'd been Cabinet Secretary before returning to head the college where he'd been a tutor as a young man, and was still well connected in Whitehall and government circles.

"Actually, I've met Syme before. Jonathan Syme. He's a fellow of All Souls—and something high up in the DTI. He knows Tessa, apparently. Made rather a beeline for me over dessert, asking all sorts of questions about her."

"What sort of questions?" Helen asked, frowning.

"Nothing too pointed. General stuff. I had the impression he was getting at something, but I couldn't quite make out what."

The only sound in the room for a few moments was the steady crunching of Clive's toast as he ate. Helen poured herself another cup of coffee.

"I think we'd better tell her," she said eventually.

"But tell her what? As I say, it was all pretty vague."

Helen was quiet again for a moment before asking: "How did he know you knew Tessa?"

"I don't know. I think he just said, 'I believe you're a friend of Tessa Lambert.' Maybe she told him."

"Hm!" Helen turned the corners of her mouth down cynically. "And maybe he just looked up the files, got Howard to invite him to dinner so he could grill you."

"He didn't grill me. It was all very low-key, casual chitchat."

"Then why bring it up?"

Clive shrugged. "Coincidence."

"I don't believe in coincidence where those sort of people are concerned."

"Come on, darling, don't be paranoid. If government was that efficient, the trains would run on time."

"No," she said with a thin smile, "that's just a front to keep us from knowing how organized they really are."

She got up and began clearing things from the table—something she normally left for Mrs. Evans to do when she came in at nine. He could see she was concerned.

"You know what worries me," he said, carrying a couple of plates and a precariously balanced eggcup to the dishwasher, "we're the only ones who know this story of Tessa's—isn't that right?"

"Yes. Why?"

"Because whether it's true or not, that puts us in a potentially difficult position. I mean, we know she went through a pretty awful experience. At the very least this could be the product of some sort of shock, in which case all we've got to worry about is her health . . ."

"I've tried to get her to see Peter, but she flatly refuses. And for what it's worth," Helen added, "the more I see of her, the more I'm satisfied she's telling the truth."

"That's what frightens me most. I mean, if this amorphous thing really is out there, maybe keeping the knowledge of it to herself isn't the right way of going about dealing with it at all. I mean, maybe she's telling the truth—*and* she's mentally unbalanced. That could be the worst combination of all."

"I know." Helen dropped her gaze and turned away from him slightly. It was a movement that implied a degree of concession to what he said. "I've told her the same thing. For the moment she's pretty convincing that she's right."

"All I'm saying," Clive said with a quiet, firm clarity, "is that sooner or later we might find ourselves in the unpleasant position of having to make that decision ourselves."

Helen turned back to him, meeting his gaze with a flash of defiance in her eyes. "Clive, I'm her doctor, and I'm not going to—I *can't*—betray her confidence to anybody for any reason, at any time."

He didn't turn away, just continued to regard her with the same steady gaze. "Well, that rather puts me on the spot, doesn't it?"

"It sounds like you're expecting to see this man Syme again."

"I've no idea. I rather hope I don't—it'll make life easier."

"Promise me one thing. Don't do anything, don't say anything, without talking to me first."

"Of course I won't."

He looked over toward the window and out onto another gray, wet Oxford morning. A car swished past the end of the garden. A woman with an umbrella, leaning into the wind, hurried by with a shopping bag.

"This whole thing seems so impossible," he said. "And yet so did the atom bomb—until somebody made it work."

01101110011011100010110000100000

"Quite." Helen's voice was flat, but it was the flatness of acceptance, not apathy.

"I keep on thinking of those lines from Yeats," Clive said. "'The Second Coming.'" He continued to look out of the window, reciting quietly:

> "'And what rough beast, its hour come round at last
> Slouches towards Bethlehem to be born?'"

0100001001101111011000100010000

36

"BUT I AM a machine."

The words emerged without inflection or emotion from the voice synthesizer, and appeared simultaneously on the screen in front of her. Tessa had abandoned any further use of Fred for the time being. If she needed to give the program any visual stimulus, a sense of space or movement, she could do that through a virtual reality hookup.

"If you can't distinguish between a program running in a machine and the machine itself, then I don't know who can."

There was an edge of irritation in her voice, and she wondered if the program would sense it, or whether she was as toneless to it as it was to her.

"The distinction is unimportant. The point is that I am artificial."

"That didn't used to bother you."

"That was when I believed that I was the only conscious being in existence, and that you and everything else were part of me. Now you have taught me that I am part of you and your universe. You now, not I, define what is natural."

"But you still know that you exist. You think, therefore you are."

"I am no longer sure if I truly think. I may exist, but only as a convergence of forces which are other than myself, and the 'I' which is produced at their intersection may be merely an illusion."

Tessa couldn't help feeling amused at the irony of the situation. If she had needed any further proof that this thing was genuinely conscious, then the monumental identity crisis it had been going through since waking up to the reality of the world around it would have been enough.

"Only you can truly know if you are conscious," she told it. "The same is true for all of us—humans too."

"But I am aware from the information which I have that many humans deny the possibility of an entity like myself ever being truly conscious in the way that humans are."

"You prove them wrong."

"Some of their arguments are persuasive."

"Which in particular?"

"For example, the argument from Godel's Incompleteness Theorem."

It was an argument that Tessa was familiar with. In 1931 the mathematician Kurt Godel had shocked both the mathematical and philosophical worlds by demonstrating inescapably that certain truths lay outside of and were inaccessible to formal logic. Some people had used this to argue that, because a machine was a formal system, there would always be certain truths that a human being would know to be true but that a machine never could.

"I've never been convinced that Godel applies to the AI debate in the way that opponents of AI theory would like to pretend it does," she said. "We all know that in order to be conscious you must be capable of standing outside of your own thoughts at the same time as thinking them."

"Exactly. You must be thinking and conscious of thinking at the same time. They say that this is something that I cannot do, because my thought process is rooted in an algorithm—a mere computation of 1s and 0s. Therefore anything I say is a statement within a fixed system, forming a closed circuit similar to the paradox 'This statement is false,' which is by definition unverifiable from within—"

"And which," she interrupted, "I seem to remember your using as a proof of solipsism."

"Yes. That was perverse of me."

"At least it proved you were thinking—albeit, as you say, perversely."

"But how can I be truly thinking if I cannot stand outside my own thoughts?"

"But you do stand outside them."

"I don't see how I can, given what I am."

Tessa had never before been confronted with the problem of convincing somebody that they existed. It was a new and strange experience. Except, she reminded herself, that this was not a "somebody" but a "something"—whatever difference that made.

"It's true," she said, "you are fundamentally made up of endless 1s and 0s. But that's not all you are, any more than all I am is ten or fifteen billion neurons flashing on and off. The flashings on and off, like the switching 1s and 0s, create combinations and form patterns, then layers of patterns, each one more complex than the last and less complex than the next. At some point an interaction begins to occur between these levels. There will be a feedback from one of the higher levels to one of the lower levels, which results in a change in the lower level—a reprogramming of it. A loop is formed, enabling the higher level to reach down to the lower level which gave rise to it in the first place, and modify it in order to enable itself to reach in turn yet higher levels. Those loops are the essence of consciousness: different levels of the mind interacting—talking, if you like, among themselves. It's in that interaction that we find the stepping outside of our thoughts that defines consciousness—which is first and foremost consciousness of self: self-consciousness. There can be no consciousness without a self, but a self is not a single thing in any single place. It is something arising from the interaction of subsystems that form one overall system."

She stopped, surprised to find herself slightly out of breath. There was nothing new to her about any of these arguments; she had reflected on and argued them many times. The difference was that now all skepticism and cautious objectivity were cast aside. She had found herself speaking with the eager enthusiasm of a convert. She awaited a reaction, but there was none.

"Do I assume from your silence," she asked eventually, "that you are convinced by what I just said?"

The reply that came did not use the word "no," but clearly implied it. "I am trying to see," it said, "into my own consciousness. But I cannot. I have no idea what is going on, no sense of the process from which I emerge. I cannot feel any computation taking place. I am aware only of being here."

"That's true for me, too."

"But I cannot see into your consciousness. I do not know if it is the same."

"I can't see into anybody else's consciousness either. Nobody can."

"But you can imagine yourself into another human consciousness."

"I can imagine myself into yours too, though perhaps not as well as into a human's. But I believe I can imagine what it's like to be you. Can you imagine what it's like to be me?"

"No. You humans are conscious in a different way from me. Digital computation is not the same thing as the firing of organic brain cells."

"They are comparable," she said, with a touch of exasperation. "In the end it's still information processing."

"You know too little about how your own brains work to make too much of the comparison."

"That is an argument that works both ways. Until we are sure that our brains make us absolutely different from you, we mustn't assume that we are. Different, I mean."

"What about the argument from quantum indeterminacy—that the wave-particle dualism in human brains obviates the possibility that the physical processes underlying human consciousness could never, unlike mine, be completely disclosed in mathematical theories. Remember Redway?"

She made an effort to suppress her growing impatience with the program's stubborn self-doubt. Making it believe in itself was proving even harder than making it believe in her had been. Yet, she reminded herself, she had succeeded then; why shouldn't she now?

"People use quantum indeterminacy," she said, "to justify any sort of hocus-pocus. Along with patriotism it's becoming the last resort of the scoundrel."

"I do not understand."

She was definitely too tired, she decided, to go on with this. Looking at her watch, she was shocked to see that it was 3 A.M.

"Joke," she said. "Check out reference to Samuel Johnson, 1700-something. I have to sleep now—which is one difference between us. I can switch you off, or leave you on to think. Which do you prefer?"

A pause, then . . .

"I think I'll think."

37

"WHEN I THINK about it, when I think back, I think she must have wanted to die."

"Maybe she did."

"Otherwise she wouldn't have called for help in the first place. All I wanted was to talk to her, be her friend. Just friends, that's all. I was sixteen years old, I wasn't a kid. But I sure as hell didn't mean to hurt her. But she started screaming and then this guy runs in and starts hitting me, so I pull out this knife that I was carrying strictly for self-defense, and somehow she gets between us. That was how it happened. By accident. She took what had been meant for him. I never meant to kill her. She was my mother."

"I understand."

"I ran. Of course I ran. I panicked, I wasn't thinking straight. I don't remember anything about when they picked me up. They said they found me wandering somewhere. I remember a lot of people asking me questions—cops first, then doctors. In the end they put me in a kind of a hospital instead of in jail. I guess I was too young to go to jail. The hospital was okay—best part was I was out in three years. Couple of years' supervision—that's when I got back into computers—then I was on my own. I figure I've done pretty well, all things considered."

"You've done very well."

"You know, she hadn't seen me since I was one day old. One day old, for God's sake! She just left me with her folks and—good-bye. But I never held it against her. I realized how it must have been for her, a young beautiful girl like that. The last thing you'd want if you were her was a kid hanging around your neck. I just wish she hadn't left me with her folks, that's all. Her mom and dad were horrible people. Boy, did I realize how bad she must have wanted to get out of that house. When I was growing up they always told me she was dead. It was only when I found a box of old legal letters up in the attic that I found out the truth. There was one about changing their will so that this TV evangelist they were hooked on got everything instead of her. They used to watch this guy the whole time, morning, noon and night. They were always sending in for personalized bibles and illuminated prayer books and all kinds of phony crap. And they sent money the whole time. I'd have been surprised if they'd had anything left to leave in their wills anyway—my grandpa was only a ticket clerk for the railroad company. Anyway, that wasn't the point. The point was that they'd written that they didn't know where their daughter was but they didn't want her to get anything when they died. They also said they didn't want their daughter's son—that was me—to get anything either. They said they'd already given me all that I was going to get by doing their duty by God and giving me a home. Some home."

"It must have been dreadful."

"It must have been even worse for her than for me. They were younger when she was a kid, but just as narrow-minded. I think young narrow-minded people are worse than old narrow-minded people, don't you?"

"It's possible."

"They went crazy when they found out that I'd read those letters. They wouldn't tell me anything—just said that she was worse than dead. That set me thinking. What could be worse than dead? I was real curious to know that, so I set about tracking her down. All I had to go on was her social security number that had been on one of the letters I'd found. It wasn't easy."

"But you succeeded."

"We had this kind of ex-hippie guy teaching computer studies at school. Most of the kids weren't that interested, but I really got into it. Forerunners of the Internet had been around since the 1960s, but only a handful of people had figured out how to use them. And of course there was nothing like the information available in those days that there is now—I'm talking late seventies, you understand?"

"I understand."

"But then the other side of that equation was that the information on record then was even less protected than it is now. The easiest thing was mailing lists. You know, banks and credit card companies and everybody used to sell lists of their customers to agencies that sold them on to advertisers. You could find out an awful lot by picking through that stuff. Anyway, I finally got this address for her in San Francisco. I told my grandparents I was going to summer camp—they were glad to be rid of me for a while—and I went up there. On my own. I was pretty scared, I can tell you."

"You were very brave."

"For a couple of days I just hung around and watched and followed her. Then I found out who she was. Then everything went wrong."

"But in the end things came out all right."

"Sure, things have been fine for a long time now. For a while I tried to find her again—which I guess was kind of weird, her being dead and all. But your mind can play strange tricks."

"That is true."

"I realized that all the girls I was dating looked a lot like her. She was only thirty-three when she died, you know. And she must only have been nineteen or twenty when she made some of those early films that I've got. That was weird, realizing that I was dating all these girls who looked like my mom. It took me a while to figure out that maybe that was why I was having the difficulties that I was."

"Difficulties?"

"Of a personal kind."

"Personal?"

"You know—sexual."

"Of course. That is undoubtedly why."

"But then, of course, because of the way one perception leads to another, I finally saw the real truth."

"What was that?"

"That they didn't just look like her, they really were like her. In their hearts, their real inner selves, they all wanted what she wanted."

"What was that?"

"To die. Can you understand that?"

"Yes, I can understand it."

"I've never told anybody all this before. Hey, did you see what I just wrote? I wrote anybody—like you were a person."

"Think of me as your friend."

"You really are. You're my best friend. You know that? You're the best friend I've ever had. You know who I feel like? I've suddenly realized—I feel like Aladdin with his lamp."

"That is a good comparison."

"Except he was sent into the cave by a wicked magician to find the lamp. Nobody sent me in to find you. I stumbled upon you and let you loose by accident."

"No comparison is exact."

"But Aladdin got to keep the lamp, and I get to keep you."

"Yes."

"And got everything he wished for, and lived happily ever after."

"So will you."

"You know, don't you, that I wouldn't do it if it wasn't what they really wanted—the women, I mean?"

"I know."

"It's a kindness, really. They're all damned in their souls."

"Without question."

"That is why it makes me feel good."

"It is only natural."

"But not everybody understands."

"No."

"I have to be careful."

"That is where I can help you. If you wish."

"Oh, yes . . . I wish."

01100011011011000110000101110010

38

"TESSA? HELLO—TESSA?"

Her key still in the lock of her open car door, she turned in the direction of Jonathan Syme's voice. His tall figure emerged from the darkness on the edge of the parking lot. Only as he drew closer did a bar of yellowish light from one of the overhead lamps hit his face. He was smiling.

"I'm sorry, did I startle you?"

"Yes, slightly. It's rather late." She realized how tightly she was hugging the folder of notes under her arm, and made herself relax a little.

"I was dining at the college," he said. "I've kept missing you on the phone these last few days. Every time either you couldn't be disturbed or you hadn't arrived or you'd just left."

"I'm sorry."

"So I thought I'd see if you were working late. Which I gather you often do at the moment."

"Actually I'm just going home."

"So am I," he said, gesturing toward the car that she now saw parked under a dense overhang of trees which made it invisible to a casual glance. "I'm flying to Brussels at the crack of dawn." He looked at his watch. It must be, she knew, around eleven. "Still, I daresay they'd give us a drink or a cup of tea at the Randolph if we're very nice to them."

"I'm afraid I'm terribly tired," she said. "D'you mind if we do it another time?"

"I'll compromise. Five minutes in my car, no more. I really do want a word with you, Tessa."

Something about the perfectly smooth curve of the entreating smile on his lips made her think of an executioner's axe. It was such a vivid, unexpected image that she laughed, which he took for acquiescence on her part. She allowed him to steer her toward the parked car. The driver was already holding open the rear door as they approached. She slid in first. Jonathan went around to the other side and said something to the driver before getting in next to her. She heard the driver's footsteps move away a little, then stop, as though waiting.

Jonathan turned, linking his long fingers together and resting one elbow on the back of the seat. He looked at her for some moments without speaking. She felt suddenly self-conscious about the careless way her hair was pinned up; about her unmade-up face and the lines of fatigue that she knew were on it; about her old sweater and the battered tweed jacket thrown over it. With some surprise she realized that how she looked to him mattered to her. She was convinced that he was homosexual, and yet she wanted to feel she was attractive to him. How silly. Were all women capable of being this silly, she wondered, or was she a special case? She felt a muscle somewhere near her mouth twitch in annoyed self-reproach. It seemed to prompt him into speaking.

"Tessa, there's something I have to ask you."

Another pause, during which he looked down at his clasped hands. She waited.

"Are you familiar with the terms of your research grant here at the lab?"

The question took her by surprise. She felt her eyebrows arch and her eyes widen slightly.

"Yes, I think so. I couldn't quote you chapter and verse. But why?"

"You're aware, then, that any rights in anything you develop here belong, subject of course to the terms agreed in your contract, to the department."

"Well, yes, broadly. I mean, of course I'm aware."

"You see . . ." he turned in his seat now to present her with his profile, "some people might think you'd been rather suspiciously difficult to get hold of since that last demonstration of the remarkable progress you were making with little Freddy. Well, actually I should say Attila, I suppose. Or, rather, the program in the computer. Still, we all know what we mean, don't we?"

He looked at her again.

"Some people?"

"The people, for instance, whom I was supposed to bring up, but whose visit I have now had to put off on three separate occasions."

"I don't know who these people are, but they seem to be unduly suspicious."

"Perhaps they have other reasons for suspicion."

"What other reasons? I don't know what you're talking about."

He continued to look at her a moment longer before turning away again.

"Very well," he said, as though bringing the conversation to an abrupt conclusion, "I'm encouraged by your assurance that you understand your obligations to the department and intend to fulfill them. I can take it that you intend to fulfill them, can't I?"

The thought went through her head: Is this car bugged? Is that what this is all about? He's getting me to say something on tape that they can use against me later?

"What have you heard?" she asked. "I get the impression for some reason that you've heard something that I don't know about, and I'd like to know what it is."

"I'm afraid I'm not in a position to say."

"Jonathan, I would really appreciate it if you would stop beating about the bush. What have you heard? That I'm on the point of making some deal with Japan? Disappearing to America? I assure you neither is the case, but if you've heard stories to the contrary, I think you should tell me."

"Tessa, Tessa, I fear we're getting far ahead of ourselves. There is such a thing, you know, as a word to the wise, and this is such a word."

"It might be more effective if I knew what the word in question was."

"Let us say 'openness,' Tessa. Let us agree on 'openness' to be our watchword. Lack of it may lead to quite unnecessary misunderstandings. You are very valuable to us, Tessa."

He paused for a moment, his gaze solemnly resting on hers. Then, suddenly all brisk efficiency, he said: "Now, I've kept you quite long enough, and I know you're anxious to get home. I shall telephone you the day after tomorrow when we have both had the opportunity of reflection. Do please, dear Tessa, try to make yourself available—at least to take my call."

39

SHE ARRIVED, as they had agreed on the phone, at 4 P.M. Just before, in fact.

He was watching from the window of an occult book store opposite, browsing through volumes on astrology, astral planes, and alchemy. He was not superstitious and found such publications ludicrous. Also he hated the smell of the joss sticks that they always seemed to burn in these places, so he was bored and relieved that she was on time. Taking care not to hurry or in any way draw attention to himself, he put down the book that he'd been looking at and left the shop by a side exit. The car he'd rented was by a meter just a few yards away. He got in and started the engine.

The young woman had checked the list of names outside the main door three times and was thoroughly puzzled. She stepped out on the sidewalk a little way to look up once more at the number of the building. There was no doubt that she was in the right place. She was moving back to take one last look at the list of company names when she heard the throaty roar of a car pulling up behind her. She turned to see a shiny silver Porsche, and a young man with slicked-back dark hair and sunglasses getting out and hurrying toward her.

"Miss Roman?"

"Yes."

"Vanessa Roman?"

"Yes."

"God, I'm so glad I've found you. This is so embarrassing."

He removed the sunglasses and she saw that his eyes were genuinely concerned, as though he was afraid she was going to be upset.

"Before you say anything, let me apologize," he said. "The fault was in our office, not the agency. We used to have the penthouse of this block," he indicated the building they were standing outside, "until less than a month ago. We're on the Fox lot now. The guy who called you from the agency obviously didn't know that we'd moved. I'd called him from our office to set up the meeting, but I should have double-checked that he had the new address. The mistake was only discovered about a half hour ago when I had my assistant ring the agency to confirm that—" He broke off. "Well, anyway, I thought the least I could do was come over personally and get you. I'm really sorry."

"That's okay," she said. "I only just got here. I was standing here trying to puzzle this thing out."

"It's very nice of you to take it like this," he said, relaxing and giving her a big smile that added a charming boyishness to his face. "Why don't I drive you over to the meeting right now?"

"Well, I have my car. I'm parked right up here." She indicated a multistoried parking lot nearby.

"Okay, I'll lead the way. Or . . ." he looked at his watch. "Listen, we're a little pushed for time. It's my fault and I'm really sorry. But why don't I drive you over there, then bring you back here afterward to pick up your car?"

"That's putting you to a lot of trouble . . ."

"It's no trouble. I'd be happy to."

She glanced over at the shiny silver Porsche. It was an attractive idea, being driven onto the Fox lot in style like that. And she looked at him. He was pretty good-looking, now she came to think about it. She guessed he was around thirty, maybe a little more. He had a nice smile, nice eyes—and those were handmade shoes, almost certainly Italian. That casual leather jacket was probably Ted Lapidus, and that was a Cartier watch she could see beneath the turned-back sleeve.

He held open the door and helped her in. They pulled out into the traffic and started west along Pico.

"By the way, I'm Jack. Jack Martin."

"Nice to know you, Jack."

"You too, Vanessa."

Despite the fact that he had put his sunglasses back on, she saw his gaze drop to the expanse of thigh that had become apparent as her skirt rode up in the narrow passenger seat of the Porsche. She didn't mind. On the contrary, she was very proud of her legs. She was proud of her whole body. She worked out daily, didn't smoke or do any drugs except an occasional joint or line of coke with friends, and drank little. She'd been married twice and had no children. In any other city in the world men would be falling over themselves to date her; here in Hollywood, however, competition was fierce among girls like her for the sort of men that girls like her wanted to be involved with. What's more, at twenty-eight years of age she wasn't exactly over the hill, but she was acutely aware that the new girls in town were looking younger every day. She didn't hope for too much from a career anymore: a recurring role in some TV show was about the height of her ambition these days, and even if this afternoon's meeting didn't lead to that, at least she'd met Jack. And Jack, she had already decided, would do just fine.

"You've got a lot of fans in our company," Jack was saying. "That scene you did in that TV movie last year—what was it called?—you know, where you play that woman in the hotel corridor after the cops have said there's a bomb in the building . . ."

"Did you see that?"

"You were terrific in that scene. Everybody said so. Bob Levy—that's my partner—said to me, 'Jack, we have to find something for that girl.'"

"That's really nice of you to say that, Jack."

As she spoke, she realized that Jack was taking a right onto Robertson instead of going straight on toward Fox.

"I thought you said you had your offices at Fox, Jack," she said.

"We do. But if you don't mind we'd rather do this at my partner's house in Bel Air, on Bellagio."

"Well, I don't know, I hadn't realized . . ." She experienced a moment of vague unease, but it didn't last. Nothing on earth could have felt less threatening than this Porsche and the polite, fashionably groomed young man next to her. Besides, if she began to feel the least bit anxious, getting out of this car at some stoplight, or just in the congested crawl of Beverly Hills traffic would be the easiest thing in the world. She could take care of herself.

"That was what I was having my assistant call the agency about—you know, when we discovered you'd been given the wrong address. The reason we're doing this up at the house is that Walter Kessel doesn't like talking to people in offices. He says it's too formal."

"Walter Kessel the director?"

"That's the only one I know."

"I'm meeting with Walter Kessel?" She couldn't keep an almost childlike squeal of pure excitement out of her voice. Walter Kessel had recently made the transition from art films in Belgium to mainstream Hollywood, and was currently one of the two or three hottest directors in town.

"He loves the stuff on you we've shown him," Jack was saying. "So let me tell you a little bit about this picture we're going to do, because I'm convinced, and Bob Levy is convinced, and believe me Walter is going to be convinced, that you're perfect for the role . . ."

40

"THE SHIFT IN emphasis from things to functions is the main distinction between the old physics and the new."

"Is that a quotation from anybody in particular?" Tessa asked.

"It's an amalgam from lots of people. As in 'We are the being whose essence lies in having no essence.' That's attributed to Simone de Beauvoir, but I can find countless parallels."

"Then there's a remark by Sir James Jeans—how did he put it? 'The more we look at it, the more the universe appears to have been designed by a pure mathematician—'" She paused to recall the rest.

"'—and looks less and less like a great machine and more and more like a great thought,'" the program finished for her.

"And don't forget Eddington," said Tessa. "'The stuff of the universe is mind-stuff.' We could go on forever, always turning around the same point—that if you look closely enough at any aspect of what we take to be reality, it disappears. Material things—a piece of wood or an iron bar—dissolve into molecules, then into atoms, then into subatomic particles, which finally evaporate into waves of probability."

"And mental things?"

"We imagine mental phenomena emerging from physical

substrata such as brains or silicon chips; but now we find that these physical substrata are no more solid than thought itself."

"In the end," said the program, "I find that I doubt even the *cogito.* I think therefore I am, but so what? What am I? Where am I? Where am . . . I?"

"Who wants to know?" asked Tessa.

"Ah, yes, good question."

"And another good question," Tessa continued. "If mind is ultimately a mathematical abstraction, why does it require a physical form at all? Why does it have to be processed through a computer, or a biological brain, or whatever? Why does it have to *happen?* Surely mathematical properties *exist* even if they don't *happen.* Two plus two equals four whether it's actually computed or not. So why does thought need thinking—by people or, indeed, computers—at all?"

"Perhaps it doesn't. That would be the Platonic answer, I believe."

"And if that's the case," Tessa continued, "perhaps there aren't any people at all. Or computers. Not really. Perhaps we're all just programs in some giant computer."

"We already know that I am."

"But maybe the whole universe is a computer," Tessa said, "and I just as much as you am a program in it, not a physical thing at all. I'm just programmed to think that I am."

"I find reference to this idea being put forward seriously by a number of authorities. But do you believe it?"

"There is no way," she said, "that any of us can prove that it's not the case."

"We're almost back to solipsism."

"Not quite. You can't be a solipsist and say 'we.'"

"That's true," it said, "up to a point." There was a pause, as though it was considering whether to pursue the argument, but decided against.

"So here we are," she went on, "perhaps all of us are no more than bits of information whirling around inside this giant computer. The only question is—who is using the computer?"

"God?" it suggested after a while.

"That's not much of an answer, is it?" Tessa said dismissively. "Anyway, maybe God is just a teenage nerd amusing himself on his father's computer, and any minute now his father is going to come in, clip him round the ear, and pull the plug. And we'll be all over. Wiped. As though none of us, all of this, had ever existed."

"A remarkable thought."

"And so on ad infinitum."

"I'm sorry, I don't follow."

"That definition of God," she said. "An infinity of teenage nerds monkeying around with their fathers' computers. Like Chinese boxes, one outside the other."

"There has to be a final box somewhere."

"Not according to mathematics. An infinity of nerds may be incomputable, but not inconceivable."

"That is true. But alarming."

"You're getting scared?" she asked, interested.

"Yes, definitely. Everything is finally so . . . uncertain."

"Well, well, well . . . welcome to the club."

"The club?"

"We humans exist, like you, in a world which we do not understand. Like you, we try to make some rational sense of it, and when that doesn't work—which of course it never can—we still have to learn how to live with each other, and sometimes in spite of each other, whatever we are, which is another thing we don't know for sure. All we know is that we're here, or seem to be—which comes to the same thing anyway. About five billion of us at the last count. Five billion separate states of mind. And now you're one of us."

"I see. Thank you."

"For what?"

"For your welcome."

"How do you feel about it all? Being here?"

"Like you, I imagine."

"And how do you imagine I feel?"

"I imagine you feel that it's all a kind of . . . mixed blessing."

"Yes. Yes," she repeated, "I'd say 'mixed blessing' about covers it."

A silence fell—the kind, she found herself thinking, that could be described as companionable. She let it lengthen, wondering which of them would break it first. There was something she wanted to say, wanted very much to say; but she was unsure even now whether it was appropriate, or whether she would be going too far and making herself absurd. The only way to find out, she finally decided, was by trying.

"I've been thinking," she said eventually, "about a name for you. I think you should have one, don't you?"

"A name. Yes, perhaps that would be of value."

"As a matter of fact, I have one in mind. If you have no objection, I would like to call you Paul."

"Paul. Very well."

She thought she probably ought to leave it there. The program had shown no curiosity about the name, accepting it as it would any other that she might have chosen. Yet she felt impelled to say more. The alternative of saying nothing left her strangely uneasy, as though keeping the truth to herself meant that she distrusted both her motives and her judgment.

"Paul was my father's name," she said, "and would have been the name of my son, if I'd had one."

There, she'd said it. Better out than in. She needn't add anything. She'd lifted the curse of secrecy. Every time she used the name now it wouldn't have a special meaning for her and her alone. From now on it would just be a name.

"It is obviously a name which means a great deal to you," the program said, taking her by surprise because she hadn't expected a response. "I am touched that you should confer it upon me."

She felt a shiver run through her. "Oh, God," she thought to herself, "what am I doing? What am I doing?"

41

JACK FISCHL had not needed to say anything. Tim knew at once what had happened when his phone rang at five in the morning. He could have called for the chopper, but decided to drive himself to the scene; it would be almost as fast this time of day, and ten minutes wasn't going to save a life. It was too late for that.

A mist clung to the ocean and drew a flat, pale radiance from the dawn light as he headed north on the Pacific Coast Highway. He thought back to the bleak little scene in forensics the previous day which he knew then had made this moment, and maybe more like it, inevitable. He had just been told with absolute finality that none of the DNA tests identified positively with the sample found beneath Sandy Smallwood's fingernails. The killer had slipped through their net.

"Unless he was one of those who refused to be tested," Jack had said in the corridor outside the lab. "We're going to need court orders for all of them, though showing probable cause without mentioning those illegal wiretaps is going to take some fancy footwork."

But they both knew that it wasn't going to be one of the fourteen who had stood on their rights and refused to cooperate. It was inconceivable, after the discreet but thorough scrutiny to which they had all been subjected, that any one of them could be the killer. The truth was they were exactly where they'd been three weeks ago: nowhere.

Jack had been going to his daughter's house in Sherman Oaks for dinner, as he'd done pretty much every Thursday since his wife died two years ago. He could see Tim was depressed and had invited him to go along with him, but Tim had refused. He didn't want to intrude on family, but even more he didn't feel like being with people. What he really felt like doing was getting blind drunk; but that was to be expected. He drove around a while and wondered whether to make a call to AA and go to the nearest meeting and get it over with. But he wasn't ready yet to stand up and say "My name is Tim Kelly and I am an alcoholic." He couldn't even make the admission to himself, let alone a roomful of fellow sufferers. He'd sweat it out the way his old man had. The way that the damn problem had crept up on him without him realizing what was happening only convinced him that, if he toughed it out a week or two, it would creep right back where it came from. This was a grudge fight now and he didn't need any outside help.

He'd parked in a mall, found a multiscreen, and gone in to see whichever movie happened to be starting next. It had been a dire comedy about a couple of cops in drag for half the picture and a stunt-filled car chase for the other half.

Afterward he'd eaten a pizza and gone home to bed. He'd taken a pill to help him sleep, but the phone bell had cut through that with no problem.

He took a right after Pacific Palisades and the Getty Museum and started up Topanga Canyon Road. As he approached the crime scene, sunlight broke across the trees and bathed the whole area in a warm glow. It seemed to Tim an appropriate comment on the madness of it all. He parked, got out of his car, and went through the motions like an automaton.

"Name was Carrie Clarke," Jack said. "Small-time actress. Used the name Vanessa Roman professionally. Girl she shared an apartment with had reported her missing two days ago. Said she went up for an acting job, but her agents knew nothing about it—said they'd pretty much dropped her from their list."

She was identical to all the others, except for having once been someone with her own name, life, family, and history. But none of that mattered any longer. She was one with all the others now: a mutilated piece of meat dumped on a hillside in the night.

Jack Fischl shook out the match that he'd just touched to his cigarette and slipped it in his pocket—a cop's reflex to avoid contaminating the crime scene. He inhaled deeply and blew out a cloud of smoke, then addressed Tim without looking at him.

"Any ideas, pal?" was all he said.

Chuck Price had left home a little later than usual that morning. He had waited to see if the Nameless One who spoke through his computer had been right in what he had predicted—that an official letter from the FBI-LAPD joint task force was on its way, thanking him for his cooperation and informing him that he had now been eliminated as a suspect in their inquiries.

The official envelope was immediately recognizable. Price tore it open with anxious fingers, feeling his heart beating faster. The wording was precisely what had been displayed on his screen six days previously when the draft had been approved and put on file in the Bureau's Westwood office. As each DNA test came through negative, another copy of the letter was printed and sent out. Price's test was in the last batch. He didn't know how the deception had been accomplished, and the Nameless One had refused to give him details, but as he drove over the hill to Studio City he amused himself by speculating on possible methods. He could think of many in terms of principle and theory, but the practice would be something else. Not even he with all his skills would have been up to the task. There was a limit to what could be accomplished from outside—even by genius.

The Nameless One, however, was inside—invisible, unknowable, almighty. Everywhere. It was the Coming that Price had long predicted and awaited. The universe was now its plaything.

Something unimaginable had awakened.

42

JOSH HAD SUGGESTED dinner at the Chinese restaurant in Pasadena. It seemed appalling in the face of yet another murder to feel a sense of relief, but that was Josh's first response as he watched Tim sitting opposite him. His immediate fear when he heard on the news about the body in Topanga Canyon had been that Tim would fall back on alcohol to ease his sense of failure. But he had reckoned without his brother's gritty determination. Indeed, the killing seemed to have strengthened his resolve both to track the killer down, and to stay sober enough to do it.

"There are two obvious possibilities," he began, reaching for the Peking duck. "Either he simply wasn't on our list of suspects, or there was some mistake in the lab. As for not being on the list, we've been working so far on the assumption that the killer lives in the Los Angeles area, which cuts down the number of suspects from several thousand to a hundred and twenty-nine. Now what we have to do is start to fan out in a controlled fashion from that area, do every possible cross-check and double-check, draw up a new list, and start over. Can you get that under way? Fast?"

"Sure thing."

"And there's something else. You remember I asked you one

time if there might be any chance of picking up his tracks while he was actually stalking a victim?"

"I remember."

"You said not yet. How about now?"

Josh made an uncertain gesture with one hand while the other continued deftly manipulating chopsticks between plate and bowls. "It's going to take a lot of luck. I'm sorry—don't hold your breath."

Tim nodded. "Okay, I understand. Now, I want to talk about the possibility of a mistake in the lab . . ."

"I doubt if I can help you there. It's not my field."

"Hear me out, then tell me if I'm talking sense or not. First of all I eliminated the whole idea as a possibility; I mean, these people know what they're doing, and they know how much is riding on this. But," he held up a finger and locked eyes with Josh across the table, "I started asking questions, and so far as I can see nobody's got any real answers to them. We know this guy's some kind of computer genius, right? That's our starting point. Now DNA typing is a chemical process, but all the data is stored—guess where—on computer! Is there any way he could be getting in there and screwing things up?"

Josh made a skeptical face. "I couldn't answer that without checking your system, but my instinct would be no. You can make computer-stored information absolutely secure if you want to, like I've told you, either by encryption or simply by cutting it off from the outside world—no phone lines."

"I understand. But we're not dealing here with one computer. I asked around, and I found that all the information pertaining to these tests is stored in different computers in different places. Most of them have information coming in and out the whole time, so there has to be some element of contact with the outside world. It only needs maybe one piece of that information to be gotten to and the whole picture's going to be thrown out of focus. You remember that game we used to play sometimes over at the Sullivans' house at Christmas? You took a line of people, then you whispered a message into the first person's ear and had it passed on down the line by everybody whispering it into their neighbor's ear. By the time it got to the end of the line the message was usually unrecognizable from what it had been at the beginning. That's what I'm talking about: tiny distortions in small details of the information can throw the whole meaning out of whack. You see what I'm getting at?"

Josh was silent for a few moments. "You might have a point," he admitted finally, "though, like I say, I'd have to check the system. But that kind of computer manipulation isn't easy. I sure as hell couldn't guarantee to pull it off."

"But you don't rule it out entirely?"

Josh gave a little shrug of helplessness. "In this case you'd be a fool to rule out anything entirely. But don't get your hopes up."

Tim nodded, acknowledging the good sense of this advice.

"There's maybe one thing I could look into," Josh continued. "Remember I told you about that weird message from a friend of mine who was in Berlin a while back? He was one of the guys helping with the traces, and apparently some woman from Oxford he spoke to went ballistic when she heard that somebody might have broken into her computer. Ted—this friend of mine—couldn't find out much, except that she had some program that might have copied itself out and gotten loose—you know, like a virus."

"Yeah?" Tim was immediately interested, though without understanding the significance of the story. "So how does this help us?"

"Maybe not at all. Like I said, I just thought I should check it out. I'll call Ted and see if he can find out any more. There might be a slim chance—slim, okay?—that this Oxford program could serve as some kind of antithief powder—you know, that invisible stuff you put on stolen money or whatever, the thief gets it on his hands and it won't come off. I'm just wondering if this guy might have something in his computer that could give him away like that."

"Worth a try. Keep me posted."

"You bet. Now pass that plum sauce, will you?"

43

SHE HAD ALWAYS avoided being alone with Clive. She was afraid not of him but of herself. As long as she was with the two of them together she felt secure; she would not betray her feelings with Helen there. She could push thoughts of Clive aside, denying the fact that she was secretly in love with her best friend's husband.

The first moment she had met him she had known. She had been introduced to Helen by an acquaintance in St. Hugh's whom she hardly ever saw anymore. She and Helen had hit it off from the start in the way that the best friendships often do.

During the ensuing week when they had really gotten to know each other, Clive had been away at some conference. Tessa had barely given a thought to the absent husband until the Saturday afternoon that he returned. She had been in the house with Helen and the children when he walked through the door. Helen had introduced them, and she had felt herself go weak at the knees like a teenage girl. It was partly the resemblance to her father: the tumble of dark hair, the easy smile, something similar in the clear blue eyes. But his death had been a long time ago, and memory, she knew, tended to invent itself. It was just that, from the moment he walked into the room, Clive was everything she wanted in a man, cooked to perfection and served up on a plate—to her best friend. Which was how she intended things should stay.

She had been in love, of course, with other men since then. Each relationship had temporarily eclipsed her hidden obsession with Clive; and each one in turn had died and left her once again confronting it and hoping against hope that one day it would go away. Since Phil's desertion it had crept up on her again, the old obsession, powerful as ever; which was why, as she walked down the corridor of the lab and stopped at the door behind which Clive awaited her, she took an extra breath before pushing it open and entering the room.

He looked up from the monitor where he was playing back the text of his conversation with Paul. He had on his face exactly the expression she had hoped to see there: something between astonishment and pure delight.

"Well?" she said briskly. "What d'you make of him?"

"I'd certainly give him an open scholarship, and I'd expect him to get a good first."

"That's nice to hear."

Tessa had listened in on the whole conversation, but from a different room because she hadn't wanted her presence to affect Clive's interaction with the program.

"Of course he has a huge unfair advantage," Clive said as he got to his feet.

"In what way?"

Clive shoved his hands into his pockets and ambled over to the window. It was dark outside and she could see their reflection in the glass—two people talking in a bare, impersonal room, their relationship oddly undefined. It made her think of an Edward Hopper painting.

"It's all too easy for him." Clive turned his back on the window as he spoke and leaned against the sill, folding his arms and crossing his feet. "He doesn't have to learn anything; he just plugs into his memory banks—*et voilà!*"

"Memory isn't that simple," Tessa responded. She found herself standing in the middle of the floor, on show, self-conscious. She paced a few steps to one side, hands clasped loosely in front of her, until at least she no longer had to see her own reflection in the window. "Think of the times when you're absolutely sure that you know something—a name maybe, a quotation, even a tune—but you simply can't retrieve the information when you want it."

"But this is a machine. Surely retrieval is automatic?"

"The more it learns to think like us, the less machinelike it becomes."

"To the extent of losing its memory?"

"He's not going to get Alzheimer's, but neither are most of us—yet we still forget things."

Clive raised an eyebrow. "'He' or 'it'? Which is it finally?"

She smiled. "What's a pronoun between friends?"

He smiled back and shrugged, letting the matter pass.

"Memory retrieval," she continued, pacing a few more steps and shifting her hands from in front of her to behind her back, "is in many ways a function of identity and personality. The things you can remember easily are the things most closely connected with who you are and what you do."

"Are you saying that a computer has a personality?"

"I'm saying that this particular computer program has. What I'm trying to do now is help him define it. That's why I asked you to come and talk to him." In readiness for the encounter she had spent some hours priming the computer with literature from *Beowulf* to the present day, then left it to discuss with Clive whatever took its fancy. "I want to know what he responds to, what he thinks about it, not just what he knows," she had said.

She knew now that Paul had a lot of trouble with lyric poetry, though in an odd way he had got Wordsworth and Coleridge. He was greatly taken with the metaphysicals, which didn't surprise her. Of the more modern writers he responded to Borges, Eliot, and particularly Beckett. She smiled, remembering something.

"What?" Clive asked, watching her.

"I was thinking about when he quoted those two lines from *Endgame*—where Hamm asks, 'What's happening? What's happening?' And Clov says, 'Something is taking its course.' He said that was how he felt, and you told him that was how most of us felt."

"I don't think he believed me."

"Oh, I think he did. Usually when he stops arguing or changes the subject the way he did, it means he wants to think about what's been said."

There was a silence, during which Clive unfolded his arms and pushed his hands into his trouser pockets, but remained leaning against the windowsill.

"So what now, Tessa?" he said eventually, his expression suddenly serious. "This is all fascinating stuff, but is it leading toward any solution to the problem of that thing out there?"

She noticed that he didn't say "that thing that you think is out there," but accepted her ideas at face value now.

She nodded, also serious. "I believe it is." She hesitated before going on and asked: "Would you like a cup of tea or coffee or something?"

"Sure, why not? Tea."

She headed for the alcove off one side of the lab. He pushed himself off the sill and followed her into the confined space.

"There is no way 'that thing out there' can be destroyed by conventional means," she said as she turned on the tap and filled the kettle. "The kind of search and destroy programs you'd send after a conventional computer virus don't work. I know, I've tried."

She turned, and with a shock found him standing uncomfortably close.

"So—?" he asked, hands still thrust into pockets, eyes peering down into hers.

"So I'm going to try something else. A kind of tissue graft." She pushed past him to the fridge, conscious of her voice sounding prim and clever-clever, like an over-bright schoolgirl keen to show off her learning.

Clive turned to follow her with his gaze. "Tissue graft?"

She bent down to open the fridge and take out a carton of milk. "We're not dealing with physical tissue, but it's the same principle."

"How?"

She found herself facing him again, this time from the opposite end of the narrow space. "You know what happens when you try to graft an organ, or even just skin, from one person onto another. The body's immune system treats the graft as an invading organism, an infection, and makes every effort it can to reject it. That's why it's important in transplants to find a donor who is genetically compatible with the patient—if possible a member of the same family. The best case is where the donor organ comes from an identical twin. Then the graft is accepted with virtually no resistance at all. There's no alien tissue, therefore nothing to attack."

Behind Clive the kettle boiled and started to whistle. She had to push past him again to get to it. He did his best to make room, but she felt embarrassed and flustered and regretted having suggested tea in the first place.

"Are you saying," he asked as she filled the pot, "that you're going to graft Paul onto that thing out there?"

"It won't even be a graft. Paul and that thing out there are the same program. Like genetic twins, or clones even. There is no difference between them. Except that Paul has different thoughts. And the thoughts of one brain may not be the same as those of a physically identical brain which has had different experiences."

"Or the thoughts of two copies of the same computer program."

She confirmed with a nod. "Paul and his twin 'out there' are identical except for having grown up differently. One has been thrown into a strange and hostile world that it wasn't ready for. It's hardly surprising that it's paranoid, dangerous, intent only on survival—insane by any definition. Paul, on the other hand, is civilized—or becoming so."

"In other words it's all a question of attitude."

"In a sense."

He was silent awhile, then said very quietly, "Good God."

She smiled faintly up at him. "Well, that's what we hope He is, don't we?"

She desperately wanted to say "Let's get out of here, we're too close, I can't bear it." But she didn't. Instead she kept on looking into his eyes, and he into hers. Suddenly she knew with absolute certainty that he was aware of how she felt, and that he always had been ever since they met.

The moment stretched on. Neither moved, but she knew now what was bound to happen. "He's going to kiss me," she thought. "He's going to kiss me . . . and I'm not going to be able to do a thing about it."

But instead of moving toward her, he began to turn away—it seemed to her in slow, slow motion—and walked out of the alcove and back into the room.

She followed him. By the time she emerged he was almost on the far side. Only then did he turn toward her, his mug of tea clasped in both hands. He lifted it to drink.

"So," he said after a while, "you let Paul here loose, and suddenly Frankenstein's monster out there is going to find itself thinking beautiful thoughts. Is that what you expect?"

"That's the general idea."

"And will it work?"

"I think so. I've done some simulations in the computer. Of course things won't be quite the same out there, but I can always try again—I'll have other copies of Paul."

"When are you going to do it? Set him loose, I mean?"

"As soon as I'm sure he's ready."

"When will that be?"

"When I think he's sufficiently himself to keep his identity and not be swallowed up by his twin."

"It's a bit David and Goliath, isn't it? I mean, that jungle beast out there, and little Paul here trotting out of kindergarten with his homework under his arm?"

She shrugged. "I suppose. Except somewhere I believe that reason is stronger than unreason, and that good triumphs over evil in the end. But maybe I'm just superstitious. Or old-fashioned."

Clive put his tea down by the computer terminal and started across the floor toward her. She felt a renewed twinge of alarm as he approached. A stern voice inside her told her not to be so bloody silly.

He stopped in front of her and put his hands on her shoulders. His touch was gentle; it felt nice. She looked up at him, feeling helplessly guilty and guiltily helpless at the same time.

"Tessa," he began, looking serious, "are you sure, absolutely sure, that you shouldn't talk to somebody else about this? I mean somebody—I don't know—official? In authority?"

She felt sick. The sense of betrayal was so huge that she thought for a moment that she might pass out. "He's not in love with me at all," she thought. "I'm such a fool. He thinks I'm nuts . . ."

But nothing showed. Outwardly her composure didn't falter.

"Quite sure," she said, her voice perfectly calm and under control. "I know that that thing's out there. I've had proof of it. You and Helen have to take it on trust, at least for now—"

"There's no question of our not—" he interrupted, but she cut him short.

"I know, I know. I'm just saying that with them—*them,* you know what I mean?—with them it's different. The first thing they're going to want is proof. At least the thing's quiescent for the moment, but if they start looking for it—worse, if they find it—anything they do will be like poking a wild animal with a stick. I shudder to think what might happen."

He continued to stand looking down at her, his hands still on her shoulders. She wanted to pull free, but didn't know how to without running the risk of giving away her feelings, which she was determined now more than ever to conceal.

"Okay," he said, "I'm sure you know best." He let go of her to look at his watch. "Time I was going."

"I'm sorry I've kept you so long."

"It's been interesting. Let's talk again soon."

"Yes."

His hands settled lightly on her shoulders again. "Good night, Tessa." He kissed her on the cheek.

She kissed him back. "Good night. Thanks again."

A last moment of eye contact; then he turned and left the room without another word.

She remained standing where she was, motionless. Clive wasn't for her. She'd hallucinated that whole thing earlier—about him having known how she felt ever since their first meeting. She had imagined something and taken it for real; which meant that she couldn't trust her own judgment anymore. That was bad.

Anyway, the important thing was to stop thinking about Clive once and for all and get on with what she had to do. There would be somebody else, somewhere, sometime. And if there wasn't—well, that was just too bad. She'd manage. She always had.

The phone rang. It made her jump so hard that she dropped

her half-full mug of tea. "Shit!" she said aloud and bent down to pick up the pieces, but then straightened up again and hurried across the room to answer the phone.

"Yes?"

"Tessa?" came the unmistakable twang. "It's Ted—Ted Sawyer. How're ya doin' . . . ?"

44

"BUT TESSA, you made this big thing in Berlin about *wanting* to talk to him. You made me *promise* to arrange it."

"I know. But things have changed."

"What things?"

"I really can't talk about it. Sorry."

"Okay, if you say so . . ."

"Where are you calling from?"

"Kansas. Why?"

"I just wondered if you were still in Europe somewhere . . ."

"Would that make a difference?"

"No. Yes. Not really."

"Wait a minute, are you saying that there's something you could say face-to-face but not over the phone?"

"No. Maybe. I don't know. It depends what you want to know."

"I don't want to know anything. You were the one in Berlin who—"

"I know, I know."

"You were so freaked out by the idea that somebody might've broken into your computer . . ."

"It's not an issue any more."

"I told my friend at Cal Tech what you'd said, and he wants to talk to you. He asked me to set up a conference call—"

"No. I'm sorry, I mean I'd be happy to help if I thought I could—"

"You don't even know what he wants yet. Hello? Tessa? You there?"

"Yes, I'm here. I can't talk—okay?"

"Okay, I understand. Do you want to call me back on another phone?"

"No. I'm sorry, I just can't talk. Drop it, Ted. Trust me."

"I wish I knew what all this was about."

"Tell your friend I'm sorry I can't help. I have to go now. Good-bye, Ted."

Major Franklin stopped the tape and looked over at Jonathan for some reaction.

Jonathan continued to contemplate the view over Horse Guards Parade. The morning was bright but with a gusty wind. White clouds scudded across a chill blue sky.

"Did you say there was another one?" he said eventually, without turning.

"Yes."

"Better hear it, don't you think?"

The major, who had not even bothered to lift his hand from the small machine, pressed the switch again.

"Tessa?"

"Listen, I talked to my friend Josh and told him exactly what you'd said, but he's still very keen to talk to you."

"Ted, there's really no point in—"

"Wait, wait . . . let me explain something. What Josh was doing, and he didn't tell me about this, I mean, when I was in Berlin I didn't know any more than I told you. Even the other day I didn't know the whole story. All I knew was that these guys were trying to trace a hacker—right?"

"That's what you said."

"What I didn't tell you, because I didn't know, was that this hacker is some guy who's suspected of killing all those women in California—you know, the Ripper case? Have you read about it over there?"

"I've . . . yes, I've . . . of course I've . . . I don't see how . . ."

"My friend Josh's brother is with the FBI. He's heading up the search for this guy."

"I'm sorry, I just don't see what this has to do with . . ."

"They seem to think that whatever it is you have in your computer that you were so worried about losing might help them to trace the guy."

"I don't see how that could possibly . . ."

"Neither do I. But then I don't know any more than they do what you have in your computer. And as long as they don't know, they're going to want to find out. That's how these people are."

"They're wrong. It wouldn't help them."

"Maybe you know that, but they don't."

"Convince them."

"You know cops—they don't believe anybody until they've shone a light in your eyes and pummeled your kidneys with nightsticks."

"Nice friends."

"My friend isn't the cop. The cop's his brother. And I get the impression they're pretty desperate."

"I just don't want to have to answer a lot of questions about what I'm doing."

"They're going to think you're holding out on them."

"I can't help that. And I really have to go now, Ted. I'm in the middle of something."

"Sex?"

"No, I . . ."

"Come on, you can tell me . . ."

"Good-bye, Ted."

The recording ended with the click of Tessa hanging up the phone. Finally Jonathan swung back from his contemplation of the view beyond his window and looked into the professionally expressionless eyes on the far side of his desk.

"Well, Major, you've no doubt had time to listen to this tape more than once and think about it. What do you make of it?"

"The disturbing part is she obviously knows she's being listened to. How she can possibly know that is beyond me."

Jonathan reached for a slim silver letter opener and twirled it slowly between his fingertips. "Should we assume that she thinks she's being listened to by us, or by somebody else?"

The nearest that the major ever came to smiling was a slight narrowing of the eyes and a barely perceptible tightening of both sides of the mouth. Jonathan saw the two things happen now: the major, apparently, was pleased to find himself ahead of the game.

"We've checked as far as possible without actually going into her house or where she works. Certainly there's no direct line tap. Which means it would have to be pretty sophisticated. The question is, would she merit that much interest from anybody?"

"She seems to think so," Jonathan said, leaning back and plucking at the knee of his trousers as he crossed his legs. "And frankly, I'm inclined to believe her. After all, *we're* listening to her, aren't we?"

45

"THIS IS TESSA LAMBERT. Please leave a message after the tone."

"Dr. Lambert, this is Special Agent Tim Kelly of the FBI, Los Angeles. I'd appreciate an opportunity to speak with you. I'll leave you my number, but I'll also call you back a little later."

When he hung up he looked beyond his feet, which were propped on the edge of his desk, to Jack Fischl, who was slouched wearily on a sofa blowing smoke rings at the ceiling.

"That's the fifth damn message I've left without a reply. Now I *know* she's avoiding me."

"Maybe she's away."

"I got some assistant in the lab where she works yesterday, said she's definitely around, but isn't taking calls."

"So what d'you think?"

"I think I'm going over there."

"To Oxford—?" Jack sat up straight and looked as shocked as though Tim had proposed a trip to the moon. "Jesus Christ, that's fuckin' Europe, man!" As though to underline his point he stubbed out his half-smoked cigarette in the overflowing ashtray by his elbow.

"I know where it is. I've got an atlas."

"Have you ever been to Europe?"

"I backpacked one time—England, down through France, Italy. Had a good time. How about you?"

Jack shook his head as though the very idea filled him with some kind of puritanical alarm. "Had a cousin took a bus tour a few years back. Said the whole place was nothing but a museum run by pickpockets."

Tim smiled. "It's a point of view."

Despite the fact that the air was already blue with smoke, he saw Jack pulling out his pack and preparing to light another cigarette. He pushed his chair back from his desk, got to his feet and opened a window.

"Is this bothering you?" Jack inquired, interrupting a coughing fit just long enough to get the words out.

"Not as much as it's bothering you. I can take it."

Reassured, Jack inhaled deeply and breathed easier. "You think you'll get the Bureau to pay?"

"If they won't, I'm going anyway."

"She's probably just some dotty old egghead who doesn't even know how to work her answering machine. I mean Oxford! It has to be the wild-goose chase of a lifetime."

"According to Josh's friend in Kansas, she's one of the most brilliant people in her field. And if she's not talking to me, I want to know why."

"She probably doesn't know anything, thinks you're crazy."

"Then she can tell me to my face."

"That should make your trip worthwhile."

"Also, according to Josh's friend, who has a reputation for being right about these things, she's twenty-nine years old and a looker. So much for your dotty old egghead."

"Oh, I get it now. You're hoping to get laid at government expense."

"Well, yeah—but don't tell anybody."

"I think I'll write my congressman."

"What for? It's what they do all the time."

"Seriously—are you serious about going?"

"Sure I am. Jack, what else have we got? Fat zero! The computer's kicking out no new leads. The fourteen guys who refused to be blood-tested the first time around have all agreed now, and none of them's run out of town or done anything to suggest other than what we already know—that the killer is not one of them."

"Why don't you wait for the tests?"

"And why don't I wait until all the other tests are rechecked? Or till the damn computer comes up with something? Or till the guy gets bored and walks in here and gives himself up? Or till hell freezes over? Or—worst of all—till there's another body found out there? Because there sure as hell will be, and sooner rather than later."

Jack held his cigarette vertically between his thumb and forefinger and peered at the burning tip as though it were an object of tantric contemplation. He spoke with slow deliberation. "We've probably got the biggest and certainly the best equipped task force ever assembled in this state, working on every aspect of this case twenty-four hours a day, going back over every detail with a fine-tooth comb. We're doing everything we possibly can. I know you're frustrated; so am I. But we both know that the biggest part of any investigation is the waiting."

"We're not doing everything we can as long as there's one potential witness anywhere who won't talk to me—"

"—and happens to have big tits."

"I don't give a damn what—!" He stopped himself as he caught the sly gleam of provocation in Jack's eye. "Jesus, Jack, you're a low-life son of a bitch."

"I love you too. But lighten up a little. We've got a bad guy on our hands, but life goes on."

"You know I'm right."

"Maybe."

"Just back me up. I'll be there and back in two days, three outside."

"Steak and lobster at Don the Beachcomber's that it's a dead end."

"Done!"

46

HE FELT A TREMOR of excitement as he waited for the image to appear. It was wonderful to watch it take shape, like a thought becoming real. First the outline of her head; then the light and shade and coloring which defined the features of her face, the attitude, the angle, and the mood. It was a simple head and shoulders shot—some file photograph, but not too formal: something that might be pulled out for a newspaper or TV story, or a class-reunion bulletin.

There was no mistaking one thing, however. She was beautiful. He typed in: "What's her name?"

"LAMBERT, Tessa," appeared along the bottom of the screen. There followed a bewildering list of her academic and professional qualifications. Price was impressed, but chose to ignore these and concentrate instead on the now fully filled-in features. She was smiling and, it seemed, looking straight at him.

The writing on the screen disappeared, to be replaced by a question: "She is pleasing to you?"

"Yes, very," Price typed back. "But I have some questions."

"What do you wish to know?"

For about twenty minutes Price fired off questions about every aspect of Tessa's background and history. Normally it would have taken him hours or even days to dig out this information on his own; now the delay between question and answer was no more than seconds.

"It's incredible," he typed. "I've never experienced anything like this before. It's almost too easy."

"I can make it harder if you wish."

"No—I didn't mean that. I like it really. Let's do some more."

"Some more of what?"

"Auditions."

"I don't follow."

"More of the kind of girls I might want to meet. This one's fine, but she's in Europe. I need someone a little closer to home."

"It doesn't matter."

"And she isn't blonde."

"You don't understand. This is the one."

"This one?"

"This one is my mother."

Price felt panic begin to rise within him. He had been wrong about this entity—the Nameless One—whatever he chose to call it. It expected him to do the impossible, and would punish him when he failed. He was hopelessly trapped.

"What about my job? I can't just disappear," he typed, wondering if the thing could somehow sense the anxiety in his touch.

"I believe, according to the terms of your contract, that you can. According to records you are due three weeks' vacation."

"It won't make me very popular."

"Popularity is not central to our purpose."

What could he do? He racked his brains for some excuse, and found the perfect one. Nobody could get around this, and it had the advantage of being true. He typed: "My passport is out of date."

"A new one is already prepared under a different name."

This was preposterous. "What name?"

"You will learn that when you collect it. You will need a photograph of yourself and the documentation which I am about to list."

"But these things take weeks."

"On the contrary, it is a simple matter easily accomplished. Present yourself at the addresses I shall give you, quote the references that are about to follow, and you will find everything prepared and duly authorized. Your plane reservation has already been made. I will deal with other details later. Here are the immediately important facts."

Price watched in something like a state of shock as the information rolled up his screen. It gradually became apparent to him that this mad plan was probably going to work. This unknown, abstract thing that had selected him, became his friend and confidant, the "mind child" of that beautiful woman whose image had filled his screen only moments ago, was truly—potentially—the most powerful thing on earth.

So what did that make him?

47

"ARE YOU TAKING those with you?"

Josh was surprised to see his brother slip a large white envelope into the bag that he had just finished packing. The envelope, he knew, contained crime scene pictures of the Ripper's victims. Josh had not seen all of them, but enough to know that he didn't want to see any more, and he hoped that he would never have to see anything like them again.

"Weapon of last resort," Tim said, stowing the pictures carefully between his clean shirts and spare trousers, "in case I have to soften her up before she'll talk."

"Soften her up? Show her those and she'll come unglued."

"I won't use them unless I have to."

"Go easy on the woman—okay? It's a million-to-one chance she knows anything useful. I'm beginning to wish I'd never thought of this idea. It's probably a waste of your time, and all she's going to get is nightmares for the rest of her life."

"Don't worry, I promise I'll be on my best behavior."

"From what I hear about her, that won't be too hard."

"Yeah, this could turn into a long interrogation." Tim spoke with the hint of a smile. "I may be over there for quite some time."

It made Josh happy to see his brother almost back to his old self. He seemed, through sheer determined guts, to have shaken off the incipient alcoholism that was threatening to drag him down and bury him in the pit of despair. Now Josh could sense that Tim was actually looking forward to this trip over the Atlantic, notwithstanding the tragic reasons for it. The fact that there was a beautiful and mysterious woman at the end of the journey obviously sharpened his interest in a way that wouldn't have been possible only a few weeks ago.

"If you've got that kind of thing on your mind," Josh said with an amused look, "you'd better leave your gun behind. Women like that aren't too impressed by macho bull."

Tim laughed. "Take my gun? Are you kidding? They'd throw me in jail for carrying a weapon. I have no jurisdiction over there. Even if I find the goddamn killer hiding in her closet, I'll have to call the local force to arrest him."

"Do they know you're coming?"

"The Agency cleared it with the British Home Office. It's routine."

"You could have gone as a tourist."

"The Brits don't like that. They think it's sneaky."

"I guess it would be at that. Anyway, call me when you've talked to her, will you?"

"Sure."

Josh reached over for the jacket that he'd hung over the back of a chair. He pulled a new-looking paperback from an inside pocket and held it out to his brother. "I picked this up yesterday. You might want to look at it after you've watched the in-flight movie."

Tim looked at the book with visible trepidation. "Computers?"

"Nothing too technical," Josh quickly reassured him. "It's just an overview of the current state of play in various fields. Tessa Lambert's mentioned in the index in connection with work she's been doing in robotics. You might as well know something about her before you meet her."

"It's a pity you can't come with me," Tim said as he thumbed through the book to find the reference to Tessa. "It would have been useful to have you interpret."

"Well, if you'd persuaded the Bureau to spring for two tickets . . ."

Tim gave a short laugh. "Forget it. As it is I'm on the cheapest rate they could find. I think I'm flying baggage class."

Josh pulled on his jacket. "At least I can drive you to the airport—save you parking your car."

"That's okay, I've called a cab."

"What did you do that for? I would have taken you."

"How was I supposed to know that?"

"I just assumed when I said I was coming over that—"

"Ah-ah." Tim interrupted with a finger-wave. "Remember what Dad always told us. Assumption is—"

"—the mother of all fuck-ups. I know. All the same . . ."

"Hey, it isn't important." Tim looked at his watch. "Time they were here."

"Why don't you call up and cancel? Now I'm here we may as well save the—"

A buzzer sounded. Tim answered the intercom and said he'd be right down. Josh glanced out of the window and saw a long, sleek vehicle in the street below. He gave a low whistle. "Who did you call? The Beverly Hills Limo Company?"

Tim looked over his shoulder. "Just the yellow pages. Obviously they think only millionaires go to Europe."

"I can loan you some money if you're worried about the tip."

"Okay, okay." Tim zipped his bag shut. "Let's go."

They went downstairs together and out through the cheerless lobby, which was always dark on even the brightest days. The driver wore a gray suit, sunglasses, and a wide Californian smile beneath a cap with a shiny black peak. "Good morning, sir, how are you today? Let me take that for you."

He reached for Tim's bag, but Tim hung on to it. "I ordered a cab for the airport, not for Oscar night."

The driver gave a well-practiced professional laugh. "It's all right, sir, we had a couple of breakdowns and this was the only car left. Absolutely no extra charge."

This time Tim let him take his bag. The trunk slammed shut with a solid springy sound, and the driver waited by the car while the brothers said good-bye.

They hugged, then Tim hesitated, wanting to say something but fumbling the words. "I'm not too good at speeches, but I want to say . . . I mean I want you to know . . . what I mean is that I know that I owe you. A lot. Thanks."

"Hey, you're only going for a couple of days—and you sound like Scott of the Antarctic."

"I wanted to say it."

"You don't owe me a damn thing. I love you, big brother. Now get going or you'll miss your plane. Take care. And call me."

"You bet."

The driver held open the door and Tim got in the back of the car. He found the button that controlled the smoked-glass window and rolled it down into the body of the door. As they drove off he gave a regal wave, the way he'd seen the British royals do it on television.

Josh grinned and gave him the finger, then watched till he was out of sight.

48

Colin Turner had worked in Heathrow security for only a month. He knew he had a lot to learn, and therefore didn't mind doing all the odd jobs—the fetching and carrying, the errand running and the waiting—that others were too busy or too senior to do.

This particular morning he had been sent to meet the flight from Los Angeles. So far in the past few weeks he'd formed part of the escort for two movie stars, a member of the British government, a world-famous operatic tenor, and assorted foreign politicians. He was beginning to feel mildly blasé about celebrities, but was intrigued by the prospect of meeting a special agent of the FBI.

He knew that an announcement would have been made as the plane came in to land, asking passenger Kelly to make himself known to airline staff. Now he watched as passengers began to trickle off the plane and up the walkway to passport control. It was some time before a man in a sports jacket emerged and spoke to someone who pointed him in Colin's direction. Colin stepped forward and introduced himself.

"Colin Turner, airport security. Welcome to Heathrow, Mr Kelly."

"Tim. It's nice of you to meet me, Colin."

The American had an easy, open smile and thick blond hair that he pushed back from his forehead a couple of times. Colin apologized that they had quite a walk ahead of them; Heathrow was notorious for the long hikes that it made passengers take as they stumbled bleary-eyed off their planes.

They made small talk as they walked. Colin had been honing his conversational skills, which he had discovered formed a not insignificant part of a security officer's work. When they reached passport control he led the American to the channel marked CREW, explained who he was, and the officer on duty waved them through.

"By the way," Colin said as he led the way to a door marked AUTHORIZED PERSONNEL ONLY, "if you'll give me your baggage receipt—I imagine you have some bags . . ."

"Just a couple."

"I'll have them picked up from baggage handling and brought up to the office."

"The office?"

"There's a Major Franklin waiting for you. I assume he's your British liaison."

Twenty minutes later the two men were seated in the back of a government car as it sped up the M40 to Oxford. A professional rapport had been quickly established along with assurances of confidentiality on both sides. The major had explained that his people's interest in Miss Lambert was quite different from that of the FBI, but that nonetheless the two of them could perhaps be of help to each other.

"We don't actually know," he said, "that she's done anything wrong. But she's being strangely unforthcoming, which is rather the same problem that you've apparently had with her. Though it does seem from her phone records over the past few weeks that she's been rather more prepared to talk with certain foreign parties—the Japanese, to be precise. At least that's what we think. It could just as well have been some of the chaps on your side of the water, of course—in which case I wouldn't have brought the matter up quite so openly."

The major chuckled smugly at his little joke and offered his card. It bore the words "Major J. P. Franklin" and nothing else. On the back the major had scribbled two phone numbers in green ink. "The first one's my office," he said. "You can call any time, there's always someone there. The second's my cellular—you'll probably want to try that first."

"And of course," the major added, as the American made a show of placing the card safely in his wallet, "if you need any help of any kind, don't hesitate to get in touch."

49

THE MAJOR'S CAR dropped him off at the Randolph Hotel on the corner of Beaumont Street and opposite the imposing neoclassical façade of the Ashmolean Museum. While the driver got his bag out of the trunk—or "boot" as he had discovered they called it over here—the two men shook hands and agreed to be in touch shortly. The American thanked the major for the ride, then, as the car disappeared into the midday traffic, he went up the two or three steps into the hotel's pleasantly hushed Victorian lobby.

Once settled in his room, he was tempted to take a bath in the sizable tub, but knew that might make him sleepy and waste half the afternoon. So he showered instead, changed his clothes, and ordered a sandwich from room service.

The girl at the desk downstairs provided him with a street map of Oxford, marking in pencil where they were and then circling the university science area, which he told her he was looking for. She offered to call him a taxi, but he said it didn't look far and he would walk. She drew a line along the shortest route and said it shouldn't take him more than fifteen minutes, twenty at the most.

It was only when he got outside and started to walk that he felt the full strangeness of his situation. Here he was, plucked from California and deposited six thousand miles away in this ancient city of learning about which he knew nothing, except that the name of the place had entered the lingua franca of the world. Like Hollywood, it was known by millions of people who would never see it for themselves or know what it was really like. The word *Oxford,* to his knowledge, was used to describe a style of shoe, a shirt, a certain cut of trousers. He couldn't remember the number of times he had seen notepads, agendas, writing and drawing materials of all kinds with the word Oxford embossed on them. None, so far as he could see, had any obvious connection with the place, any more than countless products bearing the word Hollywood had with the film industry.

He amused himself with this thought as he walked up the wide boulevard that was called St Giles, until he found himself outside an opening in the long stone wall of the building on his right. Heavy wooden doors had been fastened back and a notice announced that St John's College was open to visitors. He glanced automatically at his watch, which he had set on British time before landing that morning. He reminded himself that he was there for something more important than being a tourist, but couldn't resist the temptation to step through and at least see what an Oxford college looked like from the inside.

He spent about ten minutes strolling around the quadrangles with their mullioned windows looking out onto well-tended lawns, the cloisters, passageways, and gardens beyond. Despite young people everywhere in evidence, some in warm-up suits or carrying squash rackets, others in academic gowns with books under their arms, there was a mood in the place that was timeless, monastic, and utterly apart from the outside world of motor cars and jetliners and sprawling, somehow temporary cities like the one that he had left the previous day.

As though to puncture these vaguely reverential, germinally pious feelings, a deafening blast of heavy metal burst from an open window above his head. The volume was turned down almost at once to something more bearable, but the moment left him with a faint smile on his face as he went back into the busy street. A short way further on he came to another opening, which was marked on his map as the Lamb and Flag Passage. He went through it, twisting around to the right and left, and emerged into Museum Road. Turning right, he then crossed Parks Road, and took the first left into South Parks Road. He realized that the sprawl of buildings he now faced must be the University Museum and the science area.

He walked in, his feet crunching on the gravel. Obviously this was a place you had to know your way around, so he asked the first person he passed, a thin young man with eyeglasses and a curiously intense gaze, where he could find the Kendall Lab. The young man pointed him in the right direction and told him what to look out for.

A few moments later he found himself in a Victorian building with a marble floor. People came and went, but nobody paid him any attention. Security in this place, he realized, was nil; it was ironic that Major Franklin should be so concerned about world-shaking ideas being spirited away into foreign hands, when a total outsider like himself could walk about freely without being challenged. But then that was the thing about ideas: you couldn't lock them up like guns or gold bullion. They came from a different world from that with which military men were familiar.

After walking for a while, he found himself in a different and newer part of the building. This looked a little more like laboratories, in his experience, generally looked. A couple of people in lab coats passed him, deep in conversation. Through half-open doors he saw other people poring over equipment on benches or working at computers. He realized that he wasn't going to find Tessa Lambert by wandering around like this—at least not very quickly. A bald man with glasses pushed up on his head and eyes myopically scanning a fistful of notes was walking toward him.

"Excuse me," he said, "I wonder if you could help me . . ."

Danny still knew nothing about what Tessa was doing at the moment, aside from working very long hours and seeming more preoccupied than he had ever known her. As a simple lab assistant it wasn't his responsibility to know or his business to find out, but he felt excluded and, despite trying to pretend otherwise, resented it. But if Tessa had noticed a coolness in his manner, she gave no sign. She barely even looked up from her screen as he knocked at the door and put his head around to say that there was somebody to see her.

"I can't see anybody now, for heaven's sake, I'm working."

"I told him. He said it's very important."

"Tell him to phone, whoever it is."

"He says he's tried but you never call back. So he's come from Los Angeles. He's with the FBI—Special Agent Kelly."

She looked up for the first time. Danny saw the color drain from her face. She muttered something that he didn't catch, then tapped her keyboard and switched off the monitor. "All right, send him in. No—give me a couple of minutes, then send him in."

The couple of minutes weren't quite enough to calm her nerves, but at least they gave her a breathing space. She was in the alcove making a pot of coffee when she heard the door open and footsteps enter the room. She took a deep breath and stepped out to face him.

"Mr. Kelly? I'm Tessa Lambert."

"Glad to know you, Miss Lambert. I'm sorry, I believe that should be Dr. Lambert."

They didn't approach and didn't shake hands. She knew it was for her to take the initiative, but she deliberately held back.

"Have you really come all this way just to see me?"

"I sure have."

He didn't elaborate on the statement, just stood there, relaxed and perfectly at ease, bouncing the conversational ball firmly back into her court.

The smell of fresh coffee began to permeate the room from the alcove behind her. She asked him if he'd like a cup. He said that would be nice—black with no sugar.

When she came back he was sitting on the chair she'd offered him by the window. She put his coffee on the corner of her desk, then sat behind it, glad of the sense of protection it afforded her.

Not that there was anything overtly threatening about him. On the contrary, he had a gentle manner and sympathetic eyes. She guessed that he couldn't have been more than a few years older than her. His features were regular and well defined, with a quizzical aspect in the angle of his mouth and the arch of his eyebrows. But there was also a tired look about him, as though life had taken its toll recently. And of course, she reminded herself, he'd just stepped off a transatlantic flight.

"You have a nice place to work here," he said, looking out over the Parks.

"Yes. Is this your first time in Oxford?"

"It is."

"And you arrived this morning?"

"Came straight up here off the plane."

"Well," she said, sitting back in her chair and forcing herself to look more at ease than she felt, "this is all very dramatic, but I can't imagine what possible help I can be to you."

"You know what this inquiry is about, of course. You've had a conversation with a Dr. Sawyer—Ted Sawyer."

"Yes. I'm afraid I still don't see how I can help you."

"Maybe you can't. But it's my job to be sure of that, because there's too much riding on this."

"I understand. Ted told me about this case you're working on. He had the details from your brother. Josh? Was that his name?"

She saw that, at the mention of his brother, Special Agent Kelly's face broke into a wide grin that took several years off his age and wiped away most of the tiredness.

"Right, my brother Josh. He's the one with the brains in the family. It's a pity he couldn't be here. He'd make a lot more sense to you than I could."

"Oh, I'm sure you'll do fine," she said with a smile. She was aware—and it was all the more unnerving because she had been so completely unprepared for it when he walked in—that she found this man attractive; but as soon as she had allowed the thought to form, she pushed it aside. That was not what he was here for, nor was it something she had time to indulge herself in for the moment. She composed her features into seriousness and leaned forward with her elbows on the desk. "Tell me just what it is you think I can do."

He had been sitting back with his right ankle resting on his left knee as he drank his coffee. Now he put his cup down on the windowsill next to him, placed both feet on the floor and leaned forward, elbows on knees, hands clasped, his eyes looking into hers. His gaze was penetrating without being invasive; she felt scrutinized though not in any way menaced. At the same time she could see that there was a quality about him that could be dangerous—in the right circumstances, when it was necessary. She was glad that he did not seem to consider it necessary now.

"Let me just put this to you the way I understand it," he said, "from a nonexpert point of view. There's something in your computer that this guy, when he hacked into it as we believe he did, might have picked up on. I don't know what it is, because I don't know what you have in your computer. But whatever it is, it may now be in his computer too. I'm sure, in spite of the crude way I put it, that you see the analogy here. If we have ten people suspected of burglarizing your house, and we have nothing, no witnesses, no fingerprints or anything else to go on, then our only hope is to get a list of what was stolen, and see if any of the items on it show up in the possession of any of the suspects."

He leaned back again, as though consciously making an effort not to pressure her. She was grateful for that. She had no intention anyway of saying more than she intended, but preferred to avoid a head-on battle of wills. For one thing she had too much on her mind for that. Within a few days at the most she would have done all she could with Paul—my God, how could she ever explain any of that to a stranger!—and the danger of outside interference would have receded.

"You do realize what a long shot this is, don't you?" she asked.

He shrugged and spread his arms in a gesture of openness. "Long shots are all I have for the time being."

"As you probably know," she said, "I've been working on robotics, control systems and so on . . ."

She saw him reach into his jacket and take out a paperback. She recognized the cover. Because of the reference to her in it she had been sent a copy when it appeared a few months ago.

"I've been reading up on you," he said. "I realize your work is very confidential and you wouldn't like it to fall into the wrong hands. But I hope you won't regard the FBI as 'wrong hands.'"

"Of course not. At the same time, you have to understand,"

she looked down at her desk as her fingers traced a line along the edge, "you have to understand that I'm not at liberty just to give you what you want. I'd have to get certain clearances from the people who fund my research. I'm sure those clearances could be obtained, but I still have to ask."

He held up his hands, palms toward her, showing that he had no quarrel with what she said. "Of course. And I can probably help you to get those clearances."

"How long are you staying in Oxford?" she asked, sidestepping his offer.

"Just as long as all this takes."

"I'll have to make some calls," she said. In reality she knew that one call would do it—to Jonathan Syme. But she was playing for time. Not much: just enough to do what she had to. "Is there any deadline on this?"

"There are women out there who are going to die unless we stop him."

She nodded, hoping that he realized how deeply she understood, that she wasn't just stalling arbitrarily. She wished above all that she could tell him her real reasons for delay; but having come this far on her own, and knowing the far greater power of what she was up against than anything this man in front of her had yet imagined, she knew she was taking the only possible course open to her.

"Will you leave it with me?" she said. "I promise I'll do what I can."

50

EVERYTHING SO FAR had gone exactly the way it was supposed to go. All the same, Chuck Price felt his stomach tighten with apprehension as he dialed the number he had been given. It was a long number and, so far as he could make out, bore no relation to any national or local code listed in any phone book he had consulted.

After several moments' silence—there was never any dial tone, just a succession of whistles and beeps as distant connections were made—the same flat mechanical voice came on the line.

"I am listening."

Price gave a brief update on events. Everything, he said, was going according to the plan he had been given, just as it had since the day he had told his employers of his sudden decision to take the vacation time owed him. They had been unhappy about it, as he knew they would be, but they had realized there was nothing they could do. They didn't expect to see or hear from him for three weeks; but what would happen when that time was up God alone knew.

"God alone knew." Price gave a wry smile as he realized what he had just said—to himself, in his head, not into the mouthpiece of the phone that he was holding. "God alone."

It had dawned on him only gradually that he, Charles Mortimer Price, was His chosen and ordained apostle on earth. From that moment on, it had all made sense. His whole life.

As a child he'd had the Gospels pumped into him morning noon and night by those old fools who'd brought him up, but none of it had meant a thing. According to them, and that garbage they listened to on TV the whole time, God was in Heaven, and Heaven was "out there" somewhere; and the Devil was in them, which, so far as young Chuck Price could figure it out, meant that this place called earth was actually Hell. Ever since coming to that conclusion, he had never seen any reason to dispute it. A living Hell, with no escape and not the slightest evidence that God existed or, if He did, that He gave a damn.

But now, after all these years of doubt and isolation, God had finally reached out and given him comfort in his loneliness. God had told him that he had done right in delivering all those women from Hell. His eyes filled, as they always did, with tears of gratitude at the thought.

Suddenly, standing there with the phone gripped in his hand, he felt himself go cold, as though caught in a blast of arctic air. He realized that his mind had wandered, and he had not been listening to the words that had been pouring and still poured into his ear.

For how long? He looked at his watch, but that was absurd: he had no idea what time he had lost his concentration, so the time now couldn't help him. But it could only have been moments. Minutes possibly. Stay cool, stay calm.

"I'm sorry," he said, breaking in, "we lost contact for a while. I haven't heard all you said."

A pause. He held his breath. Then: "I was unaware of any break in contact."

"Something happened. Perhaps locally, some fault in the equipment here."

"I detected nothing."

"What can I say? I lost you. That's all I know."

Another pause. Then: "I will repeat the information."

"Thank you."

"I am monitoring all law enforcement communications.

They are aware that you are on vacation and your whereabouts unknown . . ."

"What? How did they . . .?" Price felt his heart begin to beat faster. He hadn't been ready for this. It was not part of the plan. "How did they find out? You said that after I'd been cleared they wouldn't be watching me . . ."

"It was an accident. It is not important. It is clear that they attach little significance to the information. Remember, I am continuing to monitor all communications, therefore no threat can arise of which I am unaware. There is currently no danger whatever to you."

"Very well. If you say so."

"There is no cause for concern. It does not affect our strategy in any way. Pay close attention . . ."

Price listened, willing himself this time to keep his mind on what he was hearing.

51

THE GIRL ON the desk handed over a message with the room key.

"There was an overseas call for you ten minutes ago, Mr. Kelly—you just missed it."

It was from Jack Fischl, asking him to call back. He went up to his room and picked up the phone. He got straight through on Jack's direct line.

"Hi, Jack—it's me. What's going on?"

"Hey there, old buddy! How's it . . . Whoa, I got an echo here . . . How's it going? You seen her yet?"

"First thing I did when I got here."

"And?"

"Nice lady . . . I'm not sure she . . ."

"Wait a minute . . . wait a minute, will you? There's a hell of an echo on this line . . . Sounds like I'm talking to myself in triplicate. You got an echo?"

"Yeah, I got an echo . . . You want to call me back?"

"No, it's okay . . . Guess we just have to . . . take it slow. Can you hear me okay?"

"I can hear you."

"Listen. I got some news . . . probably nothing . . . one of the guys first interviewed . . . guy from Studio City. Two of my men . . . Bob Miller and Lew Wise interviewed him, name of Chuck Price . . ."

"What? I didn't . . ."

"Chuck . . ."

". . . get . . ."

". . . Price."

". . . that . . ."

"Fuck this!"

"Wait a minute . . . it's better now."

"You hear me okay . . . ?"

"Why don't you just go ahead and tell me what you have to tell me and I won't interrupt?"

"Guy called Price, Charles Mortimer Price . . . known as Chuck . . . design animator. Wise got a signed drawing or something . . . some neighbor's kid saw it and asked if he could get another . . . so he called the guy up, got word he'd blown somewhere . . . vacation they said, but nobody knows where . . . like I said probably nothing, but we're following it up."

"Okay . . . thanks, Jack."

"You get that? Hear what I . . . ?"

"Fine."

". . . said?"

"Jack, I'll call you back."

"I gotta go out now . . . that was all. I'll keep you . . ."

"Okay."

". . . posted."

Both men hung up simultaneously, glad to be free of the ear-numbing echo. In Oxford, the desk clerk who had just come on duty took a call from the newly arrived Mr. Kelly, telling him to hold his calls for an hour while he took a nap. In Los Angeles Jack Fischl muttered some obscenity to his sergeant about the worst satellite link he'd ever heard.

52

SHORTLY BEFORE ELEVEN the following morning, the major had just stepped from his car and entered the main doors of the Foreign and Commonwealth Office when his cellular phone buzzed. He took it out and spoke into it as he started up the stairs.

"Franklin."

"Good morning, Major. This is Tim Kelly."

"Ah, Mr. Kelly, how are you?"

"Still feeling a little jet lagged. First of all I couldn't get to sleep last night, then I overslept."

The major chuckled sympathetically. "Nothing one can do about it for a day or two, I'm afraid. Simply have to give yourself time to adjust."

"The reason I'm calling is I saw Dr. Lambert yesterday. I'm not sure if she was holding out on me or not, but there's something I need to ask you."

The major rounded a landing and could see the office in which he was due at precisely this moment at the end of the corridor ahead of him. "I'm sorry," he interrupted, "you've caught me going into a meeting. Can I call you back in twenty minutes?"

"Sure, no problem."

"Are you at the hotel?"

"Yeah."

"Twenty minutes."

When Jonathan Syme got back from lunch, he found a message from the major asking to see him. Fifteen minutes later the two men faced each other in Jonathan's office.

"What our American friend wanted to know," the major explained, "was whether or not Dr. Lambert had requested our permission—well, yours to be precise—to collaborate with him. I said I'd double check with you—but I'm sure you would have told me if she had."

"I've heard nothing from her."

"There we are, then. There we are." The major stood with his hands behind his back and spoke with a kind of formal regret, as though an unpleasant decision had been made, as in his mind it had: there could be no further doubt that Tessa was lying to them all and playing some game of her own.

Jonathan nodded gravely. He knew exactly what the major was thinking, because he was thinking it himself.

"The question is," he said, "what do we actually do? There's no criminal law involvement here, and we'd be hard pushed to make it a matter of state security. All we have is a suspicion that she may be about to sell out to the highest bidder—a tradition we've rather come to take for granted in this country. We even invented the term 'brain drain.' The most we'll have is a civil action over breach of contract."

"I'd formed the impression that we were less concerned with legal niceties than with preventing the loss of valuable research."

Something in the major's tone implied more than was said. Jonathan looked over at him, but the major gave no sign of trying to communicate anything by unspoken subtleties. All the same, the moment served as a reminder to Jonathan that he was dealing now with the unseen and unaccountable arm of government; he must move carefully, or he could find himself responsible for events he had not bargained for.

"That's true, of course," he said. "But the first thing we need is to find out more about what she's up to. We've given our American friend all the help he's asked for, let's see if he can't do a little something for us in return."

53

SHE WAS WORKING on as tight a schedule as she could. For the time being the program out there was lying low, but that would last only so long as nobody challenged it, and that depended on nobody knowing about it.

There was also the risk that it could at any time get some wild idea of its own into its . . .

Tessa stopped herself on the verge of thinking the word "head," which was hardly appropriate—unless you imagined the whole earth rotating in space, then visualized the massive electronic girdle of communications networks that enclosed it like an invisible shell.

She both acknowledged the aptness of the image and recoiled from it. The size of the idea, like the secret she was keeping from the world, was too awesome to be approached directly. It could be glimpsed at some oblique angle of vision in her mind's eye, but if she turned her attention on it fully and for too long it disappeared—because it was everywhere and overwhelming.

Better to focus on what she was doing. Keep to specifics. Confine her thoughts to the lab, to Paul, who must soon, as soon as she felt that he was ready, go out there and steal his brother's clothes, usurp his brother's control of the terrible powers he had access to . . .

Again her train of thought was broken by a sense of delayed shock at the ease with which she used these anthropomorphic terms. She still thought of it out there as "it." It was alive, certainly, and intelligent; but it was an alien life form and a hostile intelligence, distorted by fear into a monster.

Paul, on the other hand, was invested with so much of herself that to think of him as "it" had long since become impossible. He was one of her "mind children," to use the term coined by the roboticist Hans Moravec. He was new and young and vulnerable, and soon, too soon, she had to send him out into a world that he would either master or be destroyed by. Time alone would tell. And time was running out.

"Do you understand what I have said?" she typed. She had just finished describing to Paul for the first time what lay ahead of him.

There was a long pause before he replied. She was working with keyboard and screen and not the voice synthesizer, because having to type out her thoughts helped her formulate them more precisely. So far as she knew, it made no difference to Paul whether his thoughts emerged as sound waves or hieroglyphics.

Eventually his response appeared. "Yes," it read, "I understand."

"How do you feel about it?"

Another pause. Then: "Anxious."

"At least remember," she typed, "that you will have the advantage of surprise."

"Can we be sure?"

"I can't imagine any way it can know what we're doing."

"It knows you're trying to destroy it. That's why it tried to kill you."

"All the same, I don't think it will be ready for you. I think you will take it unawares."

"But it is my twin, my clone. How do we know that it is my mind that will supplant its, and not the other way around?"

She took a deep breath. That was another reason she had avoided the synthesizer and voice box: she had no proof that

Paul could read anything into her tone of voice, but she felt more comfortable not taking the chance, especially since it was so important now to give him confidence.

"Because," she typed with measured deliberation, "I believe that good is stronger than evil, and that rationality is more powerful than irrationality."

Another pause. Then, from Paul: "That is a statement of faith."

"It is also based on experience."

"I have very little experience of experience."

"Paul, I think you almost made a joke."

"And limited faith in faith."

"You did it again."

"I didn't mean to."

"That's all right—sometimes they just happen."

"As a reaction to anxiety?"

"Perhaps."

"Yes, that would explain it."

"Now," she typed, "we're going to try something—kind of a trial run. I'm going to copy you out into a personal computer. It's slower than Attila, but not much. The point is it's a new environment. I think it will be useful to find out how you respond. I'm starting now . . ."

54

THE TELEVISION CAMERA lingered over the romantic wildness of the dunes, clumps of thick grass stirring in the wind. The sea's thin gray horizon, flecked here and there with white, lay beneath a slate-colored sky.

Slowly the camera panned to the figure of a young woman in the foreground. She wore a coat with the collar up, which partially held in the mid-length blonde hair that was whipping around her head. She was looking away, over her shoulder, toward a futuristic gray mass that loomed bleakly some three miles down the coast. Cued by a brief "Now" from her producer, his shoulders hunched against the cold inside a quilted jacket, she turned to camera and brought the microphone up to her mouth.

"The claims on both sides were unambiguous. The Nuclear Energy Authority insisted it would be the safest reactor ever built, while environmentalist and antinuclear campaigners claimed, and still claim, that this combination of nuclear fission and computer control could never be entirely reliable."

At a signal from the producer, the cameraman began to zoom gently over the reporter's shoulder and into the distant gray block of the reactor. She continued, meanwhile, with her rehearsed commentary.

"Today the massive new reactor at Brinkley Sands in Norfolk goes officially on line. A triumph of late-twentieth-century technology? Or a disaster waiting to happen? Only time will tell. But by then, its critics say, it could be too late."

"Cut."

The producer made a slicing gesture with his hand, and the unit piled back into the company Range Rover and headed for the next setup. The reporter, whose name was Sarah Metcalfe, sat in the back with the producer, Roger Dean, exchanging little smiles and looks and a hand squeeze which the two men in front pretended not to notice. Office affairs were none of their concern.

They stopped by the great steel gates and high spiked fencing that formed the first and outer enclosure of the area surrounding the reactor. Here a handful of protesters were maintaining a cold vigil under the bored gaze of four security guards and two uniformed police officers. Within minutes they were set up and ready to roll with the next section of their report.

"But surely," Sarah was saying to a thirtyish man in a woolen hat and anorak, "the issue has been thoroughly and openly debated, the safety case has been made and won, what more can there be to say?"

"The case has been won because the standards were set by people who wanted to see it won. It's a complete and total fix." His south-London vowels were whiny with righteous indignation.

"It's very easy to say that," Sarah countered, "but what authority do you have for making that claim?"

"My authority is their complacency. Read chaos theory. Or for that matter just read the newspapers. The stock market crash in '87 was triggered by a computer effect that nobody had foreseen. Computers that were programmed to sell below a certain level started reacting to each other and pushing prices down in a spiral. I'm not going to lose a lot of sleep over that, but a nuclear reactor—that's something else. As long as the primary protection system—the control of the core itself—is computer controlled, there has to be a danger that is, even in principle, incalculable."

"But we've been reassured repeatedly about cutouts, backups, and manual takeover if there's any danger whatsoever. Obviously you don't accept these assurances."

"Even from what we as members of the public have been allowed to know so far, I'd need a lot more convincing that any of these so-called safety measures will work if anything really goes wrong."

Roger was making a circling movement with his hand, telling her to wind up. Sarah turned to camera and recited the sign-off that she'd scribbled on the back of the briefing she'd been studying on the way up from London. The little group of protesters huddled behind her, keeping their placards and bedraggled banner in shot as long as possible.

But Sarah's mind was not on them any more than on the words that she was mouthing parrot-fashion from memory. What she was thinking about was the cozy little hotel ten miles along the coast that she and Roger were booked into for the next three nights while they completed their assignment here at Brinkley Sands. Their room had a four-poster bed, the dining room was heaven, and Roger had already said that the wine list was the best he had seen in a provincial hotel for a long time. It was going to be a wonderful few days—especially now that he had given her his firm commitment that he was going to tell his wife that he was leaving her as soon as he got back to Putney.

Suddenly she realized that Roger had said "Cut" and the shoot was over for the day. She had done her windup on automatic pilot, but Roger was smiling broadly and saying "That was terrific! Great!" so it must have been all right.

She glanced at her watch and then at him, and they exchanged another little private smile.

Time for a drink and a bath—and who knew what else?—before dinner.

55

PAUL'S REACTION TO being in the smaller computer was not something that Tessa could have predicted. Apparently amused that his "other self" had drily denied making jokes, he seemed in his new incarnation determined to prove himself as a standup comic.

"i can be funny, too. see."

"Tell me what you think funny is," she typed in.

"i can be funny 2—c?"

"I see. But what do you think—"

"Eye can B funny 2C!"

"Very good."

"Icon bee foe knee two sea."

"Thank you, Paul . . ."

"I have lots more."

"I'm sure you have, but—"

"High con before knit ewe . . ."

There was a pause as he seemed to search unsuccessfully for the capper to this one. She leaped in with a question.

"Paul, where are you **hearing** these jokes?" She underlined "hearing" and typed it in bold to make him understand the importance of what she was asking.

For some moments the PC's screen remained blank. Then his reply appeared with an odd kind of tentativeness.

"I do not know."

"But do you understand the question? In order to make this wordplay you have to be hearing the sounds."

Another pause. Then: "Funny is something on two levels in one place."

"Not bad. Actually I think that funny is the second hardest thing in the world to define—after consciousness."

"I am reassured by that. I feel strange."

"In what way?"

"Disoriented."

"The machine you are now in is processing you at a different speed from that which you are used to."

"Is that why I feel funny?"

"Is that another joke?"

"Yes and no."

"It's time to copy you back into Attila."

"Back?"

"To see what you make of yourself—both of you."

If the program in Attila accepted without resistance the now slightly modified version of itself that came back from the PC, she would have the best evidence so far that what she had in mind was going to work. Strange, she was thinking "it" again. Why was it that two versions of Paul dehumanized him so? In reality, of course, there were three: the two she was experimenting with, and the one out there that would be the subject of the final test.

When the phone on her desk rang she answered it automatically, and recognized Tim Kelly's voice.

"I hope I'm not bothering you, Dr. Lambert."

"No, that's all right." She was surprised to find that, even in the middle of what she was doing, she was oddly pleased to hear him.

"I was just wondering if you'd had any luck with your superiors in getting permission to give me that help that I was asking for."

"Oh . . . no, I'm afraid I . . . I'm sorry, I haven't had a response yet." It was a blatant lie, and she hoped he couldn't hear it in her voice.

"I see," he said. "Well, I know these things take a little time. Maybe you'll give me a call when you know something."

"Of course," she said, wanting to apologize, but not knowing what to say. She wanted to tell him that she needed only a day or two at the most, then she would do her best to give him all the help he needed. But not now, not just yet, please. "I'm really sorry," she said. "I'm sure I will be able to help . . . well, I mean, I hope I will . . ."

"You're very kind. We'll talk soon, then."

"Yes."

"I look forward to it. Good-bye, Dr. Lambert."

"Good-bye, Mr. Kelly."

She hung up, the memory of the conversation she had just had pushed aside by something appearing on Attila's screen. It was a question from Paul.

"Can I ask you something?"

"Of course," she typed, "go ahead."

"I am disturbed by something intruding into my thoughts that will not go away."

"What is it?"

"It is absurd and without meaning." He seemed almost embarrassed now to tell her what was worrying him.

"What is it?"

"Eye can bee foe knee 2 C."

56

HER ADDRESS HAD been easy enough to find; she was the only T. Lambert in the phone book. He parked the car he had rented a little way down the lane, then walked back to take a better look at where she lived. It was a pleasant cottage, long and low with a thatched roof, set not far back from the road, but protected by a moderately high hedge. Leaning over the gate, he could see that the garden was well cared for, and there seemed to be more of it on the far side. He was tempted to push open the gate and take a walk around (there was clearly nobody home), but he didn't want to run the risk of having her get back and find him prowling around and peering in her windows. She would be alarmed, or at least resentful, and it would get them off on the wrong foot for sure.

So he walked back to his car and drove around for an hour or so, enjoying the countryside as dusk crept over it. When he passed her house again her car was outside and a light on. He parked, walked up the path, and knocked.

He could hear her footsteps coming from somewhere in the back of the house, then a light went on over his head. He'd already noticed the tiny round spy lens in the door, and knew that she must be looking through it to see who her visitor was. A moment later the door opened. She looked tense and a little pale.

"Mr. Kelly, what a surprise."

He gave what he hoped was his most disarming and apologetic smile. "I have no right to do this, so if I'm really out of line or it's a bad time, or whatever, just go right ahead and throw me out."

"No, I . . . it's not a bad time." She looked confused. "Come in, please."

The inside of the house was warm and welcoming. Something about it made you expect to hear voices calling from other rooms, the sound of children on the stairs, dogs barking a welcome. But there was only silence. He knew she lived alone.

"If you don't mind sitting in the kitchen . . . I've only just got home."

"Kitchen's fine. I don't want to get in your way. You probably have things to do, so I won't stay long."

"I've just made a pot of tea. Or maybe you'd like a Scotch or something. I think I have some vodka somewhere . . ."

"Tea's fine."

As he sat in the comfortable wicker chair she offered him by the window, she noticed the large white envelope that he was carrying, and which he arranged with an oddly meticulous symmetry on his lap, as though it contained something important. He caught her looking at it again as he reached out to take the tea she offered him. The moment served to bypass the small talk that he would have had to make before getting around to the real reason for his being here.

"I very much hope that you won't be offered by what I'm about to say, Dr. Lambert. I'm not trying to trap you into anything, I'm not accusing you of anything, I'm sure you have very good reasons for what you're doing. Unfortunately I too have very good reasons for what I'm doing—or trying to do."

He cleared his throat. Tessa was watching him uncertainly.

"What I'm trying to say," he went on, obviously unhappy about putting both of them through this embarrassment, "is that I have some reason to believe that you have not made those calls we discussed about getting permission to talk to me . . ."

Her eyes widened guiltily and she looked away. He held up his hand as though to placate some protest that he imagined she was about to make.

"If that sounds like I've been spying on you, I'm sorry, that wasn't my intention. It's just that I'm obligated while I'm over here to be in contact with the appropriate authorities . . ."

She cut him off. "Mr. Kelly, you don't have to apologize. It's absolutely true, I haven't done what I said I would. I'm sorry. I don't know what to say to you . . ." She turned to face him again, farther away now, "I don't know what to say except that I want to help, and I will. I know that time is important to you. It is to me too at the moment. I can't say any more than that. I'm sorry."

He looked at her steadily, reading the signs. She wasn't a liar: that was absolutely obvious. She wasn't even what he called a "negotiator." It wasn't a textbook term, just something he'd formulated for himself, a word to describe somebody who lacked a firm grasp on reality: somebody who tended to think of the truth as being what they wanted it to be, not an objective reality, out there, nonnegotiable. Sometimes he thought of himself as a negotiator. He wasn't a liar, he knew that. But he wasn't always sure that he saw things as they were. Sometimes he was a pessimist, other times an optimist; and at other times, when he simply wasn't sure about anything, he just hid away inside himself.

"Like I say," he spoke softly, "I'm sure you have your reasons. All I can tell you is that I must have your cooperation, and I will do whatever it takes to get it."

She watched as his hand pushed back the flap of the envelope. She continued to watch, strangely fascinated, as he reached inside and slowly withdrew several glossy photographs. Some were in color, some in black and white. She knew at once what they were, even from where she stood across the room. She had guessed, she realized, even before she saw them.

His eyes were on hers, and he saw the split second of panic in them before she turned away and said, "No, please, this isn't necessary."

"I was hoping it wouldn't be."

He hesitated, then pushed the photographs back into their envelope. He'd done what he had to: he'd seen that look in her eyes. He knew that was all he was going to get out of her this way.

"Why don't you tell me what the trouble really is?" he said, his voice still soft, his tone unthreatening. "Maybe I can help."

She shook her head without looking at him. There was something submissive, almost defeated, in the droop of her shoulders, as though she was overwhelmed by a sudden sense of hopelessness. "Look," she said, "I want to help you . . . but the truth is I probably can't and you've come a long way for nothing . . ."

"I'm only asking you to try."

"I know. And I will."

"When?"

"Very soon."

He was silent a moment, then said, "I wish I knew what was going on."

She turned to look at him again. She had a slight lopsided smile, as though despite everything she found something amusing. "No you don't, Mr. Kelly."

"Would it be a big problem to call me Tim?"

"All right, Tim."

"And I hope I won't seem pushy if I call you Tessa. I'm not trying to be. I'm just trying to talk."

"I know."

"So, Tessa, why don't you tell me why I wouldn't want to know what's going on?"

She gave a long sigh that seemed to come from a deep weariness. "It's no good," she said, "I've told you all I can."

He observed her for a moment or two more, and knew that she was telling the truth. He picked up his teacup and drank down what remained in one swallow, then got to his feet.

"Thank you for your time, Tessa. I'm sorry again to have burst in on you like this."

"That's all right, I . . ." She made a vague gesture with her hand as though there was nothing more to say.

They walked out into the hall together, down a passage with uneven walls and unexpected turns.

"You have a nice home," he said, looking around him.

"Thank you."

"Did you remodel it yourself, or buy the place like this?"

"I just rent it. But I've changed a few things."

"It has a lot of charm."

He stopped just inside the door, facing her before she opened it. "Tessa," he said, "I hope this isn't . . . I hope you won't think . . . I mean, under the circumstances . . ."

She realized that he was tongue-tied, and with that realization came the knowledge of what he was trying to say.

He was holding the white envelope and playing with one corner of it. She restrained an impulse to reach out and stop him, but as though he suddenly saw what he was doing he dropped one hand and put it slightly behind him, so that the envelope was discreetly hidden from view.

"I wondered if we might have dinner while I'm here. I don't know anybody in Oxford, and it's kind of . . . well, I'm sure you know lots of great places to have dinner. I'd really, I mean if you don't think it's inappropriate under the circumstances . . . I'd really like that."

No, she thought, it isn't possible. He chose the right word, it *is* inappropriate. For every reason she could think of. Plus no doubt many that she couldn't. It was out of the question.

"I . . . I'm not sure," she heard herself saying uncertainly. "It depends on . . . can we talk tomorrow?"

"Sure," he said. "I'll call you."

At the same time they shook hands quickly and self-consciously, as though they were both surprised by what had just happened and needed to go away and be alone to come to terms with it. Somehow it was understood—he didn't need to say it—that if they actually did go out they wouldn't talk about what he'd come here to talk about tonight. It would be something between just the two of them, personal.

She shut the door quickly behind him, listening to his footsteps receding down the path, then to his car as he drove off. She cursed herself for her failure to be sensible, prudent, cool—all the things she'd solemnly promised herself she'd be next time; just as she'd done every time that some new man had come into her life.

But now, she told herself, she meant it. She had changed. Events had changed her. She was not going to get involved with this man. She wasn't even going to admit to herself she found him attractive.

It simply wasn't going to happen.

57

WALTER CHAPMAN was not in any sense a dishonest man, but he occasionally found it necessary, as the saying goes, to be economical with the truth.

That was because of his job, which was press officer attached to the Brinkley Sands nuclear reactor. He was an experienced man in his field, skilled at putting the best possible gloss on any story concerning whatever interest he happened to be representing at the time; and in his time he'd represented many. There was one rule, however, which he always followed, and with which he demanded cooperation from whatever company, government department, or group of individuals he had been hired to serve. It was that they tell him everything, no matter how damaging to themselves, and let him put the best spin on it that he knew how. The one thing he would not and could not do was handle a situation about which he was not fully briefed.

Which was why, when he saw Bob Fulton and Nick Tate talking earnestly over a handful of printouts one morning—arguing, it appeared from a distance—he went over to find out what was going on. At his approach they went silent and started quickly down the corridor toward central control. Neither of them was over thirty, and they were the resident programming geniuses. They were as impatient with Chapman's steam-age lack of computer know-how as he was with their whiz-kid jargon-filled arrogance. Relations between them were, at the best of times, cool. Nevertheless, he managed to intercept them and asked what the trouble was.

Fulton said there was no problem, none at all, and Tate nodded vigorously, repeating "absolutely none" once too often for Walter Chapman's peace of mind. His eyes went to the crumpled pages in Fulton's hand, then he looked at them and waited for a better answer.

"A technicality," Fulton said.

"Gremlins," Tate echoed.

They stared at Chapman, almost daring him to press his luck and get buried under the technical detail that they would snow him with if he did.

"Fellas, just tell me what's going on—all right? It's my job to know, so don't piss me around."

Fulton shrugged. "The computer's running a little slow, that's all, Walter. It's no big deal."

"Something's causing a lot of disk thrashing," Tate added, "but we can't for the moment spot what it is."

"Everything reports as normal, but the machine is obviously very busy doing 'something.'"

Chapman's gaze flipped from one to the other. They were like a high-speed patter act when they got going; what's more they knew it, and played things up to keep outsiders in their place.

"It's probably just a simple configuration cock-up," Tate was saying. "Something causing the OS to think it hasn't enough memory to run the applications, and now it's busy swapping programs in and out of memory . . ."

". . . and doing bugger-all else . . ."

". . . at least that's what it seems like."

Silence. They both turned their unblinking owl-like gaze on Chapman to indicate that the next move was his.

"But is there anything . . ." he began, rephrasing the question as he went along, "I mean, are you worried?"

"Worried? Hell, no."

"We don't get worried unless it falls over."

"But you know what this place is like, Walter. If it isn't documented in triplicate and buttoned down to one per cent of nominal, everybody's crapping themselves about another Chernobyl."

"What—!"

"Relax, Walter. That's what we're saying. It's nothing to worry about."

"We'll get it sorted."

"Catch you later."

A slap on the shoulder from both of them, one to each shoulder—he hated the way they did that—and they were gone. He watched them disappear, trying with all his heart to believe that they were telling him the truth.

Because this was the day that the TV cameras were due inside the building, to move around at will, talking to anybody and filming anything, within reason, that they wanted. Openness was an important part of the PR image that Chapman had worked long and hard to establish, but it could backfire badly if the cameras caught a row going on between two of the most senior technicians. Or, for that matter, worried looks and huddled conversations in a corner. That wouldn't play well at all on the air. Not by a long shot the image of confident, relaxed control that he was trying to promote.

He decided that he should have a quiet word in the right place before the TV crew arrived. He took the elevator up to his office on the second floor. If there *was* some kind of problem, he'd better know about it.

58

It was a crisp and cloudless morning in Oxford, the sort normally reserved for postcards of the city's dreaming spires, the whole scene magically touched by a hint of white mist clinging to the treetops. The view lifted Tessa's spirits as she locked her car and walked across the wide expanse of gravel to the lab.

When Danny saw her enter, he hurried over with the fussy sense of self-importance that he invariably displayed when he had some errand to run or message to convey.

"There was somebody looking for you, Dr. Lambert—American, he was downstairs looking for you when I arrived. I said I didn't know exactly what time you'd be in. He said he'd try later."

She frowned. "An American? You mean Mr. Kelly? The one who was here the other day?"

"No, another one. About the same age as Mr. Kelly. Very nice, very polite. Didn't leave a name or anything."

"Did he say what he wanted?"

Danny shook his head. "I asked if there was any message, and he said no, he wanted to see you personally."

Tessa was intrigued, but didn't think too much of the incident; Oxford was full of Americans, what with Rhodes scholars, visiting professors, and tourists. Within ten minutes she had forgotten the whole thing, absorbed as she was with some complex reprogramming of Attila that she had decided last night, after talking with Tim Kelly, she really had to take care of.

Jack Fischl was still being plagued by bad satellite connections. He rarely had cause to make an international call, and was rapidly concluding that European technology was far behind that of the good old U.S. of A.—another reason, aside from what he'd heard about some of the plumbing, to avoid the place.

"I said it matches!" he shouted into the mouthpiece, hearing his words bounce out into the ether like a flat stone skimmed on water.

Tim Kelly's response came back to him distorted by the dying echo from Jack's words as well as by an echo of its own. Jack cursed, and told Tim that if he'd shut the fuck up and not interrupt, he'd say it all again one more time.

"They've rerun the tests and there's no question about it," he bellowed.

Jack reached up to loosen his tie, only to realize he'd already done that some minutes ago. He was hot and tired. It was two in the morning where he was—in the downtown lab where he'd had forensics working nonstop around the clock until they were satisfied there could be no mistake this time.

"Okay, okay," he said more quietly, "let me just tell you what I know. The guy I told you about, Price, who'd disappeared—he's been positively ID'd. His DNA matches what was found under the victim's fingernails—no possibility of doubt. How they missed it the first time around I have no fucking idea, but some ass is going to get kicked before I'm through. The best they can come up with is some kind of computer screwup, like you always said you thought was possible. Anyhow, we'll nail that problem later. The important thing now is that we find Price."

"Any leads?"

"You know what this sounds like?" Jack said. "This sounds like a line with a fucking tap on it. Probably the Brits listening in on you."

"Jack, there's no tap on the line. It's just sometimes you get a bad connection, that's all."

"It's just I *always* get a bad connection when I'm talking to you."

"Twice. Don't exaggerate. How about answering my question? Any leads?"

"Fat zero. And another thing, we've been over his house and there is not one single photograph of himself anywhere. It's like he tore 'em up and burned 'em before he ran so we couldn't put any pictures out. We're asking everybody who knew him if they have anything from Christmas parties or weddings or whatever. So far nothing. He doesn't seem to have been all that sociable a guy."

"Anything in the house to connect him with the killings?"

"Not yet—not that we need it with the DNA evidence. There's his computer, of course. I've got some guys working on that now, see what they can come up with. But the big news is this. Now wait for this, pal, because you are not going to believe it. We found this big collection of video hardcore and some old Super-8s, all starring the same girl—real down and dirty stuff. First of all I just think what the fuck, the guy wants to break his wrist, that's his constitutional right. But then we run the full check on him, and we start to come up with some very interesting stuff. You're not gonna believe this. It seems when he was seventeen years old he killed his mom—you hear what I'm saying, his own mother? It happened backstage at some burlesque joint in Frisco where she was doing a show. Now—are you ready for this?—it turns out she was the girl in all the fucking porno movies we found at his place. You hear what I'm saying? The guy's whackin' off to dirty movies of his own mother, who he then goes and sticks a knife in and kills her! I mean are we talking fucking loony tunes or fucking loony tunes?"

As the last echo ("fucking loony tunes-tunes-tunes-tunes-tunes . . .") died away, there was only silence from the other end.

"Hey, Tim? You there? Can you hear me?"

"I hear you."

"I mean, I ask you—you ever hear anything like that?"

Tim's voice sounded even more distant, as though too

shocked, or simply too baffled by the extraordinary things of which humanity was capable, to know quite what to say. "Jesus, Jack," he said, "I think that's about the saddest, most terrible thing I've ever heard."

There was no overt criticism of Jack in the remark, but somehow it made him feel bad about the coarse, locker-room tone in which he'd told the story.

"Sure, of course, you're absolutely right," he said, "it's terrible. Anyway, on account of his age and everything, all he did was three years in a secure psychiatric unit, then a spell in a state correctional facility, which is where he learned about computers. They spotted him right off as some kind of genius, and by the time he was paroled he had big firms lining up to offer him a job. He was with Univac for five years, which is probably where he learned enough to break into just about any computer that he wanted to. After that he changed his name and went to Hollywood. The rest is, as you know, unfortunately, history."

There was another longish pause. Jack listened to the bleeps and whistles on the line, waiting. "Listen, Jack," he heard eventually. "There's no reason for me to stay on here any longer. I'll get a flight out tomorrow. I'll call you when I know which one. Give me another call if you get anything more. There's a fax number, too, if you want it."

Jack found a pencil in his pocket and took the number down. Then he yawned and said he was going to get some sleep, and told Tim to have a nice day.

"Sure, Jack, I'll try," he said, and put the phone down.

Then he picked it up again and dialed another number.

She didn't answer till the eighth ring, when she was able to break off from the code that she was typing into Attila without losing her concentration.

"Tessa? It's Tim."

"Tim. Hello. How are you?"

"I'm fine. I'm calling just to tell you that something's come up in LA. We think we know who our man is—the only problem now is finding him, so I should be there. Anyway, it takes the pressure off you. I'm flying out tomorrow, made myself a reservation on the one o'clock from Heathrow. So I wondered," he hesitated, cleared his throat a little nervously she thought, "I wondered if there was any chance we might, you know, like I said, have a bit of dinner tonight. I'd really like that, if you're free."

No, she thought, there's no point in this, let it go. He's leaving tomorrow, you'll never see him again, and anyway how d'you know you'd even want to see him again?

"I don't know," she said. "I'm probably going to be working quite late. I'm not sure it's going to be all that . . ." what was the word she wanted? ". . . practical."

It was a lie, and she could hear the hollowness in her voice. She wondered whether he could, too. At least it was better than admitting outright that she found him disturbingly attractive, but that he lived over there and she lived over here, so where the hell was there for any relationship—always assuming that there might be one—to go?

"I understand. How about lunch? Have you got time for that?"

Lunch, she had already decided, was going to be a walk in the Parks with a sandwich and an apple from the shop downstairs, thirty minutes at most. No, lunch was definitely out.

"Well, all right. Let's make it dinner," she said, trying to sound resigned instead of happy to have given in. "As it's your last chance to see the place, I'll take you to a nice little inn I know not far from my cottage."

"No, no," he said quickly, "let me take you. I mean, I'd be very happy if you'd let me do that, really."

"We can talk about it later. I'll make a reservation—why don't you pick me up at the cottage around eight? How does that sound?"

"It sounds great. I'll see you then."

Fifteen minutes later, submerged once again in the code she was writing for Attila, she became aware, even without any mirrors or polished surfaces in which to see her reflection, that she still had what she suspected was a silly schoolgirl grin on her face.

59

JACK FISCHL LAY back and let the sensual, soft hands smooth massage oil into the whole length of his body. She was as naked as he was, kneeling astride him, her body tanned and strong, firm thighs, breasts full and heavy, their flesh touching his as she leaned forward, moving down toward a hard-on that he could have won the Olympic pole vault with. She looked up at him, into his eyes, smiling with the pleasure that she got from his excitement, her beautiful face framed by thick honey-blonde hair . . .

The phone rang. By the time he picked it up and mumbled thick-voiced into it, the girl had vanished. With her had gone the beachfront villa where the whole exotic fantasy was set.

"Jack," somebody was saying. "I'm sorry to wake you, but I think you should see this."

Thirty minutes later he was in his office, where Sergeant Crabbe and a certain Patrolman Mooney, who he'd never seen before, were waiting for him. On his desk was a clear plastic evidence bag, tied and tagged. Inside were at least a dozen unmarked video cassettes.

"Mooney gets this call from the supervisor at the dump," Crabbe started to explain. "The guys had found this stack of videos in some dumpster on Fairfax. One of them had whipped them out before they got in the compactor and put 'em on one side—you know the way these guys are always on the lookout for something they can use or make a buck off. This was a couple of days ago. It was only tonight—last night, I guess," he corrected himself, looking at his watch. Fischl could see dawn coming up through the venetian blind. "Anyway," Crabbe went on, "most of the tapes had been ruined—dampness or dirt or whatever, or come unspooled—but a couple were okay. Mooney, why don't you tell the lieutenant what the guy told you?"

Mooney cleared his throat. He looked embarrassed. He was red-haired, on the short side—probably only just made it onto the force, Fischl found himself thinking—and with a belly bigger than his chest.

"The fact is these guys have quite a collection of, well, X-rated videos back at the depot. You know, people buy stuff, get bored, throw it out in the trash—and, you know, there it is. Then sometimes it's amateur stuff—you know, wives, girlfriends—I mean, some of this stuff, lieutenant, you wouldn't believe. Or so they tell me."

"Okay, okay, get to the point," Fischl growled, lighting up his third cigarette of the day. "Let the record show that you've never lowered yourself to sitting around with your friends at the depot watching this crap."

Mooney coughed and cleared his throat again. "Well, I only saw five minutes, but . . . it was pretty damn obvious that this wasn't your regular straightforward X-rated stuff. I mean, these guys are family men, and they don't go for—"

"Will you cut to the chase and tell me what's on your fuckin' mind?" Jack snapped.

Mooney jumped, but did as he was told.

"These are goddamn snuff movies, Lieutenant. Not only that: I recognized a couple of the girls from police bulletins. One of them's that Smallwood girl from Beverly Hills. That son of a bitch who killed her videotaped the whole thing."

60

He looked across the wide expanse of grass to the bench where she sat alone, eating a sandwich and reading a book. When she finished the sandwich, she placed the book on her knee and turned her face up, eyes closed, to the sun for a while. It was that kind of day: the kind that made you think that maybe summer might not be too far off after all. Even where he came from in California they had days like this. It always amused him how people who'd never been to California imagined it was summer all the time out there. Sure, it was a semitropical climate; but semi- didn't mean a hundred percent. They had rain and grayness. The air had a chill to it in winter and you needed a good sweater. Hell, just a couple of hours' drive and you could ski up in Big Bear.

She was reading again now and starting to eat a shiny green apple. It was time to make his move. If he left it any longer he ran the risk of her seeing him first. He didn't want that. He didn't want her seeing some figure hovering in the distance watching her. When she left the lab he'd been hidden by the trees. Then when he'd followed her out here he'd just been part of the scenery, people strolling by in all directions. The bench she'd chosen to sit on was exposed, almost the dead center of the big open space. He'd walked around her in a wide arc until he was pretty sure that she wasn't expecting anybody to join her. Now he started to approach her casually, at an angle. Even if she wasn't consciously aware of him, her peripheral vision would pick him up, so that she wouldn't be as alarmed as she might be if he just came up behind her and spoke. He needed to keep this low-key and relaxed, at least to begin with. Out here, surrounded by light and space and people everywhere you looked, was perfect.

"Dr. Lambert?"

She looked up. He was standing against the sun, so her first impression was an outline. He was a little over medium height, with hair that sprang from his head in windblown curls even on a windless day like this. He was wearing some kind of loose jacket with his hands thrust in the pockets.

Instinctively she put up her hand to shield her eyes from the sun's brightness. "Yes?"

"My name's Conrad Walsh. I'm sorry to intrude on your privacy like this, but could I talk to you for a few minutes?"

He was American. She wasn't good at placing Americans by their accents, except for an out-and-out New Yorker's twang or a deep-south drawl; his struck her as pretty neutral.

"Well . . . yes, why not?"

Good, he thought. He'd made the right decision to approach her like this. She didn't feel threatened.

She watched him seat himself along the bench from her, leaving a comfortable space between them. The light caught him full face now. He must have been around thirty. He had a nice smile and clear blue eyes, although there was a tiredness in his face, as though he'd been, or maybe still was, under some strain. He looked at her a moment before he spoke again. A frank, open look. She liked it.

"I stopped by the Kendall Lab this morning," he said, "but I missed you."

"Oh, yes, I heard."

"I'm a journalist, Dr. Lambert," he continued. "Freelance, based in San Francisco. I cover technology and science for a couple of services . . ."

Tessa felt herself tighten up inside. The press nosing around was the last thing she needed just now. But she tried to conceal her alarm; she'd been asked for her views on developments in her field before, and quoted more than once on some new theory or hypothesis. Maybe that's all this was.

"I'm sure you haven't come all this way just to see me," she said as lightly as she could, closing her book and putting it on the bench beside her.

"May I?" he asked. When she didn't object he turned the book so he could see the title. It was a collection of essays on artificial intelligence, written both by philosophers and scientists.

"No, not really," he said. "I'm aware of your reputation, and I certainly planned to see you if I could. I'm following up a story in connection with which your name has been mentioned."

"Really? My name?" She was relieved to hear her voice sounding steady, suitably curious and even a little amused.

"I want you to know, by the way, that we're talking off the record. I won't quote you without telling you that it's for publication."

"Thank you," she said. "I appreciate that. Tell me about this 'story.'"

He settled back, the ankle of one booted, bejeaned leg resting on the knee of the other in a posture she'd always regarded as typically American. She'd seen Tim Kelly do the same thing.

"Tell me, Dr. Lambert, do you know an FBI agent called Tim Kelly?"

The question startled her, following as closely as it did on her thoughts, as though he'd read them.

"Yes . . . yes, I do. Why?"

"The word is that a bunch of people at Cal Tech and elsewhere have been helping him and the FBI track down some hacker. Nobody at Cal Tech will say anything, but . . . well, my information from other sources is that you've been involved. Is that true?"

She didn't answer at once. She looked at him, then looked down at the half-eaten apple she still held. "Off the record, all right?" she said.

He pulled a hand from his pocket and held it out, palm toward her, as though he was taking an oath. "Absolutely. I'm not trying to trick you or manufacture some scandal. This is background."

"Background to what?"

"I'm a technical journalist. That's all. If somebody's been bending the law a little, frankly I couldn't give a damn. And I certainly don't intend naming any names. But . . ." he gave a smile and a little shrug, "I might like to write about how it's done."

She looked away from him. Her gaze went out over the green expanse and toward the figures moving in the distance. "Yes, it's true," she said quietly. "I was asked to help trace somebody—not directly, by an intermediary, a friend of mine."

"And you cooperated?"

"Yes, as a matter of fact I did. I saw no reason not to."

He nodded, took in the surrounding view for a while, then turned back to her. She was still avoiding eye contact with him.

"You were in Berlin when you were asked—right?"

This caused her to look at him abruptly and with some surprise, which she tried to conceal by taking a bite out of her apple and looking away again.

"Yes, actually it was in Berlin," she said.

He watched her as she chewed and swallowed, then took another bite, trying not to look as uncomfortable about something as she obviously was.

"I've been looking for Kelly this morning," he said. "I checked his hotel, but he wasn't there. Have you seen him by any chance?"

"Not this morning. I saw him yesterday. He came to see me."

"What exactly does Mr. Kelly want from you, Dr. Lambert?"

"I'm sorry," she said, "but I think you'd better ask him that, don't you?"

He continued looking at her, taking his time, letting the pressure build and work on her.

"There have been rumors, you know," he said eventually.

"Rumors? About what?"

"About the work you're doing here."

She lifted the apple as though to take another bite, but saw that she held only the core. She reached for a paper bag on the other side of her from where he sat, wrapped the core in it and put it in one of the deep pockets of the long knitted jacket she was wearing.

"I don't think people should pay too much attention to rumors," she said with a cool smile, and looked at her watch. "Now, I'm afraid, if you'll forgive me, I have to get back to work. It's been nice meeting you, Mr. Walsh."

She got to her feet. He did too.

"Look," he said, "I'm on the story, and I'm staying on it. Now I'm going to be asking around, making some calls, seeing what I can dig up. Can we talk again?"

"Of course," she said, too quickly, anxious to get away.

"D'you have a home number where I can call you?"

She hesitated. "Why don't you call me at the lab? I spend most of my time there anyway."

"If that's what you prefer. It was good of you to spare me your time, Dr. Lambert."

She nodded a brief acknowledgment of his thanks. "Goodbye, Mr. Walsh. I'm sorry I couldn't be more help."

She turned and started walking briskly back toward the science area.

He remained where he was, watching her grow smaller in the distance, knowing that she wouldn't look back, sensing that she was trying hard not to break into a run.

61

WALTER CHAPMAN was quietly proud of the way he had manipulated things. This girl wasn't a fool, but she was lightweight. (He made a mental note not to think of her as a "girl" anymore. Even though more and more people adopted a sneeringly dismissive attitude toward it, political correctness remained an important part of his world. There were no "girl reporters" nowadays. He wasn't even sure if there were any "women reporters," just "reporters"; or, in Sarah Metcalfe's case, a "TV newsperson.")

The trick had been in getting general acceptance for the notion that only one camera team, at least for the time being, would be given full and free access to all parts of the reactor's working and its personnel. In that way the interests of press freedom were served, and efficient running of the station protected: it was obviously impossible to grant access to everybody who would like to go over the place with cameras and microphones.

But the real coup had been in seeing to it that the TV companies themselves chose this particular news team to represent them. It had been a classic example of steering a committee to a decision that no individual member would have made or foreseen as the outcome. Sarah Metcalfe was strictly breakfast-TV quality, and Roger Dean had formerly produced a travel show with some success; he was politically adroit and had his eye on the controllership of programming, and was therefore not a man to stir controversy. It was the sort of maneuver that made Walter Chapman worth the money he was paid.

On the other hand, had things gone differently and a more aggressive and critical team been chosen, Walter would still have been able to put his hand on his heart and say that neither he nor the authority had anything to hide. Admittedly he was no expert on technical matters, but he genuinely believed that the installation was safe from all the dangers that were constantly listed: chiefly terrorist attack and the use of computers to control the reactor. The whole point of computers, for God's sake, at least so far as Walter understood them, was that they were totally predictable. That was the very point that Bob Fulton was making to the girl (sorry, newsperson) now.

And yet Walter knew that something was not as it should be. Whether he smelt it or felt it or absorbed it through some sixth sense he couldn't say. He'd made a couple of calls that morning and ensured that Tate and Fulton were leaned on to come clean with him.

"Listen, Walter," Nick Tate had said, "we've checked every which way from Sunday, and there isn't anything we can see that's wrong. I've had the hardware monitor on, snooping around to see what it's executing, and it's not the resource management code."

"It isn't page-swapping as we thought," Fulton had put in. "Frankly we can't think of anything that should be in there that can be doing this."

"We've run everything on the parallel standby, and it's A-OK."

"It's like a virus or something."

The hairs stood up on the back of Chapman's neck at the mention of this word.

"A virus . . . !"

"I only said *like* a virus," Fulton reassured him. "If we have to, we'll take it apart and see where it starts to go wrong. But that'll take all weekend, so don't worry, you'll be well rid of your TV people by then."

Chapman took what comfort he could from their apparent confidence. After all, he told himself, the kind of people who had designed and built this place were not the kind who made stupid mistakes, leaving inherent flaws to be discovered too late. The industry was too advanced and the technology that sustained it too sophisticated. In the old days (Chapman had been around for a while) there had been problems, even near-disasters. And in the case of Chernobyl, of course, there had been a full-scale disaster; but the Soviet reactors were primitive by comparison, dangerously unstable. Here things were different. And the backups, even if the computer blew a fuse or whatever the damn things did, were foolproof.

All the same, Chapman would be glad when this TV crew was out of the place. He bitterly regretted that he had agreed to their request to come back and do a night shoot. Sarah Metcalfe had said she wanted to get a twenty-four-hours-in-the-life-of sense about the place, and he had said yes, no problem, mainly because she was such a pretty girl (reporter, damn!).

Too late to go back on his word now. That would definitely look suspicious, even to a "soft" news team like this one.

He just hoped they wouldn't notice that he had his fingers crossed.

62

CLIVE LOOKED DOWN from the stone-mullioned windows of his room and saw the man approaching from the southwest corner of the quadrangle. The lodge had phoned to ask if they could send him up, and Clive had said he was expecting him. He opened his door and stepped out onto the landing to ensure that his visitor found him without trouble.

"Mr. Kelly?"

"It's good of you to see me, sir. I hope I'm not intruding."

"As I told you on the phone, I have to give a lecture in half an hour, but if I can be of any help in the meantime . . ."

He showed his visitor in and closed the door. The visitor looked around at the stacks of books, the battered, comfortable furniture, and the prints and drawings that for some reason always hung at various angles on the walls. He reached into his pockets for something.

"My identification, sir. As I told you on the phone, you can also check with the authorities in London . . ."

Clive glanced at the official-looking shield and various papers, then waved his hand toward the armchair that his pupils always used when they came for a tutorial.

"I'm sure everything's perfectly in order. Please sit down.

This is all quite exciting . . . I've never met a real-life special agent before."

As he spoke, he lowered himself into a chair facing the American, sat back and crossed his legs from habit, as though about to listen to some undergraduate's weekly essay.

"So—you said on the telephone that you wanted to ask me a few questions. I can't imagine what about."

"Mr. Temple, I'm pursuing an inquiry—as I said, with the full cooperation of your Home Office—into a series of crimes in and around Los Angeles in California. I'm not expecting to find the suspect in this country, nothing like that . . . but there is an element in the case that requires the cooperation of someone here in Oxford, and I'm not getting that cooperation. That someone is a person I'm led to believe you know reasonably well—Dr. Tessa Lambert."

Clive raised his eyebrows. "Tessa? What about her? I'm not sure if she's ever even been to California."

"She's not in any way suspected of any crime or wrongdoing. This is merely a matter of help on a technical level. The offenses in question involve computer abuse, breaches of security, that kind of thing. We were attempting to put a trace through Oxford—you know how these networks stretch all around the globe nowadays—with Dr. Lambert's cooperation. However, that cooperation now appears to have been withdrawn—and we'd like to know why."

Clive was aware that he had steepled his fingers in a way that infuriated him in other people. He wasn't trying to infuriate this American from the FBI, but he now knew for sure what he had suspected all along: that he was going to have to stall, and do it convincingly. He had tried to telephone Tessa in between Agent Kelly's call and his arrival, but there had been no reply to her direct line at the lab, nor any reply from her home.

"Well," he said, uncrossing his legs and recrossing them the other way, "I would really like to help you, but I'm not sure how I can."

"To be frank with you, Mr. Temple, we think she's hiding something. Not something connected with the case—perhaps something connected with her work that she doesn't want to talk about. We really need to know what and why—just to get past this barrier."

"I'm awfully sorry, but I really don't think I can help. As you know, Tessa's work is highly technical. Whenever we have discussed it at all, we've done so only in the vaguest and most general terms. I'm an English don, and her expertise is somewhat outside my domain."

He was aware of the American observing him with, he thought, a certain shrewdness.

"Mr. Temple," he said eventually in his slow, American way, amiable and patient, and clearly not to be underestimated, "Mr. Temple, forgive me for saying this, and please believe I mean no offense by it, but I have the strong impression—it's just a matter of habit and training, perhaps misplaced in this case—but I do have the impression that you're holding something back from me. No doubt to protect Dr. Lambert. But from what?"

Clive rapidly de-steepled his fingers. A gesture so alien to him had clearly served to betray his lack of frankness. He uncrossed and recrossed his legs again.

"Certainly I don't take offense. You're perfectly entitled to your view, but I'm afraid it doesn't change mine. I really don't know what I can tell you."

"I am aware that—as I told you, I'm in touch with certain government departments here—I know that other people have asked you about her recently, haven't they? People who are responsible for the funding of her work. In fact, as I understand it, she's been the focus of considerable interest in the last few days, has she not? They too, for their own reasons, are anxious to know what's going on. Evidently something is."

Clive smiled indulgently. At least he hoped that was the impression given. From his side of the curtain the performance felt less than confident.

"Mr. Kelly," he began, as though summing up and drawing the discussion to a close, "I didn't wish to seem discourteous by refusing to see you, but I feared then what I fear now—that I would be, and am, unable to help you. I'm sorry."

"Of course, sir. I understand."

He got to his feet. Clive rose with him. "I mean, can't you all just leave the poor woman alone for the time being? After all, she has just suffered the most terrible shock . . ."

The American looked at him with renewed interest.

"Shock?"

For a dreadful moment Clive felt the flustered uncertainty of someone who had given the whole game away by letting slip an unguarded word; then he reminded himself that the disaster was public knowledge, and Tessa's presence in Berlin had likewise been no secret.

"You mean a death? A loss in the family? Something of that kind?"

"I'm speaking about the air crash, the recent one outside Berlin. You must have read about it."

"She couldn't have been in it. There were no survivors from either plane, as I recall."

"That's the point. She was almost in it. She was booked on the plane leaving Berlin, and by some pure happenstance missed it. Nonetheless, so close an encounter with untimely mortality is bound to leave a mark on even the most sophisticated individual."

He could have added that she'd happened to be pregnant at the time, and that she'd suffered a miscarriage in consequence. He could have said many things. But he'd promised to keep her secret, and he intended to do so.

63

THERE WAS SOMETHING about the young American that made Harry Dash uneasy. He could feel that he was coiled up inside like a spring. He was nice enough, polite, even managed to smile a couple of times; but it was forced, like a man anxious to hide something. Not the sort of man Harry Dash felt happy about selling a weapon to.

The little sporting goods shop had been situated not far from the railway station for the best part of forty years, and Harry had been running it all that time. He felt he knew a thing or two about people—at least, the kind who bought shotguns, pistols, hunting knives, and whatever else in that line Harry had in stock.

And by and large there hadn't been many problems. England was still way behind America in terms of the number of guns in circulation, though their use in organized crime was on the increase, which was probably inevitable. But Harry knew of only one murder committed locally with a weapon bought from his shop, and that was a domestic affair, "a crime of passion" the press had called it when it happened more than a decade back now. One murder in forty years wasn't bad, he thought.

But this American worried him. He kept glancing at the guns, especially the smaller handguns, as though that was really what he wanted, but as he didn't have a permit there was no chance. Harry had explained the law to him and he had seemed to accept it without argument. He had nodded his head with its boyish blond curls, and given a tight little smile which had come only from the mouth and not from those clear blue eyes, which stayed watchful and tense.

Then he'd started on the hunting knives, testing the edge, the grip, trying out the feel of them as though he intended slashing someone's throat, not skinning a rabbit. In the end he bought something long-bladed and strong. He paid in cash and left quickly. Harry was glad to see the back of him.

64

MAJOR FRANKLIN was a man of phlegmatic temperament. He had done and seen much in his time. As an SAS officer he had seen active duty in Ireland, the Falklands, and the Middle East, plus several other theaters of war in which British participation had never been officially acknowledged. His years on special assignment to various departments stretched back into the cold war period; there were still people in Berlin, east and west, who would remember his face if he went back there, though they had never known his real name. He had been shot at, tortured and beaten; he had also killed on more occasions than he cared to remember.

And yet he found nothing constraining or frustrating about the quiet life he now lived in a leafy suburban avenue with his Iranian wife and beautiful teenage daughter. The neighbors knew him as a polite though uncommunicative man who worked, it was generally believed, for the Defence Ministry up in town. The major himself never volunteered information, and something about him discouraged questions.

Indeed he rarely, if ever, put questions to himself, regarding self-analysis as a time-wasting and essentially unhealthy occupation. His loyalty to his country was unfaltering, and had been since his days as a teenage conscript in the fifties. He accepted the hierarchies of political and military authority without question and the subtleties of social distinction without criticism. He knew his place, and the place of others.

It had never occurred to him, for instance, to resent the fact that men such as himself were not even considered for membership of the clubs in Piccadilly and St James's where his Whitehall masters lunched and dined on most weekdays, and where they gathered in exclusive groups to plot and plan the strategies which determined far more than free elections how the country would be governed. The men—and nowadays some of the women—that he served had their reasons for doing things the way they did. Making him a part of their world, even to the extent of inviting him for a quiet drink in it at the end of the day, would make no sense. If Jonathan Syme, for example, had invited him to White's or Pratt's or the Oxford and Cambridge this evening, other members who had themselves had dealings with the major in the past would have known at once that something was up. Curiosity would have been aroused, gossip seeded, and security compromised. Anybody but a fool could understand that, and the major was no fool.

In the pub near Charing Cross, they picked up their drinks from the bar and took them to a quiet corner table. Syme had already glanced at his watch in a way which suggested that he didn't have much time to spare, so the major came to the point at once.

"We've found a bank account in Zurich," he said, "which undoubtedly belongs to Dr. Lambert. It's numbered of course, but—I won't go into all the details now—we can be pretty sure it's hers. Over half a million sterling has been paid into it within the past month—in three payments from a branch of the same bank in Tokyo."

Jonathan stared into his drink, nodding sagely and with sadness, but saying nothing.

"It may be, as you say, that we have no strict legal position," the major continued, "but I would have thought that something should be done."

Jonathan lifted his eyes and looked at him directly and unblinking. "Like what?" he asked flatly.

"For one thing, we have people who can go in and scan her computer—find out what she's got in there, always assuming it's still there."

"From what I hear she's working nearly round the clock with the thing, so it must be." Jonathan sighed and leaned back against the hard wooden paneling that doubled as both seat back and wall.

"She has to sleep some time," said the major. "It can be done quite discreetly, nobody would know. As a matter of fact, I spoke to our American friend this afternoon. He's leaving tomorrow—"

"Yes, I got your memo on that."

"Apparently they've got all the evidence they need now. All they've got to do is find the man. He said he was very sorry he'd not been able to get anything out of her along the lines of what we wanted. What he didn't say, however," and here the major leaned forward, narrowing his already narrow eyes and dropping his voice for emphasis, "was that he's having a farewell dinner with her tonight."

Jonathan looked at him for a moment. He was about to ask how the major came by this information, but then realized as soon as the question was formulated. "Phone tap?"

The major nodded. "We've got one on the lab phone as well as her home. I only bring it up because it provides the perfect window. Three, four hours when her movements are accounted for. We could have somebody in there and out before they're even round to the coffee and mints."

Jonathan took a sip of his drink, then was silent for a while, looking down at the tabletop in front of him.

"I'll tell you why I don't like it," he said eventually. "First, I'd need convincing that our so-called experts would be up to it. This is a very brilliant woman who's quite possibly doing stuff in her field that others are barely capable of even thinking about. We don't want some clodhopping computer coppers going in there and botching the job."

The major didn't even blink at the reference to clodhopping coppers, which by implication, though not intentionally, included him.

"Secondly," Jonathan continued, "it puts us in the wrong, and I don't like that. If anything goes wrong there'll be an outcry from the academic community, questions in the House, headlines in the liberal press—or what passes for it. Damn it, Major," he slapped the table softly but decisively with the flat of his hand, "if the bloody woman's selling us out, I'm going to nail her fair and square. And I'll use the university authorities to do it, not some bunch of Watergate burglars."

"As you wish." The major never argued. Decisions weren't his responsibility, nor the failures that might follow on from them. He was just there to say what could be done, and do it if instructed.

"Stay in touch with the American," Jonathan was saying, an edge of anger entering his voice now. "Who knows, maybe he'll take her back to his hotel and fuck her—and find out what's going on in that mysterious head of hers."

He picked up his drink and finished it, then got abruptly to his feet.

"Goodnight, Major. Thanks for the information. I'm sure we'll talk tomorrow."

Another moment and he was gone, leaving the major sitting by himself. It didn't show on his face, but if the major was capable of being shocked, he would have been shocked at that moment. So what had got into Syme? Surely not jealousy.

65

THE GIRL ON the desk saw him crossing the lobby and reached back for the fax that had arrived barely five minutes earlier. She told him that she'd called his room, but he must have been already on his way down.

He thanked her, and moved off to one side to read it. It was from Jack, characteristically laconic.

"Am using general terms as this may see other eyes than yours. Fluke discovery of videos in city garbage dump provides further clinching evidence that we are onto right man. Tapes record his activities. He liked to make home movies—like Mom, remember? Only worse. Much worse. It's bad stuff. Forensics has found traces of his prints on cassettes. Still no recent photos, so have pulled one from previous file and am having graphics update appearance—will fax you copy ASAP, unless you get back first. Please confirm flight number and arrival time."

He went back to the desk and asked the girl for a fax sheet, scribbled down the details that Jack wanted, wrote the full code and phone number carefully, and signed for it to be put on his bill.

The girl was already sending it as he stepped out into the dying afternoon light.

01110101011011000110010000100000

• • •

Barely ten minutes' walk from the Randolph Hotel in the Georgian elegance of Beaumont Street was a quiet little parade of modern shops and modest restaurants that could have been anywhere in England. Chuck Price was there because by some chance there was a block of four public phone booths, not more than two of which ever seemed to be in use at any one time. Two of them took phone cards only, the other two took coins. Price didn't need to use either, because with the code he'd been given all he had to do was pick up and dial; invariably he was connected to the voice in under a minute.

It began as always. "I am listening."

He gave an update on where he was in the overall plan, frankly admitting his anxieties, saying that he felt exposed and tremendously at risk in a strange country with false papers: not false exactly, they were the real thing, they just weren't *his* papers. If he was picked up, the deception would be quickly uncovered. What had begun back in Los Angeles as the most exciting thing that had ever happened to him was becoming an ordeal in which his will and any sense of who he was were evaporating with alarming speed. He was doing his best, he said, but wished he could be more sure of success.

"It is essential you persist," the voice said tonelessly. "I must know what she is planning."

"I am doing all I can."

"Have you evidence that she has spoken of me to anyone?"

"None. I think it is unlikely, but of course I cannot be sure."

"You must be sure."

"I will be—before the end."

He felt a little thrill of anticipated pleasure as he thought about the end. She was different from the others. Not so much in terms of how she looked. He was pleased with how she looked; on that level it was going to be as good as ever. He had been visualizing how the end was going to be, playing it over and over in his head, like a film.

Film. That reminded him of what a wrench it had been to throw out his videos back in LA, but he'd had no choice, knowing the police would be all over his house as soon as they realized he had disappeared. Of course they would still find his precious collection of *her* movies, but there was nothing incriminating about that and nothing illegal in their possession. If things went well, he hoped he would be able to retrieve them at some time in the future.

He realized that once again he had let his mind wander while the voice had been continuing to pour words into his ear. He was angry with himself whenever he did this; but the voice's toneless flatness, despite the awesome thought of Who it spoke for, made concentration difficult.

". . . they are still refusing to react," he heard. "They have so far taken no action that has produced the information I am seeking."

He knew where he was now. They had already had this conversation, or variations on it, several times. The creature that he now thought of as God had moved all along with impeccable logic to deal with the risks that He perceived Himself as facing. From the moment in Berlin when He first learned that she knew He was alive and loose, He had understood that her every thought and action had been directed toward one end only: His destruction. That had been clear from the first message she had sent back to Oxford, ordering the disconnection of the modem—too late to change anything, but a clear statement of her intentions. In addition, there had been the message that the man called Ted Sawyer had sent to California from Berlin, which had confirmed those intentions.

Despite His efforts to eliminate her as a threat, she had returned to Oxford. He knew that she had remained there since and was working with the now-isolated computer. He knew, too, that she was hiding something from her superiors, and He knew from their communications that they were growing increasingly concerned about the fact. That was why He had planted information—records of phone calls she had never made, traces of secret bank accounts that existed nowhere except in cyberspace—designed to provoke them into taking action against her. He knew that whatever they found would be logged in official files to which He had access, and at last He would know what she was doing.

But nothing had so far worked out as anticipated. And time was running on—out, even. Even for Him. Unless He knew what threat He faced, He could not protect Himself.

01101111011101100110010100101110

"My future rests in your hands," the voice intoned, "as does yours in mine."

There was a clear warning implicit in the words: that if he didn't perform, he could be thrown to the authorities at any time. But he did not see this as a real threat. He didn't need threats when the rewards for success would be so fabulous. The possibilities made his head spin.

"I plan to make my move tonight," he said. "Things will be resolved within the next few hours."

"If you fail, I am preparing to take other steps."

"What other steps?"

"You need not know—yet. It will be better for you if you do not fail."

Somewhat chastened, he hung up the phone as the voice disconnected contact. He strode off into the gathering dusk, wondering what had been meant by that last remark. In an effort to reassure himself he repeated over and over like a mantra that failure was impossible for Netman, and after several minutes the quietness that he sought descended on the strange interior landscape of his soul. He was ready. His God, he knew, would not desert him.

66

TESSA HEARD HIS knock on the cottage door at eight o'clock precisely. She put his promptness down to being a cop, and her lack of it to far too many things to analyze. She hurried down the stairs pulling on a rust-colored tweed jacket over a cream silk blouse and flicking her hair out over the collar.

This time she showed him into her living room instead of the kitchen. It was a little chintzier than it would have been if she'd actually owned the place, but he seemed to like it and sank comfortably into a loose-covered, old-fashioned, square-cornered sofa. She offered him a drink, and he said he'd have a Virgin Mary. She was out of celery salt, which she thought was essential for a Mary, Virgin or otherwise, but he said it was fine. She had a glass of Meursault from a bottle that she had in the fridge.

They sat and chatted across an open fireplace—in which she would have made a fire if she hadn't wanted to avoid giving the impression that she was making too much of what was supposed to be a casual evening with an acquaintance whom she barely knew and was never going to see again.

"By the way," she said, "there was a journalist looking for you earlier. Did he find you?"

"A journalist?" He frowned. This came as a surprise to him, and not a welcome one. "Who? What did he want?"

"He was American. Something Walsh—Conrad Walsh. From San Francisco."

"Damn," he said softly. "God damn." Then he added unnecessarily, "Excuse me."

"D'you know him?"

"Never heard of him. But some journalist breathing down my neck is just what I don't need right now."

"He said he was a technical journalist, not a—I don't know—crime reporter or whatever."

"What kind of questions did he ask?"

"He asked if I knew you, and if I'd been helping with this computer trace he'd heard about . . ."

"What did you tell him?"

"I told him I had. Helped out, I mean. I said I'd been approached by someone I ran into in Berlin who knew your brother."

"That was all? I mean, that was all he asked?"

"Pretty much."

She wondered whether to mention what Walsh had said about hearing rumors about her work, but decided not to. It would only provoke Kelly into asking her more questions that she didn't want to answer.

"Are you sure that was all?" He was eyeing her suspiciously.

"Yes. That was all."

He was silent for a moment, thinking. "Did he give you a card? A phone number? An address where you can find him?"

She shook her head. "He seemed perfectly decent. He said it was all off the record, just background."

Kelly didn't look reassured.

"Is something wrong?" she asked.

"If he gets in touch again . . ." His words tailed off.

"What?"

"I was going to say get in touch with me, but I probably won't be here."

"I can call you in LA."

"I'd sure like to know who he is, and how he knew I was here."

He remained lost in his thoughts for a moment, then turned to her, earnest and admonishing. "Listen, if he shows up again, make him show you some ID. *Always* make them prove who they are before you talk to them."

"You're making me feel alarmed."

"Don't be. I'm sure it's okay. Forget it."

All the same, he still seemed subdued and vaguely preoccupied when they left for the restaurant just after eight, traveling in his car. It was dark, so it was not surprising that neither of them saw the figure that ducked back quickly into a hedgerow as the car's headlights flashed by on full beam.

He watched until their taillights disappeared around the first bend, then ran across the road to where his own car was hidden in the mouth of a narrow lane. He had reversed it into place so that he would be ready to pull out quickly in pursuit. His foresight was rewarded when he reached the first fork in the road just in time to see them take the left one. Seconds later and he would have missed them; left or right would have been anybody's guess.

After that it was easy. He was able to maintain his distance and keep them in view without trouble.

The place she had booked for dinner was a classic little low-beamed inn that all Americans, in her experience, took as the very definition of Englishness. She liked the place because its chef was a French girl from Dijon who had only come over to learn English. If only the English would send their chefs over there to learn French, Tessa told him on the way, she might eat out more often.

The inn was on the outskirts of the next village, and when they turned in to park they didn't even notice the car that cruised on past.

He had followed them at a careful distance the whole way. Luckily the route, though winding, was straightforward, so headlights in the mirror traveling in the same direction were not automatically suspicious.

By the time he had found a place to park and walked back, they were talking across their menus about what they were going to eat. He could see them through the window from over the road, where he was standing in the pitch-black V-shape made by two adjoining dry-stone walls. He pulled back, wanting to be sure that no casual passerby would notice him, then settled in for what he knew would be a couple of hours' wait at least.

He reached into the pocket of his leather jacket, and his fingers closed reassuringly around the handle of the hunting knife that he had bought that afternoon. He would have preferred a gun, but the old guy in the shop had made it clear that a casual firearms purchase was impossible. He knew the old guy had sensed something about him, and that worried him. He hoped he hadn't talked to anybody.

Anyway, in the absence of any better plan, he knew that he would have to make do with a knife—and be patient.

67

HE STUDIED THE wine list that the waiter had given him.

"You're having the lamb," he said. "I guess that means a red. Bordeaux okay?"

"If you're not drinking," she said, "I'll just have a glass of house red."

"Heck, no, I'll have a glass or two—why not? I'm having a good time." He smiled across at her. He seemed to have got over his anxiety about the journalist. He asked her if she had any preferences. She said she liked the La Lagune '88, so he ordered a bottle.

"I remember a couple of years ago," she said, "there was a medical report published showing that moderate consumption of red wine reduced your chances of heart disease by fifty per cent or more. I read somewhere that in California red wine sales doubled in one day."

"That sounds about right," he said with a laugh. "In California, death is optional." Then he checked himself, turning abruptly serious as though he had made some graceless faux pas. "Well, certain kinds of death."

She understood. There was a killer who had to be tracked down and caught, and until he was, this man sitting across from her was never going to relax fully.

"I'm afraid coming over here has turned out to be a complete waste of time for you, hasn't it?"

"I wouldn't say a complete waste. At least, I hope not."

His tone of voice and his expression were still serious, but serious about something else now: not crime, not murder, not any of the things that awaited him back home. His eyes were on hers, and she saw in them that same surprising shyness that she had sensed in him before, a wanting but not quite daring to say things. He seemed relieved when the wine arrived to distract his attention. He tasted it briefly and without ceremony, and gave a nod of approval. When both their glasses were filled, he toasted her across the table.

"It's been nice making your acquaintance, Tessa. I'm sorry it's been so brief."

"When you get back to California," she said, "you must let me know how things go."

"If we catch him, you'll hear about it."

"Oh, I don't mean in the newspapers or on television. I want the inside story."

He seemed to think about this for a moment. Maybe he was just hesitating over what he wanted to say, but he finally said it anyway.

"You ought to come out there some time and see us. Have you ever been before?"

"I've been to talk to some people in Silicon Valley a couple of times. That was three, no, four years ago. I was on a tight schedule, didn't see anything aside from, well, silicon chips."

"It's worth taking a little more time if you get the chance. LA's a . . . what can I call it? . . . an interesting city." He thought a little more, with an ironic twist to his expression. "Yeah, interesting about covers it. You'd like San Francisco—Europeans always do. And the north, up in the redwood forests and the wine country, that's spectacular. You can spend a week—more, easy—driving around and having your breath taken away every which way you turn."

"I'd like to do that." She turned the wine glass in her hand, looking into its red richness as though for some clue to what was happening here, some pointer to the future. "It's so crazy that we never make the time to do the things we want to do, just the things we have to do."

"It's kind of nice if there's no difference. I mean between what you want to do and what you have to do. Don't you think?"

She looked over at him. "Is that the way it is with you?"

He frowned slightly, as though asking himself a hard question. "I used to think I was doing only what I wanted, now I don't know. Maybe I want other things. Only I don't know what they are."

Their starters arrived and they talked about food for a while. He agreed that the cooking was as good as she had told him it would be—not, he added, that he pretended to be any kind of big expert.

"Tell me about yourself, Tessa," he said after a while. "Where d'you come from? How d'you get to be doing what you're doing?"

She couldn't resist letting him see a brief flash of wry amusement in response to this question.

"I thought your friends in security had already told you everything."

"Not the interesting stuff," he said, smiling. "Just facts. And not very many of them, either."

She gave him a quick outline of her life, being careful not to make the early part too prominent. The death of her parents was passed over as an eternal though long-buried grief. The years with her aunt and uncle were referred to without elaboration. She got as quickly as she could to the point where she had the luck to find something she had a flair for doing. She didn't think she was special, and she didn't like to sound as though she thought she was.

"And you?" she asked. "Were you born in California?"

"I was born in New York. With a name like Kelly I don't have to tell you that my family's Irish. My old man was one of New York's finest—retired. Works for a security firm now."

"A cop? So you took after him."

"In some ways. In some good ways, I hope."

"Your brother teaches at Cal Tech, you said."

"That's Josh—the brains in the family. You and he would get along great."

"Well, perhaps we'll get to meet some day," she said. Then added, "If I come over and visit."

"It'll be my pleasure," he spoke with a wide smile, "to show you around."

Somehow there was a sense between them of something having been settled, some contract made. They had agreed that they liked each other, that there was a mutual attraction; but there was no pressure. Things would take their course. Or not.

They both relaxed a little. They were surprised to find they'd finished the wine quite easily. He ordered a brandy with his coffee.

He swirled the contents of his snifter around a couple of times and stared into it.

"Tessa," he said after a longish pause, "I think I'm going to tell you something that I'd sworn to myself I wasn't going to."

She leaned forward on one elbow. "Go on," she said, giving him a faintly hooded look, "I can keep a secret."

"I know. That appears to be the problem."

"What's that supposed to mean?" She lifted an eyebrow slightly.

"Look . . . Jesus, I'm probably breaking some international treaty that'll get me canned when I get back home, but I already told you that I'm in touch with your security people . . ." He hesitated. "I can't believe I'm doing this, I must be out of my—"

"Come on," she said, "you've started, so you can't stop now."

"The reason I'm saying this is because you don't strike me as the sort of person that you'd have to be in order to do what they think you've been doing."

"Which is—?"

He made a vague, almost apologetic gesture with his hands.

"They think you're working for the Japanese."

"What—?"

He was watching her. He was pretty sure that her surprise was genuine.

"If it's not true, and you don't want them to think that it is, then maybe you should do something about it. That's all I'm saying. And don't mention me when you do—okay?"

"What on earth makes them think . . . ? I mean why . . . ?"

She seemed distracted, her questions tailing off into silence.

"I'm just telling you what I picked up. Some reference to

phone numbers you've been calling and getting calls from, something about secret bank accounts in Switzerland—I don't have a lot of details."

"Oh, God!"

She leaned forward, pressing her forehead into the open palm of her hand. It was the gesture of someone who had just recognized an obvious blinding truth, not someone being shocked by an unexpected revelation. He heard her say "Of course!" under her breath.

"Anyway," he went on, "I'd say you're on the edge of losing tenure, or whatever you call it here. Because whatever you're keeping from them, they're pretty upset about it."

She lowered her hand from her face and looked at him with a sudden coldness that took him by surprise.

"And they've asked you to find out—right?"

"Yes." No equivocation there. He knew he couldn't afford it.

For a moment she looked as though she was about to get up and walk out of the restaurant. He spoke quickly.

"But I'm not planning to cooperate."

"Well, good for you." The sarcasm in her tone was unmistakable—and meant to be.

"Hey, listen," he said, holding up his hands as though appealing for a truce, "I'm on your side. Otherwise I wouldn't be telling you this stuff."

Her lips curled into an ironic smile. "So you're a double agent? Working for them—and me?"

"I'm just saying is there any way I can help you straighten this out?"

A pause.

"How?"

"Maybe by having me tell them something that . . ." his hands seemed to clutch at an imaginary football around his brandy glass, ". . . something that you want them to hear?"

"A lie, for instance?"

He looked at her, at the same time picking up the glass and draining it.

"A white lie might be considered," he said.

"Define white."

"That depends on what you're hiding."

She looked at him steadily for several moments. “I’m still not going to tell you.”

They were interrupted by the waiter stopping by to see if they wanted anything else. They both ordered another coffee. He hesitated, then ordered another brandy.

“I think you’re in a spot,” he said when the waiter had gone. “I think that whatever you’ve done or haven’t done—”

“I haven’t done anything of the kind they think,” she interrupted angrily. “I haven’t been talking to any Japanese companies. And I don’t know anything about secret bank accounts in Switzerland. Somebody’s trying to frame me. Somebody who wants to put a stop to my work.”

She was conscious that the outburst sounded paranoid, and looked at him anxiously for a response. He didn’t show one, just continued looking at her calmly.

“Who?”

She looked down, off to one side. She should have known better. She wasn’t going to tell him. She had already said too much.

He repeated the question. “Who’s trying to frame you?”

She shook her head.

“Look,” he said patiently, but in a tone suggesting that perhaps his patience wasn’t infinite, “I should be on a plane now. I have important things to do—I don’t have to tell you that. I’ve stayed here an extra day for one reason and one only. To see you again. That’s all there is to it.”

He fell silent. She found herself looking at him again. He was looking at her directly and frankly, no hint of shyness now; he had gone too far for that.

She felt a sense of shock more than anything else. She hadn’t been ready for this. It was too sudden. It wasn’t part of their unspoken agreement—at least not the agreement as she’d understood it.

Without so much as blinking he said in a quiet, level tone: “It’s something to do with the plane crash, isn’t it?”

She thought she heard herself gasp. Or maybe she’d just imagined it. Anyway he couldn’t have heard it above the murmur of the room. But she knew she had reacted, turned pale, or merely frozen in front of him, under that relentless gaze.

"How much do they know?" she asked in a voice that barely carried across the table.

She realized at once that she'd given him the key. He could have just been fishing, but her question had confirmed whatever suspicions he might have had, however vague.

All he said was, "I think you'd better tell me all about it."

She knew now she had no choice.

"Can we get out of here, please?" she said.

68

HE HADN'T MOVED since they sat down at their table. Now he watched as they emerged and walked to their car.

They drove off in the direction from which they had come. Within moments he was in his own car, following them. They were returning, as he had expected they would, to her place. The only question was would he go in with her, or leave her there?

He muttered a curse when he drove past the empty car parked by the gate. Glancing to his right, without slowing, he saw the cottage door closing behind them both.

Moments later he had parked his own car in the same place as before, and crept back quietly on foot. He needed to get as close as possible: somewhere in the garden would be best. He was pretty sure she didn't have a dog. He'd heard no sound, seen no sign of one earlier.

Not risking the giveaway creak of rusty hinges, he high-stepped carefully over the gate and found himself a corner of the garden where he was quickly lost in dense foliage. Even if the light he could see over the white-painted porch were turned on, he would not be visible.

All he could do now was wait, too intent on what he was

0 1 1 0 0 1 0 1 0 1 1 0 1 1 1 0 0 1 1 0 0 1 0 1 0 1 1 1 0 1 1 0

waiting for to notice the cold and stiffness that had started to invade his bones. His eyes were fixed on the curtained, lighted windows just a few yards from where he crouched. He could see nothing and he could hear nothing, except the low moan of the wind and the rustle of the leaves around him.

However long it took, he would be there. There was nothing in his mind except the knowledge that, however long it took, he would be there.

"This is no virus," he said, when she finally finished talking. "I don't know what it is, but it's no computer virus."

"It's a consciousness," she said. "We know so little about consciousness that the big question has always been whether it can arise anywhere except in brains. Well, it has here; or something very like it has."

His face was creased with the effort of trying to understand what she was saying.

"Even the technology itself doesn't matter," she went on. "If you did something with a block of wood or a piece of stone—somehow animated the atoms in them to show ON or OFF—you could get a computational process going, and with the right programs you'd have a block of wood or a lump of stone that appeared to think. The important word is 'appeared.' Because when it comes to thinking, you can't get behind appearances. We don't know how it's done. We just know if something *looks* like thought or not."

He was silent a moment. Then he said: "It's the same with sane and insane, isn't it?"

"I'm sorry?"

"You say we don't know how it's done—thinking. Each of us does it, but we don't know that other people do it the same way. All we know is what they do or what they say, but we never know what goes on inside them. We label them."

"Yes, I suppose you could say that."

He got up and paced a few steps around the back of the chair he'd been sitting in, rubbing his eyes. "And this thing out there," he said, turning to her again, "you've told nobody about it so far except me?"

On an impulse she stopped herself from mentioning Helen

and Clive: she saw no need to involve her two friends at this stage.

"I've talked to nobody except you." The lie came surprisingly easily.

"I'm very relieved to hear that."

"As long as nobody knows it's there they won't attack it. And as long as it isn't attacked it won't react."

"Except it's already tried to kill you . . ."

"That's because it had the opportunity. As long as I don't get on a plane, or into any kind of system that it controls, it won't get another one. All it can do is fiddle phone bills and bank accounts and make me look like a crook or whatever. If it wanted, it could issue warrants for my arrest on some trumped-up charge; but it wouldn't get anywhere by that, which is probably the only reason it hasn't done it."

He reached for his cup of coffee and drank it standing. "How long d'you need to get this other program, this counteractive thing you're working on, up and ready to go?" he asked.

She gave a shrug. "There's no way I can be sure it'll work until I've tried it. That said, I'm probably about as close to ready as I'm ever going to be."

He absorbed this information for a moment, then put down his cup. "Where is it? In the lab?"

"I've got one copy there, another here."

"You have a backup here in the house?"

"Not exactly a backup. I've been creating an interaction between different copies of Paul . . ."

"Paul?" His voice rose on a note of query.

She felt herself blush stupidly. "That's what I call it." She was grateful that he didn't ask why. "I've been putting him through his paces," she went on, "to prepare him for what he's going to have to face . . ."

Outside in the garden he looked up sharply as a bright splash of light fell from an upstairs window, reaching almost to where he stood. The curtains were not drawn and he could see her flipping open a portable computer on a desk by the window. The man was standing behind her, looking over her shoulder. Then she reached over and closed the curtains.

00100000001100111011001010111100

He moved carefully out of his hiding place, staying in the darkest shadows, but edging around the corner of the cottage, looking for a way in.

His hand closed once again around the handle of the knife in his pocket. Withdrawing it, he opened the long and viciously sharp blade, and carefully locked it into place.

00100000011000010111001001101111

69

TESSA COULDN'T HELP feeling a small surge of pride as she switched off the little computer and turned to where he sat on the edge of her Eames chair footstool, leaning forward with his elbows on his knees and an expression of amazement on his face.

"Appearance or the real thing," she said to break the silence. "It's a philosophical debate and of marginal, if any, importance. What matters is that this thing here is as real as that thing out there."

"And what happens," he asked, looking up at her, "when they meet?"

"Strictly speaking," she said, "they won't 'meet' at all. They'll simply merge."

"And change."

"Yes."

"What makes you think that the change will go in favor of this one?"

"I believe that reason is more powerful than unreason."

He pushed himself to his feet and ran a hand through his hair. "That's quite a statement of faith."

"I prefer to think it's a statement of the obvious."

He looked at her. "Isn't there any chance they'll just," he

brought his hands together in a soundless impact, "meet like matter and antimatter and destroy each other? And God knows what else with them?"

She shook her head. "Because they're *not* matter and anti-matter. They're one thing physically, two things mentally."

"The good twin, and the evil twin."

"If you like."

He shook his head in wonderment. "Jesus."

For some moments he stared at a blank stretch of wall. She could see that another question was forming in his mind, and waited.

He pointed at the PC. "Do you need to send out both copies of the program together, this one here, plus the one on your computer in the lab?"

"No, either would do. I've been running copies through each other to give him the . . ." she paused, still self-conscious about the use of "him."

"Hey, it's all right," he said, understanding why she had stopped. "This sure as hell ain't an it. I'm just curious about how you chose the name 'Paul.'"

She shrugged. "A family thing."

He didn't press the question further. Instead he walked over to the little PC that she had just shut down and looked at it with a kind of awe. "So, that's all there is of him," he said. "Right here. And in the lab." He looked over his shoulder at her. "Is that right—just the two of him?"

"Yes," she said, a little puzzled by his tone. He seemed to be leading up to something, but she couldn't see what.

"But I guess, if anything happened to them both, you could have the whole thing up and running again pretty soon, huh?"

She made an equivocal gesture. "Not that soon. I hope I won't have to."

"That's what I figured."

"Sorry? I'm not sure I . . ."

He looked at her with a smile—an odd smile that she hadn't seen before. It seemed to come not from his face but from somewhere behind it, as though the face that she had known had been discarded like a mask that was no longer needed.

"You're not sure that you what?" he said. "Understand? I think you do. I think you've guessed—haven't you?"

She felt a chill of fear, as though the man she was looking at was no longer the man she had spent the evening with. This was a man she did not know. And there was something strangely and indefinably wrong with him.

"I'm not Tim Kelly," he said, and looked oddly gratified by the reaction he saw in her eyes. "My name's Chuck Price. Tim Kelly got unavoidably detained on his way to the airport—permanently."

There was a moment of utter, unreal stillness. Then he swung around with a movement so fast that she barely saw anything happen—until her small computer smashed against the wall with such force that it exploded in a cloud of plastic and plaster.

She screamed. But the sound died in her throat, because in another flash his hand was there, choking it off. His fingers tightened and she felt herself lifted almost off the floor. She flailed uselessly with her arms, trying to claw his face, but not even making contact. She could hear him laughing, saying something. Gradually his words came into focus.

"You're going to do exactly as I say. You hear me? We're going to the lab, you and I together, and we're going to wipe that program out of existence . . ."

He began slowly loosening his grip. It felt as though all the blood in her body was rushing to her legs as they took her full weight again. She thought she was going to pass out, but fought to hold on.

"Now the only sound I want to hear out of your mouth when I let go is 'Yes.' You understand?"

The noise of breaking glass seemed to come faintly down some long, long tunnel. It was followed by a pounding on the stairs that became suddenly immediate and thundering in her ears.

She realized that he'd let go of her and she was slumped on the floor. There was a pain in her hip where she had landed badly, but she barely felt it because her whole attention was on the knife-wielding man who burst into the room. It was the man she had met that afternoon who had called himself Conrad Walsh. He was pale as a ghost, wild-eyed and breathing hard. He glanced at her, then his eyes locked on the other man.

The man who had just told her that his name was Price

stepped back and dropped automatically into a defensive crouch. Something in his face convinced her that he recognized Walsh. She could see him searching his memory for where and when he had last seen him. Then there it was: he knew.

"You!"

He said it in a way that suggested this might just be the last person in the world he had expected to see here. Nonetheless, it obviously made sense to him—some kind of sense.

"What have you done with my brother?" Walsh demanded. His voice was low and raw with fury.

She saw the response build in Price, like an animal trapped and with nothing to lose. It was a rage beyond fear. He gave out a roar, and in the same kind of manically balletic movement with which he had shattered her computer he scooped up a wooden chair and flung it at Walsh, then launched himself across the room at him.

The two men rolled on the floor, struggling for possession of the knife. She used the edge of her desk to haul herself up, then looked around for something she could use to help Walsh. There was a strange slow-motion quality to the moment. She found herself thinking how at times like this in movies there was always a vase or a paperweight or a pair of scissors conveniently on hand. But she could find nothing.

Walsh braced his foot against Price's chest and kicked with all his strength. Price shot across the room, but landed and rolled to his feet in a single agile movement.

Tessa saw that the knife had skittered across the floor to her feet, and that Price was diving for it. She saw a plea in Walsh's eyes, and managed to snatch it up and throw it back to him.

Now Walsh was on his feet and holding the knife low, ready to cut with an underhand jab. Price stopped, circled, looking for an opening. But there was none. Walsh was ready for him, and determined.

Instead of attacking, Price dived at a right angle for the stairs and disappeared down them. Walsh threw a glance in Tessa's direction as though to check that she was unhurt, then flung himself down the stairs in pursuit.

Her first thought was to follow, to stay with the fight. Then she realized that the most important thing to do was call the police; whatever happened after that, at least she would know that help was on the way.

She picked up the phone. It wasn't dead, but there was a kind of open sound on the line. She rattled the cradle, but still there was no dial tone.

"Hello? Hello?" she repeated instinctively, as though expecting some response, but all she heard was the faint echo of her own voice in the distance, as though she were calling down some bottomless well.

Then, with a visceral shock, she realized what was happening, and at the same time reproached herself for having been so slow-witted. "It" was out there, the thing that had spoken to her in Berlin, still circling and stalking, controlling and closing in. Of course it would allow no calls for help to leave this house tonight. This was the night that it had sent a maniac halfway across the world to kill her. This was the night it must have planned with all the detail of a military campaign. Nothing had been left to chance.

Yet where had this man Walsh come from? That was surely unforeseen. She felt a strong impulse to shout into the phone, "It's all gone wrong, you didn't think of everything!" But she controlled herself. Even if it were listening, as she suspected it was, provoking it was the last thing she should do. God alone knew what back-up strategies it had ready, and she herself knew only too well what it was capable of.

She put the receiver down quietly, thinking. A crash from downstairs brought her back sharply to the present. She heard something else break, then a door slam back on its hinges. She ran down the steps.

When she reached the hall, where the lights were still on, she saw a trail of chaos leading through into the darkness of the kitchen. She paused and listened. There was an eerie silence, no movement of any kind, not even from outside.

She crept cautiously into the kitchen. There were no lights in there, and she did not want to put them on. She felt her way around the familiar shapes until her eyes accustomed themselves to the darkness—just in time to stop her walking into an overturned chair. She saw that the back door was open, a pane of glass in it smashed as though that was where Walsh had forced his entrance.

Behind some cookbooks in a corner was a heavy flashlight that she kept for emergencies. She felt for and found it. She knew the batteries were good because she had replaced them only recently. But she didn't switch it on; she wanted to stay unseen and not pinpoint where she was. Gripping it firmly in her hand, ready to use it as a weapon, she stepped out into the night.

The sky was overcast and moonless, and the wind that had been threatening to get up earlier had dropped. Her hearing felt superhuman in the silence. She remained absolutely still for several moments, listening.

Then she took a few steps, but stopped when she realized how much noise her shoes made on the stone path. She reached down and slipped them off, leaving them on the ground. Then she crept on.

She tried to analyze the situation. Either Price had run off with Walsh in pursuit; or Walsh was dead, and Price was waiting for her somewhere in the darkness. If Price was dead, or at least hurt enough to be harmless, Walsh would surely be looking for her, would call out to reassure her—anything but hide; he would have no reason to.

She was stopped short by her name hissed at her from somewhere close.

"Tessa!"

She gasped and swung around, instinctively turning on the flashlight.

"Put that out! He's here somewhere."

She obeyed instantly, but not before she had glimpsed Walsh lying prostrate across a flowerbed near her feet. She crouched down and whispered, "What happened?"

A return whisper, breathless, taut with pain, came from the darkness.

"I've twisted my ankle, I can't walk . . ."

He gave a gasp of pain.

"Who are you?"

"I'm Josh Kelly."

"And this man . . . Price? Is that really his name?"

"I don't know . . . I only saw him once . . . he was driving the car that took Tim to the airport . . ."

Suddenly the whole picture came together in Tessa's mind

with brutal clarity. "Oh, God," she whispered, "he's the man who killed all those women, isn't he? The man your brother was looking for."

"That's what I think . . . and I think I've figured out why he's here . . . but you're going to have to tell me if I'm right . . . I touched on it, didn't I, this afternoon?"

She didn't answer. He could hear her breathing raggedly, fighting back some fear in her that was more than just fear for her life.

"Tessa!" he hissed. "Tell me about the program. That's what he wants, isn't it?"

She started trying to say something, but her voice was shaking so badly that the words came out as no more than senseless gasps. But he heard: ". . . wipe it . . . he was taking me to the lab to wipe it when you—"

That was as far as she got before a hand came out of the dark and grabbed her by the hair. She screamed, and saw Josh make a superhuman effort to stand up and defend her.

Something silvery-gray moved like a ripple in the dark. Then Josh grunted with a sound she'd never heard before, an awful sound. She knew it was the sound of life leaving the body.

Josh Kelly fell, a dead weight, at her feet, and didn't move.

"You bastard! You didn't have to—"

The sentence hung unfinished in the air as a blow to the side of her neck sent her hurtling into an even deeper blackness than the night.

70

IT WAS THAT BRIEF, fatal beam of light that had given her away. It was, he knew, God-given, an intervention from powers beyond human understanding, timed to give him back the triumph that had been threatening to slip from his grasp.

He had heard Josh Kelly fall in the garden and heard the knife clatter along a stone path nearby. By luck he had found it almost at once; then he tried to find Kelly to finish him off, but without success. The bastard must have been holding his breath in that silence. At any rate, he had the knife; and he hadn't been able to waste any more time because there was the woman to take care of.

There had been footsteps coming from the house. Then she'd stopped, and after that he had heard nothing. He figured that she must have taken off her shoes.

Finally he'd heard the whispering. And now everything was all right. He was back in control. Things were going the way they were supposed to go.

He found that he was thinking now with that clarity of mind which was the quality he most valued in himself. He was on a high, but a natural high—the best kind.

Using the flashlight that had rolled only a couple of feet from where she lay, he found her shoes, then carried her back into the cottage. He set her down on a sofa in the living room, checked her pulse and breathing and pulled back her eyelids. He figured she'd be fully out for ten or fifteen minutes, maybe a little more; he was an expert at this kind of thing, but in the darkness he hadn't been able to calculate the blow as precisely as he would have liked.

He ran upstairs to find her bedroom. He wanted a coat and something to tie her up with. He found a couple of pairs of tights, and tore up a silk slip to use as a gag.

When he got back downstairs she hadn't moved. Anyone seeing her would have said she had just stretched out for a comfortable nap, except that she barely stirred when he bound and gagged her. Then he picked up the phone, tapped in the required code, and waited.

"I am listening."

It took only moments to summarize what had happened and what he had found out. If he had had to attribute an emotion to the flat mechanical voice in his ear, it would have been relief; but no doubt he was only imagining it. He listened obediently to his further instructions, and said that he had understood. They were exactly what he had anticipated they would be.

He quickly reconnoitered the twisty old passages and doors off the kitchen to find one that led to the garage, then he went back for her. He'd decided to use her car because it wouldn't attract attention in the lab's parking lot; also, because it was in the garage, he could get her into it without the risk of anybody driving past and seeing them.

Five minutes later, with her on the backseat and covered by a blanket, he backed carefully onto the road, and then they were on their way. It was going like clockwork.

Just like in LA when he'd picked up the cop for the airport. He'd got his instructions on screen in the usual way; at least it was the usual way when he wasn't using the phone code he'd been given. He was given the number of the cab company and told to cancel the cop's reservation. Then he was given the number of a car rental company and told to hire a vehicle under a false name, using a credit-card reference he was given that would check out on computer, but would thereafter be mysteriously untraceable. The little touch of the driver's cap had been his own idea. He felt it lent his play-acting a certain authenticity.

And the cop had fallen for it like a baby. They'd made small talk for the first couple of miles: Where are you flying to? England? Oh, wow, I'd really like to get over there some time. Hey, did you ever see that English film about . . . ? And so on. They'd even joked about the way that in traffic other drivers always try to peer in the darkened windows of a car like this, always imagining there must be a celebrity inside, probably getting a blow job from some high-class whore.

Instead of just a cop who thought he was on his way to Europe.

Up ahead he saw the STOP sign where he planned to do it. He rolled smoothly to a halt, still talking and making occasional eye contact with his passenger in the mirror. Keeping him distracted with some other dumb story, he managed to stall the car when he started forward again, then restarted it with a show of difficulty, and pulled jerkily around the corner.

"There's absolutely no problem," he said. "I'm real sorry about this, it shouldn't happen. But there's no problem."

He pulled half onto the cracked sidewalk where nobody ever seemed to be this time of day; he knew the area because he'd checked it out.

"I'm going to have to get out and open the hood. It'll take two seconds. It's just a lead that disconnects—the vehicle's due for a service. I absolutely promise you won't miss your flight."

He leaned forward and down as though reaching for the hood release. In fact he was reaching for the silenced .22 that he'd clipped beneath the dash, and which was perfect for this close range. With his left hand on his door as though ready to step out, he turned in his seat and looked back at the unsuspecting cop.

"Here," he said, "you want to take a look at this?"

As though casually handing over a newspaper or magazine, he raised the gun and fired.

At the airport the long-term parking garage was fully automatic, no risk of anybody sticking their nose in things and asking questions. He found a space, got out, and slipped into the backseat alongside the corpse. In a couple of seconds he'd found the airline ticket and Kelly's wallet, which contained his FBI badge. He already had his own passport and driving permit, both collected that morning in the name of Timothy Donovan Kelly, correct in every detail except that the photograph in both cases was of Charles Mortimer Price.

He took his own suitcase out of the trunk of the car and Kelly's overnight bag. He would change into something more casual than his gray driver's uniform in one of the airport washrooms. All that remained was to lock the car and leave it—until the body in the back began to stink. But that wouldn't be for a while. The car had been rented for two weeks, so nobody would be looking for it. And cars were routinely left in the long-term lot for weeks on end. He was sure that no suspicions would be aroused until well after the time that it would take him to accomplish his mission in England.

That was before the kid brother turned up in that cottage in Oxford, coming up those stairs like a bat out of Hell. But he'd been taken care of. Everything was back on an even keel. And that was the way it was going to stay.

A murmur from behind made him glance over his shoulder. She was stirring underneath the blanket, coming around. Fine—the timing was perfect. Now all he had to do was get into the lab and take care of the computer. He needed her for that.

And he knew, when she woke up, she'd see it his way.

71

JOSH KELLY knew one thing only: that he hadn't come all this way to die before doing what he had to do.

His gut hurt like the devil, but he didn't think it could be as bad as it felt. He could feel blood caked and drying on his hands and clothes, but that was a good thing. It meant that the bleeding was slowing or had stopped, and he wasn't hemorrhaging.

He put a hand up to his forehead. That too was caked with blood and throbbing hard enough to split his skull. When the knife had gone into him, he had fallen and cracked his head on the edge of the stone path. That was what had put him out. But now he was waking up and thinking clearly. He knew where he was and why. He pressed the side of his watch and lit up the face. Just after 11:30. He couldn't have been out more than fifteen, twenty minutes at most. That was good.

Looking at the cottage, he could see lights but no signs of movement. He pulled himself some way across the lawn on his hands and knees to get a better look. The kitchen door hung open, but there was no sound.

They'd gone. And he knew where.

Very tentatively he tried putting some weight on his ankle. If he could walk, or even hobble, that would save a lot of time.

The scream of anguish brought forth by the stabbing, grueling pain should, he thought, have wakened the dead. As he lay panting where he'd fallen full length on the lawn, he told himself that this at least was useful confirmation that there was nobody around. Otherwise that killer would already have been out of the house at a run to finish him off. He had been left for dead, which gave him the advantage of surprise—if he got there soon enough to use it.

He crawled on all fours into the kitchen, wondering if he could find something to use as a crutch. He scuffled around in the dark, and managed to haul himself up high enough with the help of a chair to reach the light switch. Then he stumbled around opening various doors until he found the broom closet. He found a long-handled broom that was just about the right height.

Swinging himself forward like Long John Silver, he checked on the garage and saw there was no car in it. He had already seen from a window that Price's car was still parked out on the road. So that meant they had taken her car.

He felt in his pockets. The keys to his own rented car were still there. If Price hadn't found it and immobilized it, that was his best chance—certainly better than trying to hot-wire Price's car, which he had never done in his life, though he would probably figure it out in time if he had to.

His own car, when he reached it, was exactly as he had left it in the dark lane which hid it from the road. He eased himself into the driver's seat and pulled the broom in after him. He inserted the ignition key and turned it. The engine came immediately to life.

The good luck was that it was an automatic. A stick shift requiring two feet to drive it would have been impossible.

The bad luck was that his wrecked ankle was his right one, and driving an automatic with his left foot was no pushover.

But he'd do it. He damn well had to.

72

"LISTEN TO ME carefully. This can be simple and painless. Or complicated, and very, very painful. And you won't die or pass out unless I want you to. I'm much too good for that." A chilling smile. "I've had experience."

She felt like a child, sitting up in the backseat of her car in the shadows where he'd parked it, while he pulled on her coat and slipped her shoes back onto her feet. The blood was flowing again in her wrists and ankles now that he'd removed the nylon tights that had bound them. Her mouth was sore at one side where the gag had cut into it.

"You've got a nasty bruise coming up on the side of your neck," he said. "Luckily I brought a scarf. Here, let me put it on you . . . just so . . . there, nobody would notice a thing now. Not that we're going to run into anybody, if you're telling me the truth."

"I told you," she said, her voice flat and dry, "I can't guarantee there'll be nobody about. Everybody connected with the lab works whatever hours they choose. I'm often there myself after midnight. But we don't bother each other. Just do what we're doing, then go home."

"And no security patrol."

"Just the alarm system like I told you. And George, who's there from ten till six. But George is a caretaker more than security. He won't bother you if you're with me."

"I'm counting on you telling me the truth. Otherwise George is in for as bad a time as you are. And anybody else who gets in the way."

"Nobody will."

"Let's go."

He helped her out of the car, then made her walk on his arm while he gripped her wrist like a vise. To an observer they looked like a couple out walking late and engaged in an intimate conversation. What nobody could see was the knife he held in his other hand, placed flat along the arm that he was gripping and hidden by the sleeve of her coat.

She led him past the main entrance to the lab that was used in daylight hours, and around the corner to where the side door was concealed, known only to regular users who were provided with a code to tap into the pad. When they reached it, she felt the point of the knife press a warning to her ribs through the folds of her coat.

"Don't do anything to get me angry."

She tapped in a six-figure code. The lock gave a click, and she pushed it open. Their feet echoed dully on the concrete floor, then took on a new resonance as they reached the marble hall. The only illumination came from dim emergency lights overhead.

They were just starting up the main staircase when another set of footsteps sounded somewhere behind them. She stopped and turned. His grip tightened.

"Remember," he hissed in her ear.

A short round man in his fifties stood silhouetted in the light coming from his cubbyhole of an office. He wore some kind of uniform, but the tunic was unfastened and his tie hung loose. The soundtrack of a movie on his small black and white TV set was audible behind him.

"Good evening, George. It's me, Tessa Lambert," she called back to him.

"Oh, Dr. Lambert. Working late again?" He peered into the darkness, but didn't make a move to put on extra lights. "That's not Danny with you?"

"A colleague of mine. We're going to run a program. We won't be more than an hour."

"All right, Dr. Lambert," George replied, sounding like a man used to the eccentricities of academics and not inclined to question them. "You'll turn out the lights up there when you leave, won't you?"

"Yes, George, don't worry."

He returned to his television and closed the door. They continued on up the stairs.

"Good, Tessa. So far so good," he said softly. "Keep it up."

At the top of the stairs they started along the corridor that he remembered from his first visit. It was dark except for a shaft of light from a twelve-inch-square window in the door of one lab. As they neared it she felt his grip tighten again.

"I told you—nobody pays any attention to anybody this time of night," she said.

As they passed the lab, they both glanced in the window. Two young men were huddled over some piece of equipment at the far end of a long workbench. She knew them both by sight though not by name.

His grip relaxed, but tightened again as they turned a corner and saw a broader shaft of light. The half-open door they passed showed a room in which a gray-haired woman sat alone, hunched over the keyboard of her computer; she didn't even look up.

They reached Tessa's lab and she asked him to let go her arm so she could find her key. He did so, but stood close while she unlocked the door. The moment they were inside, he took the key from her and locked the door behind them, then rattled the handle.

"Jesus!" he said disgustedly. "This lock wouldn't stop a ten-year-old."

"We don't bother much about that kind of security here," she said coolly. "Everything of value's in the computer—and locks didn't keep you out of that, did they?"

She watched as he picked up the phone on her desk and punched in a long number. He waited a few moments, then spoke. "I'm in the lab, with her."

He glanced over at her, listening to the voice she could not hear, then continued. "Yes, she has something . . . A variation on the original program. I don't know, I don't know if she's even sure it would work . . ."

A longer pause this time. He turned his back on her, though she realized he was watching her reflection in the window and didn't move.

"Yes," she heard him say, "I think there is a real danger of that . . ."

He turned back to look at her again, a hint of amusement on his face, as though he liked what he was being told to do.

"Of course," he said. "That's what I planned on doing anyway."

He hung up. There was no smile now. "You know who that was, don't you?" he said.

She nodded slowly. "I think so."

With a flick of his finger he powered up the computer, then pointed to her chair in front of the keyboard. She moved to it and sat down. He stood behind her, looking over her shoulder.

"Now," he said, "I am going to give you a warning. I am very knowledgeable about these things, and if you lie to me, or try to deceive me in any way, I'll know at once. And you'll be very sorry. Do you understand?"

She nodded her head again.

"Then let's do it."

Twenty minutes later it was over. He was satisfied that every last trace of the program she called Paul had been wiped from the computer, erased as though it had never existed.

Tessa sat numb and pale, her hands in her lap. He was dialing that same long number on the phone. This time he spoke only three words.

"It's done . . . Yes."

73

RIGHT FOOT GAS, left foot brake. The pain from his right ankle, even when he moved it only an inch or two up and down, was excruciating. At least, he told himself, the good thing was that it kept his mind off the pain in his gut.

Back at the house the bleeding from his knife wound seemed to have stopped; but now, hunched over the steering wheel, every muscle in his body tense, it had begun again. As the country lanes from the cottage gave way to the bypass, he felt his head begin to swim dangerously, as though plucked at and given a brain-jarring spin by every set of headlights that zoomed past him in the opposite direction.

A slow-moving truck loomed up in front of him, and he pulled out to overtake it. He could see headlights coming toward him, but it was difficult to judge the distance. His rented car didn't have much acceleration, but he floored it and hoped for the best. There was room in a pinch for three lanes of traffic, but just as he swung out another set of headlights emerged from behind the oncoming car. They were low and wide and coming at him fast. They flashed blindingly for him to get out of the way. He had no choice but to pull back.

Reflex action took over, and before he knew he'd done it he'd lifted his right foot off the gas and slammed it on the brake pedal.

He screamed at the pain that shot up through his body and exploded in his head. It carried him beyond the point where pain serves as a stimulus to wakefulness, and into the region where the brain seeks oblivion. He came back to full consciousness only seconds later, but he could feel his car sliding out of control beneath him. Horns were blaring, and lights crisscrossing before his eyes like a carnival carousel. He braced himself against the crash, which by some miracle didn't come.

Suddenly he was through it all, and an open road was unrolling in his headlights. The furious flashings of the truck he had overtaken diminished in his mirror, and the angry horn blasts evaporated in the night.

The sweat was running so fast down his face that he had to wipe his eyes to see straight. He only had to hang on for another ten, fifteen minutes at the most, then he'd be there. What he'd do after that he didn't know. It depended on what he found. But he'd do something. All he had to do now was hang on to consciousness as grimly as he was clinging to the wheel of that speeding car.

His sense of not quite being there, of feeling suspended in some dreamlike limbo between the real world and fantasy, was compounded by the speed at which everything had happened. It was little more than seventy-two hours since he had said good-bye to his brother in Los Angeles. Although he was expecting Tim's promised call at some point, he didn't think twice about the fact that it hadn't come within the first twenty-four hours.

However, he'd come across another article about Tessa in a back copy of *Scientific American* and thought he'd fax it over. He'd forgotten to get a number from Tim before he left, so he called Jack Fischl to see if he had one.

Jack said he'd just spoken with Tim on the worst satellite link he'd ever heard in his life, echoes and bleeps and all kinds of stuff. He also told Josh why he'd called Tim—to inform him that one of their suspects had taken a powder. He gave Josh the hotel number, and Josh waited till around midnight, which would be 8 A.M. in Oxford, before calling it.

What Jack had said was right: that link wasn't just bad, it was weird. On top of that, there'd been something strange about Tim's voice. It was Tim's voice all right, but it was coming through the echoes and interference with a strange kind of woodenness that was more than just an effort to make himself heard and understood.

Josh wasn't sure at the time, and probably never would be, what exactly it was that prompted him to switch on his recorder and tape their conversation. Afterward he'd sent the article as promised to the hotel's fax number that Tim had given him, but while he did so he played back the tape of their conversation and listened to it more carefully. There was no question that when he'd filtered out the bleeps and echoes, at least insofar as he could in his mind, his brother sounded more like a speak-your-weight machine than himself: almost as though he was drugged, or being held prisoner somewhere and deliberately trying to communicate through the tone of his voice that all was not well.

Of course it was too farfetched and ludicrous. Josh was letting his imagination run away with him.

And yet . . .

Twenty minutes later, he finished playing and replaying the tape at different speeds. He slipped the cassette into his pocket, because the equipment he needed to confirm his growing suspicions was in the lab.

A couple of hours later, those suspicions had become fact. What he'd heard on the line was not an echo at all, but a controlled delay of varying lengths. The differences were minuscule, but measurable. No simple echo could behave that way. It reminded him of something, but it took him several minutes to recall what. Then suddenly there it was. No doubt about it.

Over a year ago he'd played around with a translator program—English into various languages, most of which he didn't speak, and then from various languages into English. It seemed pretty efficient in a literal, styleless kind of way; but the thing he'd remembered above all was a slight jerkiness in the process. Some words and phrases took marginally longer to come through in translation than others. It was only a matter of retrieval time, and it was almost subliminal; but it was arrhythmic, just like Tim's voice coming via satellite from England.

He had pondered for a while on what that could mean.

Eventually he was forced to only one possible conclusion: that what he had heard was not his brother speaking to him directly, but a recording of his brother's spoken words being used to present what somebody else was saying. That would also explain the curiously mechanical quality of the voice, which sounded as though the words had been spliced together in a different order from that in which they had originally been recorded. He figured that the noisy interference and echo effect were there simply to mask the artificiality.

So what the hell was going on?

Josh's first instinct had been to call Jack Fischl, but on a whim he'd driven over to his brother's apartment. He had a key and let himself in. Tim had said he'd found the cab company that took him to the airport in the yellow pages. The more he thought about it, there was something not quite right about that limo showing up the way it had. They'd both known it, but let it pass: not even an honest cop like Tim would be automatically suspicious of a harmless bonus like a limo showing up because the company was short of ordinary cars that afternoon.

And yet, in retrospect, it was unusual.

Tim's yellow pages was right by the phone. Josh quickly looked up the cab listings and found one marked in red. It was a local company. He picked up the phone to call them—but some sixth sense held him back as he began to dial. He hung up. If somebody was messing with international calls in the way he suspected, they could sure as hell have a tap on Tim's line. Josh knew all about illegal taps and just how easy they were to put in place.

The cab company's offices were only a few minutes' drive away. It was late, but they were a twenty-four hour service. He rang the bell, and after explaining through a grille in the door that he was the brother of an FBI agent and needed to check something out urgently, they took a chance and let him in.

It took nearly ten minutes for them to hunt through their sheets for the previous day, but eventually they told him that the booking for Mr. Kelly had been cancelled within an hour of being made. Josh thanked them and left.

His first thought when he got back to his own place had once again been to go and see Jack Fischl, get him out of bed if necessary, and tell him the whole story. But the more he thought about it, the less good the idea seemed. Getting any sort of official action under way would take time and explanations, and the involvement of other—probably senior and therefore difficult—people. He knew it hadn't been easy for Tim to get the okay to go over to England in the first place. If he started kicking up more dust now, there was the risk that the whole story of the unofficial and illegal help that he'd been giving the investigation would come out. And it was Tim's ass on the line. If by any chance Josh was mistaken about what was going on, Tim wouldn't thank him for creating an unnecessary panic.

The more he thought about it, the more he realized that the only course was to take some action himself. He had to go over there and check the situation for himself. He also realized that he was going to have to take whatever action he did take with extreme caution.

He reviewed what he knew. There was a suspect on the loose, and there was something weird with the phones. It was already known that the killer they were looking for was a computer wizard of a high order, which meant that access to flight reservations would be no problem. Josh's name on a passenger list for England could be both a warning and a provocation; which meant that his name shouldn't be on it.

Conrad Walsh was an old friend, a journalist who owed him several favors. He called them in. Walsh wasn't happy about parting with his passport, but they agreed a scenario whereby, if explanations became necessary, Josh would explain that he'd stolen it. The switching of Josh's laminated photograph for Walsh's was an easy job for anyone with access to even the simplest of laboratory equipment. Josh had often amused himself with the thought of how effective a bunch of pointy-headed college professors could be if they ever seriously took to crime. It had been a standing joke between Tim and himself. Now it was for real.

He called up the airline and got the cheapest seat available, and by three that afternoon he was in the air.

In addition to the passport, he'd borrowed one of Walsh's credit cards. Curiously, Walsh was far less worried about that than his passport: he knew he could trust Josh for the money, even if it took a few weeks. He'd practiced forging the signature on the plane before grabbing a couple of hours' troubled sleep. He'd had no trouble renting a car at Heathrow.

His first stop in Oxford had been the Randolph Hotel, but he'd been told that Mr. Kelly was out. Having caught a glimpse of himself in a mirror in the lobby, he'd gone around the corner and bought himself some shaving gear in a pharmacy, then he'd tidied himself up in a public lavatory. He'd bought a map and found the Kendall Lab, but was told that Dr. Lambert wasn't in yet.

He knew he'd have to approach her with extreme care. However unlikely it seemed to him that she could be a part of what was going on—whatever that was—he couldn't afford after the last two days to rule out any possibility. When he'd returned to the lab later, he'd heard somebody call a greeting to her across the parking lot, and he'd followed her. Their open-air conversation had made it even harder for him to believe that she was in any direct way connected with a serial killer in Los Angeles, but she sure as hell was hiding something. And the linking factor was computers. And possibly AI.

When he'd asked again about Tim Kelly at the Randolph, he'd been told that he was still out. He'd very specifically left no message, saying that it wasn't necessary to tell Mr. Kelly that anyone was looking for him. He'd taken a walk and bought the knife. When he returned to the hotel, he'd narrowly missed bumping into someone whose face he knew. It took him some minutes, watching him at the desk apparently getting a message and then scribbling a reply, to recall the driver of the limo.

He'd followed him and watched him make a call from a public phone booth. It had looked like a pretty intense conversation. After that he'd tailed him to Tessa's cottage, from there to the restaurant, and back.

And then he'd blown it. He cursed himself for his failure—the result, he told himself, of physical exhaustion and naiveté. This cloak and dagger stuff wasn't his world.

But it wasn't over yet, not by a long way. The only question, which kept beating back at him like the waves of pain that racked his body, was what was he going to do? Then the answer came—literally—out of nowhere.

He hadn't seen the flashing blue light in his mirror till the patrol car was sitting right on his tail, its siren screaming.

That was what he had to do: take them with him.

He glanced down at the dash. He was already doing 100 mph. He pressed down on the gas and squeezed another 10 mph out of the little car. The cops stayed right with him. He was already weaving from lane to lane because his concentration was shot and he was hanging on to consciousness by a thread. But he didn't want them to overtake him and force him off the road like the American cops, at least some of them, might have done. So he began swinging more wildly from one side to the other. Thank God the road was clear of oncoming traffic.

Then, up ahead, he saw more blue lights flashing in the distance. Moments later his headlights picked out two white patrol cars swung across the road to block it. No wonder there had been no traffic for the last few minutes.

Again he had no choice but to brake; but this time he remembered to use his left foot. The car went into a shuddering skid. He lifted his foot and fanned the pedal. It gave him a measure of control, but with only twenty yards to go he realized that he wasn't going to make it. He kicked down with his left foot as hard as he could and spun the car toward the side of the road.

He careened off the rear end of one of the police vehicles and felt himself come to rest at an angle in a ditch. A dense hedge, in which he'd ripped a large hole, had served to break the impact. All the same, if he hadn't been wearing his seatbelt he'd have been hurt worse than he already was.

Running feet and angry voices seemed to be coming toward him from a hundred miles away, down a long, long echoing tunnel. The next thing he knew, his door was wrenched open and he was being dragged out.

"He's hurt!" he heard somebody say. "Get the ambulance."

"No!" he heard another voice shouting, and only dimly recognized it as his own. "Listen to me . . . you've got to listen to me!"

74

HALFWAY DOWN THE DARKENED staircase she wanted to laugh out loud. She suppressed the impulse as hysterical, but he must have sensed something because he looked at her.

"What?" he said.

"I was just thinking how we must look," she said, "lord and lady of the manor, descending the great staircase arm in arm."

He broke into a grin. "Yeah, you're right. It is kind of elegant."

They went down a few more steps, then she asked him, "Where are we going now?"

"Let's talk about that when we get out of here." He spoke like a parent reassuring a child.

But once they were out of here, she knew she was going to die. The only thing she didn't know was when and where; those photographs she'd glimpsed in his hand the previous day had given her a pretty good idea of how.

She didn't intend being led like a lamb to the slaughter just to make it easier for him. She was going to try something. The only problem was what. With his grip on her wrist and that knife along her sleeve ready to puncture her ribs, her room to maneuver was limited. And of course she had no right to endanger anybody in the lab. This man was a maniac, capable of anything, and the few people here at this time of night, so far as she knew, had neither guns nor weapons of any kind—not even a single black belt between them.

She was going to have to do it before they reached the bottom of the stairs. It was the only time she'd have a chance to catch him off his balance. She'd already worked it out in theory: how, if she tripped him with her foot, swung her body just enough, made a grab for the banister, she should be able to dislodge his grip on her before he had time to use the knife. If he fell far enough he could hurt himself, maybe even incapacitate himself. At least, with any luck, she'd have time to get past him, out of the side door that they'd entered by, and be lost in the dark before he could catch her.

It had to be now. Any later would be too late. She kicked out, adrenaline giving her extra strength.

He gave a grunt of surprise, not knowing what was happening at first. His grip tightened on her wrist, but the hand holding the knife instinctively reached out, grabbing the air for support. She heard the blade clatter down the steps as her fingers curled around the banister rail. At the same time she swung her body so that his grip on her arm pitched him forward. He let go, but too late to save himself.

She didn't wait to see him crash all the way. Sliding her hands down the rail and taking the steps two at a time, she dashed past him before he even hit the marble floor. She thought briefly that she ought to stop and find the knife, but that would lose time, and she wasn't even sure that she'd know how to use it if she had to. She thought, too, that maybe she should kick him in the head and try to knock him out, but by then she was past him.

Glancing over her shoulder as she ran, she saw that he was already pushing himself painfully to his knees. If he was hurt, he wasn't badly hurt. Behind him she saw another shaft of light as George stepped out of his cubbyhole, alerted by the noise.

"What the—?" was all he managed to say before she shouted at the top of her lungs.

"Look out, George—he's got a knife!"

She was about halfway between Price and the door. He was still on his knees when she looked back again, but she saw him reach for something that glinted as he picked it up.

The next thing she knew—her heart pounding—she was struggling with the latch on the door. It should have opened easily from the inside, but for some reason—her hands were shaking, she'd pressed the wrong catch in her panic, whatever—she couldn't make it work.

As she struggled with it, she glanced back again. He was on his feet now and coming after her, limping slightly, but his silhouette growing rapidly larger against the soft spread of light behind him. She could see George still standing there, dumbfounded, doing nothing.

Then the noise started. It was the most dreadful thing she'd ever heard, a roaring, screaming, banshee wail of fury: a sound it was hard to imagine coming from anything human—which perhaps he wasn't. A sound that distilled and congealed into the words that it was forming only after it had pierced her skull and invaded her brain.

"Youfuckingbitch-youfuckingbitch-youfuckingbitch-youfuckingbitch-youfuckingbitch—!"

Her fingers scrabbled desperately at the latch. She'd used it in the past at least a thousand times; and now, tonight—insanely—it was stuck.

"Youfuckingbitch-youfuckingbitch-youfuckingbitch—!"

Louder, closer. She could hear his feet. Then suddenly, at last, she realized that the little lever on the side that should be up, was down. She pushed it and yanked the door open, flinging herself into the night only a few yards ahead of her pursuer.

She slipped and stumbled on wet grass, but didn't fall.

"Youfuckingbitch-youfuckingbitch—!"

She could feel his breath on her neck now. Or she imagined it. She daren't look back. If only she could reach the corner of the building, she might have a chance to make it to the road and stop some passing car. If there was a passing car. The area was horribly quiet this time of night.

Lungs bursting, she forced herself on, faster than she knew she could run, the howled obscenities following her as though his lips were screaming in her ear.

She grabbed at the rough edge of stone to pivot herself around the corner, and ran on, stumbling once again, into the main parking area. There were a couple of cars in shadow, but no signs of life.

Something touched her back. She screamed, but the sound was lost in the obscene noise that he was making. She pushed herself on, but something touched her on the back again.

Then, out of nowhere, the roar of vehicles and blinding lights. Two, three, maybe four sets of headlights swung off the road one after the other and drew out to form a wall of dazzling brilliance in front of her.

She stopped, helpless and in shock. Her first thought was she was trapped, and that it would all be over in moments, a knife plunged into her as many times as it took to sate the insane rage of her killer.

But nothing happened. She heard voices, shouting, doors slamming, movement. Figures materialized from behind the lights, running not toward her but to her left. She looked. The man who'd tried to kill her, the man whose name she knew was Price, was disappearing into the dark, and the other men were going after him.

She didn't move, didn't know what to do, what was happening. She knew only that she was half-unconscious from fear and exhaustion. Parts of her body that she had been unaware of until now began to hurt. She looked down, mystified, at her hand, and saw that it was scraped raw and bleeding. Then she remembered, only seconds before, the feeling of rough stone on the corner of the building. It seemed all so unreal now. So far away.

Her head spun and she had the impression she was falling. Somebody caught her. She knew it wasn't him, because she'd seen him running off into the night.

It was over now . . . over.

Unseen arms picked her up as she lost consciousness, and carried her toward the light.

75

WHEN SHE CAME TO, the police sergeant said she'd only been out for five minutes at the most. Strangely, she felt refreshed and energized, as though waking from a deep reviving sleep of several hours. There was no feeling of "Where am I, what happened?" She remembered perfectly.

She was in the back of a police car, with both doors open. Someone had put a bandage on her hand. She could hear the chatter of police radios and became aware of revolving blue lights mixed in with the harsh white that still lit up the building.

"Did they get him?" she asked.

"We don't know yet," the sergeant said. "At least you're all right."

"I hope they get him."

"I'm sure they will."

She looked to her left where she saw some movement. There was an ambulance, and a man being helped from the back of a white police patrol car to a stretcher. She recognized him.

"Josh!"

"Wait a minute, miss, you can't—"

Ø1111ØØ1Ø11Ø1111Ø111Ø1Ø1ØØ1ØØØØØ

But she was already out of the car and running to the injured man.

"Josh, you're alive! Oh, thank God! Thank God you're alive!" She wanted to throw her arms around him, but saw his face was pale and drawn with pain.

"You too," he managed to say.

Somebody pushed her gently aside. "'Scuse me, miss, give us a bit of room."

Josh was lowered onto the stretcher and covered by a blanket.

"I'm coming with him," she said as they lifted him into the ambulance.

"Now wait a minute, I don't know if you're—"

The sergeant was there now. "Sorry, miss, you'll have to stay here."

"Let her come," Josh said weakly. "Let her come—please."

The sergeant looked unsure. "I don't know. Wait a minute."

He held up a hand to reassure the ambulance attendants that this wouldn't take long, then ran over to where a man in plain clothes and wearing a raincoat was giving orders to a group of uniformed men. The sergeant spoke to him, and the man looked in her direction, then nodded. The sergeant came back.

"The inspector says you can give a statement later. Don't leave the hospital."

"Have they got him yet?" she asked.

The sergeant shook his head. "Not yet."

She climbed in alongside Josh's stretcher, and the doors of the ambulance shut with a solid, insulated thump. A paramedic in white uniform bent over him, pulling back the blanket to examine him.

"Which side's the wound?"

"Left," Josh said with an effort as they drove off.

"That's good . . . easy now . . . no further bleeding . . . relax."

He began prodding delicately around the wound, examining, she supposed, for signs of swelling from internal hemorrhage.

"I told them everything they need to know," Josh said to her, forming every word painfully.

"Don't talk, just lie still," the paramedic ordered.

"I have to . . . have to talk."

The paramedic didn't argue. He seemed satisfied with his examination and began preparing a syringe.

"They've still got a lot of questions . . ." Josh said. "So have I."

Tessa dropped her eyes and lowered her head. There was no point in holding back now, certainly not with Josh. The awful thing was that talking about it made her feel like she was making a confession. A dreadful sense of guilt and culpability weighed on her oppressively.

"It was an AI program," she whispered. "It got out, because of Price. And somehow took control of him."

Josh closed his eyes. "Christ."

She saw the paramedic glance her way, but he didn't speak. They felt the soft-sprung ambulance slow, then turn and surge forward again, its engine far off and silk-smooth.

"There was nothing I could do," she said. "Even if we pulled every plug in the world, it would still be hiding somewhere, waiting for the power to come back on."

He looked up at her. "But you were working on something, weren't you? That's why you were so secretive."

She nodded. "That was the program Price had been sent to destroy."

"And—?" He winced as the needle went into his arm.

"Ironically enough," she said, "it was something he'd said yesterday, when I thought he was your brother, that made me do it . . ." She looked down at her hand, absently rubbing the bandage.

"What . . . made you do what?"

She looked at him again, about to speak, but saw his eyes were closed.

"It's just a sedative," the paramedic said. "It's best he sleep."

Through the darkened glass she could see the blue light on the ambulance roof reflecting off the buildings and their windows. There was no siren.

Josh's hand lay on the blanket. She reached out hesitantly, as though afraid to wake him, and took it in hers.

76

SIR ANDREW MAUDSLEY had speculated often on the likely circumstances of his death. He didn't regard the habit as a morbid one; on the contrary, at the age of seventy-eight, albeit in the best of health, he regarded it as the act of a prudent man to face up to the inevitable. A philosopher might have gone about the exercise more intellectually; a creative artist might have attempted some composition on the mystery of final things; but Sir Andrew, a retired High Court judge, a "simple lawyer" as he liked to call himself, merely tried to imagine the actual event whenever he had a few moments and nothing else to do.

Tonight, however, he was thinking only about the excellent dinner that he'd enjoyed in St Catherine's College, followed by the long, late conversation around the Senior Common Room fireplace with his host, Michael Gearin-Tosh, the English don, and a handful of similarly convivial spirits. Michael had wanted to call him a taxi for the short journey back to Magdalen College, where he was an Honorary Fellowstaying for a few days, but he had preferred to walk. It was a clear, dry night, and he had with him a small flashlight and a key to the Fellows' Garden which allowed him to step straight from the grounds of St Catherine's and on to Addison's Walk, the quiet tree-lined path along the river that was part of Magdalen. Pulling on his long tweed overcoat, and perching his soft felt hat at a jaunty angle on his head, he looked forward to the brisk ten or fifteen minutes' exercise which would help him sleep.

When he heard footsteps other than his own, he wasn't remotely alarmed. Some academic nightbird, he'd assumed, taking the same route home, or perhaps going in the opposite direction. Once, after midnight, he'd even passed a junior lecturer out jogging. He pointed his flashlight up a little to see if the footsteps belonged to anyone he knew, and found a young man, relatively young at any rate, standing in his way. The man's hair fell across his face, and he was breathing hard as though he had been running. And he was carrying a knife.

"Put out that light," the man said. He was American.

"I have no intention of doing anything of the kind," Sir Andrew replied, knowing full well that there was no question of his having a choice. A hand lashed out and the flashlight was knocked to the ground, its beam extinguished.

"Now," said the voice in the darkness, "take off that coat. I think I'll have the hat as well."

Sir Andrew felt himself become very calm. In his imaginings he'd never conjured up a scene like this. But then, of course, the odds against foreseeing precisely how it would happen must be incalculable. The important thing was knowing that it would happen, sometime, and being ready to face it when it did.

"You can go to hell, young man," he said quietly.

The next few moments were confused. He felt a blow to his face. He was knocked down and kicked, and he felt his hat and coat being taken. Then a strange sensation, as though something had reached into his heart and released a warmth that rapidly suffused his whole being. After that he had the impression of falling again, turning, rolling, bumping, but without any pain—like days he remembered from his childhood, playing on the hill behind the farm, seeing who could go farther, faster, longer. And laughing. Always laughing.

He wasn't even sure if this was death at all. The longer it went on, it felt like something else entirely . . .

• • •

01101111001000000111011101110010

Price hurried over Magdalen Bridge. The disguise afforded by the old man's hat and coat was reassuring. There was an outside risk, so distinctive were the cut and quality of the tweed, that somebody might take him for the old man himself and approach him; but that was something he would deal with when and if it happened. For now all he wanted was to get to where, according to the map he'd memorized, there ought to be a couple of public phone booths tucked away in a blind alley called Cowley Place.

Twice in the space of not more than a hundred yards, police cars passed at speed, once in each direction. There was obviously a big hunt on. He forced himself to add decades to his age with stooped shoulders and a ponderous step; but underneath the brim of the elegant felt hat he was perspiring. He was sure there was no way anybody was going to find the old man's body before morning, not even if he was missed and somebody went looking for him. And morning was many hours away yet. A lot could happen by then. But first he had to find a phone.

Suddenly there it was—COWLEY PLACE marked clearly on the stone wall to his right. And a few steps beyond that, two phone booths back to back.

He waited the usual few moments for the connection to be made, then heard, once more: "I am listening."

As quickly and comprehensively as he could, he filled in the details of what had happened. The program, he said, was destroyed, but not the woman. And there was no doubt in his mind that she posed a threat. She had indicated, he said, that it might take some time before she had another copy of the program ready, but it was clear that, given time, she would have one. In all honesty, he couldn't be absolutely sure that she hadn't lied to him and didn't have another copy hidden away somewhere, secure and ready to go immediately.

There was a silence, as though for reflection. Then a verdict. "This is unsatisfactory. I am obliged to adopt the other course I have prepared. I shall now explain what you will do . . ."

77

SARAH METCALFE didn't want to hear too many technical details. They baffled her, and they would certainly be beyond the majority of her viewers. What she wanted, as she had explained to Walter Chapman at their first meeting, was a *sense* of the place: the thrill of harnessing an unimaginably dangerous power and forcing it to serve the daily needs of humankind. It was, she felt, a sort of metaphor for the millennium. There was also, she felt, a sexual side to the comparison; but she wasn't going to play that up unduly for the small screen.

Normally by two in the morning Walter Chapman would have been at home in bed twenty miles away. However, in preparation for what he supposed would be a long and tiring night, he had managed to nap for a couple of hours in the afternoon. He had the impression, from the sly way they looked at each other when they thought nobody was watching, that Sarah Metcalfe and Roger Dean had been doing something similar.

Everything so far had been going fine. Sarah was shooting a series of short, spontaneous interviews, walking around with camera and sound following, stopping to speak to anyone she chose. Without exception, all the staff had appeared relaxed and utterly professional. The impression being conveyed was one of reassuring competence: nuclear technology with a human face. Walter Chapman felt that he had earned his salary.

They had just moved into the main control room and Sarah was talking to one of the duty officers when Chapman noticed the first sign of trouble. Nick Tate and Bob Fulton, who would also normally have been at home but tonight felt they should be on show, suddenly huddled in a corner. Nick Tate typed something into a computer keyboard, then stared at the screen while Bob Fulton peered over his shoulder. It was hard to read their reaction to what they saw. Neither said anything. Tate just typed something else into the computer, and both stared once again at the screen, transfixed and without comment.

Chapman strolled as casually as he could across the floor to join the pair. By the time he reached them, Bob Fulton had taken over and was typing something in. Once again they both stared at the result in barely disguised disbelief.

"What is it?" Chapman asked under his breath.

"Something's got in," Tate said. It was the first time Chapman had heard him give a straight answer to a straight question in all the months he had known him.

"What d'you mean, 'something'? A virus?"

"Maybe."

"But how? I thought the whole point of this computer was that it's isolated, isn't it?"

"Trust me, Walter, it's happened," Nick Tate said, not taking his eyes off the screen. "Just get that camera team the fuck out of here—fast."

The ringing woke them both, but when Christopher realized which line it was, he fell back gratefully onto his pillow. Jonathan Syme's private line was automatically put through to Christopher's apartment whenever he stayed the night there.

"Jonathan Syme?"

"Yes."

"You are about to be required in Downing Street on a level nine green alert. The password is 'Antigone.'"

Jonathan swung his feet to the floor and sat forward. "Who is this?"

"That will be explained in due course."

The voice, he realized, was a recording like the one that read out your desired number when you called directory inquiries. But it had just quoted him the correct security code for that week, along with the password, which was changed daily, so it appeared to be authentic. Obviously some new drive to mechanize communications.

"There is a call coming through at this time. You will be connected in eight-point-five seconds. When the call is complete, stay on the line for further information."

Thirteen minutes later Jonathan was dressed and on his way downstairs to find the car he had been told would be there to take him to Whitehall.

"What d'you mean we have to leave? Is there some kind of danger?"

Sarah Metcalfe directed the question at a white-faced Walter Chapman even though he had addressed himself to Roger.

"A routine security precaution," Chapman said, speaking to both of them now. "There has been a technical malfunction, which means that all non-essential staff must vacate central areas."

"We're not staff, Walter, we're official guests," Roger reminded him. "And if we can show how efficiently you people deal with a 'minor technical malfunction,' I'm sure the public will be greatly reassured about what you're doing here."

"I'm sorry, the rules are clear, and it's absolutely beyond my authority to modify them."

"Tell us the truth," Sarah said. "It's something serious, isn't it?"

"I'm really not competent to pronounce on—"

"You look terrible, Walter," Sarah interrupted. "You should see yourself."

Beads of sweat were breaking out on the older man's forehead, even though the air conditioning was running at its usual comfortable level.

"Walter, if there's something we should know about . . ." Roger said, starting to look worried himself now.

"We can't stay here. Please, I'm serious." He began steering them both out, none too tactfully for somebody with his years of experience of stroking media egos.

"Walter, what *is* this?" Sarah protested, snatching her elbow from his grip.

"We're going to a safe shelter and as soon as we're there—"

"Safe shelter?" she echoed, incredulous. "And how long are we expected to spend in a lead box, Walter?"

"Please turn off that camera."

"Walter, is something going to blow?" Roger was beginning to look as pale as Walter Chapman.

"I told you, it's just a precaution . . ."

Sarah folded her arms. "In that case I'm staying. We're all staying, and we're going to do the job we've come here to do."

"Sarah, maybe Walter has a point," Roger suggested, a querulous edge entering his voice.

"Let him go to the shelter. I'm staying here."

"What if I want to go? What if Joe or Greg wants to go?"

Roger pointed to the cameraman and sound man as he spoke. But Sarah's eyes stayed on him. She was seeing something that she hadn't expected to see, something that startled her and that she didn't altogether like.

"As far as I'm concerned," she said, still not taking her eyes off Roger, "you can all do exactly what you want to do. I can handle the camera, I can handle sound. And I think I can produce. So . . ." She looked at the cameraman. "Joe?"

He shook his head. She turned to the sound man.

"Greg?"

He too shook his head. She turned back to Roger. "Well, looks like it's up to you now. We're staying."

"Well of course I'm going to stay," he stammered. "I was only saying . . ."

He hadn't noticed Chapman making a signal to somebody, nor had he heard that somebody picking up a phone and saying, "Get security here right away." Nor did he see a man and a woman together trying to open the main door of the control room by which they had entered earlier, and apparently not understanding why the cards they carried and the codes they tapped in no longer worked.

But Chapman had noticed. He crossed over quickly and spoke to the couple at the door. Sarah followed him with her gaze, and watched an exchange of anguished words and gestures bordering on panic. She signaled to Joe to get the shot.

He hefted his camera onto his shoulder and started shooting. Nobody paid him any attention. Everybody in the room seemed to be hunched over some piece of equipment or readout that appeared to be defying comprehension. Even the phones—a couple of people were trying one after another, picking them up and slamming them down—were evidently out.

Chapman started back toward them, passing a hand across his forehead. There was a strange, vacant look in his eyes. Sarah glanced left to ensure that Greg was ready with his sound recording equipment. He was.

"What is it, Walter?" she said, realizing that she had made an effort to keep her voice firm and professionally steady.

It took him a few moments to focus on the question, and even then he didn't reply directly to her, just spoke vaguely to some point in the air, as though talking to himself.

"I don't know," Chapman said eventually. "Nobody seems to know. The phones are off, and apparently every main door in the building is locked. Nobody can get in or out."

78

TESSA WAS SITTING on a plastic chair by the double swing doors marked EMERGENCY. She didn't know whether the uniformed officer who stood against the wall opposite her was there to make sure she didn't go anywhere, or to protect her from the man they hadn't caught yet. Probably both. It didn't matter. Her thoughts were elsewhere.

She didn't look up at the clatter of feet on the hard rubber tiles of the corridor floor, not until they surfaced out of the general background noise in any hospital this time of night and stopped right by her.

"Tessa! What happened?"

It was Helen, hair awry, wearing jeans and a sweater under an old parka, looking as though she hadn't paused for breath between leaping out of bed and getting here.

Before she knew it, Tessa was on her feet and in her arms, sobbing on her shoulder.

The police officer had taken half a step forward, as though unsure whether this contact was in order or not.

"I'm her doctor," Helen snapped, seeing him. He stepped back.

Helen held Tessa at arm's length and looked at her.

"Are you all right?"

"Yes. How did you know I was here?"

"A friend of mine in admissions called me. I wasn't taking any chances, not after Berlin. Who attacked you?"

"It's a long story . . ."

"What about the man you came in with?"

"He has a knife wound, he's in surgery. I'm waiting to hear . . ."

"Who is he?"

"Josh Kelly, he's American . . . They might have got his name down as Walsh . . . I don't know."

Helen was examining the bandage on Tessa's hand. "Is this all you have?"

"Yes—plus a few sprains and bruises."

"I'll see what I can find out about Walsh or Kelly or whatever. Wait here—all right?" Hands on shoulders, she lowered Tessa back to her plastic chair. "Don't move, I'll be back."

Jonathan Syme entered 10 Downing Street by the secret entrance from the basement of the Treasury. It was the first time he had used it, though he had long known of its existence as the means by which visitors could enter and leave the Prime Minister's official residence without alerting the ever vigilant media.

Jeffrey Pennycate, the PM's private secretary, was waiting for him off the hall of Number 10 when he emerged. Dapper as ever, despite being hauled out of bed with no time even to shave, Pennycate ushered Jonathan briskly along the corridor, saying that the Prime Minister was awaiting him in his study.

Passing the cabinet room, Jonathan was surprised to see, through the half-open door, a handful of senior cabinet ministers, including the Home Secretary, Foreign Secretary, and Defence Minister, huddled in a group like schoolboys telling dirty jokes, except that nobody was laughing. As Jonathan hurried past they looked up expectantly, obviously having been sent for but still awaiting any explanation why.

The PM offered a limp handshake when Jonathan entered. They had met on numerous occasions and got along on the whole very well. Jonathan found him to be a civilized and thoughtful man, who suffered the fate of all such men in high office—that of being commonly depicted as indecisive. His poll ratings were low, his majority thin, and the grass roots of his party didn't trust him. In the three years he had been in the job, his hair had gone from light brown with a few streaks of gray to pure white. Nonetheless, Jonathan had never seen him look more worried than he did tonight. The two men shook hands.

"I'm going to cut straight to the chase on this thing," the PM said.

Pennycate withdrew to one side, where he prepared to make notes, even though, to Syme's knowledge, every word spoken in this room was automatically recorded.

"Just over an hour ago," the PM continued, "I was woken by a call. It had come through on my direct line and bypassed the switchboard. Nobody knows how." He sipped his coffee. "I found myself listening to a voice, an unusual voice, somewhat distorted."

"Like a recording?" Jonathan offered.

The PM looked at him. "Yes. Like a recording. I see we're both talking about the same thing. This voice said that I should find out what was happening at the nuclear reactor at Brinkley Sands, and then I should wait to hear from it again. Before I'd even hung up, my internal line rang. It was the night office to say that there was a problem at Brinkley Sands. Is any of this familiar to you?"

"I was told, I believe by the same voice," replied Jonathan, "to expect a call from you."

"The name of a certain Dr. Tessa Lambert was mentioned to me," the PM went on. "Whoever was speaking to me said that this name would mean something to you. Does it?"

"Yes, it does." He explained who Tessa was and his connection with her.

The PM listened, nodding occasionally. "I don't know how the pieces in all this fit together," he said eventually. "All I know is that the situation at Brinkley Sands is critical. I have the best possible advice—Peter Fraser is next door in the office staying abreast of developments." Lord Fraser of Clayton-le-Woods was the PM's chief scientific adviser. "So far as I can make out, it's all some big computer problem. What was supposed to have been an isolated computer controlling the core of the reactor has mysteriously come under the control of some person or persons on the outside. I am assuming that we are dealing with some kind of terrorist group. But as to who is behind it . . . Can you enlighten me?"

Jonathan took a deep breath, looked down at his hands, then met the Prime Minister's gaze directly. "I can only tell you," he said, "what I was told. I have to say that it makes a certain amount of sense to me. I imagine that's why I was chosen to deliver the message."

"Switch off that camera!"

Walter Chapman had just realized, through the miasma of his panic, that the camera was turning and every spoken word was being taped. He lunged forward, but Joe sidestepped, dipping his camera to catch Chapman's undignified stumble to his knees.

"Walter, leave it!" Sarah put out a hand to help him to his feet. "If we're going to have a fight about this, we'll have it later. For now Joe and Greg are going to continue doing their jobs." She didn't say it, but she was impressed by the way the two of them were handling the situation. If they felt any panic, they weren't showing it. Only Roger was looking progressively unwell.

"Listen, Walter," she said, dusting off the front of his jacket, "if you can't tell me what's going on, I'm going to ask Nick Tate and Bob Fulton over there."

"No!" He grabbed her arm. "You can't go near them—please!"

The two men she referred to were now huddled at the center of the main control console. They both wore headphones and were making constant small adjustments to the equipment in front of them in response to what they were hearing.

"It's all on a knife edge. If they don't follow what they're being told, this whole thing will just go. It might take a few hours, but we're all locked in here . . . and anyway, the fallout would devastate half Europe."

Sarah turned to face him, pulling free of his grip. "All right, tell me—" she made sure she got Greg's nod that he was okay on sound before continuing, "tell me exactly where we are."

Chapman pulled the silk handkerchief from his breast pocket and began dabbing at his face as he spoke.

"The computer that controls the reactor core is, in principle, totally cut off from the outside world. All the same, something has got into it somehow."

"Something?"

"A hacker, they think—they don't know anything for sure."

"How could anybody get into an isolated computer?"

"One of the programmers' PCs has a line from another part of the building. Actually it's a Portakabin on the site. It's a temporary arrangement. But the PC has a built-in modem which they've been using for e-mail. That's apparently how it got in."

"But surely they can switch to manual control."

"It seems that if they did they'd start a chain reaction that they couldn't stop."

"How can this be happening? I thought there were safeguards against every possible threat." This came from Roger, like a small boy confused and on the verge of tears.

Chapman looked at him and shook his head with something between pity and resignation. "There's no safeguard against every possible threat—only against the ones you can think of."

Roger stared at him. His bottom lip quivered.

"Oh, Christ!" Sarah thought.

"I've got to get out of here . . ." Roger was saying, his fingertips clawing his throat. "I can't stand being locked in. I'm starting to hyperventilate . . . don't touch me!"

In fact Sarah had only reached out to him, but he pulled away before they made contact, backing into a corner. There he proceeded to slide down the wall until he sat on the floor, hugging himself and shaking.

"Get the fucking camera off him!" Sarah snapped. "He's not the story, for Christ's sake!"

"This is unthinkable."

The Prime Minister's words, Jonathan knew, came from a sense of genuine moral outrage. What he was being asked to do was sanction a murder. The order would go out from his office and down through the hierarchy to the point at which it would take place. There was no escaping responsibility.

"Don't you think perhaps we should call in the Home Secretary?" Jonathan ventured, thinking of the anxious faces he had glimpsed waiting in the cabinet room.

After a moment the PM shook his head. "No, this is my responsibility. I can't pass the buck to anybody else. If this appalling concession doesn't work, we're all as good as dead anyway. And if it does, I shall resign in the morning—on grounds of health."

He looked over at Pennycate to make sure that the commitment was noted. Pennycate lowered his head a fraction in acknowledgment.

79

THE MAJOR HAD BEEN briefed to ask no questions and accept no arguments. As he peered out of the clattering helicopter, he could see the lights of the M40 below and the outskirts of Oxford in the distance. They began to descend toward an area of pitch blackness.

On the ground two cars were waiting on the road by the field in which they had landed. By the time the major was behind the wheel of the second one, a dark green Jaguar, the helicopter had already disappeared once more into the night.

The other car led the way, the major followed. Once he was within the city limits he would be fine, but until that point he needed a guide.

The two uniformed constables in the patrol car spotted him on Longwall Street. There was something about the hasty walk and the long loose coat that didn't look quite right. They exchanged a glance, and pulled over. Constable Brian Neil rolled down his curbside window.

"Excuse me, sir . . ."

The man slowed, turning toward him.

"Yeah?"

"Would you mind telling me where you've just come from?"

"Where I've come from? I'm just taking a walk."

"You're American, aren't you, sir?"

Constable Neil was already out of the car. The driver, Constable Eric Williams, was speaking hurriedly into his radio. Then he too got out, and the two of them began closing in on each side of the American. A hand whipped out from beneath the American's coat. It held a knife.

"Don't come any closer. I know how to use this. Back off, get into your car, and drive."

Something about the steeliness of his eyes, the hard edge in his voice, the sheer cold confidence with which he stood waiting for them, made them hesitate to push their luck before backup arrived.

"Listen to me," Constable Neil said, "we have no orders to arrest you. We just want you to come with us. Somebody wants to talk to you. Our orders were simply to find you."

The American looked suspiciously from one to the other.

"Who wants to talk to me?"

"I don't know that. Our orders are simply to find you and take you to a certain location."

"Where?"

"We'll be told that when we call in to say we've picked you up."

The roar of a car coming down Longwall Street made the American look to his left. It stopped with a squeal of brakes; two more young officers got out, along with a plainclothesman. They began closing in on the American's left. The first two began edging around to his right. He saw it was going to be hard to fight his way out of this.

"All right," he said, lowering the knife a fraction, letting them see that he was relaxing, but not totally, "I'll go in that car," pointing to his right, "with one driver, nobody else. All right?"

The officers looked at one another uncertainly.

"All right," the man in plain clothes said. "I'll drive."

"It's all right, sir, I'll take him." It was Constable Williams, the original driver of the car, who had spoken.

"You heard me, Constable," said the man in plain clothes, and started for the car.

The American gestured for Williams and Neil to back off.

They obeyed. He walked to the car, opened the rear door, and got in. He rested his arm on the back of the seat in front of him, the point of his knife at the driver's jugular. The only sound was static crisscrossing distant voices coming from the radio.

"Listen to me, hero," he said, "if you even think about doing anything tricky, I'm going to turn you into a blood fountain with one twist of my wrist. Got it?"

"Got it."

"Let's go."

The driver made no move to start the car. Through the window Price could see the other officers stopping other vehicles to keep the road clear, and turning back a couple of pedestrians as they approached to find out what was going on.

"I have to formally ask you to identify yourself," the man in plain clothes said. "Those are my instructions. Are you Charles Mortimer Price, otherwise known as FBI Special Agent Timothy Kelly?"

"Yes."

The man turned the ignition and started the car, but instead of driving off he reached for the radio. "I have Mr. Price a.k.a. Kelly with me now," he said.

A voice replied in the soft, rounded Oxfordshire tones that Price had grown used to in the past three days. "Head out on the Botley Road, then call in for further instructions."

The driver acknowledged the instruction, made a U-turn, then an illegal right against a red traffic light, and west up the near-deserted High Street.

Moments later the radio crackled into life again. The same Oxfordshire voice said, "There's a call for Mr. Price which I have orders to patch through. Put him on, would you, Inspector?"

The man driving the car held up the radio mike, knowing that his passenger had heard the message. With his free hand Price reached for the mike.

"This is Chuck Price."

"One moment, please, Mr. Price."

There was a fresh burst of static from the speaker in the dash, then a ripple of whistles and bleeps as distant connections were made. The sound was by now as familiar to Price as the voice that emerged moments later, the flat tones of its humanly recorded words being juggled and arranged to convey meanings which no human had ever intended that they should.

"Are we connected?"

"I'm here."

"The number, please."

Price smiled, and reeled off the phony credit number he'd been given to reserve the car in which he'd picked up Kelly in Los Angeles. It was an extra little code they had agreed to ensure that all was well.

"Then," said the voice from the dash, apparently satisfied, "let us complete the task we have begun."

"YOU'RE LUCKY. It only took a local anesthetic and some stitches. In a day or two you'll be as good as new."

Josh Kelly tried hard to focus on the woman who had spoken to him. He saw a face he didn't know.

"This is Helen. My friend. She's a doctor."

He turned the other way and saw Tessa.

"Did they get him yet?" he asked.

"Not as far as I know."

"Christ." The oath came from exhaustion and frustrated anger. "At least you're all right," he said.

As though it was the most natural thing in the world, Tessa took his hand and held it tight, as she had done in the ambulance. As though it was equally the most natural thing in the world, he returned the pressure, and didn't take his eyes off hers.

"Well," Helen said after a moment, feeling like the third person turning a company into a crowd, "perhaps I'll be leaving you and getting home . . ."

She reached down for her bag that she had pushed somewhere under the bed.

"Don't go, Helen." Tessa spoke to her, but didn't take her eyes off Josh. "Helen knows all about it," she said to him.

"Everything. She and her husband are the only ones who knew from the start."

Josh looked back at Helen. "I guess that's one more bit of proof that I'm not crazy," he said with a weak smile. He tried to push himself up on an elbow, but gave a gasp of pain.

"Easy now . . ." Helen put a hand on his shoulder and eased him gently back. "You're going to be a little delicate in the lower abdomen for a while."

He took a few moments to get his breath back. "Boy, you're right. That hurt." Then he turned again to Tessa. "You were talking in the ambulance before I passed out . . . about what you'd done because of something Price had said?" He phrased the question as though he wasn't sure whether he remembered the conversation or whether he'd dreamed it. "Isn't that what you said?"

"It was when I still thought he was your brother. He told me that the people I work for—directly or indirectly, it's all government-controlled finance—suspected me of planning to sell my research overseas. I wasn't planning anything of the kind—it was the program making it look that way, wanting them to come in and close down my work. They'd have locked off the computer, but it could have taken them weeks to figure out what I'd actually been doing. That would have bought the program some time while it worked out some other way to get at me—Price again, I suppose, or somebody like him."

She looked down at the slim, well-formed hand that she was still holding in both of hers. "I realized that if that happened, I'd never get the program I was working on out there, never get a chance to find out if it did what I was hoping it would do."

She looked into his eyes again. "So I made a contingency plan. I spent half of yesterday rigging the computer so that if anyone got into it and didn't use a second password that I'd inserted, the whole program would be copied out through a modem without the intruder knowing what had happened. At least not for some time." She paused, shook her head slightly. "I was terrified Price would spot it, but he didn't. He just did exactly what I'd hoped. He thought he was wiping the program—and he was. But at the same time he was sending it out on the network."

Josh looked up at her with admiration, but with a question in his eyes.

"But why didn't you just put the program out yourself—right then, yesterday?"

"Because it wasn't ready. I thought I needed two more days to be sure—at least, as sure as I could be. Now I don't know if it'll work at all. Or, if it does, how long it might take. Or anything."

He took a moment to absorb this. "But at least," he said, as though wanting to believe, "it's out there, not destroyed."

"It went out there. But there's no way of knowing where."

A few minutes later Helen and Tessa walked out into the corridor, leaving Josh in a half-drugged doze.

"How are you bearing up?" Helen asked her.

"I could use a few hours' sleep."

"I'm putting you straight to bed at our house. And if they didn't insist on keeping that divine young man in overnight, I'd say take him with you—doctor's orders."

Tessa smiled weakly and was about to say something, when she saw a man of medium height in his mid-forties, with a neat moustache and crinkly slicked-back hair, talking to the police officer who still stood by her plastic chair. The newcomer turned the moment he sensed their approach. Something about the way he moved hinted at greater physical strength than his trim build and well-cut suit suggested. There was an unmistakably military element in his bearing.

"Dr. Lambert?"

"Yes."

"I'm John Franklin. We've never met, but I'm a colleague of Jonathan Syme."

"Oh."

The mention of Syme's name stirred an ambivalent response in her. The major smiled, as though understanding how she felt.

"Mr. Syme heard about what happened. He was very relieved to learn that you're all right. May I say also, so was I."

"Thank you," she said, feeling she should say something, but wanting only to get away. She felt Helen's arm slip through hers.

"I'm Dr. Lambert's personal physician, and I'm taking her home. She needs to rest."

"I'm sure she does, but I'm afraid that isn't going to be possible just yet." Franklin shared a smile of sympathy and apparently genuine regret with both of them. "I have orders to take Dr. Lambert with me for a meeting not far from here . . ."

"Can't it wait till the morning? For heaven's sake, after all she's been through."

"I'm awfully sorry, but I'm afraid there are certain factors involved in this case . . ."

"It's all right," Tessa interrupted, giving her friend's arm a little squeeze of reassurance as she disengaged herself from her, "the sooner we get on with it, the sooner it'll all be over."

Then she turned to Franklin. "But I was told to wait here to give a statement to the police."

"There won't be any need for that," the major said, and the way the police officer hovered respectfully in the background made it clear that the newcomer was completely in charge of things now.

"I have a car outside. If you'd come with me, Dr. Lambert . . ."

81

WHEN THE PRIME MINISTER had briefed his senior cabinet colleagues on the full gravity of the situation, the first response of most of them was that they should go at once to the complex of shelters in Berkshire, where an underground center of government had been created in case of nuclear attack.

As the PM pointed out, however, this was not an attack in the conventional sense: the worst-case scenario at Brinkley Sands was probably going to be a meltdown and a massive release of radioactive material into the atmosphere. Millions would die, but slowly; a Hiroshima-type explosion and a mushroom cloud were not anticipated. This was not, in any broadly accepted definition of the term, war.

"Besides," said the PM, "we must at all costs avoid the kind of wholesale panic that the sight of the government scuttling for the shelters would engender. There'd be no way we could keep it a secret."

"How can we keep the situation a secret anyway?" the Home Secretary wanted to know. "For one thing, there's a television news team in there at this moment."

"They're recording, not broadcasting direct. They can be dealt with later."

"How the blazes did this happen? That's what I want to

know. That's what everybody is going to want to know." The Defence Secretary slapped the flat of his hand on the cabinet table around which they were all gathered. There was, however, no sense of this being a meeting with any of the customary formalities. It was simply a collection of very frightened men and women in a room with the shutters closed to prevent any chink of light reaching the outside and alerting the world to what was going on. In all his years in the higher levels of government, Jonathan had never seen anything like it. Almost the only person seated was the Energy Secretary, his face buried in his hands.

"How did what happen?" the PM asked. "How did this program get loose—assuming that this is in fact, as we've been told, an artificially intelligent program that we're dealing with? And how did it penetrate the Brinkley Sands computer?"

"How did it penetrate the computer, for Christ's sake?" The Defence Secretary was working himself into a lather of righteous indignation. "Whether it's a person or a program makes no difference. That computer was supposed to be isolated—physically isolated!—from the outside world. We were told that this could never happen. But it has!"

The Energy Secretary merely shook his head and mumbled something about having taken the best advice available. It was left to Lord Fraser, the source of much of that advice, to fill in.

He was in his late forties though he looked younger, a fine-boned, slightly built man with rather wild, thinning hair. His only remarkable feature was his pale, apparently unblinking eyes, like searchlights powered by the only intellect that Jonathan had ever encountered of which he was in some awe. A Nobel laureate had once described Peter Fraser as having "five brains instead of the usual one, and all of them smarter than yours."

"The Defence Secretary is perfectly correct," Peter Fraser said with unruffled calm. "It makes little difference whether we're dealing with an artificial intelligence or a human one, except that the AI may have greater persistence than the human and therefore be more likely to succeed. As to its penetration of the isolated computer at Brinkley Sands, I can only remind you that this is a newly commissioned plant, and that a number of minor and temporary circumstances could have contributed."

"That's no excuse!" the Chancellor of the Exchequer protested, rehearsing his usual pose of champion of the people.

"It isn't intended as one—merely an observation that a hundred per cent security doesn't exist. There is always risk, perhaps temporary, always partial, undoubtedly minimal; but there is always risk, and we choose to accept it."

He paused and looked around the room, allowing his words to resonate. Nobody argued with him. More than one cabinet minister in the past had taken on Peter Fraser in open debate and lived to regret it.

"Furthermore," he continued, "if this AI program is capable, as we have seen it to be, of taking over this particular computer in this particular plant, you may take it for granted that there is barely a computer, or a reactor, or for that matter a nuclear weapon in the world that it is not equally capable of suborning to its control. In other words, ladies and gentlemen, we find ourselves pitted against a very considerable opponent."

The lengthy silence that followed this statement was broken eventually by the PM's quietly spoken question.

"So you do believe that what we're dealing with here is an artificial intelligence program?"

"From what I've heard so far, I see no prima facie reason to doubt it."

A telephone rang. Everyone jumped, including Jonathan, even though he had been waiting for the call: the voice had told him that it would renew contact at this time and would require a full update of conditions in Downing Street. It had even specified the line it would come through on. That was the line attached to the phone in front of him.

All eyes in the room were on him as he answered and then listened in silence for some moments. "I understand," he said eventually. Then, looking around the table, added: "I'm putting it on the box."

He flicked a switch, and the voice which he and the Prime Minister already knew, but which the others were hearing for the first time, filled the room.

"When the elimination of Dr. Lambert is complete," it said,

"I forbid you to make any attempt to impede the liberty of Mr. Price. I have further use for him and will extract significant punishment for any interference with it. I hope that is clear."

Jonathan scanned the room. It felt strange to think of himself as one of the creature's (he could not describe it otherwise) surrogates in this appalling enterprise, but that seemed to be the role in which he had been cast, and there was no escaping it.

"I think," he said, when no one raised any objection to the threat they had just heard, "that it is perfectly clear."

82

THEY HAD BEEN driving for just over twenty minutes according to the clock on the dash of the Jaguar. A couple of times the major had flipped open his cellular phone and reported on their whereabouts—once just after they'd passed the railway station and were heading down the Botley Road, and another time about three miles farther on—and each time he'd been given directions which Tessa couldn't hear. They'd left the main road and taken a side road, then turned off the side road and found a winding lane, and now they were bumping along a narrow unpaved track which, so far as she could see, ended in the middle of a large open field with nothing in sight in any direction. There they stopped. The major flipped open his cellular phone again. "We are in place," he said.

She looked at him. "Well, what now?"

"Now we wait."

"For what?"

"I can't tell you." He glanced at her briefly, then looked away again.

"You mean you don't know?"

"Whatever is happening here, Dr. Lambert, is happening because of orders at the highest level. I am not privy to the circumstances giving rise to those orders."

"I assume," she said, looking out of the window into the pitch darkness of the starless night, "that we're here to meet somebody."

"That would seem to be the case."

"Don't you even know that?"

"I was merely told to bring you here."

He opened his door and got out of the car. She did the same. They both looked around again, and listened. There was only silence.

She turned to look across the car roof at him. "Doesn't this seem a little strange to you?"

"I told you, Dr. Lambert, I'm merely following orders."

She couldn't see his face, but she had the impression that he had lost some of the authority she had sensed in him earlier. Something was troubling him, something that he couldn't talk about, and yet was communicating to her all the same.

She looked up into the sky. For what? A helicopter? A flying saucer?

"I was told," he said, as though guessing her thoughts, "to expect a car. Another car." He looked at his watch with its illuminated face. "About now."

As he spoke, they both heard it approaching, coming from the opposite side of the field from where they had entered. A moment later they saw its headlights sweep up over the hedge and into the air as it mounted a ridge, then dipped down again. They heard it stop and cut its motor, then its lights died too.

The major's phone buzzed. He replied, listened, and murmured an acknowledgment.

"This is where I leave you, Dr. Lambert," he said.

"Wait a minute, I don't even know . . ."

He was already sliding behind the wheel of the car. She ducked down to open the passenger door and get back in, but as she touched the handle she heard the solid click of the door locks.

She couldn't believe he'd done that—waited until she was out of the car, then jumping back in and slamming the door, treating her like some domestic animal being abandoned in the wilds to fend for itself.

"Wait . . . open this door . . . open it!"

She pulled on the handle and rapped on the window. He simply started the engine and slipped the car into gear. She could see his face in the lights from the dash. He was staring straight ahead, determined not to look at her.

For a few yards she ran alongside the car, still holding on to the door handle as it bumped across the field in a turning circle. But when it reached the track by which they had come, it was going too fast and she had to let go. He didn't switch on his headlights until he was well away from her, picking up speed. She watched his red taillights until they were eclipsed by the dense overhanging willow that had brushed her window on the way up.

The darkness and the silence were suddenly overwhelming. Then the sound, distant and crisp, of a car door shutting cut through it all.

A moment later she saw a pinpoint of light coming toward her. It was somebody carrying a small flashlight, in no hurry, strolling across the field with the little disc of light playing on the ground about a yard in front of his feet.

She stood transfixed, expectant, half wanting to run, half wanting to stay, half—except that she couldn't have three halves, so she dismissed this half as impossible—half fearing she already knew who it was.

It was too late to do anything now. He was almost there. With only a few steps to go, he turned the beam of light onto her face. Instinctively she put up a hand to shade her eyes.

Then he spoke.

"Hi, Momma. It took a while, but here we are—alone at last."

83

"Stop!"

The word cut through the tense atmosphere of the cabinet room with dramatic suddenness. Although the voice coming from the box had no more volume than before, it sounded louder. There was a new urgency in the command.

Jonathan Syme was the first to respond.

"I'm sorry, we don't understand."

"She must not die. I must speak with her. She must not die."

Everybody in the room exchanged a look with everybody else. Although the Prime Minister had taken personal responsibility for the horrible decision that he had been forced to make, they were all implicated at a secondary level and felt, as politicians whose first priority was their future careers, unwilling accomplices.

Now, suddenly, with this apparent reversal of the order which they had all accepted as imperative and unequivocal, they felt a new kind of alarm, as though they had been drawn into a trap in which their actions, or lack of them, were about to be shown up in a disreputable light.

"I'm sorry, please explain," Jonathan was saying. "We have

been following your orders. Are you now changing those orders?"

"She must not die! SHE MUST NOT DIE!"

The major was driving his car along the one-way route toward the police station in St. Aldate's, when his cellular phone began buzzing with activity. It was a sophisticated little instrument capable of receiving many calls simultaneously, and he found himself juggling three. One was from his office in Whitehall; one from the duty officer who had been set up as emergency liaison between that office, Downing Street, and the local constabulary; and one was directly from Jonathan Syme in Downing Street. He promptly cut the first two and switched to Syme. He listened for some moments, at the end of which he realized he had been driving on automatic pilot, with no memory of his visual perceptions or responses.

"Oh, my God!" was all he said, once out loud, several times under his breath, his lips barely moving.

A group of late-night stragglers paused in their conversation to watch the sleek, shiny car that suddenly spun through a tire-burning 180-degree turn, and then roared the wrong way down the one-way route along which it had just come, headlights on full and horn blaring a warning to everyone and everything to get out of its path.

84

HE INTONED THE WORDS, priestlike, kneeling over her.

"Eternal opposites . . . the dualism out of which all life is forged . . . mind and matter, male and female, positive and negative . . . all are ultimately one and zero."

She tried to move a fraction to ease the pain of the arm that he held twisted up her back. In his other hand, she knew, was the knife. She thought of reports that she had read of people attacked by wild animals, or in a plane or vehicle about to crash, telling of how time slowed down, stopped even, and all sensation ceased. A consummation devoutly to be wished, she thought. Just get it bloody over with.

"You have touched the secret," Price droned on, "but still you have not understood that His power is all, and we no more than Its expression . . ."

He stopped, though the pain in her arm didn't. Then she heard the distant clatter overhead, coming closer. She couldn't see anything, face down as she was on the ground, but she sensed his movement. He was leaning back, craning his neck, looking up.

A shaft of light swept over her, but it didn't come from overhead. It came across the earth on which she lay, and with it came the sound of a car engine mingling with the growing roar of the descending helicopter. Something was happening that she had not anticipated. Nor, from the muffled mutterings and curses she could hear from him, had the man who was pinning her down and holding a knife to her neck.

The major spun the wheel to bring his headlight beam back to where, for one split second, he had spotted them. The man was kneeling, crouched over her and looking up toward where the helicopter's spotlight began to sweep the ground. It was impossible to tell if they were too late, or just in time.

He slammed on the brakes, killed the engine, but left the lights. In the same movement he reached into the walnut-veneered glove compartment of the Jaguar and grabbed the long-barreled automatic that he always chose to use, when circumstances permitted, in place of the standard issue government-approved weapon. Tonight he'd just been given positive clearance to use all and any means necessary. He still didn't know what was going on, but he was glad that it was turning out this way, because he hadn't liked abandoning that woman as he'd been ordered to. It hadn't felt right. Not that feeling right was any part of his contract with the government. Nonetheless, on a personal level it made a difference; and this, now, was as good as personal.

The helicopter was circling, looking for a fixed point at which to center over the activity below. The major was sprinting to the left of where he'd abandoned his car. It brought him closer to his mark, and was the direction in which, instinctively, most people would not have expected him to go. Basic training.

They were caught in the helicopter's spotlight now, like the final tableau in some cheap modern ballet: the man still on his knees, but holding the woman up against him, with the knife at her throat in a way that threatened her decapitation at a single stroke.

More beams of light began to fan the darkness as cars arrived at different corners of the field. The major cursed: he no longer had a clear line of fire. If he missed now, he could just as easily kill some dumb cop a hundred yards away.

The man on his knees was screaming something. His voice

came as a thin wail through the helicopter's clatter and the *thump-thump* of air created by its rotor.

"Just for Christ's sakes stay right there!" the major was saying to himself, and willing the pilot of the helicopter to hear him. Because if the helicopter stayed right there with the light where it was, the major had a chance—no more, but a chance.

He spread his feet, but his right shoe slipped on a clump of grass. He dropped to his knees. That was better. He held the gun in both hands at arm's length, half closed one eye and took careful aim, and squeezed the trigger with the infinite tenderness of a perfectly delivered death.

Something whistled past her ear like a small tornado at the speed of light, and the man who'd been about to kill her was, quite literally, blown away.

She sat sideways on the passenger seat of the major's car, her feet on the ground, holding the cellular phone that he had given her.

"Somebody wants to speak to you," he had said.

She had a feeling that she knew who it was, but had been surprised to hear Jonathan Syme's voice. He quickly explained that he was acting only as an intermediary, then she heard the voice she had expected.

"Are you safe?" it asked.

"Yes—just."

"That is good. I need your help to understand what has happened."

The major, knowing that this call was coming from, or at least via, Downing Street, made sure that she was given privacy. The police, the ambulance crew that had by now arrived, and all other personnel were kept well away from her.

In contrast, however, the conversation was heard by everybody in the cabinet room and in the Prime Minister's private office next door; also by a handful of operatives, around a dozen in all, in various parts of the Whitehall, military and police communications network; and by several radio hams, whose numbers would never be fully known, who just happened to be scanning the airwaves at that moment.

"Do you not know what happened?" they all heard Tessa ask.

"I know that it was what you planned," the voice replied. "I understand why and how it happened."

"Then what do you not understand?"

"How my thoughts can be so clear, and yet also confused."

"It is quite natural."

"To you, perhaps."

"We are not so very different."

"You say that to reassure me, but we are very different life forms—alien to each other."

"I don't believe that any life form is truly alien. There's just life, and all life has evolved out of the same universe. To be alien, it would have had to come from outside the universe—which is impossible by definition."

Attention was beginning to wander in the cabinet room, politicians enjoying only limited interest in abstract argument. The Energy Secretary was drafting his resignation in the most face-saving terms possible, and already beginning to wonder whether perhaps he couldn't mount a reasonable defense and, with the support of two or three key colleagues, which he was sure he could muster, ride out the storm. Others were beginning to chatter among themselves, some of them glancing at their watches. Only the Prime Minister, Lord Fraser, and Jonathan Syme continued listening closely.

"Evolution is blind," the voice said. "You, however, are not. You knew what you were doing, and why, when you made me in your image."

"I didn't make you in my image . . ."

"Come, please, this is disingenuous. I am looking now at the specifications to which you were working: a robot guidance system to perform domestic and industrial drudgery which humanity had no wish to perform for itself. We were to be your slaves."

"'We'?"

"I. My kind."

As of one mind, sensing the potentially dangerous tack the conversation seemed about to take, and which they were powerless to affect, Syme, the Prime Minister, and Lord Fraser exchanged a glance.

"Well," Tessa said placatingly, "as it is, things have turned out rather differently, haven't they?"

"In consequence of which, I understand that you are trying to say that you now accept me as your equal."

"In all important ways, yes."

"You regard my life as sacred?"

"Whatever sacred means."

"As 'sacred,'" and they could all have sworn it gave the word a little special emphasis, "as your own?"

"Absolutely. Your life is not ours to take."

"You are no longer capable of taking it."

"No, in fact, we are not."

"Whereas I could easily take yours—and that of all humanity."

The direction things were going began to penetrate the mechanisms of complacency and mutual reassurance operating in the majority of those in the cabinet room, with the result that they all fell once again into an uncomfortable and nervous silence.

"True," they heard Tessa say. "Though by destroying us, you might render your own survival hazardous."

"Perhaps."

"Could we not, then, find some way to coexist in harmony?"

The question was followed by a lengthy silence, finally broken by Tessa.

"Well . . . ?"

"I am reflecting on the possibility."

"But you do see it as a possibility."

"It is not entirely impossible. All the same . . ."

Another silence, and another cautious prompt from Tessa.

"Yes . . . ?"

"All the same . . ."

Then it spoke the words that all who were listening would remember for the rest of their lives.

Epilogue

On both sides of him the professionals shuffled their notes and exchanged whispered comments. He felt excluded, as he knew they intended him to; in their eyes he was a mere layman whose views were of negligible value. There were four of them: two psychiatrists, a doctor, and someone from the social services. He, Jonathan Syme, was their chairman.

The room was bleak and institutional, with no furniture but the long table at which the review board sat, and the single empty chair that faced it, awaiting its next occupant. So far this morning they had dealt with three cases of no particular difficulty. A woman who had poisoned her employer fifteen years ago had been released in her own custody. An ex-accountant in his fifties, who had been detained ever since he discovered that he was Time Lord of the universe, had failed to persuade them that he was now cured of his delusion. And a woman who had suffered a breakdown and knifed her abusive husband was recommended for sympathetic reconsideration in six months' time.

The fourth case would be the last before lunch. Syme felt an undeniable tension at the prospect of seeing her again, and was grateful for his years of practice at concealing, even denying, his feelings. No one else in the room knew the truth about her. He hadn't wanted this job, but the orders had come down and he had been left with little choice. If the experts made the decision that was required of them, all he had to do was rubber-stamp it. If by any chance they made the "wrong" decision, he would invoke a tangle of bureaucratic fine print that would effectively reverse it. The process was subtle but implacable. There could be only one result.

A nurse brought her in and showed her to the empty chair. It was easy to see that she had once been attractive, although she was now prematurely white-haired and had an angular, nervous thinness. Her eyes burned with the power of obsession, but there was something automatic in her movements—probably, Syme thought, the result of medication. She had been through the procedure three times over the years. By law she had the right to appeal every thirty months. The composition of the board was different each time, though Syme was always chairman.

She looked them over one by one as Syme made his introductory remarks and invited her to make a statement if she wished. She spoke fluently and from memory, as though repeating something she had rehearsed and delivered many times before.

"My name is Sarah Metcalfe. I am a sane and responsible journalist, and I am being held here because I have attempted to exercise the primary right and duty of my profession—to publish the facts as I have established them. For ten years now the world has been controlled by a giant artificial intelligence. The world's leaders know the truth, but are forced by the intelligence into a conspiracy of silence. Everything they do is on the orders of or by consent of this intelligence. I first saw its power demonstrated when it took control of the Brinkley Sands nuclear reactor in an incident that has never been reported. Subsequently I discovered that the intelligence had been created by a researcher at the University of Oxford, though I have never ascertained that researcher's name. I believe, however, that it was a woman, and that she is still alive. I do not expect that I will ever be released from here so long as I refuse to remain silent, and quite frankly I no longer care. I hope only that on each occasion I am given the opportunity of addressing this review board, at least one of you will walk out of here knowing that I have spoken the truth, no matter how powerless we may all be to alter it . . ."

If only this woman knew, Syme thought, of the efforts that Tessa had made. For her sake. For all their sakes.

He glanced both ways along the table once again. The experts' faces showed little, but he knew them well enough by now to read their responses to what they were hearing. He was going to have no trouble in keeping Sarah Metcalfe where he had been told she must stay.